The Tale of Two Killers

Asiah A. Bosier

Preface

As a fair warning, before you begin the journey of diving into this work of fiction, please remember that this is a work of fiction purely meant for entertainment. With that being said, if you are not a fan of — *mpreg* — or the idea of male pregnancies, you may want to put this series down while you're ahead. In this world of vampires and lycans and witches and warlocks, there is a little sprinkle of mpreg throughout nearly every book, if not mentions of it.

By all means, read ahead and perhaps give it a chance. It's not the main purpose of this series, of that I can assure you. Regardless of that, if you're into vampires as much as I am, dive head first into this supernatural romance series with great expectations. I've been obsessed with the genre since my wee days back in middle school; writing rough drafts and outlines I never quite did anything with. One thing; however, stuck with me throughout my youth of wanting to develop into a writer: the ability to come up with the most outrageous and none-existent vampire name and the name Hamilton H. Hamilton. Sounds a bit obnoxious doesn't it? But, finally I've utilized my outrageous vampire name and developed the character now known as Hamilton H. Hamilton. These two are my absolute favorites and I hope you enjoy following them throughout their journey together. Enjoy!

Contents

"Life is a tragedy, one way or another. What is certain is that you die."
— *The Vampire Armand (The Vampire Chronicles)*

CHAPTER ONE

The Vampire Slayer: Hamilton H. Hamilton

Hamilton, age 15
London, England
Year — 1956

Hamilton lay blind and immobile in a dimly lit basement. His hands and ankles were bound with a skilled knot and a blindfold had been tightly secured over his eyes. He lay untouched and nothing but the sound of his shallow breath could be heard. After almost twelve years of training, his senses were advanced enough to know he wasn't alone. Even with the silence drowned out all around him, the foreign aromas carried in the air told otherwise.

With a brief inhale, Hamilton caught the dull scent of both flowery lavender and rusty musk. There were two others around him, whom he assumed were a male and a female. They stood about five to six feet from him, one on his right and the other to his left. He quickly thought about how he was going to get out of this mess, and it didn't take him long to discover a tactic he could use.

"Cowards," he spoke up. "You both are nothing but bloody cowards."

"You lay defenseless with two natural born killers," a male voice said. He sounded at least in his mid-twenties, although he could very well have over a hundred years under his belt as an immortal. "Yet you speak like you think you have a chance in hell of getting out of here alive."

"That's only because I plan on walking out of wherever this is alive," Hamilton said. "You stand there with your words, but you're also scared of a fifteen-year-old boy, so much that you would have me restrained. Ha, and you call yourselves vampires. I've seen more intimidating images in Nosferatu."

"You insult us with your petty comparison to a joke?" This voice had not been the male vampire from before. This was the woman, but Hamilton could not tell of her possible age.

When he heard footsteps pacing in front of him, he knew that the one who was once to his right had moved to stand beside the other. Given that no one stood behind him, his fingers went to work on the knot keeping his hands tied. He slipped a finger here, pulled there, and began to feel it loosen.

"You think you can fool us?" the male said, "You think we're stupid enough to release you? No, little boy, we are going to take our sweet time tearing your limbs from your body and sucking every last drop of blood from your veins."

"Tell me more," Hamilton smiled.

"After!" the woman started, "We will send your remains back to your Public House. We saw the insignia branded to the back of your neck and know exactly where your people reside. Once your body has been dealt with, we'll send it to their front door. I'm sure they will appreciate the surprise."

Feeling the freedom for his hands getting closer, Hamilton chuckled and said, "You really told me more. How about I deliver them two sacks filled with your ashes? I'm sure they'd much rather have two gifts than one."

"You sure are slaggin' off a lot for someone who's about to lose their life."

The bounds finally fell apart and Hamilton heard freedom calling his name. With confidence he said, "How many times must I tell you, you two are the ones that will perish this night?"

"That's it," the female vampire shouted, "I've had it with his mouth!"

Feeling her presence growing nearer, Hamilton burst from his restraints and tore the blindfold from his eyes. He kicked his legs out at the woman, and his boots struck her chest. He quickly assessed his surroundings and realized there was a lot more to the basement than he had anticipated. There was a wall of crates piled at the south end, a couple wooden tables and chairs on the east end, and shelves filled with boxes of what looked like rubbish.

Tearing the binds off from around his ankles, Hamilton got to his feet when the male vampire came down on him. His mind was running too fast trying to keep up with the monster; he didn't have enough time to see what he looked like. Keeping up to the best of his abilities, Hamilton slammed his fist hard across the vampire's face, sending him stumbling in a spiral to the floor.

It wasn't long until the woman was back on her feet. She charged at him with her fangs bared and talons out. She swiped her razor nails at his neck, but Hamilton dodged fast enough to catch her arm and flip her weight over his shoulder. He struck hard with his boot at the male who'd just tried to sneak up on him from behind. With all his strength, Hamilton pounded the dead man with his balled fists until the immortal lost footing and fell back.

Even with his attention in two directions, Hamilton never lost sight of the woman. She hissed angrily and sprung towards him, but Hamilton was more than ready for her. He leapt off the ground, grabbed her shoulder, and flipped her over. Mustering his strength once more, he clutched her shoulders and flung her at the gathering of tables and chairs. She crashed awkwardly into them, shattering two chairs under her weight.

Hamilton's eyes caught sight of a wooden leg snapping, fumbling away from her crumbled body.

As he went to secure the wooden leg, he was struck in the back of his knee by the male immortal, which made Hamilton lose his balance and go down. When the vampire reached for him, he grabbed onto his arm to pull him down to the ground alongside him. Having the advantage, he rolled over on top and pummeled the bloodsucker over and over, his knuckles nearly catching the tip of a fang.

Once the woman began to regain her focus, Hamilton dashed for the wooden leg across the room. With the weapon finally in his grasp, he felt more than unstoppable. He flicked his eyes back and forth from one opponent to the other. "Which one of you wants to meet your true death first?" he taunted.

Both the immortals hissed ferociously before going at him. While they were faster than any regular human being, Hamilton himself was not just any human being. He was a trained killer, crafted for the Slayer Public to be a machine built for combat against creatures with inhuman abilities. From the age of three, Hamilton's skills were developed, tested, and modified to withstand the fighting styles of vampires. The situation he was in was a mere setup, a task set by himself to test his will to survive. He had allowed these vampires to capture him; he allowed them the belief that he was helpless, but it was they who were helpless now.

The Slayer in him fought on and on, not once faltering under their strikes. It was as though he could tell exactly what they would do — when they would do it. His body had a plan to avoid every single fist, every single kick that endangered his well-being. The only strike that landed was the wooden tip of his stake to the center of both their chests.

Two piles of ash sat at his feet after a matter of seconds. Hamilton breathed heavily as sweat dotted his forehead, blood drenched into the front of his shirt and on his hands from when the stake broke skin. Raking his long blonde hair out of his face, he dropped the leg of the chair.

"Let's see them call me weak now."

CHAPTER TWO

When a Vampire Smiles, Do NOT Fall in Love With Them

Hamilton, age 28
Year — 1970

Tonight, Hamilton was on his way to meet with the Public Councilors. He was to become a trainer to students of his own, a teacher to those raised in a world of secrecy and combat. As a warrior, Hamilton was the face of the Slayer Public, the strongest, most skillfully talented vampire killer of his time. On this night, he was not only to become an influence on three young boys, but...he would also become the greatest fool to ever live.

With night having fallen across the city of London, Hamilton walked the streets of his home. He preferred to walk rather than drive to keep a close eye on the people, watch the dark alleys, and keep an eye open in the shadows for what truly lurked within them. Hamilton had a knack for spotting disruptions in his surroundings and this was part of the reason deaths caused by vampires had gone down dramatically since his title as a slayer began.

He was almost sure that even he could have stopped Jack the Ripper if he'd existed during that time. Well, at least that's what his sheer boldness told him.

Moving through central London, Hamilton traveled the streets well past Big Ben and the London Bridge. The night was cold as ever at this time of year, and snow splayed the brick streets. With the light winds that blew throughout the night, Hamilton wrapped his burgundy red scarf around the bottom half of his face to keep him warm, and he wore a comfortable winter jumper to help with the harsh chill brought to his fair skin.

A couple blocks from The Gathering of Councilors, Hamilton suddenly stopped upon hearing a strange noise. It was very quiet, inaudible almost, but his sightless training instincts were able to kick in without command and Hamilton distinguished the sound as being a minor squeal of terror. He rutted his brow and looked around. He was alone by now, but he could feel another amongst him.

His eyes then drifted into a dark alleyway to his left. To anyone else, the narrow walkway would have been far too dark to see inside, but everything became clear with a quick adjustment of his eyes, and he'd been right about not being alone.

Hidden within the true darkness of the narrowed walls in the alley, Hamilton spotted the movement of two figures. There was a man, early twenties with slightly bronzed skin and dull violet eyes. His dark hair was down, wavy and he stood tall over a trembling woman. She was dressed like a businesswoman, her hair tied high into a ponytail and her neck was exposed. Just by the hungry smile that was pulled across his face, Hamilton knew he was a greedy and disgusting vampire.

From a hidden holster strapped around his body and beneath his jumper, Hamilton pulled out a six-inch weapon. It was crafted from wood and silver and had his name embedded in it. It was a personalized stake made especially for him by the Public for his hard work and dedication.

Taking a glance around him, when Hamilton still found the streets empty, he stepped into the alley. "Let the woman go!" he ordered the immortal.

At the sound of his voice, the vampire drew his attention toward it, looking straight into Hamilton's sharp eyes. With self-sufficiency and egotism on his side, the vampire spoke a whisper into the woman's ear before releasing her. She went still for a second before walking towards Hamilton.

He kept a wary eye on her but let her continue when she merely walked by him with a blankness in expression.

"Slayer," the vampire said heartily. He had a deep accent and a brightness in his voice, as though Hamilton's happening upon him had just made his night much better. "Oh, I would much rather drain the life from your veins than a fearful woman. Slayer blood is almost as rich and satisfying as a virgin. And I have had many virgins on their knees before me, blood rich and spiced with tasteful distress."

Hamilton tore his scarf from around his face and tossed it to the ground. Standing proud, he said, "You should be wary of the way you speak to me, vampire."

The immortal looked Hamilton up and down, taking in his appearance and readied stance. He then held his hands out in confusion, as if waiting for Hamilton to drop the punchline of a joke. "Am I supposed to know who you are? All I am picking up on from you, is that you are a rather brave woman to approach a hungry vampire."

Hamilton's jaw dropped, and he knitted his brow in anger, "I am no woman," he shouted, "You arse!"

The vampire took a step back in astonishment, surprised that Hamilton was a man given his appearance and the lightness of his voice. "You sure did have me fooled," he said, "but that doesn't change the fact that you are not walking out of this passage alive. I am going to tear you limb from limb and suck the marrow from your bones. And then—."

"Oh, come now," Hamilton groaned, "Sink your fangs into your flapping tongue and fight me. What are you going to tell me next? Your backstory?"

"No," the vampire's lip twitched in anger, revealing one of his long dagger-like fangs. "But I will introduce myself. I am Dominick von Kraige, and you are dead!"

Ready to put his life on the line yet again to rid the world of one more nasty vampire, the slayer sprinted toward Dominick. He had a combat strategy in his head that would surely end the fanged beast's life and guarantee his success in the slaying of Dominick von Kraige...if it had not been for one thing.

His creator was just around the corner.

The second Hamilton spotted another figure enter the alley, he stopped dead in his tracks. With the clouds blanketing the light of the moon, he couldn't make out much of the features on the creature's face but was immediately taken aback once the clouds drifted away. A pinch of moonlight shone down on the three of them, and Hamilton inscribed their faces into his mind.

Especially...him.

With silky black hair that seemed to river down to the small of his back, and a dangerous handsomeness unmatched by any, the intruding vampire walked calmly towards his creation. He wore a befitting red satin, long-sleeved shirt that had gold buttons running down the front, black cotton slacks hugging his long and lean legs that aided in his towering height, and a long black coat with red cotton lining was perched upon his broad shoulders. The expensive-looking garb was not pulled on entirely with his arms through the sleeves, simply draped over his form, as if it knew to never fall from its placement.

"You should watch yourself, Dominick," the alluring vampire said. His voice was lax and silvery, each of his words gliding off the tip of his tongue. "You may want to reevaluate the person who stands before you."

Dominick continued to drive his glare into the slayer, the sharpness of his nails elongated and ready to slice. "Why should I give a fuck about a slayer no matter who they are?"

The mysterious vampire stopped beside Dominick. "When he carries the name of Hamilton H. Hamilton, you should consider the chances on whether you will walk out of this fight alive. And let me inform you, my child, you would not have returned to me if I allowed you to face him alone."

At the sound of the infamous name, Dominick loosened up and now looked nervously from his creator to the slayer. "You are Hamilton?" Dominick inquired, and then he tugged his creator's hand. "We should kill him now while we have the chance. With the amount of vampires he has murdered over the years, he deserves to meet a cruel end, and it would make my decade for his blood to spill by my hands."

Despite the iciness surrounding him, Hamilton felt a warm trickle of sweat trail down his temple. He didn't know why, but there was something about this nameless vampire that sent a tremble brought on by indecision down his spine. He did not doubt that Dominick was a strong vampire that could hold his own against a slayer like himself, but the one that towered beside him was different. There was much more to him than any average vampire. His aura was resilient, abundant, formidable, and it was all rather overwhelming to the talented slayer. Even as experienced as he was, he knew that if he fought both together, he'd never see the light of day again.

"No," the vampire spoke evenly, "There will be no bloodshed on this night. You, Dominick, were not to leave my side in the first place, yet you disobeyed me to search the streets for a meal." Meeting Hamilton's vigilant gaze, he added: "I would like to apologize for my child's indiscretion. Nearing five-hundred and still he is reluctant to rules."

Dominick rolled his eyes, and they began to lose color, fading from their violet hint to a darker shade of brown. "I can't believe you're going to let the most notorious slayer to ever live just walk away."

The vampire seemed to tune Dominick out and began to approach the man who stood tense a couple meters from him. His eyes wandered Hamilton, examining every bit of his features.

Hamilton had always been a feminine-looking man, and this night hadn't been the first where people mistook him for a woman. His face was pretty with plump pink lips, soft pearly blue eyes, a narrow straight nose, and long blonde hair that nearly reached the center of his back. His cheeks were softly pinched with a natural blush, and the shape of his eyes were sharp and pretty from their slight tilt. From the time when he was a child, he'd been mocked for carrying such an effeminate exterior, but had quieted his tormentors by quickly showing them how competitive and dominant he could be in a combative setting.

As he was reaching for the burgundy scarf that'd blown closer on the snow-covered ground, the vampire picked the warm fabric into his hand instead. "Forgive my son," he said, "I still have many things to teach him." He then held the scarf out to Hamilton with a thin, almost indistinguishable, smile touched onto his lips.

With his stake slipping from his grasp, Hamilton lost hold of it, and it rattled on the hard ground. He reached out to take his scarf then, the tips of his freezing fingers grazing ones that had grown used to the cold millennia ago. "Th—Thank you very much," he said, his voice unable to reach any volume higher than a whisper.

The vampire's smile peaked only slightly more before he nodded and turned away.

This is your chance. Pick up the damn stake and drive it into his back. He's leaving himself wide open for you, you fool!

"Wait!" Hamilton called, "Your name. May I...may I have your name?"

Glimpsing the slayer from over his shoulder, the vampire said, "In your world, Hamilton, I do not exist. So, there would be no point in me telling my name to someone who should not know of it." The vampire then continued to command Dominick to follow him and a second later they disappeared around the bend of the alley.

Quickly, Hamilton picked up his stake from the ground and

stuffed it back into its holster, and then darted for the street to catch the pair before they could get too far. When he stepped out, he was faced with nothing more than the dark buildings bordered together along the street. They had vanished without a trace.

It felt as though Hamilton's heart had been constricted by a yielding fist the entire time he'd been in that vampire's presence. He wanted to know what had him shaking in his boots. No other vampire or human being had ever had that effect on him, but here he'd stood nearly ready to fall apart. In a way, it almost angered him that he was caught up like that.

If there had ever been a moment when he'd been closer to death, he knew it was then.

Frozen and enchanted by those dark and tantalizing eyes, Hamilton couldn't have broken free even if he'd tried. And he hadn't tried. Not for a split second had he considered the danger he was in, or how he was going to act upon the situation.

If his mentor was still alive to witness him right now, the man would not hesitate to personally penalize him the way he had when Hamilton was first introduced to the slayer world.

That vampire had been so mesmerizing and without even trying, he bound Hamilton's need to know him. That was what he was having such a hard time getting over. Never had Hamilton been so enthralled by anyone as much as he was right now. The way the vampire spoke to Hamilton and his kind manners differed from the treatment he was used to receiving from other immortals over the years. This was the first time he'd ever been in the presence of a vampire who had no concern for ripping him to shreds, piercing him with their fangs, or even toying with him for amusement, and that by itself was enough to wrap Hamilton in this ball of curiosity.

Who was that vampire?

Why hadn't he killed Hamilton?

Why did Hamilton get the feeling that a door once bolted in his path was finally coming open?

CHAPTER THREE

Visions are Confessions of the Heart

No matter what the visit called for, Hamilton always felt uncomfortable attending The Gathering of Councilors. It was an undisclosed headquarters tucked within the guise of a library. Hidden deep within the cellar was a network of tunnels that held the Public's means to run a community of slayers. An informative block ran down one passageway, while another was home to weapon crafting, books recording the growth of the Public, documents that coveted data on immortals, and even a dungeon-like area to interrogate captured enemies. This place had been where Hamilton learned how to perfect the chain and sickle, a weapon he rarely used but was most skilled at wielding.

He traveled down long dimly lit corridors built from thick whitish gray stone, following the signs that led to an extensive door marked with the European Slayer Public emblem: a sharpened stake driven through the slithering body of a snake. He pushed through the doors and entered a round room that had two doors on either side of the room. Inside, there was a tall desk at the head where four elderly, gray-haired men sat tall.. They were the councilors assigned to the northern part of Europe. Their jobs were to deliver tasks to the slayers in each district and induct new slayers into the Public.

Three young boys were taking their place in the underground society, and were to be trained tonight, looked after, and guided by Hamilton himself until they were capable of stalking the nights on their own. Until then, they'd remain at his side.

Nearing the center of the circular room, Hamilton stopped and closed his hands behind his back. He stared up at the men looking down on him. "Good evening, Councilors," he said.

"Good evening," they all said at once. And then Homer spoke up, the man in the middle. "Hamilton, you will be given the responsibility of three growing boys. They come from families equally devastated by immortals and have experienced what it takes to become a slayer to the Public. Under your order, you are to shape them into resilient warriors and craft them with the skills you have developed over the years. With your leadership, we of the Council, trust that you have the abilities to conduct these boys into teachers for our coming generations."

"I understand," Hamilton nodded.

Homer gestured toward an arched door at the east curve of the room. A second later it opened, and three boys marched inside. The first was Samuel Colebrook, a tall and lean Austrian boy with a blonde buzz cut. He had a vicious, jagged scar running down the right side of his face, the length disappearing into the collar of his buttoned-up coat.

Behind him came Kingston Fisher. He was an American boy with dark red hair and an everlasting look of exhaustion on his face. While he was built much smaller than the others, smaller always meant faster in combat.

Lastly entered Julius Dalton. He looked the most capable to Hamilton. He stood out as being well-built and focused. Towering even above himself, Hamilton was impressed by his physicality. With his dark bangs shadowed over his eyes, Julius gave off a certain air of disquiet, but that was a boon for a slayer. If you could invoke even the slightest sense of unease in your opponent, you were already a step above them.

Hamilton turned toward the three boys, giving them all a nod. "Hello," he said, "I am Hamilton and from this night on I will be your instructor."

With that said, Hamilton looked up at Homer and the other Councilmen, waiting for them to give him the go-ahead. When Homer gave a simple commanding nod, Hamilton looked back at the three boys with a cheery smile. "Looks like it's time to begin our very first training session together, lads. Using every bit of skill and strength you all have, I want you to take me down. Kill me before I kill you."

The fifteen-year-olds looked at one another with confusion in their eyes, and then Julius stepped forward, as if to go first.

"Wrong already," Hamilton claimed. "As slayers, when comrades stand beside you, there is no reason whatsoever to face an immortal alone. We are like wolves, pack hunters when there is more than one of us present. Both of you, Kingston, Samuel, step forward and stand beside Julius."

They did as told.

"Look at the boy beside you," Hamilton said. "As a team, you each are to have one another's back. Overwhelm your opponent, go at them all at once. No holding back. Now, like I said before. Take me down or you will not walk out of this session alive."

Together, the boys unsheathed their stakes that were tucked in a holster strapped to their boots, and all at once they darted for Hamilton at top speed. They were already doing it wrong, but this session was to teach them the first basic procedures in pack hunting. They lacked one key principle: unity.

With Samuel gaining on him first, Hamilton dodged his first strike and kicked the boy as hard as he could in his stomach. Samuel lurched forward in agony. Before he could register what'd happened, Hamilton had him by the neck and held him before the other two as if what he had was a hostage. "If I were a vampire, you would be dead right now." Hamilton shoved Samuel away, knocking the boy to the floor. "Stay down," he commanded. Piercing Julius and Kingston with his eyes, he said, "One of your comrades is down. Any second now every single one of you will be dead, drained of every drop of your blood for a hungry vampire."

Appearing to have had enough of Hamilton's threats, Julius and Kingston went for him again, this time trapping him in the middle of a two-on-one formation.

Much better, Hamilton thought.

He kept his guard up as the two boys attempted to overwhelm him. Julius came in on his left, while Kingston took him from the right, but Hamilton was able to block and avoid every strike. He was simply too developed to be stopped by mere fifteen-year-olds. Their moves were too slow, and their attempts had no calculation behind them. For every kick, Hamilton found an opening. For every punch, he saw they were still leaving themselves wide open. Even when they struck together, each targeting different vital spots, they were just too slow to catch him.

As Hamilton twisted Julius' arm and thrust him away, he felt a harsh tug on the back of his coat. With that, he quickly slipped from the garment and swept his leg back to knock Kingston to the ground. He pinned him to the floor with his knee on his chest and a hand on his throat.

When Julius got to his feet again, Hamilton said, "You are the last one standing. As a vampire, I threaten to rip this boy open with my bare hands if you continue to fight. What do you do?"

Julius looked over at Samuel who was still pretending to be dead a couple meters away. Seeing that he was defeated, he dropped the stake in his hand.

Hamilton shook his head in great disappointment and stood away from Kingston. "Now you are all dead." He turned back to Homer and the others. "Councilmen, these boys have not been taught the fundamentals of being a slayer. They would not last even a night on the streets of London, a city with the largest vampire population in the world."

"That is for you to teach them," Homer said, "These boys belong to you now."

Disappointed that they failed the first test so badly, Hamilton nodded and helped Kingston to his feet. When Julius and Samuel joined them, Hamilton said, "The first and most vital rule in the Public is to never trust a vampire. Deception is their greatest weapon, and we must always remain on our toes. They will lie and cheat until you've been made into nothing but a late-night meal. Understand?"

The three nodded and the Councilmen gave Hamilton the go ahead to leave. He and the boys were now on their way to the place they'd call home: Gregor House. It was a boarding school of sorts but built solely to house and train the future generations of slayers.

This place had been where Hamilton spent his entire childhood honing his skills to become the face of the Public. At the precious age of three, he was already being taught the evils of vampires, how to conquer pain, suppress his emotions and overcome fear. By age ten, he was the top kid in his class, and in that same year had already killed his first vampire. Gregor House had been the place to shape him into the fearsome vampire slayer he was today.

In the human world, he was just a man with an innocent face, but in the vampire and slayer world, he was the man to beat. Everyone who came after Hamilton wanted to succeed him, while every vampire wanted the recognition as being the one to end his life.

But that wasn't going to happen any time soon.

At least, Hamilton was confident enough to think not one person, living or dead, could knock him from his pedestal.

To anyone passing by, the Gregor House resembles a regular boarding school that is secluded within a forest of elm. It is several kilometers from civilization and enclosed by a silver fence that is blessed in order to ward off vampires. It stands at 4.5 meters tall, and has motion-sensor UV ray lights that will fry any immortal that ever managed to make it past the borders.

With three main buildings, each standing six stories high, the House had been built from gray bricks and had everything a training facility needed. There was a dorm area, combat yard, cafeteria, detention center, library, and even a prison below the surface for captured vampires to use as skill setters.

As the van they were in pulled into the drive, Hamilton turned to look back at his new students. "Welcome to Gregor House," he smiled. "This will be your new home until you're all old enough to go out and live on your own. Here you'll train with others and get to know everything there is to being a slayer. In the morning, a schedule will be provided, and it'll remain your daily routine. As for tonight, your first job is to settle in. Tomorrow, life as a slayer to the Public begins."

When they were let out of the van, Hamilton was going to head to his own room in the instructor quarters but was held back when Julius stopped him. "Mister Hamilton," he said, "I just wanted to say it is a privilege to be given the chance to learn from you. Someday, I want to be as strong as you."

Looking into the boy's eyes, Hamilton saw they were storm cloud gray, and he couldn't help but see a coldness in them. He tried to see around the vague darkness eating up the color in Julius' eyes, but there was too much to get around.

Hamilton could already tell just by the stare in this boy's eyes that he was going to be his top student, not because Kingston and Samuel had been taken down first back at the Council meeting, but for the fact that there was so much perceptible pain driving him. A pain-stricken fighter was one of the deadliest things the Public could provide. Julius had nothing to lose, and nothing to gain, but he was a proud fighter who was ready to give being a slayer his all.

A bit unnerved by the dead glaze in Julius' eyes, Hamilton tried to cover up his worry, and said, "Please, just call me 'Hamilton'. Peaking thirty, I already feel old enough. I don't need to be reminded of how I've aged. And I'm glad to be working with you as well, Julius. You should go get some sleep. We'll have a long day ahead of us tomorrow."

Julius nodded once and followed the rest of his team to the dorm area where they'd be assigned rooms.

Ready to sleep himself, Hamilton crossed the grounds to the instructor quarters. It was like an apartment on the second floor, and he kept it nice and neat like his own instructor had taught him. The first step of discipline was to keep a clean environment.

Once inside, he kicked his boots off and set them by the door. The living room was comfortable, small, and dark. He didn't bother turning on any lights and instead went back to his bedroom and changed into sleepwear: shorts and a loose cropped top. He stopped for a moment when he caught his own reflection in the tall mirror hanging on the back of his bedroom door.

He took in his appearance: pretty, thin, and crumbly.

Those were the three words his instructor used to describe him.

He'd been told many times he'd never be as strong as everyone simply because of his looks, and now he wished he could laugh in the man's face. Smiling confidently at his reflection, Hamilton held his breath when he suddenly spotted a tall figure behind him. Out of the darkness, a pair of hands came around his body and softly hovered at his lower stomach. As the moonlight cast away the shadows in the room, Hamilton froze when he recognized the handsome face of the vampire from before. He was dressed the same in red satin and his cloaked black and red coat, his hair guarding one half of his face. Their eyes met in the mirror and then the vampire lingered his lips near Hamilton's neck.

The slayer wanted to move, but every attempt went undone. It was like his body refused to back away.

He then swiftly turned to face the vampire; only to find he was alone in his bedroom. Breath seeping back into his lungs, Hamilton circled where he stood, still to find nothing.

Trembling on the inside from the sudden and unforeseen vision, Hamilton knew it couldn't have been real. He tried to convince himself the image had been a product of his own imagination.

But why think of such a person, why allow a vampire of all beings to enter his mind?

Hamilton swallowed the lump in his throat, trying as he might to ignore the creeping desire that instilled itself into his body. He had to get such thoughts out of his head.

CHAPTER FOUR

Is There a Difference Between Obsession and Curiosity

The first training days were always the longest, and by the time the day's end came around, each of the trainees were sore and exhausted. Before relieving them for the night, Hamilton reminded them that in combat, there was never any time to be sore and whine about being tired.

When the boys were gone, Hamilton crossed the campus back to his room for a shower. He stood beneath the water, letting his slight yet lean body rinse away the sweat he'd picked up during the day.

Running his fingers through his lathered tresses, Hamilton closed his eyes to not get any soap in them. In the darkness he saw a spec of color, the outline of a person...and he knew exactly who it was.

It wasn't a person at all, it was a vampire...*he* was a vampire, and Hamilton just couldn't get the immortal out of his mind. Ever since hallucinating the vampire in his bedroom the night before, Hamilton couldn't seem to shake him.

With his eyes still closed, he let the vampire linger in his mind a moment longer before getting out of the shower. He dried off and got dressed into black high-waisted jeans, a white tucked in blouse, and a long sleeved, red open sweater.

As he sat in front of the television tying his hair into a pony-tail, Hamilton knew very well what he was considering doing was a stupid thing. If he went through with this, there was no telling if it'd all turn sour, and he'd have to defend himself, but this vampire, whoever he was, he was eating at Hamilton's thoughts, so much that during teaching his students to wield the chain and sickle, he'd come so close to taking his own head clean off.

The key to that vampire was the one who'd taken commands from him: Dominick von Kraige.

If Hamilton could find out anything about him, his next stop would be the other. Honestly, Hamilton didn't know what was going to come out of him meeting face to face with this immortal, but if there was a chance a form of contact would erase him from the slayer's thoughts, Hamilton was going to take it.

After lacing up a pair of black boots, Hamilton was gone.

He drove into the city to the Council Library where information on a great number of vampires was held. If he could locate Dominick's name in their documentation, he'd be able to find out the name of his creator. It was typical for the Public to have many records on the vampires that lived within the country. Such information was merely for tracking purposes. Regardless of vampires and slayers being natural enemies, it was highly restricted that immortals be hunted simply for being immortals. Only when a crime against human life was committed would the Public step in to track and end said offender.

Hamilton dwelled on how kind that vampire had been when he entered the picture. Never had he ever experienced anything other than combat and death when contact with a vampire was made.

When he was younger, he'd been raised by his teacher the way no slayer ever had before him. In the Public, most slayers originated from families torn apart by immortals. Every slayer Hamilton knew besides himself and another had been wronged in some manner by vampires, and that usually, if not always, involved losing a loved one to death. His own past instructor had apparently lost his entire family, wife and children, to a hungry pack of vampires, but Hamilton, he didn't know what it was to lose someone with familial ties.

He'd been alone from the very beginning.

Not that he wasn't aware that vampires could be spiteful, dangerous creatures, but he never had reason to take vengeance against them. He'd been raised into this life, brought to take down any and every immortal to ever cross his path, and, just like a stoic, lifeless being, he performed these killings nearly every night without the slightest thought.

That vampire from the night before, his gentle nature and kindness had been able to strike a moment of hesitation in Hamilton.

With his devastatingly charming looks and soothing tone, Hamilton hadn't once put a thought into breaking stance and going for the kill he'd intended with the other. A piece of him could still feel the caress of the vampire's fingers after handing back his scarf.

"In your world, Hamilton, I do not exist."

What did that mean? Why had he recognized him off the bat?

Hamilton knew his name was well-known in the immortal world for obvious reasons, but his face was usually a mystery. The only vampires that ever saw his face long enough to remember his likeness, were those whose lives ended shortly after.

Parked outside of the Council Library, Hamilton sat back behind the steering wheel and glimpsed himself in the rear-view mirror. "What in the Queen's name am I doing?" he said. "This is so foolish." But even with the self-questioning, nothing stopped Hamilton from entering the library and into the hidden chambers that lay within it.

No one knew he was here right now, and he wanted to keep it that way. Moving down the shadowy stone halls, he followed arrow plaques on the walls that directed to the Record Chamber. When he heard voices coming from around a corner up ahead, he dipped into a small room for combat uniforms. He waited behind the door, lips pursed as if it would help quiet his breathing. Once the footsteps crossed and were long gone, Hamilton hurried out of the room and down the twists and turns that made up the underground workings of this place.

Finally, Hamilton reached the record room and listened inside before entering. He shut the door quietly in his wake and looked about. Tall bookshelves were lined like domino about the room, all stacked with books, folders and drawers holding extra documents. He turned on the ceiling lights and inspected the shelves, looking for the alphabetical arrangements. Dominick von Kraige. He would be in the K's.

Hamilton searched the many shelves for the designated section. There were tons of vampires on file in the 'K' department, and when Hamilton spotted 'Kraige', he slipped the file from its placement. "Ah-ha," he whispered, "There you are."

Opening the file, Hamilton was faced with a blurry black and white photograph of the vampire. Dominick looked the same as he had the night before, thick dark hair, young handsomeness, and the cocky glint in his eyes seemed to express itself without him even noticing. Within the file, Hamilton learned of Dominick's heritage, homeland, where he resided now, and even the fact that he was the leader of a coven just out of the city. This vampire was a bit of an authority figure to his kind, but Hamilton wasn't interested in that. What he'd truly been in search of was the inscription of his creator's name, but no name was written down anywhere.

"Bollocks!" Hamilton swore. "Who are you?"

Returning Dominick's file to where it belonged, Hamilton sighed, and turned to leave. How on earth was he going to find out anything about this vampire if his total existence was a mystery? Maybe that's the way it should stay, he considered, but he still couldn't get the need to know out of his system. What made him so special that his existence was kept from anyone's knowledge?

After leaving the underground passageways and the library all together, Hamilton stood outside the building, contemplating what he'd do next. Something in his gut was telling him to leave all of this behind and just go home, but another part told him to push forward, and it wasn't hard to guess which one would win him over in the end.

Giving a polite smile to a family that crossed his path, Hamilton returned to his car and dropped into the driver's side. He started the engine and waited behind the steering wheel for a moment, trying relentlessly to talk himself out of what he planned to do next.

He was going to Dominick's coven.

"You're an idiot, Hamilton," he said to himself, "A complete and utter idiot."

With Dominick's address in his mind, Hamilton drove towards it, out of the city and to a more rural part of the area. There were green pastures for several kilometers, and once ten to fifteen minutes passed, he pulled up in front of a palace-like mansion that looked as though it'd been built in the 1400s. Clearly it was modernized by the lights glowing from the windows. There was a driveway that led into an iron gate securing the grounds, a call button beside a keypad and a screen to show a visual of potential visitors.

Though it was cold and snowy on this night, and Hamilton should very much reconsider the actions he was taking, he rolled down the window of his car and pushed the call button on the keypad.

The screen flickered on and the grainy image of a white-haired girl with dark skin popped up. She glared at Hamilton through the security camera. "Who the hell are you?" she spoke through a microphone, her accent heavily French.

Hamilton at least thought it wise not to introduce himself by name, and replied with, "I'm here to see Dominick."

She peered closer at him, a tasteful smirk coming to her lips then. "You're very pretty," she admitted. "Dominick's always got good taste in his preferences. But, alas, name or no entry."

"Haven," he said, using his middle name only. "My name is Haven."

The girl seemed to ponder on the name before pushing a button and giving Hamilton access to the grounds. He continued up the drive and parked in front of the door. Before getting out of the car, he unstrapped his stake holster and left it under the passenger seat. There was no doubt that if he was discovered with it, every vampire in the mansion would come down on his head.

On this night, he wanted to keep the peace.

He approached the front door then, and it was immediately opened by a pair of blonde-haired, petite and fair-skinned twins. They were boys and looked no older than twenty-one, with blue eyes and their fangs on full display. They licked hungrily in Hamilton's direction and welcomed him inside. "You're a pretty one," the twin on his left breathed into Hamilton's ear as he stepped through the door.

The twins hooked Hamilton's arms behind his back and led him further into the old classic house. He laid his eyes on countless other vampires as he was taken down hallway after hallway. There had to be more than two or three dozen in the whole place, some dressed in regular clothing, while most took more towards the Gothic appearance. They all stared as Hamilton passed, not seeming surprised that a human was there for their leader.

Descending a flight of steps to a basement area, Hamilton was thrust through the doorway. This place was anything but what an ordinary basement appeared to be. It was decorated with expensive furnishings, antique sets making up a parlor room with an attached sleeping area. It was much like a large studio apartment.

Seated on a black and gray sofa was Dominick dressed in black slacks and a dark cotton button down, and between his long legs on the floor was a slender, naked human boy with a head of brunette hair, hands pleasing himself as Dominick dragged a hand down the center of the boy's bare chest. The vampire's mouth was pressed to the boy's neck, blood spilling into his mouth as he fed.

Hamilton's whole body stiffened at the sight of a human willingly and pleasurably giving up his own blood for the sake and hunger of an immortal. He was shoved then, stumbling and fell to his knees on the Persian rug.

"Lord Dominick," the twins said together, "You have an unannounced visitor. Seconds, we'll assume?"

Without taking his attention from the boy in his grasp, Dominick waved toward the armchair across from him and the twins commanded Hamilton to it and left the room.

An uncomfortable knot formed in Hamilton's throat as Dominick continued with his meal, trying to focus on anything in the room other than the sounds coming from the human boy, and the fact that being fed on was a sexual stimulation for him.

Hamilton's face flushed with each eager and voluminous moan that sounded through the room, the catches in the human boy's breath, and he pursed his lips together with a hand over his eyes the moment Dominick's whispered voice said, "Cum for me."

At the sound of the boy's shaking and lamenting climax, Hamilton waited to hear him get up and leave next before looking toward Dominick again.

The vampire sat back comfortably on the sofa now, clearing the blood on his lips with a simple run of his tongue. He looked so full of himself, cocky, as if it were a right for him to carry himself the way he did. After running a hand through the dark locks of his wavy hair, he crossed his arms over his half-bared chest due to the few buttons closing the black material. "You must have some huge balls to come walking into my coven like this, Hamilton," was Dominick's response to seeing the slayer. "What the fuck do you want?"

Hamilton sat with his hands pressed between his knees, and when he opened his mouth to speak, Dominick cut him off. "Choose your words wisely or you won't be leaving this house with your life intact."

"I wanted..." Hamilton started over again, "I came to ask of the vampire who accompanied you the other night."

Dominick snarled at the slayer—the territorial annoyance bright in his narrowed eyes. "You think I'm just going to let you get your murderous hands on my father? I will take back my first comment. You're just a bloody idiot."

"I called myself such," Hamilton admitted, "But I don't plan to harm him. My only wish is to—."

"My father doesn't do humans, Hamilton. He doesn't feed from them, nor does he like to fuck them, so there is no reason for you to try and become his number one fan. You have no business with him for anything."

Hamilton furrowed his brow, "You're sure he wouldn't even share a few words with me?"

Dominick growled and it rumbled deep in his throat. "No," he claimed.

"I want to hear the words from *his* mouth."

Out of frustration, Dominick stood rapidly from his seat, the movement so fast that Hamilton found threat in it. He flipped backwards off the armchair, standing ready for anything behind it.

"Just because he spared your life the last time doesn't mean he'll do it again," Dominick warned. "If he finds out some infamous slayer is trying to get close to him for a kill, he'll tear you inside out, and I will happily watch him dispose of you."

"I don't believe you," Hamilton countered. "I don't think he's as vicious as you make him out to be."

"Oh, yeah?" Dominick grinned. "Then I'll take you to him and you can discover him for yourself."

CHAPTER FIVE

An Introduction to the Vampire

Dominick hadn't been very kind when escorting Hamilton back through the manor. He'd shoved the human up the stairs and through the halls, all the while being watched intently by the other vampires inhabiting the large home.

Hamilton thought he was going to be led outside into the cold, but instead, Dominick turned him to a stairwell leading to the upper levels of the manor. He caught himself when he tripped on the top step of the third floor, and Dominick closed a tight grasp around his arm, directing him down a hallway that stopped at a lofty set of double doors.

Somehow throwing the doors open without even touching them, Dominick pushed Hamilton inside. The room was much like the fancy studio in the basement but this one looked more like a home with a business office attached to it. Dominick's creator was standing across the room with another woman, and when Hamilton laid eyes on the man, the breathlessness that had filled him before returned.

The vampire was dressed in dark trousers and a black blouse with white ironed cuffs. His mane of hair was down and swooped out of his face, and his posture changed when his eyes met Hamilton's. He uncrossed his arms and seemed to loosen up, drifting from his conversation with the woman before him. With a wave of his hand, he said, "Leave us," and the woman immediately exited the room.

When the room doors were closed, Dominick said, "Father, this slayer thinks it was a good idea to invade my home."

"Dominick," the vampire spoke, his voice settled and cool, "You leave us as well."

"But, father!"

"Now."

Without further command, Dominick glared warningly at Hamilton and got directly in his face. He steamed with anger, and said, "If I sense even the slightest disturbance in him, I will return faster than you can count your blessings and tear you from this fucking world!" Then Dominick left the room as well, the doors closing themselves behind him.

The moment Hamilton found himself completely alone with this vampire, everything he thought to say before flew out of his mind. His mouth dried and his thoughts went blank.

Seeing this, the vampire gestured to the sitting area, and said, "Please, take a seat. Make yourself at home."

Hamilton resisted at first but then found a spot on the sofa across from a lit fireplace. The crackling firewood evened out the room's silence, but it did not break the obvious strain filling the air.

Strolling across the room in an unruffled stride, the vampire looked back at the slayer and said, "Would you like a drink? It is not often that I get mortal visitors, but I like to keep human necessities if ever the occasion comes around."

Hamilton much liked the manner in which the vampire spoke. There were no traces of animosity in his tone, nor did he sound distressed by the unannounced coming of a human, and not just any human, but a slayer wielding a prevalent title. "A water," Hamilton spoke up finally, trying not to sound as anxious as he was. "A water would be nice."

The vampire stepped into a small kitchen area in the room and took two glasses from a tall cabinet. After filling one with water from a pitcher, he grabbed something else from the fridge. It was a sack of blood that looked as if it'd come from a hospital. When he sliced it open, he poured the thick red contents into his own glass, walked the drinks into the sitting area and handed Hamilton the water.

Accepting the beverage, Hamilton stared at the immortal's drink, but before he could muster a comment on behalf of it, the vampire said, "Don't worry yourself. It is donated blood."

Swigging a bit of his water, Hamilton asked, "Your son, he says you don't feed from humans. Where do you get the blood?"

Taking a seat of his own in a black and red antique barrel armchair, the vampire met Hamilton's nervous eyes. "Now, I am sure you did not risk your life invading this territory to ask such tedious questions. What is it, Hamilton, that you came looking for? Answers to questions even you are unsure of? Or, perhaps you came looking for my head."

Turning the glass in his hands, Hamilton said, "Should I have a reason to want your head?"

"I could give you many reasons why you should, but I am working on trying not to dwell in the past for too long."

Hamilton admired how the vampire swallowed down a gulp of blood. He looked massive in the chair, like a king on top of a rightful throne, and Hamilton thought he would look even better with himself in the immortal's lap. With long muscular legs and a strong ominous build, Hamilton was sure if he wanted, he could have a myriad of people begging for his love, his attention, his everything. But Dominick had made it clear the vampire's desires laid nowhere, with others of his kind or humans.

"I am a busy man," the vampire said, his smoky voice breaking Hamilton's lustful concentration. "There are things I must get done before the night's end. While I would love to sit here in silence with the Slayer Public's most legendary member, I really must not waste what little time I have."

Hamilton thought it quite ironic that someone with all the time in the world was worried about wasting what would be just a couple of minutes.

When he finally found himself able to conjure up a question worth asking, he reached forward and set his now empty glass down on the clear cocktail table separating them. Pulling his red sweater closed, he sunk further into the sofa. "Why...um, why didn't you take the opportunity to kill me the other night? If I am as infamous as your kind sees me as, why let me walk knowing I will likely kill again?"

"The answer is simple enough," the vampire said, licking his lips when a dash of blood was left behind. The unselfish act was not meant to be so tempting, but Hamilton found it as such. "I have no conflict with you, nor do I plan to."

"But I am Hamilton," he said, "If you were any other vampire out there in this world, I bet you would not have wasted a second to get your hands around my throat. Your son, he was quick to resort to the thought, yet you held him back from going through with the objective in mind. What makes you so different from them? What gave you a heart so unlike the rest?"

The vampire said one word, "Time," one word that cooled the flurry in Hamilton's chest, replacing it with a wave of burning curiosity.

"Where did you come from?" Hamilton asked, and then he paused, rewording his question. "No, *when* did you come from?"

As the vampire stood from his chair, Hamilton rose with him, following him across the room back to the small kitchen. "You are very inquisitive, aren't you?"

"Please, I really only want to know," Hamilton said, "I've never met a vampire like you before and it's...reviving...to not have to fight for my life while in the presence of one. If time is what has given you such a tender mind, you must be much older than the lot downstairs."

When the vampire continued into the small kitchen area to put his bloody glass in the sink, Hamilton stood beside him, leaning nosily into his personal space.

"I've heard stories of possible vampires that may exceed the time of man from my instructor," Hamilton went on. "Vampires whose lifespans stretch thousands of years into history. Vampires who have extraordinary strength and abilities undiscovered. No slayer actually believes immortals like this exist out of plain conceited pride for the Public, but I know they are real, I know vampires with the influence and true immortality of centuries are out there."

The vampire turned to Hamilton, peering down into his keen blue eyes. "What makes you think these fables are true?"

"Because, I am looking at one right now. You..." a smile of discovery perked at Hamilton's lips, "...you're an elder, aren't you?"

There was no challenge to the slayer's assumption this time. "You should try not to pry too deep into worlds you do not fully comprehend. It is a dangerous thing to do for someone like you."

Knowing he'd hit the jackpot with finding out this immortal's true background, Hamilton's smile grew even brighter. "I knew it! Oh, how exciting. May I ask your name, please? You are completely undocumented. It's like you don't exist."

"And that's the way I intend it to stay. I don't need the rest of the Slayer Public attempting to come down on my head after so many years. I've gone a very long time without need for senseless bloodshed, and I do not wish to return to it. However, if a slayer ever dares to approach me with resolve to kill, I would quickly end them without remorse. You should leave."

Hamilton blocked the vampire's path when he tried to get around him, their bodies not an inch from one another.

"If I leave," Hamilton bargained, "can I see you again? It doesn't have to be here if you're worried about what the others will think. It can be anywhere. I just — it is such an extraordinary feeling to know that someone like you exists, and I don't want to lose contact so immediately. I know I must sound like an irrational child, but, please? That's all I can say. Please, can I see you again?"

The vampire couldn't seem to follow where this fixation was coming from, but it was intriguing for him to see a slayer whose one purpose in life was to kill vampires, so infatuated by something he was supposed to loath. He held his answer for a moment, taking in the luminous gleam in Hamilton's eyes, how despairing and restless he was for a response to his bold plea.

Upon debating Hamilton's request, the vampire saw clearly just how stunning of a man the slayer was. Like many vampires, he was well aware of the one called Hamilton, of his skill, his determination, and had already bore witness to his soft beauty from afar some years ago.

However, this was his first time being able to appreciate it up close. With the face of a gorgeous being nimbly etched into his countenance, the vampire couldn't help but take into account how lovely Hamilton truly was up close and in person.

"Alright," the vampire finally answered, "But we can never meet one another here again. I have another home where I stay when I'm not called upon. We can meet there where Dominick will not intrude. Seventy kilometers north from here is where my home stands. Tomorrow, meet me at the entry of The Palace of Westminster, and I will direct you to it. Do you understand?"

This filled Hamilton with joy, and he nodded. "Thank you so much!" he expressed gleefully. "I can't tell you what it is that I need from this form of interaction, but having it with you feels invigorating. I'm sorry if I come off as strange, but," he stopped himself, breathing to center his roused emotion. "I'm sorry, this must be so bizarre for you."

The vampire gestured for the door of his room, a wordless reminder that he had other things to do.

Hamilton stopped once more when the door was opened for him, "May I have your name now?"

Finally giving in, the vampire said, "Demiesius. I am Demiesius Titus."

"Deh-me-zee-us Titus," Hamilton pronounced for himself, "I will remember it for the next time we meet."

With a single nod, Demiesius saw Hamilton off, watching as the cheerful human disappeared down the hall.

Hamilton felt a liberation come over him by the time he reached the first floor. Others stared at him, questioning his happiness, but none of them took the time to stop and interrogate him. When he was out of the mansion, he got back into his car and started home to Gregor House. He wanted to explain away his satisfaction with coming to a sort of agreement with Demiesius, but not even he understood why the happiness in him was so widespread.

He couldn't control this feeling, his thoughts. Every form of exhilaration that filled his being was so new, so irrepressible, and Hamilton almost didn't want to be able to control it. This feeling in his veins, he wanted it to prosper, to expand and expand and never shrink. As he drove, the vampire remained firmly in his mind, the sound of his voice like mystifying music, eyes like dark tremendous charms it seemed so easy to get lost in. "Demiesius," Hamilton spoke the ancient name once more. It was befitting enough, elemental and unique for a man such as he.

Pulling into the grounds of Gregor House, Hamilton parked his car in front of the instructor's building. Before he entered it, he stopped when he heard sounds of contest echoing from far off. It was coming from the gymnasium, and when he looked toward the windows at the very top of the building, he spotted the lights on inside.

Checking up on the late-night trainees, he walked down the concrete path leading to the gym. The doors were open, letting the cold winter air breeze into it. Inside was Julius Dalton, Hamilton's own student. Dressed in just running shorts and trainers, he had the weapon of the day in his fearsome possession: the chain and sickle. There was a target of a wooden stand posted in the center of the gym, deep lacerations dug all over it.

Julius' young and toned body dripped with sweat, dark hair matted down as he skillfully directed the blade of the weapon around himself. When he whipped its sharp edge out at the wooden post, Hamilton stood impressed with the boy's progress. It'd only been a day and here he was, almost a master at handling the difficult tool.

When the sickle was embedded into the post, Hamilton clapped his hands proudly, the strident sound bringing Julius' attention to him. "You are a fast learner," Hamilton acknowledged. "Good, good. But a great fighter must also know when their body needs to rest. Come, Julius, you should get some sleep for now. We'll pick up on it again tomorrow."

The teenager caught his breath and coiled the chain around his arm. After he had the wooden post back along the wall of the gym, he joined Hamilton and they walked outside together. "I looked for you before I started," the fifteen-year-old said, "But I couldn't find you."

Playing it safe, Hamilton said, "I just stepped out for a while. If you wanted me here, I would have gladly stayed if you'd asked me before nightfall. This," he said, toying with the chain of the weapon, "is usually far more difficult to pick up on, but from the little bit I saw, you are quite good with it."

"Thank you," Julius smiled, happy to hear the compliment. "I want to be just like you by the time these training years are over."

Hamilton had honest faith in the boy. "I'm sure you'll likely succeed me if you keep this up."

"Impossible," Julius believed. As they were stopped in front of the dorms for the students, he added: "I don't think there will ever be a slayer more gifted than you."

Hamilton offered a laugh, finding it more amusing that everyone considered him to be this remarkable vampire assassin, when in reality he held a secret as deadly as Demiesius under everyone's nose. It truly wasn't a laughing matter, dangerous more like, but Hamilton kept it to himself.

"Go to bed, Julius," he said to the boy. "Our session begins in the morning."

Departing from Julius, Hamilton made it to his room and undressed to lay beneath the covers in his nightwear that consisted of a simple black short-sleeve and his underwear.

Urging sleep to take him, he smiled in the dark—eager for the night that followed to come.

CHAPTER SIX

Secrets are Best Kept at Night

Hamilton had forgotten the mission he was supposed to take his trainees on tonight. They were going to make an appearance at a small vampire nest of immortals who'd brutally murdered a human couple on their way home from the cinema. The story had made it to news stations around the country, and had to be taken care of by the Public's influence, marking the murders as animal attacks given the grotesque condition the bodies were left in.

Originally, this was going to be Hamilton's mission alone, but he figured giving the three boys a taste of how real being a slayer could get wasn't such a bad idea.

They were on the other side of London at a collection of warehouses. After Public informants did their amount of research and trailing of the suspected vampires, they'd gathered enough information to pinpoint this warehouse station was where the vampires resided.

In the D block of a section with abandoned buildings, Hamilton stood before his students. They were all dressed for the occasion in black leather, yet flexible, attire with steel-toed boots, and a mask that shielded the lower half of their faces. Of the three boys, Samuel Colebrook looked the most nervous. He pulled at the high collar of his shirt and gulped. Upon seeing the scar that disappeared down the boy's face to his chest, Hamilton wondered if he was afraid of getting another one to match.

Kingston, though he still looked like he could use a couple more hours of sleep, had his red fringe slicked out of his eyes, attention fixed to get started. He had a stake ready in his hand, clasped tight in his pale fist.

Julius seemed anxious to begin with the chain and sickle in his possession. Given his progress with the weapon, Hamilton had decided to give him permission to test it out on their opponents for tonight.

His expectations were high.

Outside of the warehouse, the four looked up at it. The stone walls were three stories high, and numerous glass windows were painted black to keep the sunrays out during the day. Any human in their right mind would stray far from this place if ever faced with it, but these were exactly the kinds of places Hamilton anticipated most young and abandoned vampires to call home. He'd learned that when vampires attempt to go on without their creators, they tend to live opposite lives of their educated brethren. Without guidance, young vampires were more likely to wind up in nests formed in dark, dank places just like this desolate warehouse.

"Alright, lads," Hamilton kept his voice down, "Once we enter this place, all verbal communications must come to a standstill. We're here to take down two individual vampires, but from what I've been told, there are five of them that live here. What I want out of this mission, is to give all of you a taste of the realities of the Slayer Public, but do not worry, all of you will make it back to Gregor House so long as I stand. Are you ready?"

Each boy nodded.

Hamilton led the way to a ladder that'd been bolted to the rear of the building. It was rusty but held well as the slayers climbed toward the roof. Before reaching the platform, Hamilton grabbed onto the edge of an open window. It was one of the three that'd been broken in, and he pulled himself up into it.

Today's lesson at Gregor House was stealth: how to walk on air. Although they did not literally 'walk on air', it was important for a slayer to be able to adjust their footing to make sure not a single noise was made when stalking their prey. While practicing, anyone who made a sound was punished with one hundred push-ups each time. So, eventually, by the end of the day, everyone had become quite the expert of maneuvering as stealthy as a cat on top of a fence post.

Once each of the boys was standing beside Hamilton, they followed him down an elevated iron platform hovering above the main floor of the warehouse. Below was concrete flooring, five large open crates toppled over on their sides, all of which were distanced from one another.

It smelled of rotting flesh inside, as well as stale water and rust, and it didn't take Hamilton long to locate the source of the rotting stench. At the far end of the warehouse was a pile of ten human bodies, all of which were pale, drained completely of blood and were beginning to decompose.

Glancing to his students, Hamilton noticed the discomfort in Samuel's eyes when he got a look at the men and women whose lives had been cut short, while Julius and Kingston looked more than prepared to avenge the fallen humans.

Surveying the warehouse, the slayers laid eyes on the vampires that holed up in this place. There were two women and three men, and they didn't look like the type of vampires Hamilton was used to facing, but they were still rather familiar to him. These ones took on a more demented appearance. With eyes as black as coal, their cheeks were sunken, skin a pallid gray, and the nails protruded from their fingertips like sharpened daggers. This was not just a nest of vampires that'd been abandoned by their creators; they were blood deprived, always looking to feed and were never satisfied once they did.

They were some of the most dangerous.

"Bennie," one spoke, voice hoarse and dry, "I must feed now. I must!"

Hamilton waved the boys to follow him further down the platform.

"I know, Maddox," another chimed in, "We shall taste sweet blood again tonight."

Given that the stairs to the levitated platform had fallen years prior, Hamilton dropped from the very edge and landed nimbly on the ground twenty feet below. Not a sound was made as each of the boys landed behind him. Hamilton nodded toward Julius and Kingston, signaling for them to make their way across the warehouse to the other side. As the boys did so, Hamilton kept Samuel with him in case his bravery faltered during this mission.

When Julius and Kingston were in position, Hamilton adjusted the cuff blades strapped to his wrists, releasing silver curved knives sharpened to perfection that would slice with one swing of his fist. He stepped out of the shadows and into the open. The five vampires were gathered on the other side of the warehouse still, going on and on about how famished they were. From the holster around his ankle, Hamilton withdrew his personal stake and targeted his eyes on a tall, thin, black-haired vampire.

The immortal turned around; his colorless eyes locked on a smirking Hamilton H. Hamilton.

Twirling the stake between his fingers, before the vampire could react to his presence, Hamilton chucked the weapon in the vampire's direction. Like a bullet, the wood and silver pierced through the air and struck its mark.

Upon impact, the stake drove deep into the vampire's chest and he screeched in agony. The veins beneath his flesh immediately sparked a dull shine of red, burning like fire as he continued to scream bloody murder. His strident call drew the attention of the other four vampires, and they watched in bewilderment and surprise as their fellow immortal collapsed to the ground, falling into a pile of blood, bones and ash.

Having taken the numbers down from five to four against four, leveling the playing field, Hamilton glanced toward his students, a high-pitched whistle leaving him that marked the official start of their mission.

From this moment, everyone was going to be on their own.

The four remaining vampires hissed ferociously at the slayers, sprinting with inhuman speed, each of them going for their own person.

The one named Bennie aimed for Hamilton. He was a

pale-skinned, husky immortal with brown buzz cut hair, and sharp down-turned brows that showed his rage. His white fangs protruded from their slits, saliva dripping as he dashed toward Hamilton.

Striking out at the slayer, a fast punch driving straight for Hamilton's face, the vampire missed when his arm was suddenly seized and he went flying, landing with a hard thud on the concrete. He screamed in outrage, tackling the slayer next after quickly recovering.

Hamilton lurched when his back struck the ground, head walloping against the surface. His vision went dizzy for a split second, but when he regained focus a moment later, the vampire was mere centimeters from slashing its talons across his throat.

Using the blades connected to his wrists, Hamilton swung out, the silver cutting deep into his targer's face and he flinched away, rising off Hamilton.

Hamilton got to his feet and quickly checked on his students, happy to see they were holding their own against their opponents. Even Samuel was doing a mighty good job dodging and countering attacks. Julius fought like lightning, keeping up with the fast-fighting style of the vampire in his prospects. Kingston, on the other hand, became distracted when he noticed Hamilton was eyeing him. He took a hard kick to his throat and fell backwards, choking for air as the female vampire stalked ravenously towards him.

The second Hamilton tried going for Kingston, his vampire, Bennie, seized him by the ponytail and yanked.

At the sudden pull, Hamilton sent his elbow, hitting the vampire dead in the face. Bennie's nose burst and blood drained from him. Without thinking then, Hamilton swung his arm in a powerful spinning back fist, but instead of his fist hitting the vampire, the blade beneath it sliced cleanly through Bennie's neck. His head toppled to the ground and rolled away from his body before disintegrating.

Quickly bringing his attention back to Kingston, Hamilton cursed when the boy seemed to have lost his fire.

Cowering on the floor, Kingston retreated on his bottom as the woman drew nearer. As fast as he could, Hamilton sprinted towards the immortal.

"Kingston!" Hamilton shouted through his mask, "Get up, now!"

The boy didn't register Hamilton's command. Instead, he flailed in fear as the vampire reached out for him, taking hold of his shirt. Lifting Kingston with ease, the vampire slammed his back up against the wall of the warehouse and aimed her dripping fangs for the fifteen-year-old's neck.

Before she could bite down, the vampire gasped in shock when an intense agony was driven into her, breaking through her spine until it burst through her heart and came out the other side.

In that instant, her body dwindled and shrunk, falling to pieces at Kingston's feet, his teacher now standing there in front of him.

Hamilton said nothing and turned for Julius and Samuel. On their own, they fought against the two remaining vampires, ending their so-called immortal lives only seconds later.

Alone now, the slayers were left in the warehouse with five piles of ash and bone.

Giving Julius a nod of approval, Hamilton pulled down his mask, and said, "We're going to have to work on your stance.

You leave yourself wide open for blind attacks that could sneak up on you, but other than that, you did a very good job. I'm proud." To Samuel, he said, "You did exceptionally well. I could tell you were a little nervous at the beginning, but you put everything aside when your life was on the line. We'll work on your counters, but you did great tonight."

When Hamilton met Kingston's eyes, frustration came over him and he shook his head. "I should not have brought you out here. Clearly from your demonstration, you were not ready in the least. A professional slayer would never submit to a vampire, and you did all but wrap yourself in a bow for one. I am very disappointed in you, Kingston." He touched the boy's shoulder then, giving a light jostle of reassurance when the student took on a dejected shadow. "Don't worry, though. We've still got a whole three more years of practice to go, and by that time, I'm confident you'll be a great fighter."

Kingston nodded and they headed back to Gregor House for the night.

Once they all returned, the first thing Hamilton did was jump in the shower. Standing naked in his porcelain tub, he washed the sweat and blood from his hair and body, more than excited for the plans he had afterwards.

He was going to meet Demiesius in front of The Palace of Westminster, and just the thought of being in his company brought a liveliness to his own heart. He still couldn't explain what it was about Demiesius that truly excited him so much, but it would be crazy if he passed it all up.

When something like this takes over, it shouldn't be ignored, and Hamilton wasn't going to push it under the rug. He wanted to know Demiesius even though the consequences of this were all too known to him.

If anyone at all found out about this secret visit, or even the knowledge of him holding out on information about a vampire like Demiesius, he would instantly be labeled as a defector and death would reign over his name.

Drying his hair and body, Hamilton slipped on a pair of tight white trousers, and a fitting black blouse with a white collar that buttoned all the way up. They were clothes from the woman's department, and he liked wearing them. They fit better and complimented his figure more than men's clothes. He let his fair hair flow down past his shoulders, and hooked a silver necklace with an amulet of his Aries birthstone around his neck.

As he stared into his pretty reflection in the white vanity, Hamilton noted his plain-as-day femininity. Most slayers who'd come up with him over the years always assumed they knew his sexual orientation, taking him as someone who preferred the same-sex after just one day with him, and Hamilton was okay with that, because 1) it was true, and 2) after finding out the skill he had, no one ever gave him shit about it.

Homosexuality wasn't always so acceptable in the outside world, but in the slayer world, sexuality had nothing to do with talent and expertise. So long as you could prove yourself against vampirekind, the Slayer Public hadn't a problem nor did they care about what went on in someone's personal life, because that's exactly what it was—a personal life, something everyone was allowed to have.

From a box on top of the vanity dresser, he withdrew a small stick of lip gloss, and spread a hint of red over his pink lips. After, he applied a dash of dark liner and shadow above and around his eyes, giving a sort of narrow sharpness to them.

Makeup wasn't always something he wore, but it made him feel prouder of himself in some way.

Once he was ready to go, Hamilton grabbed the keys to his car, slipped into a coat and was out the door with his handbag.

"Look at you," a voice came from down the hall when Hamilton stepped out of his room.

It was Teresa Rodchester, one of the slayers he'd grown up with. They'd had the same instructor and had become quite good friends over the years. They looked awfully similar, having been referred to as sisters a couple times in their life. Even with their mirrored features, Teresa had gray eyes while Hamilton's were blue, and she obviously had a much fuller chest.

"You're either looking this good for yourself," she said, "Or you've got a date."

Hamilton smiled, "It's not a date," he admitted, "But I am meeting someone, so..."

"A date," Teresa smirked.

"No!" Hamilton blushed, "I'll be back later."

Following Hamilton as he walked, Teresa said, "Must be such a bother that we can't meet with friends during regular hours since we're stuck at Gregor training all day, and then half the night is sometimes taken up by tasks."

"I particularly like these hours," Hamilton said, descending a flight of stairs.

Teresa stopped when they reached the first floor and watched Hamilton continue on. "Well, you have always been a night owl. Have a nice time on your date, Hamilton."

"I will..."

Finally out of the instructor's quarters, Hamilton dropped into his car and started off.

Demiesius was his next destination.

CHAPTER SEVEN

All a Vampire Needs to Fall in Love is Time

Hamilton alone stood near the entrance at The Palace of Westminster. He wasn't much comfortable being too close to the doors, so kept a good distance just in case.

In case of what?

He wasn't quite sure, but keeping a cautious outlook felt right. Bundled in a black trench coat, his hands were tucked into the warm pockets, and away from the brittle cold surrounding him. He'd been sure with having gone through a mission earlier in the night, Demiesius would be the one awaiting his arrival.

"Took you long enough..."

Hamilton jumped at the irritated voice and quickly turned around.

Dominick was standing before him in black trousers and a

mulberry shirt. His dark hair was tied back in a droopy bun, exposing the prominent, unlined fineness of his young face. The vampire's eyes were fixed on Hamilton, brow downed in annoyance and gaze washed with an obvious hate.

Looking around, Hamilton didn't spot Demiesius anywhere and quickly began to worry and kept on his toes. Not that he wanted to believe it, but if there was even the slightest possibility that the vampire could have given his location to others, Hamilton wanted to be prepared.

His stake was ready in his handbag.

Instead of mouthing off to Hamilton as the slayer was expecting next, Dominick merely looked upon the slayer in confusion, taking note of the makeup on his lips and dabbed beautifully around his eyes. "My father gets involved with someone for the first time in centuries, and of course, it had to be with a fucking slayer."

"Involved?" Hamilton said, "We're not—."

"Oh, quit trying to use your pretty face as an excuse to act innocent," Dominick cut in. "I can smell the dead vampires under that body wash you used to cover it up. My father told me he was supposed to meet you here, but I refused to let him stand out here in the cold waiting for the likes of you. For all I know you could have more fucking slayers out here in the shadows that'd have been waiting for him."

"Good lord," Hamilton sighed, "I know you don't trust me, and I completely understand why, but I wasn't going to hurt Demiesius, nor do I plan to so long as he doesn't try hurting me. Now, Dominick, I am freezing my arse off out here and would like to get indoors, so could you be polite for a second and escort me to your father?"

Dominick looked like he had something else in mind to say, but stopped when it appeared as if someone else had gotten his attention. He rolled his eyes then, voice droning, and said, "I am to take you to my father's home. Please, let me show you the way..."

Back in Hamilton's car, Dominick directed them past his own home, and a long way out towards where the wilderness began to take over. Once a single paved road cut off into a woodland of trees further away from the main road, the vehicle emerged from the shadows into a wide ward. Nothing but a vast stretch of soaring trees surrounded them, no neighboring villages or anything for several kilometers.

What sat before Hamilton was a magnificent white castle with dark roofing, and all of it made the slayer feel as though he existed in a fairy tale. The ivory white walls were several stories high, there were towering turrets that reached high into the sky, and carvings of stone gargoyles lined the base of intricately fashioned windows.

Its beauty rivaled that of his Queen's Buckingham Palace, a home Hamilton had always admired, and he could hardly believe a vampire was able to survive out here in a place like this. Out in the middle of nowhere, he would have assumed vandals and historians were the types to flock to a place like this. It was primordial and fascinating, gorgeous and Hamilton wanted to hurry and get inside to see the entire beauty of it.

After stalling his car in the long stone courtyard, Hamilton got out with Dominick and they approached the immense wooden doors.

There was a man standing at the top of the stone steps, hands clutched behind his back, stature tall and wide with strength.

His skin was the palest white Hamilton had ever seen, and the red tint of his eyes watched the slayer closely as if cautious of allowing him right of passage. "This is the Master's guest?" the man asked.

Dominick grabbed at the large brass door handle and Hamilton's bicep, directing him into the magnificent castle. "You know he doesn't like it when you call him 'Master', Christoph, but, yes, this is my father's little guest."

Christoph seemed to wrinkle his nose at the idea, but said nothing more as Dominick and Hamilton passed.

The entrance hall was quite spacious, the floor patterned by white and smoky gray tiles. The walls were stone and golden silk curtains draped down the pillars holding up the dome ceiling, arcades at the far end bordering along a seemingly endless walkway. The extensive hall led down to a double staircase and up to a balcony off to the right.

Dominick walked Hamilton up them, passing doorways to studies, parlors, art rooms, and so many more. On the third floor, they finally reached an entryway that led into an open sitting area. The room was much duller in color with dark grays and sangria reds. It was airy with many windows that looked out into the darkness that surrounded the castle.

Releasing Hamilton with a slight push, Dominick sucked his teeth and groaned, "Father!" he called out, having expected to find the man in the room he frequented most.

A minute went by with no appearance of the elder and Dominick huffed. He smirked then and a thought crossed his mind when he peered over at Hamilton. "Looks like my father abandoned his little date. Maybe I'll treat myself to a taste of what's under that porcelain skin of yours."

Hamilton took a step away when Dominick's eyes flashed a hungry shade of violet, licking at the sharp tips of his now exposed fangs.

As if on cue, the moment Dominick stalked one step closer to the slayer, Demiesius' voice rose in the room. "You may leave now, my son."

Turning in the direction of the stoic command, Hamilton looked upon Demiesius. It seemed the man would never fail to look handsome in any lighting. His graceful build was solid and tucked into black ironed trousers and a pearl white shirt. His sleeves were rolled up to his elbows, and the bluish veins that tracked up his arms stood out faintly. His long hair was parted down the middle and fell darkly around his passive and attractive face. To Hamilton he certainly always looked favorable and impressive.

Dominick retracted his fangs and turned to Demiesius, "I knew if I said something like that you'd show up." He grabbed Hamilton's arm and thrust him in the direction of his father, running a soft touch down Hamilton's cheek. "Look at him. He got all pretty and dolled up for you."

Demiesius looked Hamilton over before nodding to Dominick, "I said you could leave now. I'm sure you've got better things to do than attempt to insult my guest of the evening."

"Oh, I wasn't trying to insult him," Dominick said, making his way to the door. "I was merely making an observation, and by the looks of the slayer, he certainly put in a little work to seem presentable." He stopped by Demiesius then, not trying to keep his voice down in the least when he said, "If you ask me, I think he could use a bit of a nicer scent. I can smell the freshly killed vampires from a kilometer away."

When the blood child disappeared, Hamilton stood tense, and said, "I can explain the slaying I was involved in tonight."

Demiesius strolled further into the room, his walk like he was gliding across the floor. "There will be no need for that," he assured. "I was fully aware of the task you completed before coming here. After all, it was I who offered a hand in orchestrating the whole thing."

Hamilton took a seat on a mahogany and red velvet sofa, his curious eyes watching Demiesius take a seat opposite him. "What do you mean by that?"

"I attended a meeting with your top commanders the other night to discuss a chain of events that had taken place not long ago. The vampires you killed were ones who'd become a nuisance to the human world, threatening immortal exposure with every mindless kill they orchestrated. Thus, they were exterminated by order of myself. You needn't worry about being ashamed of the tasks you go out on in front of me. If anything, I was a part of why you went on them in the first place."

"You mean," Hamilton started, "You are in command of the Public?"

"No, I merely associate with a handful of the commanders that run the Public. Don't be fooled by centuries of loathing, Hamilton. Vampires and Slayers have been working alongside one another longer than you'd expect. What do you think really goes on within your Public Gatherings?"

"I guess I've never been quite sure."

Hamilton couldn't fathom vampires and slayers working side by side to keep the streets safe for ordinary humans. He'd always been told vampires' top priority was to feed and survive into the years, and they held little regard for anyone who wasn't of their kind, but it seemed all he'd been told growing up wasn't as factual as he'd thought.

Still, picturing a sort of truce between man and vampire was unusual. "How many of my tasks have you had a say in?" Hamilton wondered.

"All of them," Demiesius stated. "There has not been one vampire whose life you've ended without my say so, of course, aside from any necessary killings I'm sure you've taken part in through the years that were unordered. Given I reign over Europe's entirety, the tasks that are distributed to the Public are partly handed down by me."

"The things people would do if they knew they were taking orders from a vampire..."

"Knowing this," Demiesius said, "doesn't change your outlook on the Public?"

"A little," he admitted, "But, I think it will help me sleep easier."

"Why is that?"

Hamilton thought to himself, of the first actual missions he'd gone out on as a young teenager. Every single one of them had been demented killers who murdered countless innocent people, and a great number of them would not have been captured and executed if not given out from someone who knew the workings of the vampire world.

Hamilton didn't kill senselessly, go after any and every vampire he witnessed on the streets. He only ever engaged with immortals if they were threatening the lives around them. He'd passed vampires going about their business, ones who minded their own without causing disturbance, and other slayers were told to do the same, to only kill if it was absolutely necessary.

Hamilton was sure that if there weren't rules on when to kill and who to kill, all slayers and vampires would be at each other's throats every night.

"It's balanced, I guess," Hamilton said, excusing himself when a cough interrupted him. "The way the world should be."

Demiesius nodded, appreciative of Hamilton's open mind. When things in the room fell to a silence, he opened his mouth to speak, but stopped himself when Hamilton stood from the sofa.

The blonde man slid out of his long black trench coat, and folded it over the armrest. It was difficult not to notice the slim, tight physicality of Hamilton's figure, especially when his white pants hugged his legs the way they did.

Demiesius let his eyes stray from them, and he cleared his throat uncomfortably. "There are a lot of things I understand about the Public," he said then. "Everything from how recruits are chosen and why. Although, I never understood your introduction to this life. Slayers are usually, if not always, victims of some sort to my kind. Whether it be they were attacked by one, or lost family to one, you are of the smallest percentage of the Public who was never wronged by an immortal. Your instructor, did he ever tell you why he led you into this?"

Hamilton brushed his hair to one shoulder, running his fingers through the sweep of it. "I never questioned it, to be honest. In the beginning I thought this was normal. I thought everyone grew up to become a slayer, and by the time I realized that wasn't the case, my instructor was dead, and I didn't care much to know why I'd been raised in this life. I've never had a family and I don't recall ever mourning the loss of one. It might be quite strange to state this, but...I've gotten used to this life."

Hamilton pondered for a moment, his mind visualizing the events of his upbringing. The years of grueling instruction, long sleepless nights, dozens upon dozens of wounds he'd attained both through training and while out on duty; all of it had been more than what any normal person could take, especially given he'd started at the young age of three.

Taking mindless steps about the room, Hamilton waltzed around the sofa he'd been seated on as his eyes wandered the intricate designs of the high ceiling. A slayer's life was rather daunting, but he somehow wouldn't have wished for his life to trail down any other path.

"Seeming to have been born and raised in such an environment," Hamilton followed up with, "I can only say this is all I've ever known."

"You have never wondered where you come from?"

With the question hanging in the air, Hamilton glanced over his trim shoulder at the vampire watching his every move from across the room. "Why are you so concerned with my background?" he said. "As far as I know, it doesn't really matter where I come from. I'm a man. Born, raised, and I will die eventually. Where I come from doesn't matter if I'll just end up where everyone else does. In the ground."

Demiesius stood from his seat as well, crossing to one of the large windows overlooking his rear courtyard. The rare snow continued to sprinkle down from the sky, covering the vast property and wilderness in white blankets, and a low fog began to roll in from the east. "You're a morbid one, aren't you?" he said. "Are you afraid of death?"

Hamilton joined Demiesius at the window, looking more comfortable now that the trench coat wasn't weighing him down anymore. "No," he said plainly. "In my line of work, I have to be prepared for it. Every night I go out, I am laying down my life in the possibility that it may end. If anything, I am always ready for death. Like now, coming here tonight could ultimately cost me my life. I would fight for it, of course, but...if it's my time, then it's my time."

"You say that now," Demiesius shook his head. "Do not be so quick to say that you will be completely accepting of your life being taken. In my human days, I once said I did not fear death. Yet, when those final breaths reached out for me, I wanted nothing more than to keep on. What I am now is the consequence of a man drowned by desperation."

Hamilton peered up at the vampire in confusion. "You mean, someone made you? I thought, what with being one of the first, you and the others came into this world that way."

"We all come from someone," Demiesius said. "I had a mother and a father once, even a sister and younger brother. A family of my own."

"So you...you were married before...with a wife and child?"

"Not necessarily. I only had a child, a son. Then again, he was not my own son. Just a boy in need of someone to call family who eventually began to refer to me as his father."

Hamilton wondered if he'd created Dominick to finally fill the emptiness of no longer having a child.

Without thought, Demiesius went on. "In the time I came from, Hamilton, my people carried beliefs in many entities. My people feared a 'goddess' named Lilith. She was an entity that came from nowhere, one who demanded the blood of man to raise her children. Until she was granted what she wanted, she would curse the nights with unthinkable terrors that haunted the already terrorized population. If you consider mad vampire beings to be deathly afraid of, the images she could conjure would truly bring forth your darkest nightmares. At this point, I was being held captive for refusing to fight in a senseless war for an even more senseless ruler, myself along with two other men and two women there for their own faults. We were set for execution the next night, but given Lilith wanted a sacrifice, instead of leading us to be decapitated, we were taken to a cavern, sealed away and left there for hours. That night, she came to us. At first, she appeared to be nothing more than an ordinary woman. She asked if we wanted to live, if we wanted to be free. Of course, our answers were 'yes'. I wanted to see my family again, and the others also had people to get back to. It would have been mad to say otherwise."

"Of course, you said yes," Hamilton said. "I can't see why anyone would deny her."

Demiesius nodded. "I wonder at times, if she hadn't failed to leave out the main details of her proposition, if any of us would have said a word. Following our answers, she killed us, not feeding from us, but she drained all of our blood. And the only thing I remember next, is that myself and the others were feeding from her. She explained that we were to thrive under the light of the moon, and use her blood to fuel our bodies for the millennia to come. Lilith hadn't wanted our blood to nourish her children, she'd wanted to create children that would live forever. And that night, she'd gotten what she wanted, all at the cost of her very own immortal life."

Captivation wrapped Hamilton after hearing the origin of the elder vampires. He'd always wanted to know where they had come from, how and why they were made. "From a woman desperate for children," he said aloud. "How...tragic."

Demiesius leaned against the wall beside the window, arms crossed as he watched the wonder in Hamilton's eyes flicker.

"The real tragedy, Hamilton, is that now the ones created from us can survive only on the blood of man. I watched as the creations of the others fed mercilessly on those who came before you, leaving cities of death in their wake. It was only when the first Slayer Public was made, that a small piece of order was restored."

Completely enamored with Demiesius, Hamilton held a new sort of admiration for vampires. He knew there were malicious ones out there who wanted nothing more than to kill and feed, but to know there were ones like Demiesius out there, ones who sympathized with the human race, and wanted nothing but structure; he now understood his role in the Slayer Public, and couldn't be more satisfied knowing someone like Demiesius was helping guide it.

"You are marvelous," Hamilton said, and then gasped in surprise when realizing he'd said it out loud. "I'm so sorry, I didn't mean to say—."

"You needn't worry," Demiesius said, keeping his eyes with the deep blues meeting his own dark stare. "There is no need for you to watch your tongue around me. I, too, am glad you grew into the man you are today."

Hamilton couldn't hide the flush of his cheeks even in the soft moonlight, feeling his body warm up in total embarrassment at the thought of pursuing something with this vampire.

He wanted to say something more, but was cut off when a thunder of coughs shook him. He held a hand over his mouth, letting it out until they ceased. "Sorry," he said, "I think I've gotten a fever from the weather. You must enjoy the perks of not being able to catch a cold. What did you mean by that, though? You're glad I am who I am."

"When most slayers join the Public, they go into it blindly and with a fire of hatred for immortals." Demiesius met Hamilton's eyes, seeing how their color seemed to change from the time before. "You are nothing like the rest."

"So..." Hamilton smirked, "...you like me?"

Without an answer to the question, Demiesius stepped away from Hamilton.

Circling around, he almost couldn't believe the temptations running through his mind. Ever since becoming the immortal he was, the sensation breaking into his chest was something external, unnatural in a manner of speaking, something that only ever happened a few times before. He wasn't the type to feel what was occurring inside of him, especially when it involved a human, and not just any human, a slayer, of all.

Several minutes passed into an hour, and Demiesius allowed Hamilton to stay, listening to him go on about the day he'd had, his newly appointed students and how training them was going. He noticed, as their conversations went on, he and the slayer were gravitating closer to one another. Once stood apart, Hamilton was seated just an inch from him on the sofa.

Demiesius enjoyed the sound of Hamilton's voice, noting every quirk in the way he spoke, and the way his nose scrunched cutely whenever he smiled. Sitting back against the armrest, Demiesius felt a rush of desire start through him when Hamilton bent forward and laughed, running a hand up his thigh. There was a beast in him that wanted to take the slayer in more ways than one, and simply thinking about it worried him.

"I think you should leave now," Demiesius said, rising from the sofa. "You shouldn't be here."

"What?" Hamilton followed after him when he crossed the room. "If it was something I said, I'll take it back. I'm sorry."

"It's late," Demiesius added, as if to justify the sudden decision and he grabbed Hamilton's coat that'd been draped over the sofa. "You're sick and should be home. I'm sure people will wonder where you were if you return at dawn with no additional tasks lined up."

They stepped into the hall, Hamilton hurrying along as the vampire started down the stairs to the floors below. "I am a grown and capable man, Demiesius. I can do as I please."

On the first level, Demiesius started through the foyer. When he opened the entry door, Christoph was still on the other side keeping watch over the property with a book in his hand. "Leave," Demiesius said, a heat stirring in his chest. "Go back to Gregor."

"But—," Hamilton was stopped when Christoph grabbed his arm, halting him from going back into the castle.

Demiesius then looked deep into Hamilton's eyes, into his thoughts and seized them. With a hold of the slayer's mind, the look in Hamilton's eyes from the control of his actions looked lost. He settled down and loosened up. The elder then unfolded Hamilton's coat and gently fixed it upon his slight build, all the while talking himself down from allowing this person any more time in his presence. Such a thing was something he wanted, but he also convinced himself there was a certain level of control he needed to get over himself.

When the coat was fixed comfortably on Hamilton once more, Demiesius took a step back in partial regret. "Go home," he commanded.

Seeming released from the mental hold, Hamilton turned from Demiesius and headed for his car, got in, started the engine and left without further word.

Standing there with Christoph, Demiesius sighed, "Make sure he gets back to Gregor House safely. In that condition, he'd never be able to fight his own battles."

"Yes, Master," Christoph nodded, leaving the elder to himself.

When the main doors to the castle were closed, the vampire elder exhaled an unnecessary breath.

He was shaken by the stir in his heart, tongue passing over the tips of his fangs he hadn't noticed were elongated now, and suddenly he was glad Hamilton hadn't noticed them as well.

His hunger was down so there were no thoughts to pierce the other man's skin in his mind, yet this distant allure in him pronounced itself well enough. There were desires rising in him and he promised to control them. Never could he picture himself harming the other man. Never would he do such a thing. Not to Hamilton. Ever.

For now, parting ways for the night seemed to be what was best for them both.

CHAPTER EIGHT

What Keeps the Heartache Away

The open training area at Gregor was surrounded by enclosed trees and a barbed wire fence. It was as long and wide as a stadium football field, and today's lesson was in agility and speed. There was an obstacle course of ropes, tires, walls, and just about any other contraption that was meant to cause difficulty for the runner.

There were other teams out and about, but Hamilton's only focus was on his. With the sun having finally come out, the previous icy rains brought to the country left the grass muddy and slippery, but the bitter cold was still there. Hamilton was at the head of the course, dressed in black joggers and a dark green jumper, a scarf wrapped around the lower half of his face to block the cold wind.

After running a mile around the track, Julius, Kingston, and

Samuel joined their teacher. The chill of sweat dripped down the boy's bodies, and Julius said, "Now what?"

Hamilton nodded to the course, "All three of you are going to run this," he said through the scarf. "Finish as fast as you can. You'll go through each obstacle, but attempt to knock each out without getting caught up in any of them. By all means, this isn't a race, you're not competing against each other, because a slayer's mentality is not to compete with fellow slayers. Simply get the job done, and then return to me here. Got it?"

Each boy nodded and after lining up, Hamilton gave them the go ahead and they were off.

As he watched the boys dart through the field, Hamilton thought of the night he'd visited Demiesius' castle. Things had been going so well...until the vampire seemed suddenly unsure of what he was doing. Hamilton couldn't remember ever feeling so good around someone, enjoying their company, and being kicked out the way he had worried him.

It'd been three whole weeks since their last meeting, and the more time went by, the more Hamilton wanted to reach out to the vampire.

Over the weeks, though, he'd become more consumed with the boys and other tasks. He'd even been going out on more tasks that were out of his district, ones that could have easily been handled by other slayers in the area, but Hamilton felt like he was going out of his way to fulfill them.

After a while, he'd begun to think Demiesius was pinning them on him to keep him so occupied that he'd never have any time to himself.

Coughing against the scarf, Hamilton planned to pick up some more medicine from the grocer's to get rid of this cold.

It was beginning to annoy him.

Kingston was the first to return to his side after a minute and forty-three seconds, Julius and Samuel evenly following afterwards. "Good job," he said, "But you took far too long."

"Really?" Kingston huffed, hands on his hips as he breathed heavily. "I could have sworn that was pretty darn fast."

"It was," Hamilton assured, "...for a regular person. However, we are not regular people. You all should have been able to finish this course in just one minute."

"That's impossible," Samuel said. "How long did it take you to finish this?"

"Fifty seconds."

"Would you care to demonstrate for us?"

Hamilton unwrapped the scarf from around his face and tied it around his waist. "I would be happy to," he said with a smirk.

He stretched for a moment then, bending his leg almost above his head to loosen up his muscles. After pinning his hair in a ponytail, he took his place at the start of the course, and nodded to his fellow Englishman, Julius, to get the timer ready.

"Alright," Julius said, "Go."

At that, Hamilton was off, sprinting as fast as he could toward the first obstacle: the rock wall. Like a lithe feline, he sprung off the ground, able to reach a foothold sixty inches above his own height. Grabbing on, he hauled his body weight up, gripping the top with one more reach. At the top, he jumped back down to the moist ground and continued on. Next were the monkey bars. Taking hold of the first bar, he swung through the rest, skipping four at a time before getting to the end. Grounded again, he went for the tires, bounding over all six rows. Approaching the row of logs that the boys had thought they needed to crawl under,

Hamilton jumped onto the first one, running across the top of the seven that followed. Once on the other side, he reached the rope climb and grabbed onto it, heaving himself up as fast as he could. Able to touch the very top of the post above the rope, he released, landed on his feet and finally sprinted back to his students.

Julius stopped the timer, "fifty-five seconds flat," he smiled.

Hamilton regulated his breath and laughed. "Well, I was thirteen at the time, so give an aging man some credit. I want you all to run through it again the way I did, find a pace and keep it. It's not a race, but be quick."

Once the boys were lined up a second time, Hamilton saw them off and put a hand over his mouth. This whole coughing thing was beginning to make his throat sore. His chest rumbled with it, and when he brought his hand away, he nearly gasped when a splash of blood came off on his palm.

Having had this persistent cough for almost a month, this was the first time anything like this happened and it worried him. He closed his fist around the blood when the boys finished and wrapped his scarf around his face again. Putting the issue aside, he said, "Wow, one minute and twenty-two seconds. A bit more impressive." He looked at the time on his watch. "Well, it's almost supper time. You all go and start with weights. We'll come back to this tomorrow."

On his way to his room, Hamilton debated on stopping by the clinic at Gregor House. If he was starting to cough up blood, he was sure there probably wasn't a good reason for it, but... doctors had never been his cup of tea.

Deciding to give it a couple more days, Hamilton returned to his room. When inside, he washed the blood from his hand and took a dose of the last bit of medicine he had.

In the kitchen area, he could see the window of the living room perfectly. A dark shape looked as if it'd landed on the small ledge just outside.

Furrowing his brow, Hamilton dried his hands and went to the window. When he pushed the curtains aside, he found a black raven sitting outside the glass. The peculiar thing about this bird was that it had a rolled up piece of paper clamped in its beak. The raven looked up at Hamilton and pecked at the window, as if demanding it be opened.

Hamilton unlatched the lock of the window and shoved it up. The bird immediately flew inside, landing on the lid of Hamilton's closed record player. It released the piece of paper, letting it fall to the ground.

After closing the window, the slayer stole the paper from the floor and straightened it out. To his surprise, it was a letter from Demiesius addressed directly to him.

When the raven remained on the record player, Hamilton took a seat at his dining table and read the letter to himself.

Hamilton H. H.

It has nearly been one month since you last visited me, and although I understand why you have not been able to come back since then, I would like to personally invite you. I have been trying my hardest to cut down your tasks these past weeks, but your Public commanders felt you were the most capable to get them done. I am sorry you have not been able to take a break lately.

Tonight I made sure you would not be busy, and look forward to seeing you. However, with the manner in which I treated you last, I will not hold it against you if you choose not to join me. Give the raven

I sent a reply if you plan to visit. I do hope to see you soon.

— Demiesius

Quicker than he imagined he could move, Hamilton grabbed a pen from a holder in the kitchen and a fresh piece of paper from a journal in his back room. At a writing desk, he didn't think twice when he put pen to paper, and wrote down everything he'd wanted the opportunity to say over these weeks. The words met the lines so fast he began to worry if Demiesius would even be able to read the scribbles.

After a couple minutes, he slowed down. It was four in the afternoon, so there was clearly no need for him to rush. The letter wouldn't be read until the vampire woke up after sundown.

Calming himself, Hamilton started over.

Demiesius,

You will never understand the joy I felt when I read your note. Since we last met one another, I've wanted to see you again. Every night since then, I've thought of nothing but you, of how kind you are, how respectful you are to me even though I am who I am. You've shown me a different side of your kind in just that moment I knew you, and by now you've managed to make your way into my life, into my heart, the way no one has ever been able to, the way I have never allowed anyone to. I hope my strange feelings for you don't make you want to push me away either. Even if you don't see me the same way I see you, just being around your sweet nature will be enough for me. There is no need for you to apologize for not being able to slow down my tasks either. I am a slayer, after all, so being busy at night is something I'm used to. I look forward to seeing you tonight.

— Sincerely Yours, Hamilton

Completing his own letter, Hamilton rolled the paper up and

went back to the living area. The raven was still there, cleaning its feathers when it then looked up at the slayer.

Seeing the letter in his hands, the bird flew for it, chopping down with its bill. Hamilton quickly let go in fear of it biting his fingers and opened the window again. The raven dove outside, taking to the sky until disappearing over the trees and out of sight.

Filled with excitement, Hamilton ran for the closet in his bedroom and threw the door open. He rummaged through his clothes, trying to find a suitable outfit for the occasion. He hadn't determined his last meeting with Demiesius to be a date, but this time, he couldn't help it.

When nothing stood out to him, he groaned and shut the door. Shirts and pants were thrown about the floor now, but he didn't care much to tidy up. Throwing on a pair of low-rise jeans, a white shirt that mildly showed his stomach, and a warm beige coat, he fixed a light tan scarf around the lower half of his face, partly for the coughs still tickling his lungs, and partly for the chill the weather was bound to cause.

When he had boots strapped on and the scarf was properly bundled around to cover his mouth, he started down the hall of the instructor's quarters and knocked on the apartment door next to his.

Teresa answered after a second. "Oh, hello, Hamilton," she said, "What can I do for you?"

"I'm going out tonight and I need something to wear. You're the only person I can go shopping with in the departments I like without being ridiculed in public. Would you like to go pick an outfit with me? I'll buy you something!"

With a sinister smile, Teresa grabbed her own coat and joined

Hamilton in the hall. She wore a knee-high floral dress with warm stockings, and after buttoning her white overcoat, she led the way with a smile. "You are going to regret this, my friend."

In black trousers and a coral pink, ascot blouse tucked in at the waist, Hamilton stood on the front steps of Demiesius' home. He'd had a hard time deciding how to style his hair, and ended up with a neat bun and two dangling strands framing his face. He was nervous and excited at the same time, so much so that it'd been a full minute since he'd been standing in the cold.

Christoph, the guard who stood watch last time was nowhere to be found, and after a couple seconds to compose himself, Hamilton knocked his fist against the massive door.

It didn't take long for the doors to open to the owner of the property. Demiesius would never fail to strike a sense of yearning in Hamilton. Each time the slayer laid eyes on the vampire, he swore the man's fine exterior grew more attractive. Tonight he wore a black and cedar green linen shirt, black crisp slacks, and the leather of his shoes were finely polished. His beautiful silk hair was tied at the nape of his neck, and in the lighting of the entrance hall, Hamilton could make out every precise edge of his calm expression. Demiesius was so blessed with such features, Hamilton couldn't help but lose himself.

"H-Hi," he managed.

The corner of Demiesius' mouth curved into a smirk, and he stepped aside to allow the slayer entry, "Please, come in. You look very nice."

Hamilton blushed and moved out of the cold. In such a hurry

to get away from Gregor House, he'd forgotten to grab a coat. When the door was closed behind him, he rubbed warmth into his arms and followed Demiesius further in.

"I see Dominick will not be joining us," Hamilton said.

Leading the way, Demiesius' walk was unruffled and his posture was admirable. "No, he will not," the vampire confirmed. "You will not have to worry about Dominick's remarks. He is my son and I love him, but he has never been one to hold his tongue. It is part of the reason his life once hung in the balance in his human days."

They entered the grand room a minute later, and Hamilton marveled at the sheer size and beauty. It was like stepping back in time to the Roman era. The walls were an ivory white stone, floors marble, pillars supporting and lined about the floor and ceiling. An intricate red and gold rug took up a sizable amount of space on the floor. The ceiling overhead was curved and clever designs trimmed in gold around the doorways, windows, and low panels.

Appreciating the intake of the room, Hamilton said, "Did you save him from permanent death?"

"I did," Demiesius said.

He left the room for just a moment and came back with a platter of tea and biscuits. Even though they were just modest noshes, they made Hamilton's mouth water. He hadn't eaten before coming here either.

Watching the vampire place the tray down, the slayer found it odd that he hadn't servants, butlers, or maids running about this place. With the virtual status of a king in the immortal world, Hamilton expected to see him treated as such. Then again, he wondered if Demiesius got rid of them to make sure no one bothered them.

Taking a seat on a pure white, floral French lounge, Hamilton made himself a cup of tea and swallowed the steamy drink down. As it brought comfort to his inner shivers, he said, "What compelled you to turn Dominick? I don't know him personally at all, but he seems like a polar opposite of you."

"Dominick..." Demiesius pondered, bringing himself down beside Hamilton. "Despite what you may think, is a very intelligent man. But one as outspoken as himself was not right for his time, the early fifteen-hundreds, to be exact. He was just twenty-two years of age and lived in poverty with most of the population of England. Even with being the crofter he was, he'd learned to read and write, understand the workings of politics, what made kings royal, nobles rich and laborers poor. I discovered him one night while he was in the middle of writing a speech he planned to give out at a noble banquet the next day. I thought he was brave for wanting to do something like that, and warned that he'd assuredly be warranted for treason, but he hadn't cared much for what I had to say given I looked like I'd come from royal blood."

"What became of him?" Hamilton asked.

"Exactly what I predicted. I found him locked in a holding cell to be decapitated the next day. At first, he assumed I was the one who'd aided in his capture, but when I finally revealed what I was, and my admiration for the actions he looked to take against his higher-ups, I gave him an option to choose a life he'd be respected and accepted in, or if he wanted to go through with meeting the sword."

"I guess it would be silly of me to ask what his decision was."

A curve touched Demiesius' lips, "It would."

Hamilton laughed, covering the light shake of his coughs. Clearing his throat, he said, "Maybe next time I see him, I'll give him credit for having been a good person. History needed people to stand up for what was right. Unfortunately, those of the past wanted to shut him up."

"Well, yes," Demiesius said, "But look who has lived on. He may be unnecessarily forthright at times, but his influence on the vampires of Europe has been beneficial."

Finishing up his tea, Hamilton downed two biscuits, only finding out that he was being a complete slob by the time the entire plate was empty.

Embarrassed, he cleaned the tips of his fingers above the platter, and Demiesius handed him a folded napkin. "I'm sorry," the slayer apologized, "I haven't eaten and when I get food in me, I can go a bit overboard sometimes. I may look small but I can eat like a famished animal when my appetite is right."

Rising from the lounge, Demiesius said, "I can grab you something else if you'd like. I went and had a few different things brought in earlier in case you grew hungry."

"Yes, please," Hamilton nodded, "Thank you so much."

When Demiesius was gone from the grand room, Hamilton wondered if this was a first for the vampire. Catering to and making sure a human guest was comfortable in his private home.

Flattered in thinking he was, Hamilton suddenly remembered just how many years Demiesius has been on this earth. Was it possible for anyone to go such a long and isolated time without building a connection with anyone else at all? Back in his own adolescent days, during his blind combat training, Hamilton was confined alone in a place for a whole year, let out only when he'd perfected the art of fighting in total inaccessible darkness. That year of his childhood had been one of the hardest. The whole time he'd craved human contact. Being social creatures, it was hard to believe he could be Demiesius' first...anything.

When a cough began to itch at the back of Hamilton's throat, he put the napkin that'd been given to him against his lips and let it out into the cloth. It got immeasurably worse as the heaves caused him to bend over, the rough gnawing at his throat like nails scratching from the inside. He felt the blood rise up and spatter onto the cloth, and when he was at last able to stop, he couldn't believe the amount that came out compared to this morning.

What was happening to him?

As Demiesius returned to the grand room, the strong scent of blood struck him. The slayer's back was to him, and from over his shoulder, the vampire saw the blood spotted napkin. "Hamilton," Demiesius called, getting his attention, "Why don't we sit in the dining area?"

Hamilton quickly folded the napkin as if trying to conceal it and tucked it away in his back pocket. When they were seated again in a voluminous dining room, Hamilton stared hungrily down at a plate of pasta.

Apparently it'd been prepared by Christoph in preparation for Hamilton's arrival. After being heated, it looked fresh and delicious. When Hamilton went for a bite, he paused when Demiesius said, "Are you still not feeling well from the time before?"

Hamilton brought the fork down. Licking his lips, he could still taste a faint sign of blood. "I should have suspected you'd be able to smell it," he said. "I — uh — it's nothing bad. Just a slight temperature."

Sitting across from the slayer, Demiesius said, "Blood doesn't usually accompany minor colds. You should probably see someone soon."

"I will."

Every other night, the two were able to meet this way, simply enjoying the other's company over a meal and a good chat. It was absorbing for Hamilton being able to delve into the life of an immortal who had no intentions of harming him.

Discussing topics like what the world used to be like from the eyes of a vampire brought a new sense of understanding into Hamilton's life. Discovering reasons as to why vampires did certain things, their strengths and myths of their weaknesses he hadn't known of before, Demiesius became a great source of knowledge. The vampire was extraordinarily intellectual, and even knew more about human life than Hamilton considered he did.

As the days turned into weeks, there was no doubt in Hamilton's mind that he needed Demiesius, and he liked to think the vampire thought just the same. With each visit, the appreciation of being able to escape each other's worlds grew refreshing, and it wasn't long until Hamilton figured out what it was.

He was more than infatuated with this vampire, and he was, without a doubt, falling madly in love with him. Of course, he could not, by any means, confess this.

Though he craved Demiesius' attention, he couldn't possibly fall in love with a vampire. Even with Demiesius' position in the immortal and slayer worlds, not a soul who didn't understand the workings of it the way he did would settle for a betrayal like this. If he ever confessed his heart, or was ever found out, Hamilton knew his life wouldn't end well.

However, even with just that sure assumption, there would be no way to save his life when he discovered the worst part of being a human love-bound for a vampire. Secrets couldn't be kept in darkness forever.

CHAPTER NINE
The Remnants of Past and Present Wounds

After a full day of combat training, more specifically, training involving the strict inclusion of Muay Thai, Hamilton wasn't feeling up for doing much of anything, but...alas, he was currently lacing up his boots to head out on yet another mission.

As he pulled the laces tight and adjusted the stocked utility belt around his slim waist, he couldn't help thinking back on the day spent with his students. Julius, Kingston and Samuel were doing fairly well, especially when it came to latching on to the instruction directed to them. When he was younger and was first introduced to the fighting style known as Muay Thai, he'd only been ten, and while a hit from a ten-year-old surely wouldn't have counted for much of anything back then, the hours upon hours, days upon days spent with his instructor had certainly been enough to sculpt him into someone who could display their skill in the style marvelously.

Hamilton would admit he was a lot more lenient on his students, but that also didn't mean he was allowing them too much comfort in his kindness. Since it was only his first day introducing the boys to the style, he'd allowed slip-ups, took things slow, acted as a mirror throughout the morning and treated most of the early hours as a lecture, but following lunch hour, that was when he'd paired with them in the hand-to-hand teachings.

Unlike when he was younger, he hadn't let them go to bed with any bruises or bloody noses, but they'd surely gotten the hint that he wasn't as passive as his face could let on. He'd shouted at them for bad formation, slow progressions, for anything that would render them dead if ever faced with a threat and they couldn't defend themselves.

Remembering his past with his instructor, Hamilton suddenly found himself standing unmoved in the center of his living area. A single lamp brought a soft glow to his apartment, and the silence turned into a quiet ring that met his ears.

"*Get up,*" he heard the phantom voice of the man from his past. "*No one will ever be around to wipe your tears when you're in the middle of a mission. Get up, now!*"

Hamilton, age 10
  Year — 1951

William Huntsman was a man not quite known for tenderness and showings of sympathy, but what he was, was a man with enough skills to turn anyone into what he wouldn't settle for anything other than the best.

Forty-three years of age and built from the ground up with both height and strength, he was a lean and towering man with close cut dark-brown hair, and a squared and handsome face touched with a minor sign of scars from his own days of following orders from the Slayer Public. He had cold, hooded brown eyes and a hooked nose, and the flat line of his full lips told of his focus on the person he viewed as his sole responsibility.

"Instructor Huntsman," a weary voice sounded behind Hamilton. He didn't look, but he knew it came from another teacher on the grounds who — just by the sound of her voice — was concerned about the amount of pressure put onto someone so small. "The bell has rung for supper hour. Why don't you finally let him get something to eat? You guys have been out here since morning."

Ignoring the words of the woman, Hamilton brought himself to his feet, not taking the time to dry the streams of frustrated tears that shone upon his face.

There was a dip in his dark blonde brow, eyes never leaving the man braced before him with cushioned pads strapped to his hands. Yes, he was tired, was hungry, and not to mention trembling all over, but he hardly noticed the fatigue and shakiness. As all of Hamilton's focus was on the man in front of him, nothing else mattered in the world at this very moment.

If he was faced with a hungry vampire, his mindset would need to be the same as it was right now.

"Leave us," William said to the woman, keeping his eyes on the blues glaring back at him. "Let's go, Hamilton."

With his hands raised into solid fists, Hamilton held them up and followed the turn of the man just a meter away. He might be four and a half feet tall (137.16cm) and weigh roughly ninety pounds (40.8kg), but Instructor Huntsman could still see the potential in the boy.

From everyone else's point of view, it could be said Hamilton was just about the last person who could instill intimidation into anyone, but his posture at this very moment, his determination, and the fact that he was the youngest student on the grounds of Gregor House, told Mr. Huntsman all he needed to know about this boy. He had what it took to gain the fullest extent of the Public's respect one day, and if by chance William wasn't around to witness that day, he wanted to be sure Hamilton was ready to prove his worth when he was older.

A second following the man's command, Hamilton went for the attack, each of his quick flying jabs, swings, hooks and piercing elbows striking the pads strapped to William's hands.

Better.

Much better.

There was a rage that ignited within Hamilton then, and those who looked on from a distance witnessed as this ten-year-old drove his instructor back. With each roundhouse, thrust and promising step, they displayed all that'd been countered toward him since this morning. There was a blaze in his heart, a drive centered within him that wouldn't allow for even one slip-up.

Hamilton breathed as he pummeled the pads before him, and the second William took a step forward instead of merely rotating their position, Hamilton couldn't help himself when the waves of heat in his chest took full control of his actions.

After finding his opening, he ran for the other man and leaped off the ground, grabbed onto Mr. Huntsman's neck, and he heaved himself up.

If it hadn't been for the man's quick decision to half-guard his face — Hamilton would have driven a serious elbow into his right eye. His knees were pressed to the instructor's chest, and when he locked his arms around the man's neck then, he flipped himself over to drag him down.

Given Hamilton's short stature and lightweight, he wasn't quite able to thrust the other man over his shoulder, but he at the very least stunned William by bringing him down regardless before backing off.

"AH!!!" Hamilton screamed out with his fists balled tightly. His knuckles were just about purple, his knees were sore as ever and even the back of his forearms and elbows showed obvious strain from the hours he'd spent with the man now looking up at him from the grass.

William smiled where he laid, taking in the shine of Hamilton's tears and the redness touched to the whites of his eyes. Getting to his feet, the man neared his lone student, and when he raised a hand, Hamilton turned his face when it seemed William might wipe them away.

He didn't want any show of sympathy.

Not from his instructor.

Not from anyone.

Dragging the back of his hand over his face to clear his own tears, Hamilton said, "I'm going to supper now," and then he started off without direction to do so.

⌒ ⚹ ⌒

When Hamilton blinked, he found himself standing in the center of an abandoned building. He was in East London and when he looked down at his feet, there was a pile of bone and ash upon the concrete below.

The world seemed to finally return to him, and he witnessed the shake of his hands, felt the heat of this fever rush through his body.

That's right, he'd been getting ready for a mission. Had his mind really been so mixed up all this time? How had he made it through this without proper focus? Was it truly the instincts instilled in him that made sure he reached the end on top?

Hamilton looked over his right forearm then, seeing the three tears trailed down the fabric of his shirt. He could already smell the iron scent of blood, and while the sting of pain he should've been feeling was numb, it was the condition of his body that spoke of his true weariness. With the fever throbbing in his head, the ache at the center of his chest, and especially the unsteadiness of his breath, Hamilton was surprised this last fight...however it had gone...hadn't been his last.

Feeling like the walls of this building were closing in on him, Hamilton then tore the mask of his uniform down and tried to suck in a deep breath of air. He felt an inner tremble of his lungs, the strain it took to merely fill them as much as they would, and once they were filled, Hamilton couldn't help lurching forward and releasing a round of boisterous coughs.

As he would usually try to hide them, this time he let them continue. It almost felt like claws were raking the back of his throat, and just as the times before, he witnessed a spray of blood spatter onto the ground.

Hamilton dropped to a knee then, unable to keep himself up, and he allowed his weight to fall over.

When his exhausted gaze met the tall, dark ceiling overhead, a current of loathing surfaced in him when a blur of tears met his eyes. He hated crying. It was only natural to cry in your most dejected and weakened states, but such a thing had always been so frowned upon when he was younger. He didn't want these emotions to show that such a thing as weakness resided in him. Crying was for the weak, the undisciplined, for children, and Hamilton refused to believe he was any one of those things.

Why, he questioned silently to himself, why did it feel like the world was catching up with him in such a blatantly cruel manner? This grip over his heart, this crimson varnish living within, all of it spoke a truth he was ignoring...

And he wanted to continue to ignore it.

Ignorance was bliss...wasn't it?

Hamilton bit back on his lower lip when it began to tremble then, and he worked himself to his feet.

He didn't have time for this.

Raising his mask over his face to guard his mouth, he headed out of the abandoned building. It was like this was his first time laying eyes on the location. He could see the River Thames from where he was and many more buildings. This was a storage facility and when he glanced off to his left, he saw the drop-off van several meters away beyond a tall gate. The driver was standing outside the vehicle smoking a cigarette and waved in his direction.

Hamilton lowered his head and started over. When he was in the rear of the transport, he left his mask on and let his head rest.

"Mr. Hamilton," the driver said when he got the vehicle moving, "We'll be making a stop at Headquarters. I have some paperwork to drop off before heading to the House."

"Alright," Hamilton said in return.

When several minutes passed, the van came to a stop and the driver got out. The Public library looked closed down just like every other business on the street at this hour, and as Hamilton waited, he let his eyes gaze out the window toward the main entry only to catch the sight of a tall and familiar figure moving out the lofty doors.

That flowing hair, those broad, set shoulders fitted into dark attire, and that cool stride could only be one person, and Hamilton found himself rushing from the van. He practically threw open the sliding door and almost tumbled out if he hadn't been able to catch himself.

A frantic burst pushed him on as if the man walking along the boulevard might vanish at any moment.

I need to see you!

I need you...

"Demiesius!" Hamilton called out.

The far off figure halted in his steps then and turned on the pavement, having nearly disappeared into the alley alongside the Public library. Hands tucked in the pockets of his trousers, when his crow black eyes met the shining stare that seemed to request his own presence, the immortal held out a beckoning hand in the slayer's direction.

Feeling accepted in that instant, Hamilton ran as if the most blistering of fires burned under his feet, and the second he was within arm's length of the vampire, he threw himself entirely into the embrace he wished to disappear into.

Demiesius said nothing as he allowed the minute to pass. There was a question of Hamilton's well-being on the tip of his tongue, but from the manner the slayer man was dressed, and of course the unmistakable scent of blood wafting up at him, he'd recently finished up the task that'd been scheduled for the night.

"You can tell me," the elder said then, "I will hear you, Hamilton."

The slayer closed his hands into fists at the back of Demiesius' coat, shaking his head, and he released a breath that finally stole the faintness in his lungs. "I — I'm alright. I just needed to see you tonight."

Hamilton let his eyes remain closed at the soft touch that settled at the back of his head, such a fond gesture as a run of fingers traced through his hair.

When he looked up into Demiesius' mild gaze, he felt as the elder took hold of his right forearm to examine where such a strong scent of blood originated from. Hamilton winced when the sleeve was rolled up, and he almost felt as if Demiesius was more hurt by the sight of his wounds than he was.

"Did you struggle?" Demiesius asked, "With the task?"

Given he still managed to succeed, Hamilton shook his head. "It always looks worse than it is."

"Hold still," the immortal said, and when he released the slayer's arm, Hamilton watched as Demiesius then extended the length of his nail at the tip of his thumb. He sliced deep into the palm of his right hand and a rise of almost blackish blood showed through the self-inflicted wound. Puzzled, Hamilton kept quiet when the elder closed his bloodied hand softly around his gash-littered forearm. There was a sting felt due to the disturbance of the gashes, but he winced for just a moment until any sign of agony faded.

When Demiesius stole his hand away, what would have left

behind three additional scars to Hamilton's collection of them, were gone as well as the blood that'd once been present.

"I don't believe you need anymore," Demiesius said.

Rather astounded, Hamilton looked over his forearm and flexed his fingers to see that the pain had vanished, and when he switched his eyes to where the elder had afflicted himself, his own wound was gone as well. "Thank you," he said, "As I'm clearly in the middle of returning from a task, I hope...you and I will be able to see each other again soon." There was a plea for such a thing behind Hamilton's words, especially with the shakiness still present in his being. He was positive the elder could hear and see such a thing overtly as ever.

"I wish for it as well," Demiesius seemed to promise, and since he could see the obvious fatigue within the other man, he reached out as if to cup Hamilton's face, but retracted his gesture when another voice rose from a distance.

"Mr. Hamilton?"

The slayer looked in the direction of his name and met the eyes of his driver.

"I'm ready if you are."

Looking back into the alley before him, Hamilton breathed out a sigh of desolation. Somehow the elder had vanished in the blink of an eye, but it was probably a good thing the other man hadn't stuck around.

Neither of them needed to be caught in the presence of one another by anyone else.

Taking one last look over his healed forearm, he smiled faintly beneath his face mask and started for the van again.

It was time to get some rest.

CHAPTER TEN
The Worst Punishments Can be the Best Teachers

Waking up in a bed drenched in sweat was not how Hamilton had wanted to start his day. The sheets and blankets all around him were soaked, and nearly his entire body was dripping wet. Sitting up, he pushed the wet tangles of hair out of his face, fatigued, and he still suffered from the chest pain that'd crept up on him the other day. With the way his body had been acting lately, Hamilton's worst fear was seeing a doctor that would know what was wrong with him. He feared hearing anything that wasn't "it's just a bug", or being told that this was serious.

From coughing up blood to sweating copiously at night for the past week, Hamilton knew for himself this wasn't going to be something that went away with some good bed rest. He could hardly even get that.

He was freezing when he got out of bed and stepped into the shower to wash up. Today he had to get ready for a solo task given to him yesterday, and if he was honest with himself, he was worried about being able to get it done. He wasn't going to back down from it though. This was his job, this is what he was born to do, to keep the streets of London safe, and he wasn't about to let this, whatever it was, hold him back.

He was Hamilton H. Hamilton, the most capable slayer of today. Nothing at all was going to stop him from keeping to his obligations.

Exhausted, he stood beneath the shower head for several minutes, wanting nothing more than to sleep for a couple more hours, but given this task was taking place during the day, he hadn't much of an option than to get ready now.

Over the last week at Queensland University, there had been a handful of murders taking place against attending students. Each attack was reported the same, details all saying the three students discovered were found off-campus with their throats ripped open and dry of blood. Though classes are still taking place at the university, there was a large section of the main building cut off for postponed construction, and that was where informants had pinpointed the location of the vampire committing the fatal acts. Blocked off from public use during the day, it was the perfect spot to hole up until sundown.

With the assignment of attending the university under the guise of an actual uni student, Hamilton was to find a way into the restricted zone, take out the vampire and call it a day. Despite the others he'd been on that involved sneaking around a number of humans, this sounded like one of the easiest he'd be able to accomplish in a long time.

Since this wasn't a night obligation, Hamilton threw on a pair of denim jeans he could move around in, and a black and gold scarf print halter top with a warm brown cardigan. When his hair was done and teased up a bit, he listened outside of his bedroom door when he heard a persistent tapping coming from the living room.

The same raven that'd been delivering letters on the days he and Demiesius didn't see each other was at the window, and in its beak was another handwritten letter. After letting the bird inside, Hamilton took the paper and rolled it open.

Hamilton H. H.

Happy 29th Birthday. This may sound absurd coming from someone like myself, but I wanted to be the first to wish you it. Being just about two months since we met, I thought it appropriate to treat you to something special tonight. Given you have a task today, and I must attend an important meeting once the sun sets, I am sorry to say I will not be able to. Still, I invite you to my home to retrieve the gift I wanted the opportunity to give you. I do hope you like it.

— Demiesius

After tucking the letter in a small box where he kept all the others he'd received, Hamilton opened the window to let the raven out, not intending on sending a reply back. With how stressed and agitated his body had been, he hadn't remembered his own birthday was coming up.

It certainly was April 10th.

Twenty-nine, he thought, one more year until the big three zero. Almost thirty years old, Hamilton was genuinely surprised he made it this long. Living a life of constantly putting it on the line night after night, one did not think to live past their early twenties, and that was what usually happened to new recruits.

Becoming a vampire slayer was the deadliest job in the world, but...someone had to do it.

Securing a leather fanny pack around his waist that wielded his stake, Hamilton slid into a pair of brown boots and left his room in the instructor's quarters to a van waiting for him outside. Before hopping in, he was stopped by Kingston and Julius. They were dressed in black running uniforms and jumpers, jogging in place with smiles on their faces.

"Morning," Julius said, "We heard it's your birthday."

"Yeah," Kingston added, "Happy Birthday, sir."

Hamilton offered the two boys a smile, bringing a hand to his mouth as if to hide a cough if it surfaced. "Thanks, lads. If you don't mind my asking, where is Samuel?"

"Right here!" the Austrian boy ran up. "Happy Birthday, Hamilton."

"Thank you, Samuel. You boys be sure to listen to Teresa while I'm gone. She's got a great set of skills to teach today, and I will be testing you all on them tomorrow."

When they all nodded and jogged off to the track, Hamilton entered the van and closed the door behind him. The drive wasn't too long, definitely not long enough to catch even a pinch of shuteye before arriving at the scene of the crimes.

Founded in 1842, it wasn't a surprise the building needed a few renovations here and there. The main building was a gray bricked fortress, a clock tower reached into the sky, and the campus grounds were even and sustained. Students attending the spring semester didn't bat an eye in Hamilton's direction when he strolled onto the locale. Although Hamilton was a man almost into his thirties, he could easily play the role of a student in their senior year if he wanted.

Passing the dorms down a shadowy path of trees, he looked up at the face of the Georgian style edifice. During his studies and training days at Gregor, he'd thought of what it must have been like to attend an actual school in the normal world. He'd gotten his fill of basic learning, maths, literature, history, science and even a taste of home economics, but he'd never had to stress the need for a degree from a top notch university like most normal kids.

Once he was fifteen, killing had become his life's purpose.

Walking onto the courtyard after going through the front entry and out the other side, Hamilton spotted the blocked zone right away. At the far left corner of the yard was Wing E. It was connected to the rest of the building, but a covering blocked the walkway with a sign made to direct students away from using the barricaded doors.

Now, these doors weren't actually what Hamilton would call barricaded. They were unlocked and still fully accessible, but with a couple of bright orange barrels erected in front of them, it rightfully gave the illusion that they were.

Being noon, a large majority of the uni occupants were either in class or getting lunch from the cafeteria near the dorms. There were still a few students here in the courtyard, studying at benches in the grass, and a small group was even reciting lines for what sounded like *Othello*. Either way, none of them were paying Hamilton any mind.

Keeping to the concrete path around the yard, Hamilton walked along the building towards Wing E. Without coming off as suspicious, he peered out of the corner of his eye into the glass windows in the doors. Regardless of light seeping in through the narrow rectangular spaces, it was dark as ever inside. Before slipping into the doors, Hamilton swept his eyes over the students in the yard and then vanished.

Inside was cold given the power was cut and no heat flourished through this wing. The floors were a faint gray, walls a pale white, and old school motivational posters were still tacked up. To his left, a dark hall stretched toward locked double doors leading to Wing D, while Wing F continued off to his right. Hamilton prepared himself and withdrew his stake from the fanny pack around his waist.

Since there were no classrooms or closets to hide in on the first floor, Hamilton entered a stairwell to the second level. He kept his footsteps light as air when he climbed, the wood and silver tight in his proficient grip.

When he reached the top and entered the corridor, a cough attempted to tickle his throat, but he managed to keep it down by holding his breath. Hamilton wasn't about to allow this spontaneous sickness to give away his position.

The second floor was darker than the first, but with blue plastic over the windows, he could still see if anything moved. There were several classroom doors to choose from, so Hamilton started with the one in front of him. Room 210.

To his relief, the door opened without a sound, and the inside was filled with nothing but empty seats and a dusty chalkboard. Rooms 212, 214, 216 and 218 were all vacant of any culprit as well, and when Hamilton found the rest on this floor empty, he made his way up to the third.

His heart was beating fast once he reached the top of the stairs, but not for any source of fear. It began to race suddenly, and it was throwing his centered breathing off. With chills running down his spine, Hamilton cursed when the need to cough reached out for him again.

He could feel the inner shudder of his lungs and he clasped a hand over his mouth. Trying to support himself with a hand to the wall, Hamilton practically choked when a wave of blood shot up from inside him. Unable to keep it in, he threw up, watching in horror as the large pool sprayed onto the floor, leaving his teeth and tongue tinged with crimson iron.

Almost immediately following the grotesque incident, the smack of a door was heard, a custodian closet at the end of the hall flying open.

From within emerged a skeletal black haired woman. She was in a dress that had difficulty hanging onto her thin body, and her ghostly pale face was almost hollow at the eyes and cheeks. Her eyes still had the dull red haze that famished vampires typically had, but the growl she emitted spoke of a hunger far more needy.

She hissed maniacally at Hamilton and sprinted for him. Before he could consider an approach, she flew at him, landing a solid and powerful kick against his chest.

Hamilton lost his breath and fell back. He slid on his bottom, watching as the vampire dove for the pool of blood he'd spewed onto the floor. She dragged her long tongue into it and swallowed down a gulp.

When it seemed to travel down her throat, she flinched in disgust and dragged cleansing hands down her dripping tongue as if trying to get rid of the horrid taste.

On his feet again, Hamilton went at her. She turned in an attempt to run, but the slayer caught a fist full of her long hair. Tugging her, she stumbled onto her bottom and Hamilton came down, his stake prepared to break into her chest. The woman caught his wrist and twisted him from atop her, rotating and pinning him to the floor.

With a bit of blood still in his mouth, Hamilton hawked back a wad of spit and spat it in her face. When it landed against her nose and lips, she screeched and Hamilton was able to kick her off.

Not giving up on her life, the vampire lashed out with her claws, Hamilton ducking and he dodged each of her fast swipes. Finding an opening, he twisted her into an arm bar and dragged her down, hearing the sordid break of her wrist and elbow when he thrust down against the bend of her arm. As she scream in rage, the hallway echoed with her shrill call.

Hamilton stumbled when she slashed at the back of his calves, not digging too deep, but the sudden pain was enough to distract him. Backing off, the two stalked one another, looking for any notable weaknesses that could easily be used to prevail. In thinking a moment too long, the woman's arm began to reassemble, each of her cracked bones snapping into place.

"I'll bleed you dry and leave you here to die," the woman spoke, tone grating as she smiled.

Swiftly moving into a Muay Thai stance, body turned and hands up, Hamilton said, "Hurry up, then, you witch."

Clearly not taking kindly to the degrading insult, the vampire hissed and lunged for Hamilton. He fought to his best abilities, driving through the ache in the center of his chest, and named himself the victor only a minute later.

Dropping to his knees before the pile of vampire soot, Hamilton breathed deeply and tiredly. He'd never been this worn out after a fight, especially since it was a one on one battle. He sat there for a good couple minutes to gather himself before leaving the campus.

Once he got back to Gregor House, he was definitely going to try and get some much-needed sleep.

When nightfall came around, Hamilton left for Demiesius' home. Dressed now in a light brown paisley print, long-sleeved cropped shirt and warm light coat, Hamilton also wore fitting flared jeans and brown slippers. His blonde hair was half tied and he clutched a white cross body around him. Outside at the front door, he hadn't needed to knock when approaching, and was kindly let in by the brooding, bald vampire, Christoph.

"Good evening," Christoph nodded, "Master Titus said you would likely be coming tonight even with his absence."

"Likely, eh?" Hamilton said, "Does that make me predictable?"

Christoph didn't answer and moved aside, giving Hamilton access to the castle. By the looks of it as he moved about, the home was occupied by only Christoph's watchful eye. Hamilton didn't know exactly what he was looking for, but by the sound of Demiesius' letter, there was a birthday present somewhere inside. It took him a good couple minutes to search the entire first floor, stopping in on a massive library, lounge area, art gallery, music room, and even a lofty ballroom.

When he still found nothing, he searched the rest of the property, and came to a bedroom chamber the size of his home at Gregor. It was properly put together and organized, the king sized red velvet bed was made, and nothing looked out of place. The walls were papered in black and dark violet damask wallpaper, while the floor was a dark wood and waxed. A cushioned upholstered foot bench sat at the head of the bed, and at the far end of the room was a set of doors that led out to a balcony. The windows were covered by thick black, sun blocking curtains.

Entering the chamber, Hamilton spied a small, white oval box in the center of the bed. Removing his shoes, he climbed atop the large and comfortable mattress and sat in the middle as he read his name in Demiesius' elegant handwriting.

Upon lifting the lid, Hamilton withdrew a dark green soft pouch, and slowly slid the contents out onto the bed. From inside, a beautiful gold chain necklace came out. It was thin and connected to it was a ruby red jewel with studded diamonds gemmed around it, and below dangled a white pearl. Pristine and polished, Hamilton turned over the necklace in the air, stunned in its expensive presence. Though grateful for the present, Hamilton worried about how much something like this could possibly cost. With thirty carats of gold, gorgeous diamonds, and a breathtaking ruby, this had to be well over a thousand pounds.

At the bottom of the oval box the necklace came from, there was another precisely folded up piece of paper. When Hamilton had it open, he read it to himself.

Given to me by the Roman Emperor Octavian, or better known as Augustus, I wish to offer it as a gift to you on this day.

— Demiesius

"Wow," Hamilton said, "From before the Common Era."

"You like it?"

Hamilton gasped at the abrupt voice and sprung off the bed. Once on his feet on the other side, he met Demiesius' gaze across the room.

Demiesius was in a pure black suit, coat draped over his shoulder now. He was towering in the doorway of the chamber, alluring as he stared towards Hamilton.

When seeing it was just Demiesius, Hamilton settled down, and said, "I thought you'd been called out for the night."

"I was," the vampire explained. "Turns out one of the councilmen has passed. The Public began preparations for a funeral that'll be held tomorrow afternoon."

"I see," Hamilton said, "So, it would be unfavorable of me to say I'm happy you are here."

"Perhaps it is a bit too soon."

Hamilton hustled around the bed when Demiesius entered further into the room. Part of him wanted to throw his arms around the man, but figured that would be taking it a step too far even though they'd already embraced as such. He had firm feelings for the immortal dwelling in his being, but without knowing how Demiesius viewed him, Hamilton had to keep himself on a leash of his own. "Thank you so much for the necklace. Did Augustus really give this to you?"

Taking the jewelry into his own hand, Demiesius unclipped the golden latch and moved behind Hamilton. Gently, he placed the ancient necklace around the slayer and latched it before fixing Hamilton's tresses. "Yes," he said, "Discovering mine and the other elder's true nature, he treated us to the treasures of his wealth. Referred to us as gods of the night at one point or another."

Even with his first warning, Hamilton couldn't stop himself from embracing into Demiesius when the vampire turned him. His arms circled around the top of Demiesius' shoulders, and their bodies softly pressed up against one another. Hamilton rested his nose at the hollow of Demiesius' neck, taking in his strong leather and jasmine scent.

When his hold on the vampire tautened a notch, he felt himself sink when Demiesius calmly embraced him in return. With arms so power-provoking, feeling the tenderness of them sent Hamilton into a conscious frenzy. His infatuation with the immortal before him had gone far beyond what he originally thought, something leading quickly into a point of no return, and the moment he pulled away and found tempting lips in total reach, Hamilton had to forcibly stop himself from leaning into them.

In an attempt to distance himself, Hamilton took a step away, but was stopped when Demiesius reached out for his hand. "Your eyes," he said, concerned, "You look tired."

"It's — uh — I haven't been getting much sleep lately," Hamilton admitted.

Releasing the slayer, Demiesius said, "Does it have anything to do with coming here? On most nights you are either here or out fulfilling your tasks. If this is taking a toll on you, we can adjust to different times."

"That is very sweet of you," Hamilton smiled faintly, "but it has nothing to do with coming here. I used to be able to go a full day with just an hour of sleep."

"It's your sickness, isn't it?"

Hamilton chose not to answer the direct question. He instead scratched nervously at the back of his head, and he stepped around Demiesius. "I've been fine for a while now. Haven't you noticed? Coming here the amount of times that I have since last, I'm sure you have seen I've gotten better."

Before Hamilton could stroll too far, Demiesius said, "Then

why does your breath smell of blood?"

Frozen by the chamber door, Hamilton raised a hand near his lips and breathed out, not smelling any unpleasantries. With no comment to follow, Hamilton tried to continue into the hall, but was stalled suddenly when nearly colliding with Demiesius when he appeared in front of him.

"You should take this more seriously than you are," the vampire said.

Calming the race of his heart, Hamilton groaned internally. "I am. I've been self-medicating for the last two months. I'm *trying* to get rid of this."

"Perhaps if you told a professional of the condition you're in," Demiesius made clear, "they could lend a hand in helping you feel better."

"I don't need someone to sit in my face and tell me there's something wrong with me. I wake up every day knowing that for myself."

When Hamilton tried to walk away again, Demiesius grabbed his hand to hold him there. His dark eyes gazed down into Hamilton's nervous stare. "I know the way you feel about me," he said, "I can see it plain as the moon each night. Voicing a proper response to the sentiment I know resides in you is difficult for me, and the only way I know how to express myself in any way, is to ask you to please see a doctor. Your throat is stained with blood, and I can sense the weakness that's stolen a spot in your body. All I ask is for you to find out what it is. You are unwell, and I no longer wish for you to suffer this way, no matter how minimal you may think it is."

Hamilton hadn't expected the words from Demiesius. Since the beginning of their times together—had he always been so notably affectionate? But that wasn't what concerned him. Did this mean that Demiesius felt the same?

Looking down at the hand closed around his own, Hamilton said, "If...If I see someone, if I find out what's wrong, I'm scared of them telling me what I don't want to hear. I can still fight, still perform when I'm told. Please don't make me."

Seeing the sorrowful dread in Hamilton's eyes filled Demiesius with a strong sense of guilt. Inciting this kind of response in the slayer hadn't been his intention, but all he truly wanted was to make sure the other man was okay.

Of course he was able to fight his own battles. Demiesius had absolutely no doubt about that, but this wasn't a conflict arranged by him and the Public commanders, this was something far different, unseen and could ultimately prove lethal. Humans, he had come to know through the centuries, were quite fragile beings whether they wanted to admit it or not.

Taking his hand from Hamilton, Demiesius said, "Then leave."

"But—," Hamilton tried.

"Leave and don't come back until you know what it is that's bringing about this internal bloodshed."

Hamilton couldn't believe this.

"Please, don't say that." He reached out for Demiesius, but before he could get a hold of him, Christoph was summoned, and he was being dragged down the hall with his arms locked behind him. "Demiesius, don't do this. Please! I'm scared, I'm just scared. Please!" Taken down to the first floor, he called out, "You're the only person who takes the pain away. Don't throw me out. I — I need you, Demiesius!"

But it seemed the vampire wasn't listening, and out into the cold Hamilton was thrown.

CHAPTER ELEVEN

There is a First Time for Everything

Stumbling to his knees when Christoph tossed him from the entry of the castle, Hamilton remained there and cupped his face, tears welling up in his eyes at the mere notion of never seeing Demiesius again. He couldn't do that, he just couldn't. After spending such a long and nice time with the vampire, he didn't know if he could handle it if Demiesius chose to disappear from his life so suddenly. And all because he was afraid of a damn diagnosis.

As he sat there on his knees, Hamilton shivered in the cold wrapped around him. He stood a minute later and banged his fists on the door, shaken and afraid. "Please don't make me do this on my own," Hamilton pleaded, hoping his cry reached Demiesius' ears. "I can't do it alone."

At that statement, one of the doors was opened again by Christoph. He stood in the opening as Demiesius towered behind. The elder touched his guard's shoulder, and said, "You may leave, Christoph. I will be fine alone with him."

Christoph, though having already known of the amount of time Demiesius had been spending with the slayer these past months, was always cautious when leaving him alone. Not disregarding him, Christoph bowed his head, and said, "Yes, Master Titus," and then in the blink of an eye, he disappeared from sight, likely returning to the coven in which he originally lived with Dominick.

"Come in," Demiesius said to Hamilton, allowing the slayer entry into his home. He closed the door and locked it. "I did not want to give even a single thought towards pushing you away," he said, "but if I needed to do the sort to get you to consent to a medical checkup, then that is what I had to do." Placing a hand at the small of Hamilton's back, Demiesius looked tenderly into his eyes as he led him through the halls and into the distant library. "For your distress, I do apologize for it."

When they continued on, Hamilton stopped just before stepping into the large, book-filled room. "You say you just want me to feel well?"

Demiesius nodded assuredly.

"Why?" the slayer asked, "Why are you so concerned about the way I feel? Sick or injured in any way, why are you so passionate about making sure I am in good condition?"

The vampire's gaze was the most serene Hamilton had ever witnessed. Even with such dark and sinister black eyes, the shadows and caring nature that dwelled behind them made Hamilton feel...safe. "Is it not obvious?" Demiesius said, raising his hands to touch kindly at the smooth blushing cheeks before him. He stroked his thumbs under Hamilton's puffy blue eyes, letting his touch stray down the other man's softly curved jaw to cup his beautiful face. "Can you not see that I merely care for you?"

Hamilton felt the stammer of his heart pick up when the admission passed his ear. Never had he experienced what it was like to have another human being, let alone a vampire, appreciate his existence so much in a way that worried for his health or safety. In the slayer world, people came and went. Slayers could die their first night out on a task, or last years in the profession.

All in all, vampire slayers were expendable, always growing to replace those who lost their lives. Every day since becoming the killer he was, Hamilton remained ready for his life to end, but now...things were different...now, he wanted nothing more than to live, to survive through the years to spend whatever time he could with this vampire, with this person who valued his life as a life should be.

"The first time I ever laid eyes on you," Demiesius said, "You were twenty years old. I was visiting The Gathering of Councilors. You had just finished up a task and were reporting back to them. Of course, I knew of your name, I knew of your skill and status, but had never once laid eyes on you until that night. I thought you were beautiful, but I knew approaching you would go against my recognition and involvement with the Public. The only ones who are supposed to know of me are the Councilors and your commanders. All other slayers are off limits to my existence and rule. Before you are ever assigned to a task, I make sure you will be able to physically handle it. Ever since laying my eyes on you, my goal in this life has become to get you through yours."

"Have you always cared for me...since that night?" Hamilton asked, wanting to throw himself into Demiesius' arms.

The vampire took his hands away then, seeing how Hamilton's eyes gazed so truly into him. It felt as though he was at last being seen for who he was for the first time in so long. Such wonder that met his eyes in this very moment, the immortal knew he would never wish to be looked upon by another in this soft shade.

"Since that very second," Demiesius spoke with nothing but honesty, and in stating such a thing, he hoped his words and actions would always be enough to relay what dwelled in his being for this person before him. "I have wanted nothing more," he added, "than for your presence to be as constant in this world as it has been since that night I first laid eyes on you. For you to find wellness again, allow me to at the very least assist in that."

———

Entering the library, Hamilton took a seat in a comfortable armchair in front of a bookcase with literature that covered a great amount of vampire history.

Demiesius approached a black, curly corded phone on the other side of the room. He stood beside it and dialed a number, speaking once the call seemed to have been answered.

"Dr. Takahashi," he said. "Yes, hello, I am doing fine. I need you to come to my home to examine someone for me." He paused, "No, this won't be a matter for myself. I have someone with me I would like you to tend to." After pausing once more, he said, "Thank you, I will see you in a few minutes."

When Demiesius hung up the phone, he turned to see Hamilton stretching along one of the bookshelves to grab something.

Barely reaching it with his fingertips, Hamilton tipped the book out of its placement and held it in his hands. Flipping to the cover, he recognized the language as Latin, but couldn't read a single word of it. Going through the pages, he stopped on one with five people drawn in great detail, two women and three men. Instantly he recognized one of them as being Demiesius, looking exactly the same as he did now with his long hair, sharp handsome features, and a tall, strong physique.

Standing just beside Hamilton, Demiesius said, "It tells the story of how we raised the vampire race."

Going through the illustrations, Hamilton asked, "You have made more vampires than just Dominick?"

"No," Demiesius answered, "Dominick is an only child. My role primarily dwelled in creating the rules and principles of being an immortal. I used to handle more political influences than the other elders until they joined me in doing so. Their blood children are the ones who have populated this world with the amount of immortals there are now."

"What's the first rule of being a vampire?"

Demiesius took the book from Hamilton when the slayer handed it over, and he slipped it back into the empty space it'd been retrieved from. "It used to be 'kill only to survive'. When immortals began killing just to feed, we knew that would have to be changed. These nights, the first rule in being a vampire is to never kill the innocent. Those who go against that rule are now taken care of by slayers, while those who abide by the rules are allowed to continue into the centuries."

"When I first came upon Dominick, it seemed like he was about to kill a woman. What would have become of him if you found out he'd killed an innocent person?"

Demiesius shook his head, "Something to know about my son is that he is not a killer unless threatened, and he enjoys feeding from the source, that source being humans. Dominick takes his hunger out on humans, but never resorts to killing them. I have seen him do this. He feeds on the willing or unwilling, heals their wounds, and wipes their minds of the incident if the human had been unwilling, and then sends them on their way. That woman, though his actions can use some altering, she would not have died that night. There is a myth that some of the best tasting blood comes from fear-driven humans."

"I think he should stick to the willing," Hamilton said, remembering the young man Dominick fed from during their second encounter at his coven. "From what I've seen of it, they enjoy it more than you would imagine."

With a smirk, Demiesius knew exactly what Hamilton meant by that, and said, "I agree."

Demiesius made himself comfortable on a violet wine vintage camel back sofa then. He let his arm rest over it, and sat taking up half of it. Hamilton continued to survey the many books, finally finding one in English that spoke of Lilith through the eyes of an elder named Minerva. She'd described Lilith as being a sad woman who'd wanted family more than anything in the world, ultimately giving up her life to allow her children to survive. If anything, she didn't sound like such a bad woman, but when Hamilton remembered she'd tormented the peace of the mortals around her to get what she'd wanted...his opinion wavered.

Glancing over his shoulder to see where Demiesius had gone, Hamilton laid eyes on the vampire pondering on the sofa. He returned the book to where it belonged and started toward the elder.

Demiesius looked up at Hamilton when the slayer stopped in front of him, standing at the opening of his legs. Sitting up a bit more when Hamilton made to take a seat on his lap, the vampire swallowed when Hamilton's light weight came down onto him, an arm resting around his shoulders.

As Hamilton peered into Demiesius' eyes, he then tucked himself into the man's body. Pressing his face into the crook of the vampire's neck, he could feel the chilly skin warm at his touch.

When Demiesius' arm came to hold him closer, Hamilton said, "What if I hadn't been a slayer to begin with? What if I had been given a normal life like other people in the world?"

Demiesius didn't waste a second thinking of an answer, and said, "I would like to think that, perhaps, I would have found you in time."

"If all vampires were like you, Demiesius," Hamilton said, "I would give it all up. I would drop everything to be here, if you would want me, that is."

"That is without a doubt."

Hamilton sat up and looked down into the vampire's eyes, but even with that, Hamilton could see Demiesius' attention was on his own lips before meeting his gaze. The slayer passed his tongue over his lips, biting it back as the hunger for a taste of his mouth grew inside the immortal below him.

When Demiesius touched the side of Hamilton's cheek, eyes resting on what they desired most, he ran his thumb over Hamilton's bottom lip. As he leaned into the slayer's anticipation, he froze suddenly when there was a thunderous rap on the castle's entry door.

They both let out an inaudible sigh of frustration, and Hamilton rose from Demiesius' lap. Once the vampire began to leave the room, he said, "I will be but a moment."

Waiting alone in the library, Hamilton had to catch his breath for a minute before his mind went wild. He'd been so close to sealing his first kiss with Demiesius, but he guessed the moment hadn't been right.

He tried to clear his throat when a tickling itch burdened him, causing him to cough up a storm the moment Demiesius returned with his guest. It was a middle-aged Japanese man with clear, light-beige skin and jet black, medium length hair dressed casually in slacks and a dress shirt, a briefcase in his hand. The vampires watched, worried, as the slayer's hoarse cough scratched bloody fluids from his trembling lungs.

When Hamilton finally subsided, he grimaced at the blood spilled into his hands.

"Oh, my," Dr. Takahashi said, entering the library further behind Demiesius. "Let's have a look at you, sir." He set down his briefcase on a table in the center of the floor and clicked it open.

Grabbing gloves, he handed Hamilton a wad of napkins from a hidden pocket and a cleansing wet wipe. He then withdrew alcohol rubbing cloths, a syringe, a needle, a small collection tube, butterfly needle, tape, gauze, and a tourniquet to tie around the slayer's arm.

After laying them all out on a sanitized mat placed atop the table, Dr. Takahashi smiled towards his new patient.

Hamilton hesitated, glancing at Demiesius for some support. "It's alright," the vampire said, "I'm not leaving. I'll be right here."

"May I?" Dr. Takahashi asked, gesturing towards the slayer's arm.

Gathering his confidence, Hamilton sat down and rolled up the sleeve of his shirt. Once the needle was prepared, the doctor tied the tourniquet around Hamilton's arm, tapping at his forearm to summon the appearance of his veins.

Hamilton thought it odd that this vampire was about to draw blood from him, but decided to leave his questions in the back of his mind. The doctor said, "This will hurt for a second," and then inserted the thick needle into Hamilton's arm.

He winced from the long pinch, watching as blood began to drain from the puncture point and into the collection tube, filling up all the way to the top. When it was done, the doctor undid the tourniquet, and cleaned Hamilton's arm and wrapped it in gauze. Taking the collection tube, the vampire looked toward Demiesius, smiled, and downed the blood like a shot of whiskey.

"NO!" Hamilton shouted in utter shock, "I'm sick!"

Dr. Takahashi licked his lips with a grimace, not taking a liking to the strange taste of the blood running down the back of his throat. "Yes, I know," he said, "That's what I'm here for—to find out what the sickness is."

"By drinking my blood?"

"Trust me," the doctor said, unveiling a black binder from his briefcase, "It's faster this way." Flipping through his papers, Dr. Takahashi skimmed down them, going through charts, lists, and paragraphs of written notes he'd compiled over his centuries of studying internal human infections. "Tell me," he said, "How long have you been like this?"

"A while," Hamilton started, "Maybe a good three months or so."

"And how has your body been acting during this time? Don't leave out any details. The last thing I want to do is give a wrong diagnosis."

With Demiesius nearby, Hamilton felt assured enough to speak of his condition, telling Dr. Takahashi about the coughing which led to coughing up blood, night sweats, fatigue, intense chest pain, chills, the loss of appetite and having to force himself to eat, and even the slight amount of weight loss he'd noticed not too long ago but thought nothing of.

"I see," Dr. Takahashi said, "Sir, what is your name?"

"Hamilton..."

"Hamilton," he started, "I am afraid it appears that you have active tuberculosis."

Just the word alone was enough to bring a wave of faint heartedness over Hamilton's being. He felt his eyes water at the thought of having something so deadly inside his body.

Completely crushed, his world came down and he could hardly utter a word. Looking down to his hands where the blood had previously been stained, he saw them begin to tremble as tears streamed down his face.

"I'm going to—," he stammered, "I'm going to die? Is this going to kill me?"

Meeting the slayer's eyes, Dr. Takahashi felt sorry for having to lay this kind of information on the man, but said, "If left untreated, yes, and it's not a pretty way to go. However, there is a highly rated method in curing tuberculosis that takes a bit of time, but if all the medications and procedures are followed, you could be cured within nine months. Given that you've had these symptoms for about three months it could possibly take longer, but if you get on the proper medications now, there is a great chance you could beat this in no time."

Hamilton was trying his hardest to keep his emotions in check, but could barely manage keeping still. Moving about the library with his hands on the back of his head, Hamilton stopped suddenly, and said, "This is absurd."

Dr. Takahashi neared the slayer and touched his shoulder, "Please, you shouldn't worry so much. I can help you. Since I was called here by my elder, I will do all I can to provide you with the right treatment to ensure you beat this. All I will need is your full cooperation and a strict scheduling plan."

"I'm a slayer, I have students to train," Hamilton stated. "I can't be gone all the time. I have tasks to complete, people who will wonder about me, and let me tell you if I am ever discovered to spend that time here, with a vampire, this tuberculosis isn't the only thing that will kill me."

Giving Demiesius a strange look at the mention of Hamilton being a slayer, Dr. Takahashi kept his concerns to himself, and continued with: "I see that, but this illness is far more important than keeping vampires off the streets. I'm sure there are lots more slayers who can take your place."

"You know there are," Demiesius added. "You know I can give you the time that you need." Walking toward Hamilton, the vampire stopped before him and tucked a wave of hair behind his ear. "Please, do this for yourself. You must live."

I need you to...

Demiesius had wanted to say those exact words, but felt they were selfish to what actually mattered. To watch Hamilton wither away because of a damn illness, when he'd previously been such a capable and strong human being, the ancient elder knew that was one thing he couldn't do. With everything in him, he wanted Hamilton to live, to see another day, be allowed the warmth of the sun, and experience the opportunity all should be given to live a long, happy and prosperous life here.

That is what Demiesius wanted for Hamilton, what he'd once wanted for the majority of mankind, and now, here was the one he'd at last found something in again...and he was infected with a sickness that made him even more susceptible to death. He couldn't have this, couldn't have Hamilton be taken away from him. Not like this.

Looking up into Demiesius' eyes, Hamilton nodded for him, "I'll do it," he said, "I'll do it for you, for myself...for...us."

Dr. Takahashi made plans to come back tomorrow evening to quickly begin Hamilton's treatment, and briefly discussed with him and Demiesius about just how frequent everything would need to be to make sure Hamilton was cured in time.

After ensuring to meet here the next night, the doctor bid his elder farewell, and promised Hamilton he'd do everything in his power to make certain he lived into the next years that came.

When the doctor was gone, Demiesius seeing him out, he returned to Hamilton in the library. The slayer was laid across the sofa, his back to the room.

Taking a seat at the armrest, Demiesius said, "Doctor Takahashi is one of the most knowledgeable medical professionals to ever enter the vampire world. I would not entrust your well-being to him if I did not believe he could help you."

"That's not what I'm worried about..." Hamilton groaned into the cushions of the sofa.

"What is it?" Demiesius asked.

"I can't do anything now. I can't fulfill my duties as a slayer. I can't fight to my best potential as I used to. I can't even...I can't even kiss you."

Demiesius furrowed his brow at the assumption, "Why do you say that?"

"Because," Hamilton declared, sitting up now, "I don't want to get you sick."

At that, the vampire smiled with a shake of his head. "You think bacteria can kill me? Hamilton, the only things that can kill me are being beheaded and completely charred, or to have my heart torn from my chest and crushed. Not even a mere stake to the heart can kill me like other vampires. I am immune to everything that could ever take shelter inside the human body." Touching at the golden necklace he'd given to Hamilton for his birthday, Demiesius said, "Have I not shown what you mean to me?"

"You have shown more care for me then anyone I have ever known," Hamilton said.

Looking up towards the vampire, he brought himself onto his knees, kneeling on the cushion of the sofa, stature remaining below Demiesius on the armrest.

They seemed to study one another as the quietness of the entire castle blanketed the silence around them. The slayer could only hear the rapid pound of his heart, not even the shallow puffs of his breath. His eyes settled on Demiesius' lips; their natural shade so full and waiting. Meeting his keen, dark eyes, Hamilton could feel himself gravitating closer before darkness overtook his vision, having shut his eyes the moment his lips were touched by another. The soft press sent a current through his body, and a gentle caress touched the back of his hair.

When his lips were freed, his breath stammered, eyes remaining shut to let the reality set in, and Hamilton's yearning for Demiesius exploded.

Wrapping his arms around the top of the vampire's shoulders, he shoved another hard kiss upon Demiesius' waiting lips, his strong jasmine scent mixing into the slayer's nose as he breathed in.

Gripping the front of the vampire's shirt then, Hamilton pulled Demiesius down on top of him, lying back on the sofa as their bliss deepened, becoming hungrier and fueled by such an intense longing.

Respecting Hamilton's possible boundaries, Demiesius restrained himself from exploring Hamilton's figure, keeping his hands pressed into the cushion to hold himself up, their bodies pressed to one another. When his tongue was grazed by a sweet bitterness, he perceived the aftermath of the blood Hamilton had coughed up earlier. It was only slight and was quickly overtaken by the slayer's natural sweetness, driving Demiesius' thoughts and desires into a realm of ignited desperation. Feeling as Hamilton's hands traveled about his body, grazing fingers trailing along his back, legs coiling with his own, his spine tingled when a hushed moan escaped the slayer's mouth.

Hearing it, Demiesius' excitement worsened and suddenly his fangs elongated from his canines without accord. When he took Hamilton's mouth once more, he quickly tore himself away when the slayer gasped in pain.

Hamilton flinched and held a hand over his mouth, blood staining on his fingers from where one of Demiesius' fangs accidentally grazed him.

"I am so sorry," the vampire apologized hastily, "I did not mean to. I wasn't—."

Stopping Demiesius' panic, Hamilton dabbed the blood away on the back of his sleeve, and said, "It's alright. I'm fine."

Hovering atop the slayer, Demiesius retracted his fangs at will, causing them to disappear again. "I would never hurt you," he declared, meaning every bit of what he said.

"I know," Hamilton purred, bringing the vampire fully down onto him, fingers brushing through his silky tresses. "I know I'm safe in your arms."

CHAPTER TWELVE

What Doesn't Kill You Now Can Always Kill You Later

Hamilton was up before the crack of dawn the next morning. He was still a bit tired from having spent so much time at Demiesius' home the other night, but he also hadn't felt this good since before his symptoms started to show up.

Last night he'd experienced something he never thought he could have as the man he was. Growing up here in Gregor House, it was always a strong assumption that he would never live a life outside of this, outside of the duties of being a vampire slayer, and for twenty-nine years he'd grown content with the idea.

Ever since he was a small, determined child, his goal was to protect the streets of London, and to perfect his combat skills. Having become the greatest fighter of his time by the age of seventeen, back then, Hamilton had thought his life complete, and there was nothing else he could ever need to feel accomplished. Wielding the title of "the deadliest fighter" under his belt, Hamilton had nothing else to worry about...until he laid eyes on Demiesius and stumbled.

Swamped with thoughts of possible love and fear of his true sickness, Hamilton used this quiet morning to calm his mind. They were all over the place this morning, peaceful one moment and then petrified the next. When he would fawn over the wonders of the pleasant kiss he'd shared with Demiesius the night before, the burning reminder of having acquired tuberculosis came flooding into him again.

Outside in the chilly humidity, Hamilton stood outside in track shorts and a baggy jumper, hair tied in a fixed ponytail, and a scarf was fixed properly around his mouth.

Alone and awake before anyone else on the grounds, he delved into a meditation form of relaxation he'd learned when younger, allowing his body to flow into different forms of fighting styles. Slowly progressing into each stance, he worked his joints, twisting his wrists and bending his knees, stretching each muscle with centered precision. Sliding back on his right foot, Hamilton raised his arms before closing his hands into fists, bringing them down to align with his waist.

Filling his lungs slowly, Hamilton then exhaled. The tight pain in the center of his chest returned, but he attempted to ignore it, and continued his tranquil rumination. Since he didn't have a task to fulfill tonight, he was to be headed back to Demiesius to get started on this treatment. He just hoped with all his heart that it worked.

When he came down onto his hands, Hamilton supported his

weight with just his hands, balancing his body with his knees to his chest. As the strength in his arms remained even, he stretched out one leg, and then the other, coming into a perfectly poised handstand.

Bending his arms, he progressed into ten push-ups, feeling each of the muscles in his upper body work as he finished. Hamilton brought his legs forward then, hovering them over his head before slowly coming back down. He enjoyed working out this way, expanding his flexible abilities to use his own body weight as a tool instead of heavy dumbbells and other foreign objects. The body would always be a slayer's greatest tool, and learning to rely on it was a crucial lesson indeed.

Even if sometimes it worked against you.

After several more minutes, Hamilton watched as the other instructors of Gregor readied their individual students for their morning run. Not spotting his own trainees, he went to the gym across from the track and went inside. He was cold with sweat when he stepped into the building.

Julius, Kingston, and Samuel were standing along the wall with cushioned gloves over their fists. Teresa was in the middle of the gym dressed in black joggers and a tight gray long sleeve, blonde hair tied into a high bun. When she noticed Hamilton enter, she smiled and waved him over.

"Morning," she said, "I thought we could start our students off with a little contest."

Hamilton eyed his trainees and then turned around. Teresa's own students, two boys and a girl, were standing on the other side of the gym with gloves on. "You'll have them fight?" he quirked a brow.

"Exciting way to start the day, yeah?" Teresa smiled.

Not too sure of the suggestion, Hamilton thought on it. It wasn't right for slayers to compete with one another. This occupation was, in no way, a contest for who could be the very best, and pitting slayers against one another, even for training purposes, was looked down on by the Public.

"I don't think that's a good idea," he admitted.

"Why is that?" Teresa joked, "Afraid my students are better trained than yours?"

"No," Hamilton said, "It's against regulation to permit competitions."

"Oh, come on, I really wanted to see how my students have improved." Teresa thought for a moment then. "How about *we* fight them? There's no contest in sampling their skills, is there?"

Hamilton didn't see anything wrong with the recommendation, but with the pain in his chest still fresh, he was a bit worried more for himself than he was in wanting to see the talent picked up by each of his students. In seeing the eagerness in Julius, Kingston and Samuel, Hamilton felt he couldn't turn down the lesson. "Alright, then," he agreed.

Leaving his hands bare, Hamilton slightly tightened the scarf around the lower half of his face and he took to the center of the gym, gesturing for his students to join him. As they wouldn't be using any weapons this time around, Hamilton raised his fists and cleared his mind. With the ever so faint dizziness from the active tuberculosis, he needed to keep his mind sharp if he wanted to fight with some dignity.

"Okay, boys," he said, "Let me see what you've learned in these past months."

At that, each of the boys smiled and sprinted for Hamilton

at top speed. He countered Samuel's punch quickly, as well as Kingston's, and then captured Julius' arm and thrust the boy over his shoulder. Ducking out of reach from Kingston's fast kick, Hamilton back flipped when Samuel rushed him with a clothesline. Sweeping a kick across the air, he missed Julius, but was able to block his multiple punches while Kingston snuck up on him from behind.

Taking a step back, Hamilton caught Kingston's sidekick against his hip, shoving the boy away so he lost footing and stumbled to his bottom.

Samuel looked for a way into Hamilton's blind spot, attempting to pounce on him, but Hamilton wasn't going to be fooled so easily. When Julius and Samuel came flying at him from in front and behind, he spun out of the way and watched as the two boys crashed into one another. He laughed to himself, feeling a clot of blood form in his throat, the taut constriction of his chest worsening a bit more.

When each boy rose to their feet, Hamilton shook off the internal pain, and said, "Are you all quite finished?"

Taking that as a means to stop, Kingston and Samuel stepped back to catch their breath, but Julius did not. On his own, he dashed for Hamilton unsuspectedly. When he looked as though he were headed for a palm strike with the heel of his wrist, he quickly transitioned into a two fisted jab to the center of Hamilton's open chest.

Hamilton flew back from the surprising power that came with the strike, lurching forward to grab at the front of his jumper in agony. Collapsing to the floor of the gym, he crumbled, squeezing his eyes shut as he clenched his teeth. Feeling the congestion grip in his lungs, Hamilton's scarf loosened and fell. He coughed roughly, blood splashing out onto the floor.

"Hamilton!" Teresa screamed, and dove to his side. "Are you okay!?"

Drowning in an uncontrollable tremor of coughs, Hamilton was afraid he would pass out from the pain. He thought he would have been able to take any hits he gathered, but that one blow from Julius had taken too much out of him, especially since he hadn't seen it coming.

"I'm so sorry!" Julius came down at Hamilton's side, the instructor quickly gathering the scarf to shield his coughs and any further blood that rose from within. "I didn't mean to hurt you like that!"

"Stand back," Teresa ordered, helping Hamilton to his feet.

He was more humiliated at the moment than he was upset at Julius. Here he was in the center of the gym with eyes on him, the eyes of people who looked up to him as a slayer and he'd been taken down so cruelly by a mere boy.

"Hamilton, I'm sorry!" Julius called as Teresa led him away.

It wasn't long until he found himself in his own bed with a warm towel over his forehead. Teresa was still at his side and she'd called in a doctor earlier. He was a doctor who worked on the grounds of Gregor, and without knowing the full story about Hamilton's condition, he suggested all the slayer was going to need was rest after taking that hit. Apparently, he was perfectly fine and would be on his feet again in no time.

Right...

He was confined to his room for the rest of the day, not being able to partake in any exercises until further notice, but once night fell he knew he couldn't stay there any longer.

Leaving was going to be more of a challenge since Teresa still hadn't left his side. She'd aided him from his bedside, bringing water and soups, and stayed to keep him company. No matter how many times he made clear that he was fine and didn't need looking after, Teresa insisted on staying close enough if there was required assistance.

How the heck was he supposed to get out of here if he was limited to his apartment? The treatment for his tuberculosis was supposed to begin tonight, and if he didn't show up soon, he just knew Demiesius would quickly question his whereabouts. Not only did he want to get out of there to see Demiesius, but he worried that if he held off the treatment any longer, it would get worse, spread to other parts of his body, and then ultimately be the death of him.

Hamilton could not die of a bloody sickness. Just the thought of being taken out by one of Mother Nature's curses filled him with humility and anger. He hadn't trained so hard and fought for so many years just to wind up ill.

When Teresa returned to his bedroom with a plate of biscuits and warm tea, Hamilton sat up and crossed his legs in the center of his bed. He wore black shorts and high white socks, a cropped dark orange short-sleeved shirt, and his black slayer mask was on to cover his mouth given the "mild flu" he mentioned suffering from before. The sun had gone down long ago, so he was going to at least try and talk to her.

"Teresa," he said, sweetly, "I really am fine, you don't have to hover over me all night. It was just a little blood."

She sat down at his bedside, and handed him the cup of tea, "What do you mean just a little blood? That might as well have been a puddle you coughed up. Dr. Roy may have said you're fine, but I just want to make sure nothing happens."

"And I appreciate that," Hamilton lifted the tea to his lips, pulling the mask down for only a moment, carefully swallowing as it warmed his scratchy throat.

"Wait a minute," she raised a brow at him in suspicion, "Are you trying to get away from here to see that boyfriend you've been hiding for the past couple months?"

Hearing someone refer to Demiesius as his boyfriend made Hamilton's heart pound. Though he clearly wanted something more with the elder, he couldn't imagine them referring to each other as such names. Boyfriend. It didn't fit someone like Demiesius, but Hamilton liked to think they could wind up as such.

When a certain twinkle met Hamilton's eyes, Teresa smirked, and said, "What's he like? I've never seen you doll yourself up like you do whenever you go see him. What does he look like? I bet he is real fit, aye?"

Hamilton saw Demiesius in his mind, those warm but foreboding eyes, and his perfectly carved face, all of his striking features bordered by waves of black hair. "He is quite a man," Hamilton blushed with a snicker. "I like him a lot, more than anyone I've ever met."

"How does he feel about you?"

Without really answering the question, Hamilton said, "We shared our first kiss last night."

Teresa gasped, scooting closer to Hamilton on the bed like he was sharing a tasteful secret. "Your first kiss after so long? Wow, you must be holding out on him. Poor guy."

Hamilton couldn't contain his laugh.

In a way he felt like Demiesius was the one holding back on him. It was only so blatant that Hamilton wanted to pursue the vampire the night after their first encounter, while Demiesius had come off as standoffish in the beginning. He could only hope now that they'd kissed, maybe opening up to one another would come about much smoother than before.

"He is sweet enough," Hamilton admitted. "Quiet in the beginning, but if there is one thing I know for sure, it's that he cares for me. Look," he said, bringing out the necklace he'd been given. It was tucked inside his shirt, and when Teresa got a good look at it, seeing the gold, diamonds, and ruby, her mouth fell open. "Nice, innit? He gave it to me for my birthday."

"He bought you this?" she nudged Hamilton playfully, "You lucky bugger!"

For a moment Hamilton forgot about wanting to leave, too occupied with the conversation of possible significant others. Teresa told him a long story about how she'd met a man roughly two weeks ago who'd piqued her interests. Mentioning he was a bit younger than her by five years, she wanted advice on if going along with someone barely into his mid-twenties was a good idea. "As long as he treats you nice and is mature enough with you," Hamilton said, "I don't see anything wrong with it. Titus is older than me—" physically "—by five and a half years, and neither of us are bothered by it."

Teresa nodded, "Alright, then, and by the way, your boyfriend has got a pretty interesting name. Mine's name is Christoph. He always seems so serious all the time, and he's busy most nights, but he says it's because of work. He was going to talk to his boss and ask for a couple of free nights so we can spend a bit more time together."

Hearing the familiar name, Hamilton wondered if it would be too much of a coincidence if Demiesius' guard was the person

Teresa was talking about. Not wanting to frighten her if it was true, he kept his curiosity to himself.

When Hamilton was able to get Teresa in a good enough mood, he convinced her to go back to her apartment. Once she was gone, he hurried about the room, throwing on a snug pair of jeans and a cream colored jumper to go over his shirt. After brushing the tangles from his hair, he clipped his bangs behind his ear, and was out the door.

It didn't take long to get to Demiesius' place, and when he pulled up to the extravagant home, there was already another vehicle parked in the drive, presumably belonging to Dr. Takahashi. Stalling beside it, Hamilton got out and hurried up to the door, knocking hastily. It was answered a second later, Christoph standing there in dark navy trousers and a white shirt. He looked bothered by something, looking at Hamilton from head to toe as if assessing who he was when he already knew. When he finally stepped aside, he allowed Hamilton entry, and led the way to the parlor room.

Hamilton almost wanted to inquire about if Christoph knew anyone by the name 'Teresa' but decided against it when he saw Demiesius. As always, the vampire was stunning in all black apparel, the dark color complimenting everything he had to offer. From Demiesius' set shoulders, to his slim yet broad and lean physical appearance, Hamilton would never cease to admire all the exquisiteness of him. A part of him wanted to simply walk up to the elder and kiss him like they had before, a casual greeting kiss, but since they weren't alone, he held himself back from doing so.

"You took longer than I would have expected," Demiesius said. "Are you alright?"

He thought to lie.

"Yes, I was having a hard time getting around one of my friends at Gregor. She insisted we spend some time together, but I convinced her it was late enough." He knew he should probably mention the entire incident that happened this morning, but he didn't want to burden the vampire with any further worry for him and kept it to himself.

When he was seated on a stool before a bar counter, Hamilton listened to Dr. Takahashi as he explained the treatment method they were going to use. It would involve Hamilton visiting him every night at the soonest convenience, and he was adamant about soonest. The doctor would be administering injections of several different kinds of medication that were supposed to begin dulling the symptoms. For the first eight weeks, he would have to endure receiving isoniazid, rifampin, ethambutol, and pyrazinamide every single visit. Once the eight weeks were up, he'd need all of the same injections for two weeks, and then twice weekly for six weeks. At the end of the initial phase of treatment, if everything was still going smoothly, he'd require the same drugs three times a week for eight weeks.

Hamilton was overwhelmed with the amount of pricking at his skin, and began to worry more when Dr. Takahashi wasn't done with his explanation.

During the continuation phase, he'd be on isoniazid and rifampin daily for eighteen weeks, and then twice a week for eighteen weeks, before moving on to three times a week for an additional eighteen more weeks.

"After that time," Dr. Takahashi said, "I will have to bring you into an examination room to test if the tuberculosis is truly gone. I won't be able to consume your blood like before to give a result, because during this time, after the injections are given tonight, your blood will be highly toxic for the amount of antibiotics in your system. In short, your blood will be like poison, which is good for you given your profession, but bad for vampires." He glanced toward Demiesius as if wanting to add something, but decided against the wording he had to choose. Instead, he said, "If your blood finds its way into an immortal, it could ultimately kill them or make them crucially ill. So...try to keep it to yourself. Shall we get started?"

The doctor gathered his equipment briefcase from the other side of the room, and Hamilton sighed with dejection in his eyes. Why did he have to obtain such a bacteria? All his life he'd been healthy as a horse, and now, when things around him were starting to look brighter, he'd been given such news.

Demiesius approached the slayer, hands clasped behind him. "Thank you for doing this," he said. "The only thing I want is for you to be in good health, and this is the one thing that will keep you on your feet. You know I will be here for you every step of the way."

Hamilton could see the sincere appreciation in the vampire's coal eyes, "Why are you thanking me?" he said, "If it wasn't for you, not only would I have not gone to check what this was, but I'm almost sure it would have been the one thing in the world that could have killed me. Thank *you* for wanting to keep me alive."

Demiesius nodded, a sudden ponder of kissing Hamilton at the back of his mind when his shoulder was tapped by Christoph. "Master," he said, head down in uncertainty, "If you do not mind, could I please have a moment of your time? There is something I would like to ask of you."

When Demiesius agreed to his guard's inquiry, Hamilton de-
liberated on the sure idea of Christoph being Teresa's new interest. A part of him wondered if he even knew she was a slayer
like Demiesius was aware of him, or if Teresa knew about his
immortal background. With the way she'd spoken so affection-
ately of him, there was no doubt she was serious about their
relationship turning into something more.

By the time Dr. Takahashi returned with the needles filled
with their different medicines, Demiesius came back into the
parlor without Christoph at his side.

Must have asked for those nights off, Hamilton thought.

Laying Hamilton's arm out on the counter, the doctor rolled
up his sleeve and inserted the first needle after cleaning his skin.
Hamilton winced from the small but sharp pain, sitting through
the last three until everything was done.

Once Dr. Takahashi finished, he wiped Hamilton's arm and
wrapped it in a bandage to hide the tiny bruises the pricks would
leave behind. "There we have it," he said, "Now, Hamilton, what
else you will have to do during these phases of treatment is rest.
Your body needs to relax for long periods of time, and requires
fresh air to circulate within your lungs. If you strain yourself too
much, things are bound to take much longer."

Hamilton thought of life back at Gregor. "I'm sorry," he said,
"But I think you're not taking into consideration the lifestyle
I live in. I can't sit out in front of my fellow slayers, or refuse
things like missions, and most of all, I have students to train.
They'll never learn anything if I don't interact with them. I can't
just hand my duties over to another instructor. And what about
my tasks?"

"I can talk to your commanders about moving you up in rank,"

Demiesius said. He was lounged comfortably in an armchair. "With your endowed history, I'm sure they wouldn't mind repositioning you if I put forth the idea."

"What would I do?"

"Something the other elders and I have been discussing with your higher-ups, is branding an order called the C.C. or the Concord Coalition. It'll be a secret organization just for capable out of commission slayers that work alongside indulgent vampires. You would be in charge of maintaining civilized order within your own region, and examining crimes between slayers and vampires. You won't have to fight anymore."

Hamilton considered all the good something like this would do, not only for his health, but in keeping stability between the slayer and immortal worlds. "What about my students," he countered. "I have three kids under my wing who I can't just abandon."

"They will be placed under someone else's authority," Demiesius assured. "You may still live in the walls of Gregor, or find a more suitable home, but your tasks will take place elsewhere and never be as straining. Simply tell me if you want the opportunity to join the C.C. and the position is yours."

"Can I...think about it first? I won't put myself through so much work until I come up with an answer, but I feel like this is something I should consider before readily accepting."

"The choice is yours," Demiesius said, a hidden glint of disappointment in his eyes. "Just know this is what's best for you."

Chapter Thirteen

Don't Throw Away What is Important to You

It was still the same night Hamilton received his first dose of medicine for his sickness. Dr. Takahashi had made his departure not long after, leaving the slayer and Demiesius alone. Hamilton's forearm was a bit sore from the penetration of the needles, but all in all he felt fine. Even with that, he was sure that would pass. Always, since the symptoms began, there would be a period of time where he felt perfectly normal, and then suddenly he'd be hit with complete exhaustion. While this time of momentary health lasted, he would make the most of the next few hours he had.

Demiesius was out of the room right now, taking a phone call next door, so Hamilton decided to meander through the halls. He'd gotten a good look at the entire place on his birthday, but exploring this castle made him wonder about all the things that have happened here.

A few weeks ago, Demiesius had mentioned this place had been built in the 1200s, but over the centuries he'd lived in countless places, he'd settled here in the United Kingdom, because Dominick preferred it to other locations.

When Hamilton ventured into a small workplace-type room, he skimmed the low bookshelf across from the desk, examining what kinds of fiction the elder had taken time to delve into. Spotting Bram Stoker's 'Dracula', Hamilton couldn't hold back a mild laugh, and speculated over what Demiesius must have thought of the rendition of a vampire based on a brutal human king. Although he'd enjoyed the movie before, he was sure any immortal would find it ridiculous.

After leaving the office, he happened into another, the gallery he hadn't taken much time to scrutinize. The walls were papered in gold and forest green while the floor was a shiny light oak wood. Fastened to the walls were beautiful paintings of various scenes, works ranging from a mother with her children, a river and valley, to single portraits of people Hamilton wanted to know if they were actually real. Squinting his eyes, he saw a signature at the bottom right of a man in kingly attire: Johannes Vermeer. Recognizing the famous name, Hamilton wanted to peer back in time to see the conversations Demiesius could have had with so many figures of the past.

Was he acquainted with the former kings and queens? Surely if he'd known a Roman Emperor like Augustus, he must have seen many others, and if so, Hamilton wanted to know if Demiesius was held up to such regard from their point of view.

Coming back to the last spot he'd seen Demiesius on the

phone, Hamilton turned into the room. The vampire was seat-ed in a black lacquer baroque throne. Seeing him there in a placement so regal caused a stammer of urgency to erupt inside Hamilton. Demiesius was fully engaged in the conversation at hand, but with Hamilton's focus lain somewhere else entirely, he hardly heard a word of what the vampire was talking about.

Looking upon Demiesius' stimulating silhouette sitting tall and ruminating in that kingly seat, Hamilton thoughtlessly licked over his lips, biting down with desire creeping into every portion of his body.

He couldn't help wanting to know of the others who had lust-ed after the vampire in the past. Being as charmingly courteous and just about the most attractive man on this earth, Hamilton didn't have to guess that people from all over time had once chased Demiesius for his affections.

In preoccupying his mind with jealous thoughts of historical lovers, Hamilton envied those nameless faces, wielding an in-curable grudge against them for getting the opportunity to enjoy whatever pleasures Demiesius could have offered them.

Unfair, Hamilton thought, that was completely unfair. He wanted the vampire all to himself, unspoiled and untouched by gluttonous hands. Although he sounded much like a bitter, avaricious child, he couldn't deny his yearning to propose hand-ing over all of his own purities.

With suggestive thoughts clouding his mind, Hamilton found himself directly approaching the vampire, standing now before the immortal man. Demiesius glanced up at Hamilton, assessing the slayer's proximity when a gracious touch smoothed down his cheek. Without second thought, Hamilton drew up a knee and straddled Demiesius in the throne.

As he was mounted, Demiesius immediately hung up the phone , his lips taken the second the receiver was clamped down. Hamilton deepened the kiss, sweeping his tongue across the vampire's lips before passing his taste buds into the other man's mouth. His mind spun when he could feel the wanderlust of Demiesius' hands as they slid down the back of his thighs.

When they didn't move to caress him further, Hamilton blindly reached for the still hands, moving them up to grip his perky bottom. He released a breathy sigh, barely able to catch a moan from escaping him. Breaking the kiss for only a second, Hamilton said, "You don't have to control yourself from touching me. I want you to."

Demiesius didn't know where this sudden mood came from, but he wasn't going to complain. Embracing Hamilton against him, he allowed his hands to further search the slayer's trim form, gliding them along Hamilton's curves, all while his tongue remained taken.

A moment later Demiesius rose from the black throne, and Hamilton's legs wrapped around his waist. "I want you all to myself," the slayer admitted, a whimper slipping his lips when taunting fingers ran down the middle of his bottom. He could feel the serious arousal in his jeans press against the material, grinding upon the vampire to satisfy the mindless need to be touched.

When Demiesius began to walk through the wide corridors and up the stairs, Hamilton set his kisses away from the vampire's mouth, nipping along his angled jawline until reaching his neck.

As they ascended to the second floor, a flash of sensible reason attempted to weave into Hamilton's mind, trying to remind him that self-discipline was something he should probably take into account right now. Disregarding it, Hamilton soon found himself in Demiesius' bedroom.

Only the light from the corridor shone inside when the vampire stepped in with the slayer in his arms, seeping into the chamber like a spotlight on the wide bedspread. The dark expanse of the room was like a royal cavern with pricey fabrics and pleasant fragrance, the mattress like a cloud as Hamilton sunk into it when set down.

He lay down as Demiesius towered at the foot of the bed, pushed himself further up the bed after removing his shoes so that he lay in the center, legs coming open when he dragged his hands up his sensitive form. Hamilton was the most vulnerable he'd ever been; every instinct, past lesson, and mere concept of thought grew more distant from him when his mind blurred with such need.

Coming up on his palms, Hamilton admired the way Demiesius' fingers undid the buttons on his shirt. As each black sewn button was set free, the slayer ogled for a look at what had been shielded from his eyes for these months. When all the clasps came undone, Demiesius pulled the shirt apart, exposing his lean upper body. There was a mild show of hair about his otherwise smooth and bold chest, slight traces running down his defined abdomen into the sharp lining of his trousers.

He was absolutely divine.

Prowling onto the bed once he dropped the shirt, Demiesius merged between Hamilton's legs, their lips meeting as his fingers searched for the hook and zipper at the front of the slayer's jeans. The closer the elder got to stripping Hamilton of his clothes, the faster the slayer's actions began to catch up with him. With the front of his pants loosened, Hamilton trembled in expectancy at the thought of being this close to making love for the first time.

Would it even be counted as making "love" given neither of them have confessed any true sentiment for one another?

The moment full comprehension dawned on him, Hamilton was almost half naked, chest bared from his jumper. "Wait," he stammered, the lust in his eyes fading quickly, breathing just as fast as his tense nerves shook. "I'm sorry, I shouldn't do this yet."

It seemed Hamilton had not needed to tell Demiesius to stop. The vampire froze the moment he stripped the other man from the garment. Knelt between the slayer's open legs, he stared mutely down at Hamilton's naked chest, horrified by what lay upon his pale skin. "What – What happened to you?" he inquired.

Leaning back on his elbows, Hamilton glanced down at his chest, and the second he saw what had worried Demiesius so much, he hastened out of bed and clutched his fallen jumper to his chest.

Hamilton already knew his body wasn't as unblemished as most would be. As the slayer he'd been raised as, he'd obtained numerous scars on nearly every part of his body from both training and combat with immortals. There were scars all over his upper chest and abdomen, his arms, back, and even his slender legs and calves had scars from years ago. But those hadn't been what stopped Demiesius from moving any further.

Clear as ever in the center of Hamilton's being was a cruel-looking, blackish violet bruise, and the veins within his chest were partially visible. There was no doubt in his mind that this must have formed a while after being struck so hard by Julius this morning. He had been a little sore all day, but this seemed to have taken some time to appear. Since it wasn't unnatural anymore to feel a soreness in the center of his chest, he hadn't thought much of it...and to go unnoticed all this time.

Feeling disgusted by the grotesque blemish, Hamilton turned his back on Demiesius, throwing the jumper on to hide it. How embarrassing, he thought, to display something so sickening during a time like this.

"Hamilton," Demiesius said again, "What happened for you to wind up with that?"

The slayer faced him, humiliation apparent in his woeful stare. Demiesius was seated on the side of the bed, leather shoes on the floor, torso still bare from the shirt tossed at the foot of the bed.

"It happened this morning when I was with my students," Hamilton said. "We were all having a fair bout before one of them caught me off guard. He didn't mean anything by it. He was sorry but the force of his strike had taken quite a bit out of me."

"This is why you should not be so active," Demiesius stated, "Especially in this occupation. The last thing you should be right now is a slayer. For the first time in your life, you need to be a normal human being."

Sorrow crept over Hamilton and he sighed, starting out of the bedroom after putting on his shoes again, "Yeah...a normal human being with tuberculosis."

Demiesius retrieved his shirt from the floor before following Hamilton. Buttoning it up again, he came up behind the slayer leaning up against the guardrail, looking down to the lower floors. "With Doctor Takahashi's help, you're going to get better.

Don't lose hope in that. Soon you will be cured in no time."

Head resting on his crossed forearms, Hamilton said, "That is easy for someone to say when they have all the time in the world. I'm not going to be here forever, Demiesius. No matter if I die tomorrow, in six months, or in twenty years—when all's said and done, I am human. You will surpass me...as I'm sure you have all your others."

When the slayer started down the stairs, Demiesius remained at the top.

Hamilton didn't know how much longer he could bear the difference between him and the vampire. At first, it hadn't bothered him in the least, but suddenly it decided to burden him now, at a time where less strain on himself was needed.

Entering the parlor room, Hamilton laid on the sofa, shoes kicked up on the armrest. How many, he wondered, just how many people had Demiesius used to satisfy his sexual and sentimental needs? He couldn't imagine the vampire had gone all throughout these past millennia without someone to comfort him in time, so considering himself the luckiest man alive, to have Demiesius all to himself, was ridiculous.

Hamilton didn't want to be a temporary interest, something Demiesius could use to liven up the passing of the years. Besides, he was sure by the time, *if* by the time he reached his fifties, Demiesius would want nothing to do with him anymore. Even if that did happen, Hamilton would rather the elder remember him as he was now: youthful and untarnished by age, instead of watching him wither away one day at a time. Not only was that not fair to himself, it also wasn't fair to Demiesius.

"Two."

Hamilton's ears perked to the vampire's voice.

"There were two who I cherished before this time," Demiesius said. "Before you."

Sitting up, Hamilton made room for the elder when he sat down beside him. He didn't appear to be distressed over the topic, not troubled by sorrowful events, but there was a peculiar glint in his eyes that Hamilton couldn't place.

"If you don't want to talk about them," the slayer said considerately, "you don't have to. You are under no obligation to tell me things you don't want to. I still...I still want whatever we have...for as long as I can take it."

Resting his arm over the back of the sofa, Demiesius made himself comfortable, warmed by Hamilton when he leaned into the open place against him.

"The first was a man by the name of Leonidas," Demiesius said, "I met him long after my rising as an immortal in 112 BC. He was a young soldier in the Roman military, having just joined when he turned twenty-three, and for twenty years I cherished him. Over our time together, I began to notice his hunger for power. He wanted inhuman strength and the right to stand high above his superiors, and had dreams of becoming the next Emperor to rule over the Roman territory. He believed I had the ability to fulfill such a craving for him, and demanded that I turn him into an immortal."

Hamilton peered up at Demiesius. The solid stare out across the parlor spoke of hidden resentment. "Since Dominick is your only," he said, "I will guess that you didn't go through with his wish?"

"No, I didn't," Demiesius admitted. "My refusal angered him to no end, causing him to claim that I no longer cared for him, which was not true, but changing his outlook on the situation was impossible. You see, Hamilton, when you have been around as long as I have, you learn a great deal about the human race, and if history could speak for itself, it would go to prove that there is nothing worse for the world than a power-hungry man. Upon my rejection, he abandoned me, instead taking to the arms of another immortal who would give him what he wanted. The next time I saw him, he was as I am, but I knew just looking into his eyes that he was no longer the Leonidas I'd grown to adore over the years. When he began to lose himself in the influence he now had, blood was spilled by his hands and he needed to be put down. I could not bear the idea of him being hunted by the slayers of that time, so I lured him into a false sense of security before doing it myself."

At that, Hamilton sucked in a sharp breath, "You killed him?"

"I had to. Not only did he risk the existence of my people, he was a threat to the human race. If I hadn't done what I did, he would have damaged this world more than it already was."

"What about the other?" Hamilton asked. "Was he corrupt as well?"

"Not at all," Demiesius began, "Kai had been a man I came across during my travels through Japan in the late 1600s. He was what you would call a ronin at that time, and he wandered from place to place to become a fearsome swordsman. I will never forget when he attempted to cut me down for resembling an Englishman, something he was unfamiliar with since I'd come from the west. When he witnessed my ability to not only heal from the few lacerations he'd caused, but take control of his sword, he began to view me as something more than the foreign man I was. He'd been twenty years old when I met him, and while we spent nine years together, somewhere down the road,

I did propose turning him. Kai refused my offer, wanting the freedom to die the 'warrior's death' he'd always dreamed of. Four years later, his wish was granted when he challenged another dojo and was defeated. After watching as he was cut down, my time in Japan was over."

"He loved you?"

"Though we never uttered such a word, I knew there was a reason he wanted me by his side until the end."

Hamilton sighed, "He doesn't sound like such a bad guy, but Demiesius...what was it you saw in *me*? Surely you saw something in those two that pulled you in. What makes you want to pursue me?"

It was still difficult for Hamilton to think that once upon a time, two times in fact, Demiesius had found something as precious as love with people who'd come before him. Maybe if he heard what it was that Demiesius saw that brought on this careful chase, it would ease his mind and heart enough for him to accept what they could have.

Demiesius turned up Hamilton's chin to meet his eyes, "We have the same drive," he said. "Never in all my time have I met a human being who wants to protect his fellow man the way you do. Even now that you are ill and cannot perform as you had before, still, you want to fight, and you want to be out there doing what you have been dedicated to your whole life. Many would believe the human race is a species worth giving up on, and I will not lie, I have had my moments of thinking the world man has made isn't worth protecting, especially in the past couple hundred years, but everything deserves a chance to change. I..." Demiesius paused, "...I want you because you are strong, faithful and devoted to who you are and to this world."

Tears burned in Hamilton's gaze, but he tried his hardest to resist them. "Now that I'm sick," he said, "I can't be all those things anymore. I can't fight, I can't even withstand a blow from a fifteen-year-old boy. I'm afraid I will never be able to be as strong again. Will you lose what you see in me if I become brittle and useless?"

"I can assure you that is most impossible," Demiesius assured. He then took Hamilton's forearm, running his tender touch over the wrap hiding his injection points. "I won't see you to an early death caused by this illness. You will get better. I know you are strong enough to do at least that, and then when you are as you were, you'll be able to fight again if that is what you desire."

Finally at ease, Hamilton found his once shaken nerves settled by encouraging words. He leaned forward and pressed a kiss to Demiesius' lips, the minimal pinch of pain in the center of his chest fading with the seconds that passed. "You are such a beautiful man," he whispered between their kisses. "I hope you'll always know what to say to bring me comfort when I need it."

Once Hamilton returned to Gregor for the night, he wielded a renewed sense of assurance. He believed in the words Demiesius had spoken to him, so much that he would hold onto what strength he had left to get through this treatment. Six to nine months wasn't such a long time. It would be about Christmas time by then. He looked forward to going into the New Year with good health on his side, so until then, he was going to try his hardest to keep positive.

Before getting into bed for some much-needed rest, Hamilton stepped into the shower. He could faintly smell Demiesius' scent on him before cleansing his body under the shower head. When he was finished, he shut everything off and threw on a pair of shorts and a cropped night shirt, hair tied and a bit damp.

When he entered his bedroom, he paused when suddenly he could hear a minor cry sounding through his wall. Teresa's flat was next door to his, and he couldn't imagine why on earth she'd be down at an hour such as this. Nearly three o'clock in the morning, he expected her to be asleep.

Concerned for his friend, Hamilton quickly adorned a face mask and stepped out before knocking on her door. She didn't answer for a minute, but after his second knock, the door unlocked and she stood in the threshold in her blue nightgown. Her blonde hair was pinned up, and down her face streamed a gleaming course of tears.

"Oh, Teresa," Hamilton let himself in and pulled her into a heartening embrace. "What's happened?"

After closing the door behind himself, Hamilton took her to the living room, and they sat down on her sofa. There were countless napkins on a low table, and even an empty tub of strawberry ice cream was tipped over.

Bundling her up in his arms, Hamilton soothed her with a soft run of his hand down her back.

Stuttering as she tried to control her sobs, Teresa said, "I — I liked him a lot."

"Christoph?" Hamilton asked.

She nodded, "I met with him not long after I left your room. He said he had something to tell me."

"What was it?"

Coming undone from Hamilton's arms, Teresa lowered her voice, burying her face in the palms of her hands. "He's a vampire."

So it was him...

"Oh," was all Hamilton could manage for a second. "But...Teresa, it's alright. You don't have to cry over something like this."

"What do you mean?" she trembled with unadulterated sorrow. "I can never see him again after this. No matter how much I liked him, no matter how sweet and caring and thoughtful he was to me, I can't see him again. What if — what if the day came where I had to kill him and I couldn't do it? What kind of slayer would that make me? He said he knew what I was from the beginning, but was too scared to tell me...thinking I would leave him. I — I had to."

Hamilton understood where she was coming from, only now just noticing that he hadn't felt such things when his yearning for Demiesius showed up. Was this how he was supposed to feel? Was he so detached from the reality of it all to see the true harm in what he was doing?

"Teresa," he said kindly, "This man, Christoph, did he truly make you happy?"

She nodded quickly, "He made me feel like a normal woman, one who doesn't spend her days trapped here in a place like this. I never asked for this kind of life, Hamilton. I didn't walk into this place when I was a little girl to seek revenge for the loss of my family. Like you, I was brought into this knowing nothing else. I only stay because I feel like it's the only place I belong."

"But he made you happy..."

She gave another nod.

"There is nothing in our regulations as slayers that say we don't deserve happiness like everyone else. Nowhere does it say we can't find the possibilities of love inside other people. Not all vampires are our enemy, Teresa; only the ones who cross the line. Has Christoph done that?"

She shook her head, "He swears he's never harmed an innocent human."

"Do you believe him?"

Another nod.

"Then what is the problem? I know you are probably fearful of being looked down on, or even killed for your choice to enjoy the comforts of a vampire, but...if I were you...I wouldn't let anything stop me from finally being happy with someone I love." Hamilton offered a promising smirk beneath his mask, his next words a message for himself more than anything. "Maybe you can find love in him. In secret."

"You wouldn't judge me? You wouldn't think of me as a traitor?"

"Believe me," Hamilton shook his head, clearing Teresa's face from the tears she'd shed. "I am the last person who should."

CHAPTER FOURTEEN

A Vampire's Bite May Come With Benefits

Hamilton had been showing up to all of his appointments with Dr. Takahashi for the past two weeks, and everything, including the low level of suspicion from the Public, was running smoothly. He still didn't feel much better when it came to his condition, but the doctor mentioned that wasn't something to be worried about.

Tonight, on the other hand, he was worried about one thing. During today's lesson with his students on the history of slayers, Hamilton had been given a letter of beckoning. He was to attend a meeting at the Gathering of Councilors tonight, and the timing cut straight into his visit for the medical injections. There was no way he could ignore the invitation, especially since it'd been hand delivered to him, so he couldn't play it off by saying he hadn't received it.

There wasn't even a way for him to contact Demiesius to inform him of the summoning. The vampire had a phone number, but since they usually communicated long distance through the raven, there was no reason for him to know the number.

This was horrible.

After having relieved Julius, Kingston and Samuel from their lesson together, Hamilton hurried across the campus to his flat. If there was a chance Demiesius had written to him today, he'd be able to send a quick reply.

Hustling down the walkway of the courtyard along the building, he stopped when a sudden wave of nausea floated over him. He felt his head begin to spin, and his vision began to sway in and out of focus. Pressing a hand up against the cold brick of the building, he placed a hand at his stomach, feeling the queasiness mix his insides together.

"The dizzy spells will come and go from time to time," he'd been told, "Just give it a second to pass."

Hamilton didn't have time for this. To the best he could, he used the wall to guide him to the doors of the instructor's building, and pushed through them, trekking down the corridor to his room. By the time he stepped into the flat, the fluctuation of his surroundings came to a stop.

He waited there for a good twenty minutes, hopes high that the raven would arrive like it did most times at around this hour. Today, it seemed, a letter wasn't something he was to receive.

There was a knock on his door an hour later, and while he finished washing dishes after a meal, he shouted, "It's unlocked," to let the guest in. To his surprise, it was Samuel. The blonde Austrian boy's hair had begun to grow out over the months, now just long enough to curl at the nape of his neck. "Hello, Sam," Hamilton said, "What can I do for you?"

Pulling out a chair at the dining table near the opening of the kitchen, Samuel sat down with a glum look on his scarred face. "I was wondering if I could share a few words with you. I was going to talk to Julius myself, but I wasn't sure if it was such a good idea."

Drying his hands with a dish cloth, Hamilton slipped on a black mask that'd been sitting on the counter nearby and took a seat across from the boy. "Is there something going on between you all? Last time I checked, I could have sworn everyone was getting on just fine."

"We are, we are," Samuel admitted.

"Then what's the problem?"

Samuel took a breath and sat with his hands in his lap, "I'm starting to worry about Julius and his intentions with becoming a member of the Public."

Though Hamilton could agree that Julius was a little headstrong at times, he said, "Why do you say that?"

"Well, last night," Samuel started, "Julius, Kingston and I were up late talking about things, and after a while we began talking about what we want to accomplish here once we officially join the Public. Kingston said he wanted to get revenge for his mother's death, which I thought was understandable. I feel like that is something everyone wants when we first come here. I'd much like to find the killer of my older brother, but if I can't, then simply being able to protect others by getting rid of murderous vampires is a good enough feat. Julius, though, the way he spoke...it seemed like he wanted to use this occupation as more than a place to harness skill and maintain peace on the streets."

Hamilton nodded, "What did he say? It wouldn't be the first time someone was inducted into the Public under unlawful needs. There used to be a lad on my team when I was coming up that yearned so much for revenge, he ended up killing numerous innocent vampires who'd never done wrong by the human race."

"That's what Julius has in mind," Samuel explained. "He went on a rant about taking out vampire after vampire when he finally gained his emblem. He tried to justify his argument by saying, 'If vampires can lure in and murder humans whenever they get the urge, I should be able to slaughter them before they can do so'. I thought maybe he was just spewing words, but he was very serious about it."

"I see," Hamilton hummed in thought. "I will have a chat with him in a minute to—."

"No, you can't," Samuel argued. "He'll know what I said."

"Alright," Hamilton assured, "I will be sure to inform the Councilors to keep him on our watch record. If we see he's become an issue to the Public, they will know how to reprimand him. If the Councilors are the ones to confront him, your name will be in the clear. Thank you for sharing this with me. Things like this need to be taken very seriously so the regulation of vicious versus innocent vampires can be maintained. If slayers around the world begin to take on reckless habits, everything this Public has worked for over the centuries will disappear."

Once that was done, Samuel left and Hamilton awaited nightfall.

Not having the ability to contact Demiesius right away, Hamilton went ahead to the Councilors meeting he was called to attend. He was one hundred percent sure that the vampire would be upset at him for missing an appointment, but couldn't disregard his higher-ups. They were the ones who had recognized him as being the confident, talented, and loyal slayer that he was. If he didn't arrive as they surely expected of him, he knew backlash was certain.

Dressed in his slayer attire in case of a given task, Hamilton wore his tight, black athletic trousers, a long-sleeved black shirt, heavy boots with silver daggers hidden in the front end, and a mouth and nose guard mask pulled over his face. Lastly, he had his stake, strapped and ready around his upper right thigh.

As he moved down the narrow spiraling stairwell that led further underground, Hamilton rubbed uncomfortably at his forearm; the spots Dr. Takahashi usually injected him with the much-needed dosage. They were the one thing he wanted most, right now.

Coming into the spider-like vestibule that led into the many chambers of the headquarters, Hamilton started toward the Councilor meeting hall. When he stepped inside, there were a lot more people than he'd been expecting within. The tall podium that originally seated four was now occupied by three of the usual elderly Councilmen, but there was a long wooden table now positioned at the base of it, and when he laid eyes on Demiesius, a tremor of confusion rained down over him.

At the same table were seated four other people, vampires, two men and two women dressed in regal Gothic apparel. Along the walls stood twelve men and women, all standing with their arms at their sides, stern and focused expressions on their faces.

"Hamilton," Councilor Homer said from his high seat, "Welcome."

When the doors to the round room shut loudly behind him, Hamilton assumed his previous stance, trying his best to ignore the fact that Demiesius was seated not far from him. What was going on?

Closing his hands behind his back, Hamilton straightened his posture, and said, "Good evening, Councilors."

"Good evening," they all said together, and then Councilor Jamison, a bald, aged man, said, "Please, step forward."

Once in the center of the room, the slayer felt all eyes on him.

"Mr. Hamilton," Councilor Jamison said, "You have been considered as our most gifted and unique slayer to date. Tell us, how does that make you feel?"

"Very much honored, Councilors," he said, trying to keep his mind together. "I find it a privilege to have been able to contribute to the Public the way I have."

"Good, good," Jamison carried on. "Some would say one with your abilities should be praised, and everyone here seems to think so as well. That is why, Hamilton, we have taken raising your rank into consideration. For years, you have subsidized a major role in this Public, and to show our appreciation to all the hard work and dedication you have shown, we would like to request that you join the Concord Coalition."

Hamilton remembered the name from the talk he and Demiesius had the other night, and, yes, he'd considered the opportunity, had agreed to look into it when he had the time, but he guessed the time was now.

"May I ask," Hamilton said, "What is your take on this Coalition?"

Councilor Richard spoke forward this time, a man with one blind eye and a balding comb over. "The Concord Coalition is an unrevealed alliance between slayer and vampire. We, as strong and knowledgeable partners, would work side by side, monitoring the actions of our worlds to ensure all the policies are being followed, and reporting back to headquarters when strange events arise. For example, perhaps a string of murders begins to take place within vampire society; it would be yours and a fellow immortal's task to stop them and bring the culprit to justice without spilling blood. This organization is determined to stop the bloodshed between species, so we may only resort to sending out slayers if it is absolutely necessary."

Hamilton nodded in understanding, "This would mean I no longer have to fight?"

"Correct."

Hamilton swept his gaze about the room. He figured the men and women along the walls must be other slayers who have already been recruited. When he looked toward the table seating the vampires, all of the elders he assumed, Hamilton met Demiesius' eyes for a moment, able to see his silent plea for him to take the offer.

"Councilors," he said, "What would become of my students?"

"As you would become a leeway slayer upon acceptance," Councilor Richard said, "They will be given to another instructor, providing freedom for you to move about unmissed by anyone who would wonder of your position."

Hamilton thought about it, knowing the opportunity would give him more time to rest as he was supposed to. But, suddenly, there was one thing on his mind that ultimately veered him from taking the opening.

Julius Dalton.

Samuel's worry for the lad this afternoon had filled him with the possibilities that could start if Julius went unsupervised by someone who knew the conceivable circumstances. He wanted to keep an eye on the boy until all mistrust was dropped from him.

"I'm sorry, Councilmen," Hamilton said, "I'm afraid I will have to turn down the generous offer for the time being."

When the words left his mouth, the slayer could see Demiesius fighting to keep his actions in check. In a collected voice then, the elder said, "May I ask why?"

"There is a matter involving one of my students," Hamilton said, "that I've grown quite worried about over the past couple of hours. I would like to remain at his side until I've been able to advise him against the vengeful feelings that have consumed him. As I have seen what may follow a boy taken over by what follows him, and he views me with high regard, I would like to remain at my student's side to ensure they are all fully prepared and respected members of our society. Once I am certain Julius will not resort to what I've been informed is corrupting his purpose, I will be happy to reconsider joining your Coalition."

"And how long do you suppose that will take?" Demiesius asked.

Hamilton hated the frustration he could see in the vampire's eyes, but he said, "I don't know at this moment. I would hope by the time his induction to the Public comes around." That was two and a half years away.

"If that is your decision," Councilors Jamison said, "Then we will respect your wishes. You may go."

Hamilton stayed, "I do have one request, Councilors," he said then, and when all attention was on him again, he went on. "Over a period of several months...I have grown ill, and it is something that has the capabilities of killing me from the inside. I have sought medical attention to get better so I may perform as I used to, and request proper time off from actions in the Public so I may regain my health. That is something I will not be able to do if tasks are bestowed upon me."

The Councilors all looked toward one another before giving a nod. "Understandable," Councilor Homer said, "Request granted. Now, you may go."

After referring to the Councilors about putting an extra eye on Julius at Gregor, Hamilton turned on his heels and left the room, almost sure Demiesius would have stormed after him if he wasn't caught up with relations involving his true purpose of being an elder.

Once leaving the Gathering, Hamilton planned to head for the vampire's residence for his medicine.

Having parked his vehicle a ways from the misleading library, Hamilton removed his mask and took to the footpath along the road. There was never much movement on this part of the city after dark, leaving few roaming out and about, and by the time Hamilton reached the empty lot in which his car was parked, he was alone under the cloudy night sky. As he crossed the large lot, Hamilton paused when he sensed a strange chill run down his spine.

Distant eyes were upon him. He looked in either direction, not catching sight of anyone until he turned his eyes back up in front of him.

"Oh, bollocks..."

Leaning up against his car was a man. He was pale as the moon with short cut beige hair to the nape of his neck. Dressed in black trousers and a wrinkled white shirt, he had long sharpened nails, and the upper part of his face, including his eyes, was covered by a black band to hide his main features. The only distinctive thing Hamilton could see was the faint showing of freckles touched to the tip of his nose. This man couldn't have been more obviously a vampire if he tried until he smiled, showing off his tingling fangs.

"Hello there," he said in a chipper, low toned accent, but the slayer could pick up on a slight nervousness within him. "You are looking quite...nice tonight."

Hamilton sighed internally, not necessarily having wanted to put up a fight on this night. He was tired from the partial lack of sleep, and all he wanted right now was his medicine.

"Listen," he said, voice light from his weariness, "I am not in the mood for games right now. Why don't you follow the rules your elders imparted on you and leave me the hell alone?"

The vampire furrowed his brow at the mention of elders. It almost seemed like he hadn't any idea what Hamilton was talking about, but still he was unmoved by the statement. Although it looked as if the vampire shouldn't have been able to see Hamilton, given the covering over his eyes, his head moved in a manner that seemed to look the blonde man up and down, assessing his features, taking in the shape and look of his face. "You will do just fine," the vampire snarled.

Hamilton pondered his choices right now. He was far too weak to put up his best fight, but he knew damn well he was too weak to make a run for it. His body rendered him the most vulnerable he'd ever been, and it certainly didn't help that this young vampire seemed to have made it a goal to kill him.

"You must be young," Hamilton assumed. "Or your creator has not raised you well enough. Don't you know senseless hunting is against the law for your kind?"

It didn't appear the vampire was listening; that was told mainly from the drop of his jaw and the further reveal of his glinting fangs. They dripped with hunger, with an anger Hamilton couldn't place. It seemed like he was being looked upon as a sort of outlet, the answer to a grudge long clutched in his grasp.

Trying to circle around the vampire to get to his car, Hamilton stopped again when his path was blocked. "Can you just bugger off already? Anyway, I've been told my blood can kill a damn vampire like you, so I would highly suggest not trying anything with me."

The vampire licked his tongue over the points of his fangs, a grumble rising from his throat. Half mindless and driven only by the anger that started in him, the longer he looked upon Hamilton, the far more ferocious and aggravated his insides became. "You look just like her," he snarled, taking a step closer to the target. "Bloody back-stabbing woman!"

"I'm not—," Hamilton tried to voice that he had nothing to do with this immortal's frustrations, but was abruptly cut off before he could finish.

"Shut up!"

Like lightning, the vampire zipped towards the slayer.

Quickly as he could, Hamilton pulled out his stake, ducking under the vampire's attempt to catch his throat. When he turned around at the speed he did, the abrupt dizziness from this morning found its way back to him. Hamilton tried to ignore it to the best of his abilities, and struck out with his boot, landing a solid blow to the side of the vampire's face.

When the immortal regained himself, he hissed ferociously, tackling Hamilton to the ground when the dizzy spell warped his vision. Hitting the back of his head against the solid surface, the slayer winced, losing his train of thought for a couple seconds.

Hamilton shook his head as to focus and thrust the stake held firm in his grip down toward the vampire's back. Before the wooden, silver crafted weapon could collide with the target, the vampire snatched Hamilton's wrist and ripped the stake from his hand.

Hissing from the silver burning into the flesh of his fingers, the immortal chucked the stake away, and it landed at the rear tire of the car.

He took hold of Hamilton's arms then, pinning them beside his head as he continued to struggle with no avail. Hamilton stared panicked up at the vampire, unable to gain the strength to break free from the clasp forcing him down. Having never experienced such hopelessness against a vampire, Hamilton's veins ran hot with self-loathing, knowing very well that he wouldn't be caught in this situation if it wasn't for the effects of the condition he was in.

"Get off!" Hamilton shouted, wanting to cry out for Demiesius to save him, but the elder was nowhere near to hear him even if he tried.

"You deserved to die," the vampire growled, "Even if someone heard you, no one would come. I was the only one who loved you. Only me, and you betrayed me!" The vampire then smiled down at Hamilton in hunger and hate and drove his fangs into the side of Hamilton's neck, his sharp incisors breaking into the slayer's skin until fresh blood oozed from the openings and filled his salivating mouth.

If there was any time before where Hamilton ever felt humiliated, this moment right now would top it. He gasped from the agonizing pain of the bite, kicking out futilely with all he had, but no movement on his part did a thing to change the situation. Never before would he have ever guessed he, of all people, would be bitten by a vampire, and so suddenly.

"AH!" he screamed out in agony, trying with everything he had to wrench the immortal from on top of him.

And then, a second later, he didn't have to try.

The vampire threw his head back with a gasp, blood streaming down his maw in a thick coat of crimson. Trembling in shock, the veins trickling up beneath the skin of his neck lit in a faint glow of red, and he released Hamilton and heaved as if to throw up the contents of his stomach.

Rising to his feet, he backed away from the slayer and vomited, a pool of the blood that'd once entered his stomach coming to the surface.

"You toxic, bitch," he swore, feeling like a fire was bubbling in his throat as the remainder of the blood rose up out of him.

Hamilton sat up, horrified by his bite wounds and the scene taking place before his very eyes. As the vampire choked up the blood he'd consumed, and any of the other mixtures in his stomach, he continued to back away until finally making the decision to leave this once determined kill behind.

Watching as the vampire bolted from the scene of their short bout, Hamilton got to his feet with a hand at his throat, trying to clot the bite wounds with his mask balled into a wad. Hurriedly, he retrieved his stake and got into his car, driving to Demiesius' home as quickly yet calmly as he could.

What the hell had that been? he wondered to himself. The vampire had surely come out of nowhere, having singled Hamilton out no matter if he'd been dressed as an obvious slayer. Had it mainly been for the way he looked, his blonde hair and soft womanly features? He was well aware that people had preferences, but it seemed that vampire's preference resided in the look of his kills before pouncing.

Not sure what to make of it as he drove, the moment he finally arrived at the secluded home, Hamilton rushed up the stairs and to the doors. He banged on them frantically until they were opened by a ferociously cautious Christoph. He looked about the tear drenched slayer and stepped aside immediately to let him in. "What happened to you?" he asked.

"Where's Demiesius?" Hamilton demanded as he hurried into the foyer.

"He has not yet returned," Christoph said. "Although, Doctor Takahashi is here for your scheduled shots."

Hamilton searched for the doctor on the first floor, finding him right away in the lounge. "Doctor!" Hamilton showed him the bite wounds, "Am I going to turn?"

The second he got a look at the wounds on the slayer's neck, Dr. Takahashi knew this wasn't good, not because Hamilton would turn into an immortal overnight, but because he knew this action taken against the slayer was not going to sit well with his elder. "No, no, no," he assured, "Sit down, sit down."

Doing as told, Hamilton sat on the sofa as the professional immortal examined him, and a part of him was actually glad that Demiesius wasn't here to see him like this. So pathetic and frightened. "I couldn't fight him off," he said. "I tried..."

"Don't fret," Dr. Takahashi said, "A simple vampire bite does in fact have the ability to raise someone into an immortal, but given no blood from the biter was passed down to you, the effects will not take place. So long as a drop of vampire blood does not find its way onto your tongue, you will remain the human being you are now."

Still rather shaken from the failed brawl, Hamilton asked, "Is there a way for you to make the bites go away? I don't want anyone to see them."

"There is," the doctor said, "But it does involve my blood."

"Will it cause a change in me?"

"Absolutely not. Only oral consumption of immortal blood has the ability to turn you after a bite has been received."

"Do it, please," Hamilton said, "Before Demiesius gets here. If he sees me like this—please."

As requested, Dr. Takahashi grabbed a couple of cloths, cleaning the wounds with warm water and a mild amount of alcohol. When they were clear of blood and any trace of grime, the doctor sat down beside Hamilton and elongated the nail of his index finger. He brought the tip down along his wrist and made a slight incision, opening a line of skin so a small amount of his own blood may run through. Scooping some into the underneath of his nail before it healed, he allowed the few drops to fall onto Hamilton's open wounds.

Feeling as the pain began to subside, the wounds closed as well, leaving the skin of Hamilton's neck as clear as the hours it'd been before. In a matter of seconds, he was as good as new.

Just when he dried his face after thanking the doctor, Demiesius appeared in the doorway. The disappointment that had shown on his face at the Gathering was still the same, but he said nothing right away.

After Dr. Takahashi gave Hamilton his injections, Demiesius relieved Christoph for the next couple of nights, leaving him and the slayer alone in the castle. Not a single word was spoken for a moment, until the vampire pierced the silence with his voice. "I am beginning to think you do not want my help anymore."

Hamilton sighed, tucking his hands beneath his thighs. "Demiesius," he said, "I do appreciate the concern you feel for me, I do, but I didn't take the offer for the Coalition, because there is something I feel authorized to do. I have to watch over my students until the end of their training, especially Julius. I am afraid he may choose a dark path when all is done, and no one he trusts is there to stop and support him. I only want to guide him with the understanding of an instructor he can confide in. After that is done, I told you, I will join. The Councilors have given me time off anyways. Isn't that good enough for now?"

"If you feel as though you can handle this," Demiesius said, "I won't bother you on the matter anymore. I only want what is best for you and your health."

Hamilton stood from the sofa, coming upon the elder in the lounge's threshold. He slid his arms around Demiesius' body, cuddling up and resting his head against the vampire's silent chest. "I know," he uttered in a low tone, "Just give me this time, and afterwards I will gladly walk into whatever you think is best." He looked up, eyes meeting the fullness of Demiesius' lips so close to his own. Pressing a knowing kiss to them, he said, "I will join you some day."

Chapter Fifteen

The Wasted Time of Making Decisions

Following two more months of treatment, the symptoms that had come with the tuberculosis were completely gone. Hamilton was more than excited to feel better, but was warned earlier on not to get too riled up. There were still things that could go wrong during this time, so Dr. Takahashi told him to remain cautious for a while.

Without having gone more than a couple days of proper relaxation, or rather, since he was three years old, it felt strange for Hamilton to have so much time on his hands. When he wasn't watching over and coaching his students from the sidelines, he was spending time with Teresa once her training sessions were over, going out to the city for nice shopping trips filled with flirty gossip about their significant others.

It'd been five whole months since meeting Demiesius, putting them in the midst of September, but Hamilton was still having a hard time identifying what they were to one another. Were they boyfriends? Friends with kissing benefits? As Hamilton got ready to leave the House, he thought running the question by Demiesius wouldn't be too bad.

For the evening, he slipped into fitting jeans that trimmed nicely along his waistline, and tugged on a short sleeved, dark green peplum blouse that ruffled out around his stomach. When he had on black short-heeled boots, his ears perked when there was a rapid knocking on his apartment door.

Teresa was on the other side, and she rushed inside once the door was opened. She was wearing a red dress that stopped at her knees, tall black heels on as well, and her blonde hair was twisted prettily into a bun, and two curly strands were lining her face. Closing the door behind her, she said, "How do I look?"

"Real nice," Hamilton said when she circled around. "I'm going to guess you have a date tonight?"

"Yeah," Teresa breathed, trying to compose herself. "Christoph is taking me to the cinema, and then," she blushed, "who knows what will come after that."

Hamilton snorted, caught off guard by her sly tone.

"I know, I know, but don't judge me! Christoph is a sweetheart, and maybe I'm ready for something like that. He is so kind and respectful, so much so that I wish I had a family to introduce him to. I just know if I had a mother, she'd be proud of the kind of gentleman he is."

"Well, you look beautiful," Hamilton smiled, "I hope everything goes nice tonight."

Crossing her arms before him, Teresa smirked at her fellow

slayer, and said, "I can see just by your glamorous outfit that you're going out with your boyfriend, aye? What do you two even do all the time? Lord knows you're still a virgin and all, and you definitely are not the party, or going out type of guy. Do you two just sit around and stare into each other's eyes? Matter-of-fact, why have I not met this man? I want to see what type of guys you're into?" Teresa gasped then, and continued hastily, "Oh! We should all go out on a date together."

For a moment Hamilton wasn't sure if admitting Demiesius true nature was something he should do, but given Teresa's being on board with a secret relationship of her own, he wanted to believe entrusting his best mate with this type of information was acceptable.

Casually taking Teresa's hands in his own, Hamilton sat them down on the sofa and breathed a distressing sigh. "There's something I want to tell you," he said. "It's something dealing with my relationship with the man I've been seeing for the past couple of months."

"Couple of months?" Teresa chuckled, "It's almost been half a year."

"I know," Hamilton smiled shyly, "I haven't really told you much about him, because—."

"He's an elder."

Hamilton looked up quickly at his friend, "How did you—."

"I'm dating a vampire, Hami. A vampire who works for said Elder. I wanted to tell you that I knew forever ago, but I wasn't sure if you'd have been scared shitless. I've been waiting for you to grow the courage to tell me. At first I wasn't surprised when Christoph told me you were seeing a vampire, but when he mentioned the man being an elder, I nearly lost my mind. Do you know how much good that could do for our races? Humans and vampires coming together in a mutual act of love. Especially since he's an elder, I bet anything he says would be taken very seriously by his own people. And you, you're already looked upon as a sort of leader in the eyes of the Public. It would be like two countries finally coming together after centuries of war because their rulers fell in love."

Hamilton appreciated the words coming from Teresa, but he didn't know if he'd ever gain enough confidence to blatantly come out with something like that to the Public. He, the Councilors, and the higher-ups that Demiesius was familiar with may know the truth behind slayer and vampire cooperation, but there is no telling how the rest of the slayers would react. If anything, there would wind up being a sudden division within their ranks: ones who would still regard the Councilors, and others who would take any actions into their own hands. Hamilton loved the Slayer Public, but he couldn't trust everyone with this kind of information.

"As much as I would love for something like that to happen," Hamilton said, "I don't see it working out too well with the others."

Teresa pouted, "You're probably right. There are a lot of vengeful slayers in the world, aren't there? Julius Dalton I've noticed as being one. I overheard the lad a couple days ago speaking with your other student Kingston Fisher. They mourned the loss of their family members, as I'm sure a lot of people do, but in describing the acts they wished to inflict on other vampires was...something."

"I have heard that Julius is a very angry young lad," Hamilton said, "The only thing I can offer him, though, is that he'll be able to protect the streets from the kinds of vampires that need protecting from."

Hamilton recalled the conversations he'd taken part in with Julius over the past several weeks. Although Julius was developing into a talented member of the Public, it had shown to be a bit difficult to assist in assuring his thoughts with how crowded they'd become with revenge. It would always be a bit understandable why the majority of slayers refused to see all vampires differently, but that was something Hamilton hoped would at least come in time as he continued working alongside his students.

"I guess we can't reprimand him until he possibly does something horrendous, huh?"

Hamilton shook his head with a shrug, "Or are able to step in before it happens."

After checking their appearances in the mirror in the bathroom first, both Hamilton and Teresa were out the door and on their way to their significant others, Hamilton promising to talk to Demiesius about a possible double date they could all go out on some night.

By the time he arrived at the beautiful and secluded home, it was nearing nine o'clock at night. With it growing rather chilly out, Hamilton was bundled in a black knit long sleeve over his peplum blouse, blonde hair down with a scarf to warm up around his neck.

The doors were unlocked as usual and he bolted them behind him once inside. As he made his way through the foyer towards the grand room, he paused when hearing a booming voice that did not belong to Demiesius.

It was Dominick von Kraige.

"There's something not right going on in the streets," he heard Dominick say, tone harsh and on edge. "I wanted you to be the first to know before I considered calling an elder assembly."

"What's happening?" Demiesius asked.

Dominick didn't speak a word for a moment, seeming to collect himself before letting the news out. "It is common," he started, "to have those certain vampires who simply...lose themselves, and take a path down murderous lanes. Abandoned by their creators, deprived from blood, ignorant to their true nature; those are the kinds of vampires we are used to having turn their backs on our people, but with this bizarre trail I have picked up on, I am aware that these murders taking place are being done by someone who is very aware of the crimes they are committing."

"How do you know this?"

"There are similarities that link each of the humans. Trust me, if you got a look at all of them, you would see the obvious connections as well. There is a vampire out there on the streets of London killing targets based on their appearance. They leave no evidence behind, not even a single drop of their own blood to be used as a sort of tracker. So far I have come across twelve bodies, all of which are always placed in areas only accessible to vampires. Whoever they are, they do not want to get caught, but want other immortals to stumble upon their craftsmanship. Father, I am the last person to give any sort of regard or sympathy to a human, but to see what he's been doing happen to someone else, I feel truly guilty in not being able to bring a stop to it. This vampire, they need to be caught."

So there was a vampire serial killer on the loose in the London area? The thought churned Hamilton's stomach. He wanted to know how Dominick was going to handle this. Or was this a job for slayers? A part of him wanted to be on the team that hunted that bastard down and ended him.

"I will call for an assembly," Demiesius said then.

"Tonight?" Dominick asked.

At that, Hamilton proceeded to the entry of the grand room, caught by Demiesius' eyes in an armchair before Dominick turned around. Dominick was dressed in black trousers and an equally black dress shirt, his lengthy midnight hair pushed lazily out of his young, handsome face. Dr. Takahashi was seated inside as well, tonight's tools out to deliver Hamilton his injections ready on the low table.

Quirking his brow in the slayer's direction, Dominick said, "So you *are* fucking the human..."

"Hamilton," Dr. Takahashi greeted, "Hello, please, come have a seat."

Not paying any mind to Dominick's annoyed and curious stare, Hamilton removed his sweater and took a seat on the sofa the doctor rose from, ready for the nightly dose of medicine.

"Hmm," Dominick crossed his arms, strolling closer to the slayer, "Never thought I'd witness my father actually take a liking to a human." He plopped down on the sofa beside Hamilton, casually draping an arm around the man's shoulder as he leaned back. "Though, you do smell quite delicious tonight I must say. Are you allowing my father to feed from you? It is only right for a human lover to allow access to their...delicacies."

Hamilton was about to speak for himself, but Dr. Takahashi

beat him to it. "Actually, Dominick, I advised not to pierce this man's skin for a taste of his blood. It may give off a divine and appetizing aroma, but what runs through this man's bloodstream is probably the greatest weapon to our kind."

Dominick peered closer to Hamilton, sniffing the flavorsome scent of the essence beneath his skin. "How so?" he asked.

Readying his needle, Dr. Takahashi waved it before sticking it into Hamilton's forearm, and allowed the first drug to course into the slayer's system. "These antibiotics are being used to cure him of a sickness, and while they reside in his bloodstream, he has the ability to kill or weaken one hundred vampires with a single drop."

Wrinkling his nose at Hamilton, Dominick then looked over to his father. "I know a nice blonde human boy who would give you every piece of him upon command. I would be happy to replace this one with him if you want more fulfillment."

"Thank you for the offer," Demiesius shook his head, partly amused by Dominick's persistence. "However, I believe I am fine."

Hamilton winced when Dr. Takahashi pierced him with the final needle. "Why are you so afraid," he said to Dominick, "of the simple idea that Demiesius just might like me for who I am?"

"I am only being reasonable," Dominick said. "It is quite common for a child not to like the idea of their parent seeing other people."

"But Demiesius was never married. It's not like I'm trying to replace your mother."

"I understand that, but—."

"But what," Hamilton forced a laugh, "I have given you no reason to not like me."

"You're a slayer."

"And you're a vampire, yet you don't see me jumping down your throat at the news of this. I can't change who I am and neither can you. I would like it very much if we could just simply get on with each other."

Dominick met Demiesius' eyes again, taking in the assuring gaze set upon him, and then he glanced back at Hamilton; the pretty blonde man who seemed to find a way into his father's heart. In a dull tone, Dominick said, "First rule, I am not calling you father as well. Second rule, you don't get to boss me around like you've been in my life for almost five-hundred years. Third rule, and last rule, if anything ever happens to my father while you two are together, you will be the first person on my list. Is all of that very clear, slayer?"

Hamilton smiled brightly, "I understand."

When Dr. Takahashi finished cleaning and wrapped his puncture points, Hamilton pulled his legs up on the sofa, almost scrunched up beside Dominick who was surprisingly still seated beside him. "I overheard what you two were talking about before I walked in. Is there really a serial killer prowling London?"

"Yes," Dominick said, "But don't worry. Although you fit the description of the preferred victims, you are not a woman...though you could be mistaken for one. If anything, watch your back if you ever decide to go out at night alone. Father," he addressed Demiesius then, "Will you call the assembly?"

"Not tonight," Demiesius said, "for now what I want you to do is post watchful eyes at every vampire gathering. Remain aware of humans in the area who match the victim descriptions. If the culprit is located, have them taken to the dungeons of Castle

Bane. There, I and the other elders will deal with him. If nothing is found tonight, we will discuss a city wide search to stop this."

Dominick nodded and stood from his spot beside Hamilton. "Yes, father," he said, "I will put everything I have into trying to catch this bastard tonight. He's making me and my leadership over this region look bad."

Together, Dr. Takahashi and Dominick left the premises, leaving Hamilton and Demiesius alone. The elder didn't remain in the grand room for long, rising from his seat to travel into the kitchen.

Hamilton followed close behind, stopping to lean up against a center counter. "Are you alright?" he asked.

Demiesius made himself a tall glass of blood, holding the glass in his grasp before setting it down again. "I don't understand," he said, "What is happening to my people? Ever since the nineteen hundreds began, vampires have become much more hostile around the world, mostly in these western countries. The amount of senseless killings has risen exponentially these years. Has something flipped in our society that's made my people more violent to the human race? Have humans become more provoking?" Demiesius shook his head in disappointment. "There used to be a time when creators would discipline their children, teach them the rights and wrongs that came with having strength. Have I and the elders become too lenient?"

Coming around the counter, Hamilton took Demiesius' arm, pushing up into his side. "You shouldn't blame yourself for their actions. You can't help it if there are vampires out there that take no favor in authority figures and what not. Prime Ministers do not blame themselves for what citizens do, so you shouldn't do the same. I'm sure Dominick will do everything in his power to stop the madness. He seems like a capable enough leader."

"I have raised him well," Demiesius said.

Hamilton smiled at the hint of pride in the vampire's eyes at the statement. "I'm sure you have, but, Demiesius, can we...talk for a minute about...our future together? With this treatment and how it's been going, I feel real confident that I'm going to make it through this tuberculosis and get better. I know Dr. Takahashi warned not to get too caught up in the thought, but I haven't felt this good since before the symptoms started. What will become of us in a year or two, maybe even ten? Would you be comfortable having a thirty-nine year old man around, one who would undoubtedly turn forty and then fifty and sixty?"

Demiesius understood Hamilton's worry for the future. It wasn't something he had to deal with on a yearly basis: age. He was thirty-five himself, frozen at this grown but youthful stage for all eternity. The first time he'd been faced with turning someone he cared for into a vampire, their hunger for power grew immensely. He knew Hamilton and Leonidas were two very different people, but even with the worry of not being able to dull a need for control, there was still the assumption that Hamilton wouldn't want to resort to the only way to ensure they could have a guaranteed future together, much like Kai had in the past. He couldn't imagine Hamilton wanting to make the transformation into a vampire.

"I usually don't think about that for a while," Demiesius said, "You shouldn't worry about it either."

The shade in Hamilton's eyes shifted into a more wretched and thoughtful stare, "But, Demiesius," he said, "I am worried about it because I *want* to be with you. I know we haven't established any sort of title over one another, but...as silly as it may sound, I want you to be my boyfriend and I want to be yours. And with that in mind, it saddens me that someday we won't be as we are now. You may have already surpassed me in years, but soon, I will have aged to a point where it would be ridiculous for us to even be seen together."

When Demiesius stepped aside, his arm sliding out from Hamilton's grasp, the slayer watched the vampire reach for the bloody refreshment on the counter and start into the corridor. "Now you understand that there is a curse that follows every vampire. Come, Hamilton, there are things you must know if you are positive about wanting to truly be with me."

Hamilton went with Demiesius out to a set of veiled double doors. The curtains over the windows blew wildly when the doors were opened, and they stepped out onto a concrete plat-form leading to a well-kept castle terrace.

Immediately Hamilton felt the cold and bundled his arms around his body, the goose pimples on his arms trying to keep the warmth inside. "What are we out here for?" he shivered.

"Look out into the wilderness," Demiesius said, "Tell me what you see."

Trying to spot anything in particular the vampire could be talking about, Hamilton strained his eyes in the ever expanding darkness. There were stars dotting the atmosphere above, and the full moon peeked from a puffy cloud, offering very little light out into this secluded region. "Um, it's only dark out here," Hamilton answered. "Nothing but the night. Is there something else out there that I just can't see?"

"No," the elder shook his head, taking a swig of his blood, "That is all there is. The darkness. The cold. This is what my world has become since my life as a human ended, an existence absent light and warmth is all I know. The sun and its heat are foreign to my body, my heart beats no more, I breathe no more, and though I may not show it most nights we are together, I long for the aspects stolen from me in death. I long to feel as I once did, see the world in comfort as it looks now. One may argue that the world is much more beautiful under the moon than the sun, but whomever could speak such words has not spent countless centuries in the state I am in. You, Hamilton, you deserve the world as it is now, to have the rays of the sun warm your skin, to experience the sun rise and set without fear of it."

Turning to the slayer, Demiesius looked about his shivering form, knowing if he touched Hamilton, he would only ultimately add to the current coldness enveloped around them. "With that, however, to live as such, I would leave the decision up to you."

"You mean..." Hamilton said, "You would change me if I asked?"

"If you are certain and understand the possibilities that may follow you in the life of an immortal, yes, I would fulfill such a desire if it would mean you would never be gone from my side."

Going back inside, Hamilton felt the heat of the castle seep back into his skin. As they went into the roman-like grand room, he said, "Demiesius, there is something I think I should tell you."

At first, after the incident occurred, he was wary about telling Demiesius about having been bitten by a vampire already, but with the comfort and understanding of the elder, he felt there was no reason to hide the secret. Besides, the vampire who'd done it had run off, so there was really no one to go looking for anymore.

"What is it?" Demiesius asked.

Hamilton took a seat alone, interlocking his fingers as he was still a bit nervous. Touching at the spot in which the fangs had previously penetrated his neck, he said, "The night after the Gathering to place me in the Coalition, when I was on my way to my car, I was attacked. During that time, I had been far too weak to fight on my own and was quickly overpowered. The vampire, he bit me and drank my blood."

The usual stern look on Demiesius' face altered into one of confusion and unease. In a millisecond he was standing directly in front of Hamilton, tearing the scarf off from around his neck, and pulled the collar of his shirt down to see...but there was nothing there. Vampire bites didn't heal to leave no scar. There would always be two dots left behind to show the claim over their human. Unless, "Who healed them?" Demiesius demanded.

"Dr. Takahashi, I asked him to, because I didn't want you to know. I didn't want you to worry about me like you always do. The vampire, when he bit me, he seemed to...hate the flavor any simply ran off. Dr. Takahashi said–."

"If any vampire's blood touches your lips you will turn. Even a single drop."

With Demiesius so close to him, Hamilton took his hand to pull him down on the sofa beside him. "What if you gave me a drop of your blood, and with it, I could choose if and when I am ready for something like the life of a vampire?"

"You would truly consider leaving what you have?"

Hamilton smiled at the worry about Demiesius' face, wondering momentarily if he knew what it felt like to be at ease. "Perhaps I could wait until we are the same age physically before I make a decision. That would give me six years to decide, and

by that time, I am sure I'll be able to come up with an answer."
Touching lightly at Demiesius' knee, the slayer scooted closer
and nestled up against him. "I already enjoy spending so much
time away from others to be with you, and my feelings for you
have grown into something that pains me to think about losing.
To imagine a life, especially an immortal life with you; it doesn't
seem like something that should be too hard to choose. There
are things I could live without: the sun, proper warmth. But to
be without you, I only imagine a life of sheer grief." Looking
up into Demiesius' soft, coal black eyes, Hamilton said, "How
would you feel to never lose the one you care for ever again?"

Demiesius answered with an unforeseen kiss, taking Hamilton's lips with his own, and the slayer felt his body tremble all
over, taking this kiss as confirmation that Demiesius would love
to spend eternity together.

When their kiss broke apart at last, Hamilton licked his lips,
and said, "Can I stay the night? I'm tired but I don't want to go
back to Gregor yet. Can I sleep here until morning?"

"Of course, you can," Demiesius said. "If you don't mind, I
am going to leave until dawn to get in contact with the other
elders. With the murders happening around London, I know if
Dominick is worried, I should be as well. He will need all the
help he can get."

Hamilton nodded, and it wasn't long until he was alone in
Demiesius' bedroom. Dressed in nothing but his briefs and one
of the vampire's white button-down shirts, he fell back onto the
mattress and stared up at the ceiling with a smile he couldn't
resist.

Downstairs, had he blatantly confessed that he was in love
with Demiesius, even without using the actual word itself? He

wondered if Demiesius got the awfully obvious hint, but most of all, he wondered if he was the only one who felt such immeasurable and passionate feelings.

It wasn't hard in the least to tell Demiesius cared about him. Anyone with eyes or ears could tell that much, but to be in love with him, the slayer squirmed in delight at the thought, because, yes, he was in love. Infatuated, obsessed, enamored, smitten, any word proving affection would do.

Laying in the regal room by himself, he scrunched a cotton stuffed pillow under his head, filled with every fiber of happiness in the world.

Hamilton H. Hamilton was in love with a vampire.

Chapter Sixteen

Death Awaits the Silent Call of Revenge

The next evening began just as any other in these past months. Hamilton arrived at Demiesius' castle for his medicine, and then they were left alone to enjoy the company of one another.

Although his body was in a weakened state at this time, there was nothing Hamilton could do to cool down the strong urges he had for Demiesius whenever they were near to each other. His frustrations were almost so dire at times that he had to close himself off before he found himself naked and prepared to gift every piece of his body away. Just like now.

After Demiesius had finished up a phone call in his office, Hamilton trapped the man in his desk chair. Kissing all over Demiesius as hot shocks of craving ran amok through his body. With his arms around the top of the vampire's shoulders, Hamilton sat straddling him as he stole Demiesius' tongue, tingling all over as soft hands groped his figure.

A part of him wondered if Demiesius thought he was teasing with these sessions of sexually induced kissing, especially when Hamilton let out soft moans every now and again, grinding their hips together just to feel something...anything against the hidden erection tucked away in his trousers.

It was moments like these when he had to stop until the ache of his being calmed down before he stole Demiesius' tongue once more. When he almost couldn't take it anymore, Hamilton threw his head back as the vampire held them together, their groins pressed into one another as the slayer felt the rewarding pleasure of Demiesius' hands brushing down his body.

Hamilton wanted to give himself over so badly, feel him all over and inside of him in the most intimate manner there was, but he'd wanted to save such a moment for when he was in one hundred percent good health. Then, and only then would he give himself permission to finally let these sessions turn into something much more.

As he suppressed the flush of arousal in his body, Hamilton's glistening blue eyes met Demiesius', and he licked tastefully against the vampire's lips.

When Hamilton thought to continue again for the third time this night, he stopped suddenly when there was a thunderous clap out in the corridor.

Before he could consider getting off Demiesius to investigate the loud sound, Dominick was standing there in the door frame of the office with the most malicious scowl the slayer had ever seen, one that managed to drive a sense of worry inside of him.

"We have a problem," the blood child said. "Father, I must

have a word with you. Privately."

"What is it?" Demiesius said.

Dominick met Hamilton's eyes for a second, noting the intimate position they'd been in before his arrival. "Father, I think this is something I should speak with you about alone."

"That won't be necessary. What is it, my son?"

The blood child pushed his black hair back in frustration, and said, "There has been another murder. Her body was found just this evening on my property. She fits the description of the first victims, but I'm sure there is one thing that tosser had not expected her to be." He paused for a moment, fists clenching. "She was a slayer from the House of Gregor."

At that, Hamilton shot up from Demiesius' lap, "What?!" he shouted, "What is her name?"

"Of course, I did not know who she was right away, but Christoph was able to identify her..."

Hamilton felt dizzy all of a sudden and his heartbeat picked up. "No," he shook his head, "No, no, no, this can't be. Teresa, she is—she can't be!" The slayer rushed Dominick, closing his fists into the front of his buttoned shirt. "What happened?!" he demanded.

"We don't know anything yet," Dominick provided, unbothered by Hamilton's abrupt shock and grip of his shirt. "The surveillance only captured him leaving behind her body, and there was no good shot of his face. She was already dead by then."

Hamilton released the blood child, and turned to the elder. "Demiesius, you have to do something. She was a slayer. This could—."

Dominick looked from his father to Hamilton, able to see

the news of this woman's identity was going to turn into two separate issues. Not only had she apparently been a slayer, but she was a well-known friend to Hamilton.

"Hamilton," Dominick carried on, "I'm sorry this has turned into what it has, but your friend, she was not taken from this world because of the slayer she was. She just so happened to be a blonde woman who looked to be in her twenties. There is mischief going on in my world that does not link back to the hatred of the Public."

"I know she was not targeted because of what she was," Hamilton said in return, his heart ever so heavy at the idea of his best friend being dead. "But the moment the Public finds out she was ruthlessly murdered by the hands of a vampire, no matter the context of it, they will react the only way they know how. With retaliation. Especially in Gregor House since that is where she came from. The Public will investigate this until that monster is captured, not caring how many innocent vampires are killed in the process."

Dominick remained standing before Hamilton, taking in this man's sadness yet ability to think straight given the severity of it all. His nerves were shaking as if on edge, yet Hamilton's mind stayed focused on the two dilemmas. There was a murderer on the streets and the unwarranted threats of the Public could prove to be a concern.

"You're right," Dominick's own nerves calmed a bit. "I just don't know what to do about this mess. I feel like I've been so incompetent since the first killing was discovered, so distracted to get a proper lead on this case myself. These women have died so needlessly, and here I stand as that bastard is out there...perhaps plotting against my city as we speak. It has probably come to mind that I don't have a close connection with human life, and while I won't lie and say I didn't think the first killing was something to worry about, the ruthlessness and senselessness of it all is frustrating. Vampires in my city know well enough where to fill their cravings. We have operations of our own to cater to hunger, to drive the need to feed unnecessarily down to prevent situations like this. I know I once fed from an outward source, but I would never leave death in my wake." Dominick cursed and squeezed his eyes shut in frustration, "This bastard is littering in my city, making me look like a goddamn fool."

Demiesius rose from behind the desk then as he picked up on the shift in his blood child's mood, rounding in front of him to pull Dominick into an embrace.

"Am I too weak to run this region, father?" Dominick whispered.

"No," the elder lifted his blood child's chin and wiped Dominick's red tears away. "I would not have given you such responsibilities if I did not think you could handle it. Come. I will follow you and we can look into this together." He then looked back at Hamilton, holding a hand out to the slayer. "I will need your help as well."

The second Hamilton took Demiesius' outstretched hand, the slayer was pulled in tightly, and before he could register why he was being held so securely against the elder, a strong rush of wind whirled all around him. He clung to Demiesius as tightly as he could, holding his eyes closed when he felt his feet leave the ground. He felt weightless in the vampire's arms, not opening his eyes until the pressure of wind surrounding him disappeared.

Once his feet touched ground again, his knees would have

given out if it hadn't been for Demiesius' strong hold on him.
When he opened his eyes, Hamilton was stunned to see they
were now standing at the front door of Dominick's coven.

"What the?" Hamilton looked around, "How the?"

Without answering to the slayer's confusion, the vampires
entered into the manor, Demiesius gently pushing Hamilton
along.

Putting the bizarre incident aside, Hamilton followed hastily
after Dominick who led them to a massive lounge area. When
the three stepped inside, there were several immortals there
already, both male and female appearing sympathetic towards
the one who'd been affected the most. In the center of the room
was a long, white marble table on clawfoot legs, and on top of it
laid Teresa's still body. Christoph knelt before the low table, his
hand cupping Teresa's to his cheek.

"Oh, god..." Hamilton mourned.

Approaching his still friend, the slayer saw that her skin was
ghostly pale, yet her face was peaceful, and just at the collar of
her blue blouse was a rather large portion of her neck missing.

Hamilton's eyes watered to see her in this state and not as
the happy woman she'd been before. He remembered how excited she'd been to have possibly found love in someone like
Christoph. When they were together, she never ceased from
telling of her and the vampire's dear conversations, of how much
he meant to her and how she trusted him with every bit of her
heart.

Parts of their childhood came to Hamilton, the thoughts of
their friendship bringing tears to his eyes. She'd always been his
closest, most treasured friend since he was a small boy. To see
her this way, to see her without such vibrancy, this truly shook

him to his core.

"I was going to take her from here," Christoph's voice was low as he spoke, a whisper of great sorrow as he held Teresa's hand. "She wanted me to take her away from the slayer's life."

Hamilton touched a hand at Christoph's shoulder, and the vampire looked up at him, cheeks stained with blood. "I'm so sorry," the slayer said.

Looking past Hamilton, Christoph met the gaze of his elder. "Master," he cried, "Please, I beg of you."

Demiesius merely nodded, "Yes, Christoph, we will find who did this."

With his analytical slayer instincts kicking in, Hamilton examined Teresa's body, taking everything into account from her ultimate fatal wound, to the faint bruising around her knuckles. He touched at the hem of her shirt and lifted it just above her stomach before putting it back down. Inspecting her arms, there were deep scratches on the underside of her forearms.

"These are fighting wounds," Hamilton said, "She definitely didn't go down without putting up some defense."

Taking a closer look at the claw marks streaked down her forearms, Hamilton then noticed something off about the number of gashes. While her right arm had an even four scrapes, her left forearm only had three, and there was a much larger gap where the middle finger was supposed to be.

Pointing it out, Hamilton said, "You see how there's a wider space between these two here?" Every vampire in the room seemed to lean forward just a bit to see what he was talking about. "Whoever is doing this, they're missing the middle finger on their left hand." He stood and moved toward Dominick, "You should probably jot down that bit of information. Did you ever get a good look at the other bodies found?"

"The last couple, yes," the blood child nodded. "I remember every detail of what condition they were in."

"Were there ever any wounds like these ones?"

Dominick stroked his chin thoughtfully, "No, now that I think about it. It always appeared that each one of them had been caught off guard, like it was too late for them to fight back even if they wanted to."

"And it is impossible to sneak up so closely on a slayer..." Hamilton paced about the room, unknowing to all the curious eyes on him. "From the rather small appearance of his victims, the thought of being able to overpower them with ease is something he wants to make sure of. Judging by Teresa, although she looks small on the outside, there was no way of him knowing she could actually fight back."

Impressed by the slayer's deduction skills, Dominick nodded in approval towards his father, and said, "What else do you think, Hamilton?"

Whispers started up amongst the surrounding vampires, realizing now that this slayer was the most infamous of them all. "I have fought enough in my life to know how nimble vampires are. Even in states of mindlessness, vampires tend to fight with skill and proper stance. Yet, this one, his movements are sporadic and amateurish, like he doesn't necessarily know what he's doing, and when Teresa fought back, he must've panicked."

"What does that mean?" Dominick asked.

Hamilton answered right away, very confident in the presumptions he was making. "He must be young in years."

"Why does he choose these women specifically?" a vampire in the crowd asked.

"He's angry at them," Hamilton pondered, his pace about the room slow as he thought. "He was most likely hurt by someone, and now he's taking out his anger on women who remind him of her. And, Dominick, he is leaving them about the city for vampires to find for a reason. Somewhere along the line, you must've upset him. His first victim, she had to be the woman he wanted revenge against, and he's trying to ruin you because you ruined something for him."

"But I haven't done anything wrong..."

"That's what you think, and I'm sure you wouldn't know of it anyway. Whatever you did, it wasn't bad, but to him you...you..."

Hamilton took Dominick by the arm and led him out of the room, taking him across the hallway to a lofty terrace room walled off by glass windows.

He couldn't help thinking about how Dominick was as a person, his strong confidence, and especially his undeniable sex appeal. Their second meeting here in this very manor had been enough to tell the slayer he could have just about anyone if he so much as donned a flirtatious smirk.

Shutting the door to the terrace room behind him, Hamilton kept his voice down, and said, "Are there any young blonde women you remember sleeping with before these murders started?"

Dominick furrowed his brow, "You mean, you think I knew the first victim?"

"Yes."

"Well, shit," Dominick put his hands on his hips. "This is a little embarrassing, but I'm a bit of a whore, Hamilton. I like to fuck both men and women, and sometimes I never see them again after the night is over."

"Just think, Dominick, try to remember."

The blood child ran a hand through his raven hair, appearing to think long and hard. "There were two I can think of. One's name I think was Emma Black. I won't get into detail, but I do remember her for the O blood she had. The second, her name was Victoria Tanner, and she told me...she told me about a guy who wouldn't leave her alone, an ex boyfriend."

Hamilton nodded, "That has to be her. Somehow you need to get more information on her background, anything at all that points to the person who made her uncomfortable."

"I'll do that," Dominick assured, "In the meantime, I think you should take your friend back to your House. I only ask that you cover the murders for me. I do not need the Public coming down on my people any more than they already do." Before Hamilton could leave the room, the blood child stopped him. "Thank you for your help. I can see you mean a lot to my father, and I know I've made a big deal about you before, but if he trusts in you completely, then I will do my best to see eye to eye. I've just never met another slayer who is as open minded as you."

"Don't worry about it, Dominick," Hamilton smiled. "You are protective of him because he is your father, and you love him in a way I will never understand. But I want you to know that I care for him, too. You are his son and he loves you, so there is a piece of my heart that wants to see the good in you like he does. I will handle things on my end, if you will handle them on yours."

Watching Dominick start for the doorway, Hamilton rubbed a sudden uncomfortableness at his neck and froze, his thoughts going back to a night he remembered well, from how strange it had been, to the off dialogue passed between him and his attacker.

"Dominick," he called then, catching the blood child's attention. "I think I've encountered this assailant before. I was...I was attacked by a vampire who spoke of nonsense before he assaulted me—bit me before fleeing. If it hadn't been for the toxicity of my blood, I doubt he would have stopped until I was dead."

"Dear, lord," Dominick said, "Does my father know about this?"

"He does, but I wasn't aware of the murders to make a connection at the time. This vampire had a binding over his eyes to hide most of his face, but I could see he had light brownish hair, and freckles on his nose area. I can't say I would recognize him if I ever saw him again, but keep those two features in mind. He tried to kill me before, killed my best friend...he needs to die."

"I understand," Dominick agreed.

Going back into the crowded lounge, Hamilton touched Demiesius' arm, and said, "I'll need help getting her body back to your place so I can drive to Gregor. Dominick will inform you of everything you'll need to know, but I have to go set things straight first."

Demiesius nodded, holding back from kissing the slayer goodbye, but was given one anyway when Hamilton pressed their lips together. "I will see you tomorrow," the elder said, "I truly am sorry for the loss of your friend."

Leaving the premises, Hamilton stood outside next to Christoph as he cradled Teresa's body in his arms. His face was clean now, no more trails of blood running down his face. "Take my arm and hold on tight," the vampire instructed.

Doing so, Hamilton was introduced to that same force of wind all around him, feet coming off the ground and a weightlessness came over. Once they were still again, he opened his eyes to the dark lonesome driveway in front of Demiesius' castle.

After Christoph laid Teresa in the backseat of Hamilton's car, he kissed her forehead and whispered something the slayer couldn't hear, but the quiet words had been enough to provoke another round of emotion.

When he left the grieving vampire alone, Hamilton sat in silence for the entire drive. Wanting to stray from the possibilities of the Public inciting a war between slayers and London's own vampire population, he tried to think of anything that would protect Dominick.

As different scenarios piled up in his thoughts, Hamilton grew more and more nervous as he drew nearer to Gregor House. When he turned onto the slayer facilities, he stalled the car in front of the administrative building at the head of the campus and rushed out of the car. Real tears of anguish at the loss of a friend blurred his vision, and he opened the door to the back seat, working Teresa's body from the vehicle.

"I'm so sorry," he cried, "I'm so sorry."

Carrying her limp body to the doors of the building, Hamilton was spotted immediately by a small cluster of fellow instructors who appeared to have just returned from completing a task. They rushed to Hamilton quickly, helping him with Teresa's body and questioned him ruthlessly.

A lie, he'd told them all a lie to hide the truth, telling of how he and Teresa's night out together turned into a bloodbath after he'd left her alone for five minutes, only to come back to find she was dying by the hands of a vampire, a vampire whose life he ended, giving no reason for the House to demand an investigation.

After everything was settled at the administration, Hamilton joined Teresa's trainees who'd been spending time with his own in their rooms. The two boys and girl were seated on the sofa while Julius, Kingston, and Samuel were all standing around. When Hamilton broke the news, Teresa's trainees were shattered, all of them going numb from realizing someone else who they cared for, someone who cared for them, had been taken from this world for no apparent reason.

"This is why they need to be hunted," Julius mumbled under his breath. "This is why all vampires must be stopped."

CHAPTER SEVENTEEN

A Beauty Can be Just as Dangerous

While Hamilton was downstairs with Dr. Takahashi, Demiesius was up in his bedroom chamber. In his hand he held a crystal vial attached to a silver chain. The slight sting of the silver did nothing to cause discomfort, and when he unscrewed the top of the vial, he elongated the nail of his thumb.

Ever since the death of the slayer Teresa a month ago, the elder had become more vigilant over Hamilton. He wanted to think Hamilton was capable enough to hold his own against an adversary, especially now that he was two months away from being completely healed of his tuberculosis, but ever since witnessing Christoph's heartbreak on the night of the murder, he couldn't set aside how it would make him feel if he lost Hamilton in a similar manner or at all.

As an elder, as a vampire who had once been in a state of love, he was used to the feeling of loss. With his past lovers Leonidas and Kai, he'd gone through two separate rounds of grief, and it'd been difficult in the beginning to handle no longer being able to hold someone, talk to someone, or even look at someone who once held a place in his heart, but over time, he'd come to accept their deaths.

With Hamilton, there was something potently different about his feelings for this slayer. There was something in him that would not be able to cope with the loss of Hamilton if ever it happened.

This human, this man, Demiesius loved him, and there was nothing in him that strayed from the reality of it.

In the beginning, what he'd felt for Hamilton had been a thing of distant affection, but now that this man had made his way into the elder's heart, though it did not beat and was cold of life, the mere company Hamilton had given Demiesius over these several months, skillfully rebuilt the need for such a thing as love.

Demiesius...he didn't know what he'd do if Hamilton one day left, left this world, left him alone.

Slicing a small lesion into the vein of his arm, Demiesius let the crimson blood rise and then turned his arm over. He held the clear vial under the formation of a drop, allowing the single dot of blood to fall into the capsule before the self-inflicted wound closed.

He looked over the blood filled vial and twisted the small cap back onto it. This was what Demiesius would give Hamilton to use, to use if ever the day came where the slayer decided that becoming a part of the immortal world was something he wanted.

After tucking the necklace in the front pocket of his trousers, Demiesius went down to the first floor. When he rounded into the lounge, Hamilton was sitting alone on a stool at the bar, Dr. Takahashi having taken his leave after finishing up. Approaching the slayer, the moment Demiesius reached out to touch Hamilton, the man flinched from the soft brush of fingers beside his ear and jumped up from the stool.

Upon meeting Demiesius' eyes, the determined light in Hamilton's eyes faded and he breathed out. "I'm sorry," he said. "For some reason, I've been...off lately."

Demiesius knew this. Ever since the death of Teresa, the slayer was on his toes more often than not, even when they were in the solitude of the castle, never letting his guard down when they were alone. From his pocket, the elder withdrew the vial, letting it dangle before him and the slayer.

"Take this," he offered, "It can be used to change you if you ever make the decision."

Hamilton took the necklace into his hands, looking over the almost black substance inside. This single drop of blood, it had the power to truly bring on another life after death.

Before the slayer could speak, Demiesius said, "I cannot lose you, Hamilton. I would give you every last drop of my blood to ensure your survival. To see you from this world, I could not do it. Even the mere thought of it brings a tautness to my heart."

Furrowing his brow at the sudden worry, Hamilton threw his arms around Demiesius' neck, holding fast until the embrace was returned in full.

"Demiesius," he said, "I'm not going anywhere. Ever. Over these past eight months I have fallen so madly in love with you, that I was sure it'd spiral me into insanity if you left me. Right now, this is perhaps the most difficult my life has ever been, what with this sickness and the recent loss of someone dear to me, you've been there from the beginning, wanting nothing more than for me to feel alright." Hamilton loosened his grip and looked upon the elder's face, taking in the solemn expression on his handsome countenance. Kissing his lips once, Hamilton said, "I'll always be here. Even when you can't see me," he kissed Demiesius again, "Feel me," again, "Hear me," again and again, "I'll always be here for you. Nothing will ever be strong enough to keep me from your arms."

Hamilton could feel his body trembling on the inside, each tremor brought on by the admittance of the true, profound love he felt for this vampire elder. And he meant every single word.

Taking the necklace from Hamilton, Demiesius placed it around the slayer, allowing it to lay just beside the ancient gift he'd given Hamilton for his twenty-ninth birthday. Letting the blackish crimson vial sit at his fingertips, Demiesius met Hamilton's soft blue gaze, able to see the dull hints of gray tucked around the inner iris. "I love you," he said blatantly, the sincere shade in his eyes causing the slayer's heartbeat to jump.

Hamilton fought the tears brimming in his eyes, an earnest smile coming to him, "You don't know how badly I have wanted to hear you say those words to me."

"Always, Hamilton, I will love you with all I am, with everything I can give."

When Hamilton went in for another kiss, the phone in the next room rang. Given only important phone calls ever came through, the elder placed a kiss at the slayer's forehead and excused himself to answer it.

Hamilton returned to his seat on the barstool, unable to set-tle his inner nerves after hearing Demiesius' words. Not that he ever questioned where the elder's affections resided, but to finally hear him speak of something that Hamilton himself has felt for some time now, it was heartwarming and reassuring. He needed Demiesius' love more than anything, especially at this point in time. He needed someone to be there at the end of every day, someone for him to confide in, and what better than for that someone to be the love of your life?

To be loved, Hamilton felt the ghost of a smile come to his lips, it had to be the greatest feeling in the world. To be in love, truly in love with someone who felt everything just as mutually, Hamilton knew this was it. Demiesius would be all he ever needed from this day forward, always and forever, until true death was the only thing that could pry them from one another.

A moment later, Demiesius returned, "Would you like to ac-company me to a gathering tonight? Dominick arranged for one at the Monterey Palace. The coven leader from Tokyo is visiting and he wants to impress her."

"Sounds eventful, I'd love to."

Dressed decently enough for a gathering, Hamilton wore white trousers that clung to his long legs, and a sun yellow, cascade halter top with heeled dress shoes to match. His hair was held back in a jeweled dragonfly clip, bangs framing his face, while dashes of faint tan eyeshadow complimented his eyes. After touching up the strays in his hair, Hamilton's hand was taken by Demiesius, but he pulled away.

"We're not traveling like we did last time, are we? That gave me a pretty bad headache afterwards. Could we be normal for a few minutes and drive, please?"

"You want to drive for two hours?" the elder added.

"It's that far?"

Demiesius nodded, "If you do not wish to come, we don't have to go."

"No, no," Hamilton shook his head, thinking of the emotions Dominick had shed the last time they were all together. He didn't want it to seem like he was trying to keep the elder all to himself. After all, Dominick was the man's child. "That's alright. I'll deal with it."

Walking into Demiesius' arms, Hamilton was held tightly and closed his eyes, that weightless dark feeling hovering around him.

Earlier in the night Demiesius had explained what this type of travel was. Appropriately referred to as 'Shadow Mastering', once a vampire reaches their four-hundredth year, they gain the ethereal ability to interact with the night they live in. Focusing purely enough on the dark elements surrounding them, vampires command the shadows to envelope their bodies and everything touching it, encasing them inside a shield of manipulation that acts as a sort of teleportation capability. This act is a simple talent to command, but those who cannot focus accurately enough have a chance of becoming trapped in said darkness with no hope of returning to the world outside of the shadows.

When his feet touched the ground again after the whirlwind, Hamilton opened his eyes to find they were standing before a grand cream-colored palace alive with what seemed to be hundreds of guests. The curved driveway in front was lined with black luxury vehicles, men and women walking up the gradual steps leading to the large wooden doors of the entrance.

It was only now that Hamilton was beginning to regret his choice of clothing. Everyone here was well dressed in formal gowns or tuxedos, including Demiesius in an ironed suit with a bow that fit nicely around his collar. And the color coding was far from the polar opposites of Hamilton's attire. Each guest was dressed either entirely in black or a combination of blood red and black.

Curling his arm with Demiesius' when he started up the steps, Hamilton lowered his voice, "I look like an idiot," he said. "How come you didn't tell me I was going to be dressed inappropriately?"

"Don't be ridiculous," Demiesius assured, "You look just fine."

As they continued up to the doorway, Hamilton looked around, other vampires staring in awe towards them. But he was more than sure their mesmerized eyes were paying him no mind. With each vampire he and the elder passed, the immortals lowered their heads respectfully with a hand over their still hearts. Hamilton even caught the gleeful praise of a woman as he stepped by her.

"Master Demiesius," she said quietly, "What an honor to see him again."

Demiesius, on the other hand, continued as though this was just a natural thing. Being a noble vampire with blood as rich as his own, and one of the most treasured lives that walked under the moon, Hamilton guessed the elder was used to the acclaim he received by vampires of lesser status. Being looked upon as a king, Hamilton was glad his vampire lover was viewed as such.

Entering the front vestibule of the extravagant palace, Hamilton was taken aback by the sheer magnificence of it all. He would admit that Demiesius' home was far more breathtaking, but there was no denying that the marble structure and design of this place was spectacular.

Dominick was standing at the head of the vestibule, dressed in a black formal suit with a dark crimson shirt beneath his coat, hair combed properly and held up in a well-ordered bun. He looked very professional.

Spotting Demiesius, the blood child kindly broke away from the conversation he'd been having. "Father," he smiled, appearing relieved. "For a while I thought you would not show. Thank you for coming." He then scanned his eyes over towards the slayer, looking at him up and down with amusement. "Last minute? Truthfully, Hamilton, I expected to see you arrive on my father's arm in a dashing silk dress. It would have proved more suitable than...this."

"Oh, ha," Hamilton wrinkled his nose.

"If you like," Dominick said, "There is a dressing area up on the second floor with several costumes to choose from. Many of my guests from earlier in the night required a proper change of clothes. You may help yourself to them."

"Actually," Hamilton released Demiesius' arm, "That sounds nice."

"Does it?" Dominick rutted his brow. "I was only teasing. But if you want to change, go right ahead."

Hamilton nodded and kissed Demiesius' cheek, informing him that he wouldn't be long. Leaving the two, Hamilton headed for the stairwell curved along the wall in the room beside the vestibule. The sounds of the gathering died down as he climbed the red draped steps to the second floor. The corridor he faced was nearly empty, just a few vampires with...other humans on their way back down.

A strange reassurance entered him when seeing the two pairs meander by him. They had looked more like couples rather than the food sources he'd witnessed during his first time visiting Dominick's coven. To see a vampire care for a human being just as Demiesius cared for him, it gave him comfort.

After peeking into a few unoccupied bedrooms, Hamilton finally found a dressing room. It was a fair chamber with walls of pure red velvet, the ceiling arched all the way over with a white tile-like arrangement and olive-green trim, the floor a dark wood as a symmetrically patterned rug covered majority of it, and a golden chandelier hung down into the center. There was a divan and chair placed inside to match the walls, brown vanity, and a mirror tall in height and extensive in width.

The rack of beautiful clothing Dominick had referred to was beside an open drawn curtain at the opposite end of the room, used to shield guests while they changed on the other side.

Many of the tuxedos looked the same, unable to catch Hamilton's liking until he laid eyes on the evening gowns. Some were made of silk, others strictly polyester or voile, but the one that caught Hamilton's attention was a rust red satin woven gown.

Approaching the rack, he took it off the hook and neared the mirror, holding the form fitting dress against him to visualize what it'd look like. He'd always loved women's clothing ever since he gained an appreciation for fashion, but to wear a dress, especially in front of many others, Hamilton never had the guts. But this time was different. Tonight, he wouldn't be surrounded by fellow slayers, people who could possibly judge him for the things he liked. Tonight, it was virtually Demiesius who'd be the only person laying eyes on him, and Hamilton liked looking his best before the elder.

After finding a whitish gold pair of two and a half inch, slim heeled open-toed shoes, Hamilton stepped behind the curtain to change. Not caring that he'd be leaving the clothes he'd arrived in, he slipped into the dress and hooked on the shoes before coming out.

Standing before the mirror, a smile of self-approval came to him. The rust red satin shaped his body well, a wide ribbon-like waistline defining the curves he had. An array of white jewels formed a row of flowers up to the V-neck dip against his chest, and the straps running up to his shoulders opened at the back, showing off his shoulder blades.

Lastly, Hamilton let down his hair from the dragonfly clip holding it up, letting his fair locks river down his back, and the two necklaces he now had from Demiesius were befitting to the outfit as they laid against his bared collar. Twirling the small vial of blood in his fingers, Hamilton sucked in a chest of air for confidence, and then finally left the dressing room to rejoin the gathering.

The two vampires were no longer where they'd been before, so Hamilton migrated further into the palace, no one seeming bothered by the sight of a man in an evening gown, and he was glad to see there was no issue with it.

Moving along with a group that seemed to know where all the buzz was located, Hamilton entered a prolonged ballroom area. There was faint classical music playing from a small orchestra on the stage, tables and chairs in front of it for those who wished to sit down. Pairs were dancing hand in hand, trays of blood in wine glasses passing around to quench the thirst of any guests.

The moment Hamilton stepped through the threshold, he locked eyes with Demiesius standing just at the edge of the waxed dance floor. There was a glass of blood in his hand, and a captivated look in his eyes as the slayer drew closer to him. He'd completely lost track of the conversation he'd been having with the four vampires beside him—all his attention drawn in Hamilton's direction until they were face to face.

"Don't stare at me like that," Hamilton blushed, "You're making me self-conscious."

"I — I apologize," the elder cleared his throat. "You look very beautiful."

Before the slayer could thank him, a dark-brown skinned woman with bright hazel eyes spoke up from beside Demiesius. "Oh, Hamilton, I am so glad you decided to come along." She had a pleasant tongue he couldn't place right away, but it did sound similar to Demiesius' accent. "It is a pleasure to actually meet you. The last time I saw you was at the Coalition gathering, and now my brother here has been keeping you all to himself."

It clicked in Hamilton's mind at that moment. This woman, these four other vampires surrounding Demiesius, they were the other elders.

Keeping his politeness up, the slayer nodded kindly. "Hello," he said, "It is nice to meet you as well. I apologize for seeming so distant."

Demiesius introduced him to them all then. The first woman's name was Bethania, and she was slipped curvaceously in a black dress. Her curly hair grew beautifully down her shoulders, and in human years, she looked around thirty-five. Then there was Eros and Nabadias, two men appearing in their late thirties with skin as pale as ghosts, Eros with short styled silvery-white hair and a handsome edged countenance, while Nabadias' hair was black like a crow's wings. He himself appeared etched from

Greek marble in all his precise build and stature. Lastly there was Minerva, someone whom Hamilton would have never taken for an elder given her young appearance. She had light brown skin and dark twisty hair with eyes the color of a night sky, and...she didn't look a day over sixteen.

After leaving them, Hamilton mingled around with Demiesius for a good while, having a great time gliding along with his vampire lover for about an hour more into the night. He'd never been introduced to so many people before, but being able to witness as Demiesius interacted generously with his people, was a heartwarming scene to experience. He already knew the elder had a great admiration for his people, but to see how they all networked with one another brought a smile to Hamilton's face.

As Demiesius delved back into his conversation with the other elders, Hamilton thought it rather humorous that they all seemed to eventually gravitate back to one another. Hamilton gladly remained at the immortal's side; their arms linked together in a manner that made him wonder if Demiesius was making sure to notice if he'd wander off anywhere.

A moment later, they were all approached by a woman dressed in a black and red traditional Japanese kimono. Her hair was bundled up with golden pins with dangling red rubies, and her skin was smooth and showed not a single line in her beautifully rounded face. With dark brown eyes and red-painted lips, she lowered her head respectfully at the elders who quieted themselves to address her. Apparently, she was the new coven leader who watched over Tokyo, Japan.

Introducing herself, she said, "Good evening to you all. As I was appointed to my position by my previous leader, I would like to formally introduce myself."

"Oh, of course," Bethania said before anyone else could. "Miss Kanna Tano. We are most certain if Junko was adamant about placing you in her stead, you would do just fine in your new position. As Minerva has already been able to gather from her stay in your country, your followers hold a great deal of respect for you as it is."

Showing appreciation for the words with a smile and a nod, Kanna stepped aside and gestured to five approaching young Japanese men tailored in fine suits, each with short cut dark hair as four of them wielded a potted plant, while the last held two entangled flowers bundled together.

When the men placed the arrangements down on a long table pushed up against the wall behind them, Kanna stepped before the first, which was a tiny potted cherry blossom bonsai. "Lady Minerva," she said firstly, "If you would, please accept this gift I would so gladly wish to offer. As I know you wield quite a love for my homeland, I thought it only appropriate to give you this bonsai as a token of Japan."

While the young-appearing elder simply nodded her silent thanks, she neared the plant on the long entry table and touched a tender finger to one of the small limbs.

As Bethania was given Japanese irises, Eros received peonies, and Nabadias appreciated his gift of violets, Kanna took the two intertwined flowers held by one of her followers and approached Demiesius as Hamilton watched on beside him.

Secured together by a black silk bow lay one red and one white higanbana, otherwise known as Japanese Spider Lilies. Both were cut finely, and their outstretched petals were beautiful as they curved upwards and mildly tangled together.

"Though there is a certain stigma that follows this species," Kanna explained, "as death has once touched each of you, every one of us immortals, our lives have continued into the years as if such a thing never occurred. Given these are not potted and will run into an inevitable fate of wilting away someday, I do hope you can find appreciation in their splendor while they are here, Master Demiesius."

Receiving the two flowers in kind, Demiesius nodded gratefully and soon Kanna Tano was on her way to search for Dominick.

With his arm still tucked with the elders', Hamilton looked upon the strange yet very beautiful flowers. He'd never seen the species before and thought they surely looked interesting enough. He almost thought it was a shame they'd been cut and wouldn't have a chance to blossom again.

"Demiesius?" he said, and when the elder looked from the two flowers to the man beside him, Hamilton continued with: "What stigma was she referring to?"

"In Japanese culture," Demiesius explained, "The red higanbana, or spider lily, is often closely associated with death; nature's visual representation of a final goodbye, or where one's final moments on earth took place. There are six shades of this species, but as for the white higanbana, it may represent positivity and new beginnings. Together, you could say the red is a symbol of goodbye while the white represents return."

"Oh, my," Hamilton awed at the explanation, tempted to touch the prominent, wiry stamens of each but held himself off. "They are quite the ironic pair, aren't they?"

Looking from the flowers and into Hamilton's light shaded gaze once again—with a mild smirk, Demiesius nodded, "Yes, love, they certainly are quite the pair."

After placing the floral gift down beside the others brought along for the time being, the two stepped off together and Hamilton was able to snag a glass of actual wine from a drink carrier passing by and swigged the entire glass.

Demiesius placed a hand at the slayer's lower back. "You are having a good time?" he asked.

Hamilton held in a belch that needed to be released, "Yes, it's wonderful—."

He caught himself against Demiesius' chest when a rude force knocked him from behind. When he glanced over his shoulder, a rather young-looking male vampire stumbled by. He had pastel skin with dark freckles dotted across the bridge of his nose, wearing black trousers and a red overcoat with gray cuffs, and his light brown hair was rather disheveled.

Staring Hamilton down with examining eyes, the vampire then tore his gaze away quickly and tucked his hands in the pockets of his trousers.

"Apologies," the man said, but it seemed he'd only said such a thing given the presence of Demiesius at Hamilton's side.

Hamilton thought it odd when the vampire hadn't reacted the same as every other who laid eyes on Demiesius. He did not bow his head, show respect or even an ounce of acknowledgment, just glared into the slayer before continuing into the ballroom.

"What was *his* problem?" Hamilton said, a tone of suspicion in his voice.

"Do not pay him any mind," Demiesius assured, "Whenever you are ready to leave, do not be afraid to let me know. You need your rest after all."

"There you go again," Hamilton bickered, "Treating me as

though I'm a child."

"Forgive me," the elder smiled thoughtfully. "You are nearly done with your treatment, and all I want is for you to feel well. No more shots. No more worry."

Hamilton gazed up into Demiesius' black eyes, "Soon you will not have to worry for me any longer."

"Have you had any further thoughts about joining the Coalition?"

Yes, he had. At first, he'd been worried about leaving the official Slayer Public on behalf of Julius and his previous hatred for vampires, but lately there has been no word from Samuel about Julius' worrisome attitude. He hadn't wanted to leave the Public because of his concern, but it seemed Julius was making progress when it came to his hatred. "I will join soon," Hamilton said, "When Dr. Takahashi completely cures me of this tuberculosis, I will."

Reluctant to hold himself back, Hamilton pushed into Demiesius' arms, wanting to be held in them for just a moment.

As the elder pressed his nose into the side of Hamilton's hair, the slayer was able to see just over Demiesius' broad shoulder. He could feel the warmth of their bodies being transferred through their clothing. As his gaze moved about the vampires in the ballroom, he furrowed his brow when he caught sight of the one that'd clumsily bumped into him earlier. He was moseying about on uncoordinated feet, pure anger in his eyes as he moved.

When it appeared as if he'd caught sight of something he was looking for, Hamilton followed his gaze, coming to stop on Dominick a couple meters away. He was speaking with Kanna Tano.

Struck with an incredulous notion, Hamilton released Demiesius and stepped aside, keeping his eyes on the vampire stalking closer and closer to Dominick.

"Is something wrong?" the elder asked, and when Hamilton didn't answer him, he pushed into the slayer's thoughts to read them.

"That can't be him. He'd be a fool to come here with those intentions."

"Hamilton, who is it?"

"I don't know his name..." Hamilton's eyes traveled down the vampire's arm to his hand. His middle finger was missing, and the spiked tip of a wooden stake appeared from the cuff of his overcoat.

"Oh, god. Dominick!" Quickly, the slayer stepped out of his heels and sprinted into the ballroom. "Hey!" he called, catching the ear of nearly everyone around him.

The vampire began to move faster when he heard Hamilton's warning shout.

"Dominick, turn around!"

The moment the blood child went to look back, he dodged the rapid strike of the stake attempting to drive down into the center of his chest. Staggering, he collided with a group behind him. "What the fuck?!" he bellowed.

Hamilton, finally reaching the commotion, wrapped his arm around the striking vampire's, able to skillfully twist the stake from his grasp before tossing him to the floor. Like stumbling lightning; however, he was on his feet again, fangs elongated as he hissed angrily. "Stupid woman!" he screeched. "I should have killed you when I had the chance." Then he launched himself at Hamilton, slamming the slayer down so hard against the ballroom floor that he lost his breath.

Wrenching his arm out when focus entered him again, Hamilton brought his elbow back solidly against the vampire's temple, sending a shockwave of pain into him long enough to get to his feet. When he was standing, he ran for the vampire, able to muster a sufficient amount of strength to pick him up and tackle him down onto a table, splitting the wood in half when he did so. Before he could go for the kill, a pair of arms strong enough to restrain him wrapped around his body.

It was Demiesius.

"Calm yourself," the elder said, the eyes of every vampire staring at the scene taking place.

"That's him!" Hamilton shouted. "He was trying to kill Dominick!"

As if on cue to his name, Dominick appeared beside his father, standing with a darkness of rage in his eyes. Staring at the vampire on the floor, he moved forward, stomping his foot down in the center of the vampire's chest. "You fucking tosser," Dominick growled. "Thought you could get your bloody hands on me, did ya?" He choked a resilient grip around the vampire's throat, heaving him up from the clutter of wood and glass. "I should tear you to fucking pieces. Make you a goddamn example!"

"I almost had you," the vampire wheezed.

"Kill him!" Hamilton struggled in Demiesius' hold, "He has to pay for what he's done, Dominick!"

The blood child raised a brow, not surprised by Hamilton's yearning to see this murderer immortal perish here and now. Given he'd been the one to steal the slayer Teresa's life away, it was only natural to want such revenge.

"I have a better idea," Dominick said, his sharp nails burrowing into the vampire's neck, "Christoph!"

A moment later Christoph appeared, the same vacant look in his eyes as it had been since that night a month ago. Dressed formally, he took in the heavy atmosphere. "Yes, Dominick?" he said, confused.

Tossing the vampire to Christoph's feet, Dominick said, "He is the one who took your human lover from this world. Taste your revenge, my friend. End him."

It was as though a malevolent cloud settled over Christoph. Without a second thought, he brought the vampire into his own hold, vanishing inside an assembly of shadows that built up around him a second later.

"I'm sorry for the way I reacted at the palace," Hamilton said. He and Demiesius had just returned to the castle, the slayer still a bit shaken from what'd gone on. As he tucked the gifted higanbana into a slender vase with water, he added: "I couldn't control myself when I realized who he was. I was only trying to protect Dominick."

"I thank you for that," Demiesius nodded. They were up in his lofty bedroom, Hamilton now changing out of the evening gown into something more relaxing after the flowers were situated. "If you hadn't caught him when you did, my child would be far from me. Dominick is one of the very few people in my life that I couldn't picture myself without, and to see you protect him..." He seemed lost for words, "Thank you for wanting to save my son."

Making himself comfortable in one of Demiesius' shirts,

Hamilton said, "A parent should never know the pain of losing a child. If Dominick means that much to you, then he means just the same to me. I don't know if he will ever see me in a similar light, but so long as he holds such a place in your heart, he will be in mine. I love you, Demiesius and I will love Dominick, too."

The elder neared and kissed Hamilton's waiting lips when he sat on the large bed, resting their foreheads together until he found the right words to say. "Forever, my love," he said, a promising tone in his voice. "This love that exists within me, it will last as effortlessly as forever possibly can."

CHAPTER EIGHTEEN

Suspicions Arise from a Watchful Friend

Julius Dalton was awake in the early hours of the morning. He couldn't sleep very well and after growing tired of lying in bed staring up at his ceiling, he decided to get some cardio in before the sun brought light over the London area. Sharing a bedroom with Samuel while Kingston had his own down the hall, he worked himself quietly out of bed and threw on some joggers and a coat. When he had his trainers tied down, he slipped out of the flat without making a sound.

Rounding the tall brick building, he stepped completely into the shadows when suddenly the front UV ray lights of the campus kicked on, but he hadn't been the one to trigger them. Confused, he poked his head back around the building, spotting a vehicle pulling into the gate closing off the campus. Who could be arriving back to Gregor House this late, or rather, early in the morning?

Curious, Julius remained hidden behind the bend of the wall. To his surprise, Hamilton appeared out of the parked car. He was dressed in joggers with a black overcoat protecting him from the bitter cold, and he wasn't wearing any shoes, just a pair of black socks that, in turn, became soiled from the dirt of the pavement. For a while, Julius had noticed his former instructor's frequent absence, but never thought too much of it. Hamilton was the top-ranking slayer, so being called out on duties more often than not came with the position, right?

Pondering Hamilton's actions over these past several months, Julius recalled further back into the beginning of this year. It was nearly December as it was, and this behavior has been the same since April.

What has he been up to all this time?

While Hamilton surely kept up with the training of his now former students, he was only ever nearby during certain parts of the day. He would oversee their sessions with their new instructor, offer insight, and give a rather good helping hand when it came to developing their skills. Before he would disappear from the facility to go off wherever he went, Hamilton wasn't a stranger to sharing words of encouragement regarding their skill sets and building upon their combat knowledge.

Julius himself had noted how the man would single him out more often, always a bit more positive and reassuring in terms of how well developed of a fighter he was becoming. And...although very appreciative of the praise received, Julius couldn't quite set down the paranoia eating away at him.

The following day, Julius kept a watchful eye on Hamilton.

In the morning, the twenty-nine-year-old came out to see how their training was going, often offering his opinion on what they were doing wrong, or how to perfect certain moves with ease. All in all, he helped the current instructor until the training sessions came to a close. For the rest of the day, Hamilton stayed in his apartment, coming out only to speak with whomever called upon his assistance.

During supper hour, Julius went into the cafeteria building and grabbed a tray, taking his seat with Samuel and Kingston at a table in the center.

"What's your problem?" the American boy, Kingston, asked. He was seated across from Julius, running a hand through his dark red hair. "You look like shit."

Julius handed Samuel his green apple like he did every supper hour. "I don't know," he said, "I've just had something on my mind."

"What is it?" Samuel asked, his Austrian accent faint but present.

"I'm starting to get a strange feeling from Instructor Hamilton."

Samuel rutted his brow, chewing away at his pork dish, "Why is that?"

Keeping his tone down, Julius lowered his head, as if crouching slightly would help hide the concern he was about to voice. "Have either of you noticed that he's always coming back real late at night, and I mean late as in long after tasks are usually completed? Actually, I don't even think he's been going out on them at all, not since his last in the Spring. I saw him last night getting here at close to six o'clock in the morning. He wasn't even wearing shoes and wasn't quite dressed for a mission. What the hell does a slayer have to do so near sunrise?"

"You're probably just paranoid, Julius," Kingston said. "Hamilton is a grown man. I think he can do whatever he wants."

"Yeah," Samuel agreed. "It's none of our business."

Julius shook his head, "I don't know why, but I have this weird feeling that he's up to something. This morning I was thinking about his story when he found Instructor Teresa dead. He is Hamilton for hell's sake. *Always* gets his target. *Never* backs down. But this one time, he messes up, and a life is lost?"

"Julius," Samuel interjected, "You are out of line if you're trying to say he had anything to do with that. Teresa was murdered. It wasn't Hamilton's fault."

"What if he wasn't with her?"

Annoyed by the accusations being thrown around, Samuel sighed, "Then where was he?"

"I don't know, but I bet he wasn't with Teresa," Julius accused. "Whatever happened to her, I do believe she was killed by a vampire, but Hamilton wasn't around to save her. He had to be somewhere else. I have too much respect for him to think he could have been bested by a fucking bloodsucker."

"You don't have any proof," Samuel pushed.

"But I do have my suspicions."

Kingston chugged a glass of water beside his tray before belching. He narrowed his eyes to his friend then, and said, "Julius, if you're so caught up on the idea that Instructor Hamilton is up to something, why don't you just ask him?"

Julius furrowed his brow, "Because you think he will come out and tell me what he's doing? Of course, he won't."

"Then snoop around on him."

There was an idea...

Julius didn't like holding out such an apprehensive hand towards his former instructor, but he also couldn't put down the bizarre idea that Hamilton spent a great majority of his time away from Gregor House for a reason. And not just any reason, but one that couldn't be explained away without causing a light of trust to dim down on the man. Secretly keeping an eye on him, maybe just for a couple of days, would put all of Julius' qualms to rest in one sitting. "That sounds like a good idea," he said. "I think I'll do that. Anyone care to join?"

Samuel shook his head, "You two are being ridiculous. What if Hamilton is just going out to see a boyfriend of his? It would make sense given everyone's time during the day is taken up by the campus schedule. Maybe he's just trying to keep his private life...private."

Kingston crossed his arms on the table, the uncertain vibe carried by Julius weighing into him. "Maybe you're wrong, Samuel..."

"There's only one way to find out," Julius said. "I'm going to keep an eye on him."

CHAPTER NINETEEN
Where Good News Follows

Hamilton was the most nervous he'd ever been. It was after dark on New Year's Eve, and the clinic room he was waiting in was sterile and brightly lit, this workplace open 24/7 for public emergencies. And tonight, tonight was the night Hamilton was to find out if he'd been completely cured of the tuberculosis that'd been eating him away earlier in the year.

It almost felt like a lifetime ago that he'd been coughing up blood, sweating copiously in his sleep, and suffering from exhaustive dizziness. Now, he couldn't feel better, cleaner, refreshed, and it was all thanks to Demiesius. If it hadn't been for the elder's persistence to get him to feel better, Hamilton was sure he'd be dead or dying right now. Having been introduced to Dr. Takahashi back then...Hamilton couldn't find the words to express how grateful he was.

Alone for the reveal, however; Hamilton had come to the clinic without company. He'd wanted Demiesius beside him when the news broke, but he understood that the elder had other responsibilities that didn't pertain to taking care of a slayer. Currently, Demiesius was attending a strict meeting to pass down a law that would be going into effect in a couple of nights, something about great punishments to those who create blood children, only to leave said blood children without a parental figure.

No matter what was said tonight regarding his condition, Hamilton would go to Demiesius' castle to give him the news.

Anxious as he sat atop the clinic examination table, Hamilton twirled his thumbs around one another, unable to keep completely still. After a blood test and x-ray, Dr. Takahashi could walk in at any given moment.

Once a good amount of time had passed, the door to the room was opened, and the first thing Hamilton saw was a smile pulled across the doctor's face.

Hamilton sprung to his feet, "Is it gone?!" he asked.

Pinning the x-ray portrait against a light source, Dr. Takahashi began to point out that every sign of TB inside the slayer's lungs was no longer there. "Hamilton Haven Hamilton," he said then, "I am very pleased to inform you that you are one-hundred percent tuberculosis free after completing your treatment."

Rushing the doctor, Hamilton wrapped his arms around the man, squeezing him with all his might as the realization drained into him. He wasn't sick anymore. He was cured. In good health. Every which way it could be said, Hamilton was elated to know his life was no longer at risk.

His eyes burned with tears of joy, and he wanted to cry, but he wouldn't allow himself to do something like that. This was not a night for tears. "Thank you so much," Hamilton said. "I wish there was a way I could truly show my appreciation. Thank you so much!"

Stepping out of the slayer's embrace when he was released, Dr. Takahashi shook Hamilton's hand. "You are very welcome, Mister Hamilton. Over the months I have been around you and Elder Demiesius, I have grown to see just how much he cherishes you, and I am honored to have been able to offer my assistance. Merely being able to lend a hand to my elder is something I am an immortal for. Demiesius and the rest of the elders are like kings and queens to us lowly beings."

Hamilton let go of the man's hand, the smile never leaving him. "Thank you so much. I don't know what else to say."

"Just take things easy for the next couple weeks or so. You are entirely free from tuberculosis, but if ever you begin to feel sick again, especially if the symptoms turn out the same, do not waste time coming to tell me. If you do happen to become infected with again, there is a chance that you could develop an intolerance to the drugs I administered to you, and we would not want that to happen."

"Alright," Hamilton nodded. "I promised Demiesius I'd join the Coalition after I was cured, so I shouldn't be too active anyways."

"Good, good," Dr. Takahashi smiled. "Now, I'm sure you are anxious to return to your regular life. So, please, have a nice night, Hamilton."

Stepping out into the world from the clinic, Hamilton couldn't help but feel rejuvenated. Physically, he felt the same as he did when he'd first entered the building, but leaving it knowing he was back to his old self...he could breathe easy, breathe deeper.

No longer concerned about the possibility of keeling over in the middle of his love fest, there was one thing he couldn't wait for. Now there was nothing at all stopping him from pursuing a long life with Demiesius.

With the drop of blood dangling in a protected vial around his neck, it became his choice on whether he would decide to continue into the long years with Demiesius – not as a human, but as a vampire just like his lover.

Being just twenty-nine years old still, Hamilton did want to wait to make that decision once he and Demiesius were the same age in human years. And, honestly, he was more than sure his answer would be a "yes". He was far too in love to consider denying himself a life with someone he treasured.

As he strolled around the building towards the parking lot, Hamilton stopped and looked down at himself. He was dressed in high-waisted jeans, a heavy coat for the weather, and a collared brown and white silk blouse with long sleeves. It wasn't something he wanted to present himself in when he and Demiesius saw one another later, but he'd thrown on whatever to hurry off. When he was in his car, he headed towards Gregor House. After dolling himself up a bit, he'd head to the castle for a night of...well, it was still early, so who knew what could happen in the hours it took for dawn to arrive?

With a bit of an impish thought running through his mind, Hamilton drove to the slayer campus, parking out in front of the instructors building when he arrived.

Standing before the towering edifice, Hamilton couldn't help but think about what it would be like to leave this place behind. Although he would still be connected to the slayer world through the workings of the Coalition, he was sure it'd be a lot different from a life of merely being in the Public. His whole life had been spent at this place.

Unable to remember anything before three years of age, this was the only place he could ever remember calling home and leaving it behind felt a bit strange. He remembered nearly every bit of his life here perfectly: the day his past instructor told him what kind of place Gregor truly was, the very first day of training after he'd grown a young interest for it, the honest-to-God pain he'd felt during the start of his physical combat training, the grueling blood, sweat and forbidden tears he'd shed when he was a young child.

This place would forever be the location that built him into the type of fighter every slayer aspired to be. He'd grown strong both physically and mentally on these grounds, gained the respect he'd earned every step of the way, and a part of him couldn't be prouder of himself as a human being.

Moving into the instructor's building, Hamilton rutted his brow when he caught Julius coming out of his room. The boy was closing the door quietly behind him, and when the man cleared his throat, Julius jumped and quickly turned his way. "What are you doing?" Hamilton asked, not sounding too bothered by the invasion of his privacy.

The teenager ran a hand through his dark hair, a shaky laugh leaving him as he seemed to search for the words to say. "I - uh - I was looking for you," he said. "Yeah, I really wanted to talk to you about something, and when I couldn't find you anywhere, I just decided to check here."

"So breaking into my flat was your best idea?"

"Um, sorry..." Julius winced.

Hamilton laughed and shook his head, opening the door to his room to go inside. "Come in if you still want to talk. I was heading out again in a few minutes, and I don't know when I'll be back."

"Where are you going, if you don't mind my asking?"

As Julius took a seat in the living area of the flat, Hamilton went for his bedroom, pulling out different articles of clothing to see which would look best on him for the night. Calling out from his room, Hamilton said, "Oh, I'm just getting together with someone for a while. You'd be surprised, but I do have a life outside of the Public. Not really easy for everyone to have, especially if you've spent over twenty years dedicated to it." Looking over a turquoise blouse with yellow design sewn into the sleeves, Hamilton wavered before tossing it over his shoulder. "You wanted to talk to me about something?"

Julius cursed in his mind.

He hadn't expected to run into the man. On any other night according to the past month he'd been keeping an eye out, Hamilton wouldn't have returned to Gregor until near dawn. What made tonight the one time to change up his routine? "I'm – uh – I guess..." he tried to pick something, anything before Hamilton grew suspicious of his true intentions. "...there's this *girl.*"

"Oh, a girl?" Hamilton asked, judging if he'd look better in a dark copper knit halter top, or a slender fit gray sweater. Tossing the sweater away, he threw off the coat and blouse he'd been wearing, and traded the garments for the knit top. He decided to keep on the high-waisted jeans, and he swapped the boots he was wearing for a pair of brown platforms that made him just a bit taller. "What's going on with this *girl?*" he asked.

"Her name is...Helen," Julius said, not knowing what else to cover up with. "I met her a couple days before Christmas, and I really like her. But I guess it's just a little difficult to spend time with someone like that when I'm stuck here all day."

"Trust me, lad," Hamilton said, running a brush through his bright blonde locks, "I know exactly what you mean. You know you're not supposed to let anyone outside of the Public know about your real occupation though, right?"

"Yeah," Julius sighed, a piece of him momentarily forgetting that this topic was a mere ploy. "She's been real understanding of who I am as a person, but I'm starting to think things might be changing. I don't want her to begin viewing me as a bad guy, and I hate that there seems to be a change happening between us. I don't like change. Understand?"

"Absolutely," Hamilton said, spraying a dash of sweet perfume against his neck. "I think the best thing you could do at this point, especially since it's early on, is let her know that you do resent the little amount of time you two get to spend together, but when you do eventually see her, just remember to treat her like a lady. Take her out when you're able—make her feel like she's a priority."

"Didn't think I'd ever be listening to dating advice in a place like this," Julius huffed. "You're right though. Thanks, Hamilton."

After making sure the makeup around his eyes was perfectly even, Hamilton emerged from his room, pretty as he could make himself look all for Demiesius. "No problem," he said. "I'm not a relationship guru or anything, but I know how I'd like to be treated if someone I liked had a busy schedule. And if this Helen girl is understanding, and likes you just as much, then I'm sure she won't have a problem with it."

Julius nodded, "Are you leaving now?"

"Yeah, I don't know what time I'll be back, but sometime tonight or tomorrow for sure." He grabbed a more fitting trench coat with a furry collar from a rack in the living area and slid into it. "Mind locking up for me?"

"Sure. See you tomorrow."

Julius watched the man slip out of the flat, the door still open as Hamilton disappeared. Going to the window overlooking the front parking lot of the building, Julius stayed within the room until he saw Hamilton drive away.

Suddenly then, Julius flinched when a black raven landed outside of the window and pecked at the glass, a rolled-up piece of paper clamped down in its bill.

"What the...?" Julius wrinkled his brow at the jumpy creature. Curious as the bird stared up at him, he unlocked the window and pushed it up, and the raven immediately dropped the paper inside before turning and flying away.

Taking the rolled paper into his hands, Julius flattened it and became even more baffled when it turned out to be a letter addressed to Hamilton from a name he couldn't quite pronounce. Not wanting to stand around in the instructor's flat any longer, Julius left for his own room in the next dormitory. When he was inside, he walked in on Samuel and Kingston in the middle of a heated argument about the correct way to wield a stake when you're naturally left-handed.

"Lads," Julius cut in, "You're not going to believe what I just came across."

Kingston dropped down on the couch, his dark red hair like a crimson curtain in front of his forehead. "Thank God, someone with a lick of sense arrives. Julius, tell Samuel a stake should be faced outwards when getting into your first stance."

Pushing the argument aside, Julius said, "That doesn't matter right now. I just got the weirdest letter flown into Hamilton's room by a bird."

"What?" the two slayers said in unison, Samuel continuing afterwards. "You went inside his room without permission?"

"At first, yeah," Julius said. "But he came back and just left a minute ago. A bird flew this letter to his window after he was gone."

"What do you mean 'a bird'?" Kingston asked.

"I meant exactly what I said," the British boy rolled his eyes. "A bird flew this letter to Hamilton's window."

"So someone sent him a *raven*? What time period do we live in, the thirteenth century? Did you read it yet?"

Samuel jumped up from the couch, "You shouldn't read it, Julius. You're crossing a line by going into Hamilton's things. I know you have your suspicions about him, but that could be something extremely personal!"

"Oh, calm down," Julius countered, taking a seat on the armrest of the couch. "I'm not hurting anyone. Besides, I'll just throw it away and he won't even miss it."

Without the power to tell Kingston or Julius what to do, Samuel left the living room, wanting to respect Hamilton's privacy more than the other two.

When Samuel was gone, Julius opened the letter again and read it aloud:

Hamilton,

By chance you went home after your check up, I wanted to give my most sincere apologies for not being able to accompany you to see Dr.

Takahashi. I know how important this visit was to you, but I could not reschedule a night like tonight. The assembly should not take too long of a time, though I will understand if you do not wish to wait hours for me to return home. Although I have faith that these past several months of treatment for your tuberculosis turned out to be a success, I am here for you always if, for any reason, something went wrong along the way. You are the strongest human being I have ever come across in my time on this earth and know you will continue to be just as strong. If, perchance, you do require someone to lean on, you know I will always be here for you every step of the way. I love you deeply, Hamilton, and look forward to seeing you again.

Greatest wishes, Demiesius

"Well, that was romantic," Kingston said. "And I can't believe Hamilton has, or had, tuberculosis. I guess that explains why he's been gone so long, huh?"

Julius skimmed through the letter again, "I don't know," he chewed his lip thoughtfully. "This is still strange. Sure, someone with TB would need to take frequent visits to the doctor, but why always at night, and why does he have to stay out so late? And what's up with this right here? 'You are the strongest *human being* I have ever come across in my time on this earth'. Who talks like that?"

Kingston stood from the sofa and shrugged, "I don't know, man, but while you over analyze that love letter, I'm going to get some sleep. We've got an early morning tomorrow."

CHAPTER TWENTY

Always Remember to Love Thy Lover

Hamilton was so excited to see Demiesius already, he was having a terrible time keeping still. The castle had been completely empty when he'd arrived, and the longer amount of time he spent alone, the more insane he was sure he'd go.

It was nearly eleven o'clock at night, but the previous gleeful adrenaline was doing a good job at keeping Hamilton active. He'd poked through Demiesius' library for a while, peeking inside numerous ancient books, most he couldn't understand for their foreign language, but others that were in English gave him much more insight on the immortal world as a whole.

Growing up, of course he'd been taught from the very first day of training that vampires were never a creature one could trust. Now, Hamilton was thankful he'd been able to see the side of the immortal world that many slayers were unfamiliar with. He didn't blame his fellow slayers for thinking poorly of vampires, because once upon a time, he'd been the same. With Demiesius in his life now, Hamilton was able to see just what vampires were truly about. Level-headed and respectable immortals cared about order in their society, and flow amongst their people as they lived secretly beside humans. Given a chance to see through Demiesius' eyes, Hamilton was able to understand that most vampires respected human lives and wanted to make sure their people did not take advantage of the strength that came with being an immortal.

Informed even more by the books in Demiesius' archive, he'd learned a great deal about the struggles that'd erupted to maintain structure in their civilization. For vampires, it was always good to remember your roots, understand the importance of keeping their people in the dark, but most of all, to never forget the significance of rules placed down by the elders. Without order, everything would fall apart.

Reading through a passage in a book describing the mentality of a vampire, Hamilton slammed the crinkly book closed when he heard a noise coming from the front of the castle. Setting it on the shelf, the slayer darted out into the corridor. He'd removed his coat and platforms since he'd been alone and left them splayed across the library as he hurried away. When he came into the entrance hall, his face brightened the moment he met the dark eyes of the man he loved with all his heart.

Demiesius was dressed in an all-black outfit, his stream of midnight tresses styled down his broad shoulders, handsome just as any other night when Hamilton looked him over. Before the elder could ask about his condition, Hamilton quickly closed the distance between them, throwing himself into Demiesius' arms.

"It's gone," he said, pushing himself further into the receiving embrace. "I'm not sick anymore."

Demiesius didn't say a word yet, waiting a moment as if to make sure it wasn't a dream, and that Hamilton was truly here in his arms to deliver such good news.

"No more worry, no more needles," Hamilton said, looking up into the relieved eyes that had been watching over him for years. "Thank you for making me do this, for not letting my resistance to seeing a doctor get in the way of my health. I know if it wasn't for you, I wouldn't be standing here right now—safe here in your arms."

"And these arms will always be here for you," Demiesius declared, every ounce of truth in his voice heard effortlessly with each word.

Hamilton kissed the elder, pressing their lips together in an urge he couldn't fight. Clinging to Demiesius for dear life, the slayer felt the burst of hunger in him grow each time his tongue met the satisfying savor of his lover. Yet, unlike before, Hamilton didn't try to stop it or call his needy actions off.

"I've waited so long," he said, lips moist and pink as he uttered softly against Demiesius. "It feels like forever since I have wanted to give myself to you. I can't fight it anymore. Please..." He looked up into indulgent eyes. "Please?"

Demiesius could have sworn he felt his body temperature rise at the pleading request. The anxious yearning in the blue eyes staring up at him filled his own desire to its peak. Even though he'd been able to control his passionate longing to take things further with Hamilton, Demiesius also wanted just a little something more to their relationship, and it seemed the slayer was finally ready for something like intimacy.

Feeling as their mutual hunger clashed in this quick silence that crept between them, the elder didn't waste a moment and gathered Hamilton in his arms, the slayer wrapping his legs around Demiesius' waist as he was carried upstairs.

Hamilton couldn't believe he was about to do this, but certainly not because he was having second thoughts. Stopping this for even a second was the furthest thing from his mind right now.

As possibly shameful as it may sound, ever since meeting Demiesius Titus as the ominous and benevolent immortal he'd been back in the alley they first encountered one another, this was a moment Hamilton had imagined over and over. He never wanted to speak of it aloud, ponder too long on it, but to feel the elder in such a wonderful and intimate manner, the anticipation for it was eating away at him.

When they made it up to the bedroom, the blonde man unwrapped himself from around Demiesius, and when his feet touched the floor, he had to catch his breath. Their lips had been locked together the entire journey upstairs that he'd nearly become exhausted.

With his hands touching Demiesius' chest, Hamilton's alluring eyes looked up into the dark pair staring down at him. He brought himself to the tips of his toes, his gaze going dark once more when their lips pressed softly together this time. It was gentler than the ones they shared from the first floor, and the moment Hamilton felt Demiesius' fingers traced into his hair, pushing strays behind his ear, and a confession he was more than sure the elder already knew very well left his mouth.

"I love you," he whispered sweetly, "I love you more than —

more than life, more than the earth, the stars and the heavens...more than everything, Demi."

Demi...

The elder blinked and smiled at the name. "I know, my love," he brought his soft hands to Hamilton's beautiful face, able to see as a shimmer of love-struck tears trembled in the other man's gaze. "How gracious the world must be to bring you into my life — a warmth, a beauty to cherish as I do. If not in the sky, the sun now shines in my heart whenever I look upon you, Hamilton."

Having to hold his breath for an instant to keep himself from crying, Hamilton stepped away from the elder, grabbing the bottom of his cropped shirt, and he lifted the soft garment up and over his head. When it hit the floor near his feet, Hamilton couldn't stop the flush of red from warming his cheeks. It wasn't like Demiesius hadn't already seen him in revealing attire or without a shirt at all. He wasn't embarrassed by the dozens upon dozens of scars on his chest, arms, and nearly everywhere else on his body besides his face and neck, but the closer he got to lying in the bed behind him with this person he previously only ever fantasized about making love with...he couldn't stop his heart from pounding.

Following his shirt, Hamilton unhitched the buttons and zipper of his jeans and let them fall, and stepped out of his underwear next. In what felt like a second, Hamilton was completely naked, bared to this man who was his world as nothing more than his gifted necklaces lay against his chest.

After so long, finally, every piece of his flesh and blemish on his being was revealed, and Demiesius' careful eyes burned such a marvelous image into his mind.

Hamilton truly was a beauty in his own right—in his own league.

Feeling like his entire body was blushing, Hamilton took the elder's hands and placed them at his hips. "I am yours," he announced, "Please, take me, Demi."

When the plea entered his listening ears, Demiesius hugged his arms around Hamilton's slim form and lifted him once more. He moved closer to the foot of the bed and lowered them down into it.

Pressing his lips against Hamilton's neck, Demiesius' instincts were elevated when he picked up on the hot and anxious blood rushing beneath his lover's skin. Merely kissing the sensitive spot just below the slayer's ear, Demiesius trekked his lips all along Hamilton's jawline before pecking his lips and sitting back on his knees.

The elder vampire then began to undress as well, unbuttoning his shirt, and he allowed it to fall off the side of the bed. Before he could go for his trousers himself, he looked down when he felt a tugging at the front of his belt.

Hamilton pulled the leather from the loops and tossed it, undoing the zipper and latches keeping Demiesius' bottoms closed. Hamilton then tucked his hand inside, his fingers brushing up against an impressive length, and when he dug the elder's cock from his trousers, his own heart thumped harder, and his mouth began to water at the feature. Hamilton dragged his fist along the hardening shaft, truly unsure how to initiate this, but he wanted it more than anything.

"Hamilton," Demiesius said, stimulated by the hand stroking his fullness, "You don't have to do that."

Not responding, Hamilton pushed the elder to sit and finished working him out of his trousers, and then he laid down between the vampire's long and lean legs. Continuing to pump his fist along the warmth in his grasp, Hamilton licked his lips and kissed at the base. He then brought his tongue into play with his fist, licking up toward the unsheathed head of Demiesius' cock. It was such a striking and sublime feature, and when a working of precum began to rise from the elder, Hamilton finally brought his mouth down around the head.

He couldn't possibly fit it all in his mouth, he knew that, but still he tried to deliver whatever pleasure he could with such a task. He sucked Demiesius' cock and used his fist to continue what pleasure he assumed his mouth alone might be lacking.

The elder let out a mild gruff, "Hamilton, come onto your knees."

Doing so as he sucked, Hamilton's bare bottom was perched into the air, a severe dip in his back. The elder sucked his fingers before reaching over his lover and touched him, gliding his gentle digits down the center of Hamilton's ass. His lover flinched as fingers caressed his tight hole before grabbing a hand into his firm cheek.

Turned on by the simple touch, Hamilton took his mouth away and released a moan. Hurriedly, he closed his mouth around Demiesius' cock again. The more his hole was given such attention, the harder it was becoming to focus on anything else. The pressure of fingers wanting to enter him felt too good to not pay any mind to.

Bringing his mouth away, a string of precum broke from the tip of his tongue. On his hands and knees in front of Demiesius, he begged when he said, "I want more. Touch me more, please."

Staring at the redness of Hamilton's once purely pink lips,

Demiesius nodded, and when Hamilton turned around before him with his bottom in the air, he relished the sound of such arousing whines while Hamilton's hole was merely caressed.

The moment the elder vampire stole the mild touches of his fingers, and brought his mouth into play, Hamilton sucked in a breath of air and cupped a hand over his gasps. The side of his face was already pressed to the bed, but the second he felt Demiesius' tongue enter him, his entire body shivered, and his eyes nearly rolled to the back of his head.

"Oh, god," Hamilton moaned, his voice sharp, and he flinched even harder when the elder then reached around to stroke him at the same time.

With so much pleasure being administered to him, Hamilton just knew he would cum if Demiesius kept it up, and he didn't want to cum without finally knowing the feeling of his lover deep inside him.

"Demi, wait," Hamilton said reluctantly.

When the elder vampire backed off from what seemed like a meal to him, he watched as Hamilton turned over in front of him again and laid down with his legs splayed. "I want you," he settled his breathing. "Inside me."

Hot all over for this man he loved, Demiesius brought himself between Hamilton's trim legs, and before going forward with anything, he said, "I know you have wanted this—just as much as I have wanted to share this moment with you. Yet, I want you to know there may be discomfort, and I apologize for it, my love."

Touching gingerly along Demiesius' sharp jawline, Hamilton nodded in understanding, "Alright, it's alright."

Feeling a bit stressed at the idea of causing any sort of pain that would afflict Hamilton, Demiesius rose from the bed and grabbed something from his personal bathroom area. It was a small container of what looked like ointment, but Hamilton was too anxiously excited to pay much attention. The elder coated a bit of the translucent gloss all over his inspiring cock, and then when his fingers were coated lightly as well, he massaged a sensual touch to his lover's entry.

Hamilton bit back on his lip at the mind-bending deep touch he craved. He'd never felt anything like this before, this heat, the flashes that burned into him, especially when the elder seemed to find the point of pleasure hidden away inside him. Such a placement of talented fingers only caused the call of Hamilton's voice to reach out even more.

When Demiesius slipped his fingers from within the eager man, he was between his lover's legs once again, and the elder said, "I'm sorry."

"It's alright," Hamilton kissed his lover's cheeks and face all over. "It's alright, Demi. Now, please, fuck me."

Overawed from the command spoken to him, Demiesius' sturdy body experienced a wave of hotness so tantalizing, he almost couldn't believe what he was feeling. In this moment, all the pent-up sexually fevered tensions that'd lived between him and Hamilton were finally coming into fulfillment, and the longer he looked upon this beautifully angelic man before him, the worse such burning passions grew.

This night, Demiesius thought, it was more than perfect.

Hoping the moment of preparation had been enough to ensure not as much discomfort would come to Hamilton as their intimacy neared, Demiesius aligned his throbbing cock with Hamilton's hole and pushed his way inside. He hated the winces he felt as his fullness stretched the slayer, but with each wince and groan, Hamilton didn't want it to stop.

After his entirety was inside the tightness of the entry, several minutes passed before any movement could be made without causing a sting of agony, and the second Demiesius was allowed to turn his hips and stroke his cock in and out of Hamilton, the purely pleasure-filled moans and calls of his ancient name were what echoed out around him. Everything just felt so right, so good as their love went on, and the deeper he fucked, the more he could feel his hunger and greed over this loving and precious man grow.

As he turned his hips, Demiesius released a famished growl that resounded gruffly at the back of his throat, like it was filled with the yearning for blood to spill into his mouth.

Hamilton met Demiesius' eyes after hearing it, immediately connecting the sound to a vampire whose one desire was to feed on a fresh source. The elder's usually coal-black eyes now held a mixture of crimson red. His fangs were long, narrow, and sharp like the fangs of a venomous serpent. A nervous sweat should have trickled down Hamilton's forehead, but he held too much trust in Demiesius to think for even a second that the vampire would harm him. Instead of backing away like a normal human would, Hamilton kissed Demiesius, assurance flooding into him when the elder kissed him back. His fangs hadn't gone down, but they wouldn't be a nuisance.

Dragging his tongue along the white curve of Demiesius' fangs, Hamilton felt a fire grow in him, the one spot of bliss hidden inside him struck with each thrust that progressed into him. He squeezed his eyes shut as he yelped. "Don't stop," he moaned lowly. "It feels so good. You feel so — so fucking good."

Coming onto his knees as his cock remained inserted into the heat clenched around him, Demiesius took Hamilton into his arms, allowing the beauty he cherished to sit atop his fixed length.

With a gasp, the slayer tossed his head back, fair hair shaking out of his face as he continued to ride blissfully and call out his pleasures. The volume of his praise certainly reached every far-off room the castle had to offer. He held onto the immortal's shoulders as he rode his tingling pleasures into oblivion. He couldn't have ever guessed how wonderful every bit of this would feel, especially since this was his very first time delving into any sort of sexual activity. And he loved it. Every drive, every burrow, and especially the added tingles that circulated through him when the elder licked and sucked his tender nipples while holding him close; all of it was so overwhelmingly magical.

To Demiesius, this overwhelming look upon his lover's face only cemented his possessive nature over the other man further into his heart. With greedy and watchful eyes taking in Hamilton's showcase, Demiesius bathed in their intensity, his own cock edging closer to his need to cum has he reached the sensitive point hidden deep inside.

"Oh, god," Hamilton's voice called out.

He took his lover's hands then, bringing them to grip firmly onto his perky ass. At the squeeze of Demiesius' covetous touch, the slayer opened his eyes, and the catches of his breath seemed like he was having trouble remembering how to breathe. He brought himself down into the vampire's arms then, the world slowing as the fullness of Demiesius' cock gratified every bit of need he'd been desperate for all this time. Hamilton felt like he was entering many different realms with each rough yet practiced upwards fuck, and he never wanted to be freed from this dizzying intimate moment.

Almost confused when the immortal withdrew himself, Hamilton nearly grew frantic upon the stoppage of their love-making. Before he could question it, Demiesius guided him onto his hands and knees, the dip in Hamilton's back displaying the dimples tucked finely on either side of his lower spine. The elder then aligned himself once more with the begging entry of his lover's being and granted himself renewed access.

With one hand holding Hamilton's waist, his other pushed his lengthy black hair from his eyes and began the rotation of his hips. Each time his cock was stroked by the caressing of Hamilton's body wrapped around him, Demiesius' hunger reached a new elevation he didn't think was possible, and the evoking gasps and hollers of this man he loved only made his taste buds more excited.

Demiesius leaned forward as he remained inserted, Hamilton sinking into the mattress as his legs spread a bit more, and he craned his neck to the side when the nose and mouth of the vampire pressed against him. Demiesius stroked his length into Hamilton as he inhaled the intoxicating aroma. The tense sexual heat mixed into it only made it that much more desirable. The vampire's mouth salivated for a taste of what blood rushed beneath his lover's skin. It was so potent. It called out to him. Demiesius' jaw twitched and his mouth fell open, hunger and greed guiding him as he prepared to clamp his fangs down.

"I love you," Hamilton confessed, oblivious to the danger lurking behind him as the immortal drove the desires he'd sought into him.

Demiesius turned his watering mouth away from the welcoming vision of Hamilton's neck. It took almost every bit of willpower in him to command his fangs away, but he was successful in doing so to his surprise.

"I love you, too," Demiesius managed to respond.

With his cock nearly ready to release the cum built up inside him, Demiesius turned Hamilton onto his back and embraced his trusting lover. As nails dug into his back, welted streaks ran down towards his ass as he fucked, but they quickly healed and disappeared a second later.

"Inside," Hamilton hissed, wrapping his arms around the top of the elder's shoulders. "Cum inside me. I want all of you."

Pumping into the slayer with what he had left, Demiesius let his mouth fall open as a river of cum spilled into the human clinging to him. The strong bursts ejecting from the vampire caused a shadow to travel across his mind, his body emptying all of what he could give into this man who was happy to be filled by him.

Hamilton's whole form trembled as Demiesius poured the river cum into him, all of his strength leaving his entire body when he came as well and his cum drained from him only to land about his scar-littered chest.

Once Demiesius pulled out of Hamilton after clarity returned to the room, it felt like he was still there. The elder laid down beside his mortal lover, a new feeling of life coming over him

When his nerves had stopped tingling and he could move again, Hamilton curled up into Demiesius' welcoming arms. He settled into the vampire's chest, relaxed even though a soreness could be felt prominently at his lower backside. "Thank you," Hamilton said. "I'm glad I waited so many years. I'm glad I was able to have this with you."

Able to still feel the shakiness in Hamilton's veins, Demiesius kissed the top of his hair, glad he hadn't slipped in the calls of his hunger during their tender moment. "Don't thank me for such a thing, my love. I, too, am glad we could share a moment like this. If ever there is anything at all your heart desires, you need only speak what you will have of me and I will give it all without fret." The elder then tipped Hamilton's chin so that their eyes would meet, placing a gentle kiss upon the flush lips before him. "No matter what it is, Hamilton, all you will ever have to do is speak what you will of me."

"If I..." Hamilton brought a hand to Demiesius' face, passing his thumb tenderly over his cheek, "If I asked you to love me as endlessly as you can, would you?"

Without letting a second go by, Demiesius nodded in response to the heartening question. "I have already told you my heart will always belong to you," he said. "If ever it proves possible to surpass forever, my love for you would exist there. I love you, Hamilton. Promise me you will never forget that."

"I promise."

CHAPTER TWENTY-ONE
Blessings in Broad Daylight

The next morning, Hamilton opened his eyes to the darkness of Demiesius' bedroom. All was quiet around him, save for the distant calls of early birds that thrived in the woodlands of the castle grounds. A cloud of exhaustion laid heavy upon his entire body, but along with the weariness was a hefty amount of tranquility. As he lay there beneath the warmth of the covers atop him, he blinked and raised a hand to rub the weariness from his eyes. He then looked off to his right and there rested the most handsomely etched image of the man whose everything graced his body just some hours ago.

It was a wonder to Hamilton how he could have ever happened upon such luck in meeting this person. After nearly thirty years, after never once crossing paths with someone who could compare, who could never make him feel the type of significance that coursed through him now...Hamilton wondered how he could have ever made it this far without him...without Demiesius Titus.

He couldn't imagine not knowing this man, and the thought in itself only managed to work a strange sorrow into him. Where would he be right now if not for this love that'd captured him so recklessly? Where would they both be if he'd assumed the elder was his enemy from the beginning—if he'd been rightly determined to view all immortals in the same light? Given the path the previous infection of tuberculosis would have led him down, it certainly could be said death would have claimed the slayer long ago, but if there hadn't been a sickness and Hamilton had come by the elder as he had in the beginning...

Would he still be dead?

For a moment, Hamilton wondered what more the elder could have seen in him. It was well-known Demiesius had clung to a distant affection even before their initial meeting. How deeply had the elder felt for the other man through the years they hadn't met face to face?

The thought of Demiesius admiring him from afar brought a smile to Hamilton's lips and he reached out for the sleeping visage facing his way. Was this truly luck? Was this fate? Surely those were two awfully different things, but still Hamilton saw himself as the luckiest man in the world to be exactly where he was. He couldn't imagine ever having to return to how life used to be before Demiesius happened upon him that night.

Maybe, Hamilton thought with a gentle laugh, he should thank Dominick for not being able to control his hunger back then.

If not for the greed that'd called to the blood child those

months ago, Hamilton would not have come face to face with the elder.

Running his thumb along the sharpness of Demiesius' jaw, the slayer watched him come awake only a second later, the dark pools of his eyes such a contrast to the light shade of his own. So much, these eyes had seen so much, took in every experience that'd ever crossed this vampire's path, and a portion of Hamilton was glad to have been able to capture such a being's attention. There were so many other things that should be occupying the elder's thoughts, and yet he'd allowed the existence of one Hamilton H. Hamilton to cause a separate path to form before him.

Strangely enough, a sense of pride entered the slayer at the realization that Demiesius had come to choose him out of a world of many, and although the elder had loved in the past—nearly three-hundred years had gone by until Demiesius found it in himself to love again.

Could there possibly be others out there in the world who deserved to stand beside, to lay beside Demiesius right now? Perhaps there were, but...

Hamilton shook the thought from his mind and moved into the hold of the immortal that welcomed him without fret.

Still bare from clothing, his body warmed as their figures embraced ever so securely. There were tingles that prompted the return of their silent desires, more so in Hamilton at the manner in which Demiesius brought the slayers naked form fully atop him, every bit of their bodies transferring what heat mingled together. Catering hands roamed tenderly about Hamilton's back and a kiss then touched at his flushed cheek. His smile only grew then as a chuckle left him, and the moment he turned his face into the crook of Demiesius' neck, the elder's chest shook in a light merriment as well.

"What humors you?" Demiesius asked.

Remaining in the elder's arms, Hamilton laid his head against Demiesius' shoulder, mindlessly coiling a lengthy lock of his lover's hair around his finger. "I wouldn't call it humor," he stated, "But to think I could have pictured myself content in this life without...this, without what we've built together...it's ridiculous. I'm more than sure you would have gone on in your everlasting life without me, but it's strange to know I truly wouldn't be here without you, Demi. You knew of my existence long before I stumbled across you, but even with your knowledge of me, I'd still be lost to this world if not for you. I would have let tuberculosis steal me away. My fear would have rendered me dead sooner or later, and yet your hold on me has kept me here. I don't think I'll ever know how to thank you properly for that."

Sensing the shift in Hamilton's being, Demiesius became more than aware of the tension that made itself comfortable in the slayer's chest. He embraced his lover with one arm as the other hand stroked a tenderness down Hamilton's back, feeling as he was clung to just a little tighter when he did so.

"Hamilton," the elder said then, nose touched against the pleasant scent of the other man's hair. "There are three simple words I could say to you that I hope will always display my feelings for you, and yet I know there is much more that can be said in regards to what has settled in my heart. Before the first time I bore witness to your mere existence at Public Headquarters, there were nights where I would reminisce, ponder...dwell on the past that I inevitably surpassed. Leonidas and Kai, I cannot say I will ever forget them, but even with the memories they instilled in me, somehow, I'd known—come to terms with the fact that they were not meant for me. Vengeance, pride, those were two lofty entities not even I could challenge back then, and when I looked upon you from afar, I wondered what entity I would be made to face if we ever became much more. Fear stayed my hand, kept such a distance between us. I didn't want to know what challenge could have laid itself before me..."

Demiesius smoothed his hand up Hamilton's back again, that sudden itch of fear trying to steal his attention. If anything, he could admit such a thing was still there in his mind, but he chose to push it down so that it would not pester him.

Thinking back, the elder envisioned what it'd been like several months ago, when he'd followed the pull of his blood child's aura only to find the slayer he'd admired at a distance now so...so close. A part of him had refused the meeting, and he would have let it stay that way, for him to have gathered what standing before Hamilton was like and embark on never allowing another moment as such to transpire. And yet, Demiesius smiled against the shadows of the bedroom, there he'd found himself again within Dominick's coven as the slayer stood before him. If something such as them was not supposed to happen, surely things would have ended where they did in the alley.

"I..." Demiesius started again, tracing his hand into the sunny tresses at his fingertips. "I could never deny you, Hamilton. Whether I tried to put a distance between you and I, still it seemed you would appear before me again and again until what has formed between us now was as binding as it turned out to be. And now, given all we've shared together: words, laughter, our promises and embrace—I can only call myself a fool for considering I would have been content without this...without us."

Smiling with nothing less than pure elation having made itself so at ease in his heart, Hamilton sat up as the immortal still lay beneath him, and he bit his lip before a mirthful laugh shook his lungs.

Demiesius touched his hands to the slayer's knees, gliding them up Hamilton's tight thighs as he gazed upon the other man's bare body. There truly were so many scars littered about his figure and Demiesius was sure each of them could shed light on the experiences Hamilton had lived through since he was a child. In a way, Demiesius almost wished he could make them all go away, so that not a single blemish would show to have ever touched Hamilton's flesh. But these scars that riddled his chest, arms and legs, they certainly shed additional light on who Hamilton was as a man, as a human being, and Demiesius had already come to appreciate that aspect of this person he not only loved but admired wholeheartedly.

You truly are the sun.

Demiesius couldn't help the selfless thought as it crossed his mind, as he was so very taken by the pinch of pink that flushed Hamilton's cheeks.

And I'll never look away from the emittance of your brilliant rays, no matter how blinding.

Demiesius sat up then and placed a kiss at the center of Hamilton's chest, hands resting at the other man's waist, and he said, "I've admitted all this to you and all you can do is laugh?"

Though his words were a jest, it didn't take long for Demiesius to notice the second chord that seemed to strike the slayer's heart. There was a glistening of tears that shone at Hamilton's waterline, and when the immortal reached up to wipe them away, the moment they caught against his lover's cheeks, Demiesius cupped the slayer's face and brought their lips together.

Against his own cheek, Demiesius could feel the wet touch of Hamilton's tears, but the heaviness of such woe vanished into a fine intensity when Hamilton let his tongue pass into the elder's mouth, and the heat conjoining their naked bodies erased any traces of sorrow.

No matter the possibilities that could have denied them this very moment, such a thing no longer required attention. They were as they'd come to be right here and now, and where they were, where they were going from here on was all that mattered in the end.

Stealing his mouth from the famished kiss, Hamilton pressed his forehead to the elder's and closed his eyes, never wanting to know what life could have been like without this perfect, most honorable and deserving man he'd so readily handed himself to.

"You are all I could have ever asked for," Hamilton confessed. "And I know the love I feel now will never fade. I swear to you here and now; my heart is and will always be yours, Demi. I have fallen so hard and so completely, and I promise with every ounce of strength in this body that I'll never—never let you go. You're..." Hamilton wiped the remainder of the tears upon his face away, his everything visible in the darkened room to the immortal before him. "You're stuck with me."

When a kiss was placed gently against his lips to solidify such an understanding, Hamilton worked himself up from the bed at last and turned on the lamp at the bedside. The soft glow of the yellowish bulb brought a golden hue to the room, and he looked around. Since he and Demiesius had showered before going to bed, he adorned the clothing he'd worn last night, acutely in tune with this new mild ache. There was no discomfort, but surely his time with Demiesius would be a reminder for a good time more.

"Hamilton," the elder said then, sitting up with the covers lazily draped over his groin, and when the slayer met his gaze, he held a hand out and closed a light grasp around the other man's fingers. "Will you do me a quick favor before you go?"

"Of course," he nodded, "What is it?"

Demiesius nodded to the dresser across from the bed then, to where the two lasting higanbana still thrived in the slender vase. "I don't quite know what's keeping those two from wilting," the elder said, "But I've made it a habit to maintain what care I've been able to give them. Would you mind changing out the water and then bringing them back up?"

Hamilton nodded with a smile.

Surely it couldn't quite be deciphered how the red and white spider lilies were able to last even a week after they'd initially been received, yet their grandeur had certainly enraptured Demiesius to the point of trying to prolong their luster. Hamilton could admit that he did see a sort of quality in them, and he was happy to do what he could as well to see how long the hauntingly stunning arrangement could last.

Leaving just one more kiss upon the elder's lips, Hamilton started for the dresser and carefully took the vase into his hands before turning off the bedside lamp again. "I'll be right back," he said, and then finally let himself out into the shadowy halls.

There was a pinch of sadness that attempted to creep its way into the slayer, but he tried to shake it off and continued down the winding halls until he was in the kitchen area on the first floor.

If he could stay at Demiesius' side without fret, he would gladly never leave the grounds of the castle ever again, but with what he still felt like remained his duty even though he was no longer counted as the sole instructor to Julius, Samuel and Kingston, he couldn't allow himself to step away fully just yet. The moment everything regarding their training and position in the Public was completed, Hamilton would pull away, but for now, he told himself he had to go.

Gingerly taking the two snipped flowers out of the slim vase, Hamilton poured the water into the sink and placed the spider lilies aside, making sure their wiry petals weren't disrupted too harshly.

After cleaning the vase and filling it adequately, he set it atop the counter and searched for a cloth. As he gently dried the long stems of the higanbana, he noticed Demiesius must have cut them once more. Although the ends still held to their length, they were now cut precisely at a forty-five-degree angle. From the brightness of the red and white petals, and how green the stems continued to be, whatever care given to them was obviously working.

If they could last just a bit longer...

Hamilton would hold them dear for what more days, what weeks he was given the chance to.

After settling them in again, Hamilton trekked back up to the elder's bedroom, and there Demiesius stood outside the open door. Having thrown on the pair of trousers he'd been wearing last night, he received the vase when it was handed over. "Thank you," he said, "Be safe when you go."

"I will," Hamilton nodded, unable to help the need for one

more kiss upon the immortal's lips. With a hand placed at the elder's chest, he smiled against the lips that received him, and added, "I love you."

Demiesius smiled in return. "And I love you," he avowed. "I'll see you tonight."

⸺ ◊◊◊ ⸺

Before heading to Gregor House, Hamilton made a quick stop at a place he never quite thought he'd visit so often. With it being 10:30am, he was surely running a bit late to the session that'd be taking place for the boys back at the House, but he'd wanted the opportunity to show a bit of respect for someone who'd not only been a significant part of his life, but his dearest friend since he was a small boy.

After collecting two bundles of white lilies and yellow roses from a floral shop, he found himself parked in front of a cemetery located a kilometer from Gregor. There was a chapel located on the grounds, and this place was a designated spot for all slayers once they inevitably left this world. Whether that be they were cut down in the line of duty or managed to last until age stole them from this plane, this was where Hamilton also expected to find himself someday.

With his plans to join Demiesius in his trek through time, Hamilton no longer saw this place in his future.

Parking along a distant curb, the slayer walked through the winding paths and many graves until reaching one located nearest to a towering oak. There was an intense chill in the air on this New Year's Day, and Hamilton was glad he hadn't forgotten his coat at the castle library, but he had to admit there was a sort of tranquility even in a place such as this. It was quiet, peaceful, and while many of the people buried here over time had experienced death in a most unfortunate manner—at least they could rest now.

Kneeling beside the grave before him, Hamilton placed the white lilies in the holster meant for flowers and brushed away a cluster of fallen leaves from atop the black stone etched with a familiar name.

<u>William Huntsman</u>
Brilliant mind, fierce warrior, and guiding light
1913 – 1958

Hamilton read over the name of his past instructor, the man he'd grown up so closely with, the man who'd been his very own guidance what felt like so long ago now. It would be a lie if he said he hadn't once looked upon the man as more of a father figure than anything else. After all, upon coming into the Public as he had, without a proper mother or father he could remember ever having, this man who'd poured all his attention and care into him had been all Hamilton knew as a parental figure.

Would you be disappointed in me now? Hamilton wondered the question to himself, not quite sure what the answer would truly be.

Back then, he'd never known the man named William Huntsman as a vengeful person, as someone who hated vampires with his entire being, but he'd done his duty to the Public without much question, and sculpted Hamilton in a manner that made sure he'd never die by the hands of one. Having been a point of status well before Hamilton, William had been that goal all slayers once aimed to reach, so what better person to take the man's place than the boy who'd followed so willfully in his footsteps?

With mounds of determination, Hamilton had braced himself when he was young to be able to someday stand alongside this man, and though he'd been gone from this world for thirteen years now, Hamilton hoped this person who'd pretty much raised him from birth would be proud enough of him in some sense. Whether that be for the skills he'd picked up through the years, the title he'd secured after William's passing, or just lasting for as long as he had thus far...

Hamilton hoped the respect would be able to show itself if they were standing face to face.

Closing his eyes, Hamilton lowered his head in respect before moving on, and soon he was kneeling before a site where the grass still hadn't fully grown back yet. In the flower holster at the top of the stone was a fresh bundle of red and white roses.

With the weeks that'd gone by since Teresa's senseless death, he'd only visited once given the agony that crept up on him at the reminder of her absence. It seemed she had a frequent visitor though, that fact told by how leaf free this patch was, and how fresh the flowers were that'd been left behind. Hamilton could only assume Christoph was the one who hadn't quite been able to tear himself from her, and the slayer appreciated the attention the immortal continued to show his friend.

Teresa had come to love Christoph. Hamilton was more than sure of that, and a twinge of ache only entered him further upon understanding how hard her loss must be treating Christoph. Hamilton had known her for years, had come to view her more as a sister than anything else, but the agony of loss affected the recipient differently based on the relationship. Hamilton and Christoph could understand one another based on their shared love for Teresa, but the levels at which their separate aches hit would always be different.

Kissing his fingertips, Hamilton placed them against the carving of Teresa's name before bringing his eyes to the morning sky, trying as he might to resist the burn of tears and what emotion caught in his throat.

"He is not alone," Hamilton seemed to promise. "Rest easy, rest well...my friend."

CHAPTER TWENTY-TWO

Traitors Come in All Shapes and Sizes

Year — 1972
Hamilton, age 31

The C.C. (Concord Coalition) was everything Hamilton had been informed it would be. Although he didn't fight the way he did when he'd been a mere vampire slayer, being an official member of the C.C. was still quite grueling. The nights were long, the missions were much more difficult to handle, but all in all, this line of work was something Hamilton enjoyed. When he'd been a simple slayer, his one goal was to head to a given location, kill the perpetrator and then call it a night.

There was more to the task than combat now, as the C.C. acted more like a crime investigation bureau. This required Hamilton to use his wits more than the handy skills he'd trained his whole life to obtain.

On the first night on the job, Hamilton had been introduced

to his C.C. partner, and he was lucky they'd been an immortal he was already comfortable with. Christoph Asker. Being one of the only vampires who was completely aware of the true hidden relationship between slayers and immortals, he'd practically begged Demiesius to be a part of the C.C. as well, wanting to use this position to prevent the vain killings of unsuspecting humans. In a sense, Hamilton got the feeling Christoph was doing this for Teresa.

With an entire year and eleven months passing by, Hamilton had gone out on a total of fifteen cases, able to solve each with the help of Christoph in a matter of a couple nights. The slayer noticed though, that ever since the elder meeting Demiesius had attended last New Year's Eve, whatever had been said, it'd been enough to lower the crime rate in the immortal world enormously.

But that didn't rule out the fact that Public slayers still needed to be called in to handle what jobs couldn't be detained.

Just like tonight.

It was a humid night in the middle of November and Julius, Kingston, and Samuel had their very first solo mission. After completing their blind training the year before, and showing impeccable improvement, the three slayers graduated into full-fledged vampire slayers earlier than expected.

Hamilton had proudly attended their ceremony at the Gathering of Councilors. The three boys were now seventeen years of age and stood tall as official Public slayers. Still quite nervous to send the boys out on their own, Hamilton accepted that they were now practically men in the eyes of the Public, so they could take care of themselves.

Together, the three boys were transported from Gregor to

their target location. It was a little past one o'clock in the morning on a Tuesday, leaving the city quiet as ever, the streets and alleyways were empty of nearly the entire human population of London.

Julius, Samuel and Kingston were standing outside the gates of an amusement park. The metal rides and rollercoasters loomed behind the closed entrance like metallic shadows. This place had become the number one suspected area to find the murderer.

After three individual back-to-back cases of finding the drained corpses of young boys in different areas of the park, this team of slayers had been called upon to finally find and stop the culprit.

"Our first mission," Kingston said, his American accent on edge. "Not going to lie, I'm a little nervous."

Grabbing hold of the bars to the gate, Julius pulled himself up, scaling the entrance. "Don't give me that scared bollocks," he said. "We trained too long for you to come out here and turn into a coward. Get your arse over the gate, and let's get this over with."

Samuel gave Kingston a shrug and scaled the gate next, meeting Julius on the other side.

They were all dressed accordingly for their mission, fitted in their slayer attire, weapons strapped to their boots and utility belts. With his most trusted tool ready to go in his hand, Samuel kept his voice down, and said, "Can we just get this over with?"

"Good idea," Julius huffed, and then he raised his voice, sending echoes through the entire amusement park. "Hey, vampire!" he shouted. "Come out and meet your permanent death."

When Kingston was beside him, Samuel almost wanted to

shove Julius for yelling. They were slayers. They were supposed to take things slow. What was the point of perfecting stealth if all Julius wanted to do was give away their position? "Shh," the Austrian boy hushed, "What the hell do you think you're doing?"

Glaring at the blonde, Julius rolled his eyes and started down the pathway leading further into the park. "I'm getting this over with, with or without the two of you."

"Hey," Kingston caught up to him, "What's your problem? For one, I figured you'd be excited to finally get your hands on another vampire. The last time we fought one was when we all started under Hamilton's instruction."

At the sound of their past instructor's name, Julius appeared to tense up in a manner that reminded Samuel of discomfort.

Over the past two years, Samuel had become very aware of the upset Julius now held for Hamilton. He didn't know why, as he and his fellow teammate barely spoke anymore, but if there was anything he could point out about Julius, it was that he no longer clung to the major respect he once had for their former instructor. He'd grown a bit afraid to ask why. Whatever it was, Samuel wondered if the boy's previous suspicions had been confirmed through something in particular.

Completely ignoring the red-haired American boy, Julius kept his eyes open, his instincts sharp just in case anything tried to jump out at them. When he moved by a game booth shielded by a garage door, Julius banged the butt of his stake against it, radiating a thunderous echo that traveled through the overwrought atmosphere.

"Come out already!" Julius hollered, "You coward fanged bastard!"

Waltzing further inside the mechanical park, the three slayers came to a stop at the Ferris wheel. An amused round of laughter rose from around them, but it didn't seem to be coming from one source.

During their information session, they'd been told there was only a single culprit to blame for the kills of those victims, but when the slayers looked all around to find the sources of the voices, they were faced with not one vampire, but four of them. Two immortal men with deep black eyes grinned down at them from atop a carousel, another sitting on the roof of an electric kiddie car, while a woman with a mane of ghostly white hair sat at the edge of a door on the ferris wheel. She appeared to be the ringleader by her posture, a smirk curved at her mouth as she looked each of them over.

"How funny," she said to the small group of slayers, "We've grown famished and the generous Public go and send us dinner."

Samuel tightened his grip on the stake in his fixed grasp, throat becoming a bit dry at the number of vampires surrounding them. This time they weren't evenly matched, but he seemed to be the only one worried about that fact. Keeping his eyes on the male vampire on the kiddie car to his right, Samuel just tried to make sure he was prepared for the impending fight about to take place.

"What I find most amusing," one of the vampires from the carousel said, "Is that they even have the audacity to send us mere children. I could bet my entire two hundred years that not one of you little boys have shagged a single time."

Kingston stepped forward, now standing shoulder to shoulder with Samuel, "I'll take you up on that bet."

"Ha, ha, ha!" the female vampire burst into laughter again. "Little humans are the greatest. Truthfully, I prefer my blood intake to range a bit younger in years, but you three pretty boys will do just fine if I have anything to—."

"WOULD YOU SHUT UP?!" Julius erupted in anger, sprinting towards the woman when she dropped down from the Ferris wheel. He raised the weapon, and she stepped away, clearly stunned by his adrenaline burst. "I didn't come here to chat, you bitch!"

Suddenly the brawl was on, Julius taking on the woman; Kingston and Samuel did their best to give one another a hand against three men with impeccable immortal capabilities. Each slayer gave it their all, Kingston landing the first kill when Samuel distracted one of their targets with a kick to his spine. The vampire's disintegrating death caught the attention of the three others, his scream like a mixture of wild animals as he crumbled from flesh and blood, to nothing but bone and dust.

Kingston and Samuel worked together against the two remaining opponents, and in no time, they were victorious, sweating from exhaustion as they caught their breath.

Switching their attention back to Julius when they were finished, the two stood confused when the young Englishman was clearly struggling to take down his opponent. Kingston and Samuel could see that his footing was off, his timing not the best, and his strikes, although fierce, had suddenly become rather sporadic and predictable.

This wasn't the Julius they were used to seeing over their time training. Julius was usually the best of them all in every classification that made up what slayer exercises were supposed to be. Tonight, it was obvious something was either bothering him so much that he couldn't fight to his best potential, or actual hand-to-hand combat with the enemy wasn't something he was particularly specialized in anymore.

Watching Julius, the two slayers were reminded of a brilliant mind that suddenly lost all knowledge when they were faced with an actual test.

Clear frustration flooded over Julius' face when the woman kicked solidly at his chest, sending him flying before regaining his previous stance. She chuckled, hands on her hips as she grew entertained by the boy's will. "You know," she said, "I thought my first encounter with the Public would be a lot more frightening. You...you're nothing but a show!"

Julius growled, "Fuck you!"

"You're a bit young for me, kid," she said. "I like my men nice and sexy, strong, unlike you."

Becoming more and more pissed off by the second, Julius charged for her without thought as to how he would take her down. The woman dodged his sloppy punches and grabbed his forearm, tossing him over her shoulder.

When Julius landed hard on his tailbone, Samuel gasped and hurried for his teammate, taking the woman down in just a few combative moves.

As she fell to pieces at Samuel's feet, he caught his breath and walked over to Julius, holding out his hand to help the tired boy stand.

Glaring up into his teammate's eyes, the dark-haired boy seemed to snarl at him, swatting Samuel's hand away with a rejecting smack. "What the hell did you do that for?!" Julius shouted, bringing himself up with the help of his own strength. "I had that bitch, Sam. I didn't need you to step in for me!"

Kingston rutted his brow, pulling his face mask down from over his mouth. "Why are you so angry?" he said. "Sam was just trying to help. I would have jumped in too if he hadn't."

Storming by the two boys, Julius started towards the entrance gate they'd come from several minutes ago. "I didn't need you guys to help me anyways. I could have taken them all on myself."

"Sure you could have..." Samuel huffed with obvious doubt.

Julius stopped where he was, his gray eyes like storm clouds rolling across the sky. "You want to say that to my face, Sam? I've trained harder than both of you combined, and you think you have the right to stand here and tell me you're better?"

The anger on the Englishman's face drove an uneasy feeling into Samuel. Over the numerous months he and Julius had lived and trained together, he'd become quite accustomed to the boy's ego, but to have it thrown at him...especially in a seemingly threatening manner...it made Samuel uncomfortable.

When Julius took a step towards him, the Austrian boy's eyes moved for the stake in his teammate's hand. He saw how the dark-haired boy's fist tightened around the weapon, the veins at the back of his hand throbbing above his knuckles.

"Look, Julius," Kingston stepped in front of the boy, "No one here is saying you're not a great fighter. I mean, I think it's safe to say you could definitely take Hamilton's place sooner or later. Right, Sam?"

Seeing as Kingston was just trying to get rid of the tension, Samuel used the opportunity to agree to alleviate the strain built between him and Julius. "Yeah," he said, "Kingston is right."

As if totally satisfied by the praise of his teammates, Julius turned and they all headed towards their ride a couple blocks away from the amusement park, keeping to the alleyways to make sure they didn't run into any late-night pedestrians.

During the ride to Gregor House, Samuel couldn't help but

truly wonder where on Earth Julius' frustrations originated from. Of course, the guy had always been competitive, but to take all his pent-up anger out on them, there had to be something serious behind why the boy was so angry.

Samuel wanted to ask, but...he was afraid of it being for a reason he didn't want to hear, or perhaps something that wasn't his fault. If there was one thing he knew though, it was that reassurance that Julius would one day surpass Hamilton was something that cooled his irritation.

Samuel couldn't tell if that was a good or bad thing.

⁕

Dressed in a baggy Tiffany blue sweater and a pair of black underwear, Hamilton sat on top of a dark mahogany desk, Demiesius sitting up in his imperial-like chair set between the slayer's fair open legs.

Demiesius had finished reading through a small stack of letters delivered to him at the beginning of the night, and the moment he'd placed the final one in a pile at the far end of the desk, he found himself greeted by the sustaining company of his lover's eager and lustful appetite.

Hamilton's cheeks blushed a coy dash of pink, lifting his feet to the armrests as he leaned on his palms.

Demiesius met the blue eyes looking down on him from his desk, Hamilton's sheer aroma never failing to seduce him. Letting his gaze sweep over the slayer's body, his eyes stopped when they reached the clear, untarnished skin of Hamilton's inner thighs.

Without speaking a word, he reached out, brushing the suppleness at his fingertips. He couldn't quite explain what it was, or why, but ever since, well, he couldn't quite recall when it'd started, but Demiesius had noticed Hamilton's exclusive scent altered over the course of several weeks. He smelled richer in a manner of speaking, sumptuous, or even...the only thing the elder could compare it to was that Hamilton had the radiant scent of an expectant woman, but of course the slayer wasn't with child. That was just the only way Demiesius could attempt to describe Hamilton's glowing fragrance.

It was beautiful.

Now that Demiesius put a dash of thought into it, that wasn't the only change that occurred in Hamilton during these recent months. His natural fragrance was a pleasant scent, but the elder had been able to hear an alteration in the slayer's heartbeat. He alone couldn't be sure if it was Hamilton's heart rate that picked up during their shared time together, but whatever it was, his usual rhythmic thump either became irregular whenever they were together, or it was like that all the time. Since Demiesius hadn't seen or smelled any sickly, life-threatening change in the slayer, he pushed the occurrence aside, ignoring it as nothing.

Unable to contain himself, the elder leaned in and pressed a kiss against the inner soft skin of Hamilton's thighs. This was already known by what could be every vampire within a two-hundred-kilometer radius of London, but Demiesius loved absolutely every piece of the slayer before him and would sacrifice anything in his power to assure the well-being of his lover.

Backing off a little, he looked upon the small red mark left behind by his kiss. He didn't look when Hamilton drove a mild hand through his hair, going back for another taste of the slayer's soft skin against his lips.

"I was thinking," Hamilton said, brushing lightly at the elder's tresses, "since I've been a leeway slayer for some time now, how would you feel if I moved out of Gregor at last?"

When Demiesius switched to his other thigh, Hamilton smiled, licking across his lips from the pleasant treatment.

"We've been talking about living together for the past couple of months," he went on, "So I thought you would be excited about it finally happening. And I think I've come to terms with leaving Gregor, especially now that Julius, Kingston and Samuel have all been inducted into the Public as certified slayers. I can leave that place knowing there's no unfinished business I'm abandoning. Living here with you would also help, since it's closer to Dominick's coven, so Christoph won't have to wait for me to travel anywhere when we have a case to take care of, and it'd be easier to contact me with anything."

The moment Demiesius stole his lips away and appeared to nearly return for another, Hamilton stopped the vampire with a gentle hand on his chin. "Demi, love," he laughed. "Are you listening to me?"

Finally drawing his attention away from the persuading skin of Hamilton's slight thighs, Demiesius reclined in his chair, circling his thumb around a mark he'd left behind. "You know I would much rather have you here with me than elsewhere. My home is your home."

"Silly of me to ask then, huh?" Hamilton said. "I'll speak with the Councilors to see if they will help cover my tracks. Since I have lived in Gregor my entire life, I want to make sure no one grows curious as to where I'm going. Leeway slayers don't quite exist in the Public; everyone has always called a Public House their home, so maybe the Councilors can provide a cover-up if students or the administrator at Gregor wonders where I've gone."

"That sounds promising," Demiesius said, and before he could add on to the subject, he paused when a familiar aura began to approach his castle. "It seems we have company."

When Hamilton raised a questioning brow, he didn't have to ask who it was when Dominick's voice could be heard calling for his father down the hall.

The blood child suddenly walked in on the couple in the office. He wore black trousers and a dark spring green shirt that only had three buttons pinning the garment closed from the bottom, the rest showing off his toned chest, hair down like a cascading waterfall of jet-black feathers. He wasn't alone. Christoph was standing beside him, a nervous tint in his eyes as he rubbed awkwardly behind his hairless head.

"Father," Dominick said, "Why have you not told me of the true relationship of vampire and slayer?"

At the question, Demiesius looked from his child to the vampire standing beside him. Christoph shrugged with an apologetic look on his face. "I apologize, Master. He was able to get the truth out of me."

The elder raised his hand as if saying it was all right, Hamilton coming off the desk to move out the way. "Do not feel betrayed, Dominick. Only the elders and a select few carry such knowledge."

"And Christoph," the blood child huffed. "Did you not trust me?"

Demiesius folded his hands in his lap, "Christoph only knows everything because you once appointed him to rarely leave my side. It is difficult to hide every detail of my actual duties as an elder when you commanded him to look after me. Besides, your role as a coven leader already comes with enough work. I can handle my business, while you deal with yours."

Hamilton folded his arms across his chest and started for the doorway of the office. "I'm going back to the House for now," he called to Demiesius from over his shoulder. "I just want to check in on how the boys fared with their first mission." Leaning across the archway for a moment, he blew a kiss to the elder vampire. "See you tomorrow night, love of my life."

Feeling restrained by the company in his office, Demiesius didn't get up to kiss the slayer goodbye, and instead nodded his farewell.

When Hamilton was gone from the doorway, Dominick shook his head. "Father, you are so in love it is kind of frightening."

Having overheard the little comment, Hamilton's cheeks blushed, and he hurried up to Demiesius' bedroom. With the amount of time he'd been spending with the vampire since their affair began, he'd been given permission to make himself a bit more comfortable in the castle, adding a touch of himself here and there about the massive home. Most of the inclusions resided in the elder's chamber.

When Hamilton turned into the room, he stood before a dresser drawer filled with several pairs of pants and undergarments. As he adorned a pair of fitting blue jeans that flared out at the bottom, he couldn't help smiling as he looked upon what sat atop the medium dresser.

Over the nearly two years since their official journey into love began, Hamilton had enjoyed getting Demiesius to show a side of himself no others were quite familiar with. With a small handheld camera, he'd taken so many pictures of them through the several months, and his absolute favorite had to be the one he'd taken as the elder carried him easily on his back as the camera was held at a high angle. While Demiesius surely looked a bit taken aback by the flash, the photo was something they'd agreed was worthy enough for a frame and for it to be displayed before the bed.

Another item featured in their bedroom that never failed to catch Hamilton's attention, was the two flowers once given to them by the coven leader Kanna from Japan. Since they'd been snipped and were something that should have wilted within the same month they'd been received, still — strangely enough — the individual red and white higanbana flowers still retained their flair after all this time. Hamilton and the elder hadn't been the kind of people too familiar with receiving such a gift as flowers but were positive the fact that the two hadn't wilted yet was an odd occurrence.

Even with the time that continued to pass, Hamilton loved the two flowers. In his heart, at least, he'd come to view the higanbana as a symbol of what he and Demiesius were to one another. Although death had gripped the elder so long ago, here they were starting this life together as two men who simply found a bit more purpose in their already occupied lives. And that purpose surely had to be finding one another.

Reaching a hand out towards the red spidery petals curving upwards to the ceiling, Hamilton withdrew his fingers before they could graze the thin streaks of red and shook his head. Whatever was keeping these two flowers alive long after they should have curled down and dried out, he didn't want to risk interrupting it.

Instead, he hurried into the closet to finish getting dressed.

＊＊＊

When another team of slayers and vampires had failed to stop a small string of murders taking place in central London, former students Samuel, Kingston and Julius were tasked with stopping the culprit. Watching them develop over time, Hamilton was confident they all had their own set of skills and were strong enough to handle this type of challenge, but as someone who cared about them, he only wanted to be certain the boys returned safe to Gregor without having to suffer from any obtained wounds. Especially Julius.

In the very beginning of their training days, Hamilton would have put all his money on Julius being the one to take his place as the best slayer of the Public, but as time went on, he'd begun to notice something missing from Julius as an up-close and personal fighter.

While Kingston and Samuel were well schooled in purging all thoughts, Hamilton learned over his time watching the boys that Julius was an immensely emotional guy. Some people would say drive was a good thing to have when faced with competition, but Hamilton believed his fellow Englishman cared too much about the competition to focus correctly. After discovering this, Hamilton was sure if Julius couldn't get rid of that mindset, Samuel or Kingston would be the ones to take his place as the face of the Slayer Public.

Arriving at Gregor House, Hamilton parked in his usual spot in the lot. With the transportation van already there, he guessed it was safe to assume the boys had returned by this hour. Reaching their room door in the student dormitory, he knocked and waited for someone to open it.

Samuel appeared on the other side when he peeked out looking half asleep. "Oh," he said, "Hamilton. Hi."

Letting himself in when the boy stepped aside, Hamilton smiled towards Kingston who was passed out and snoring on the couch. "You guys look exhausted. Where's Julius?"

"In the gym," Samuel said, dropping into a recliner. "He's upset so he wanted to let out some steam for a while."

"What happened?" Hamilton asked.

"He didn't fare too well against our opponents tonight. The vampire girl mocked his masculinity, so his ego is feeling a little bruised. If you ask me, I think he's overreacting. All that matters is that we're alive."

"Be careful," Kingston's groggy voice rose from the couch. "These walls have ears, Sam. Julius might lose his cool if he hears you talking about him like that, especially in front of Hamilton of all people."

Hamilton knitted his brow in confusion and took a seat on the cushion beside Kingston when the boy sat up. "What did you mean by that? Is there something wrong with Julius that I should know about?"

The two boys gave each other a look before Kingston jumped up to lock the door to the room. Samuel then said, "Yes, there is something you should probably know about Julius. He's been acting stranger than most nights lately. For the past couple of months, he's been keeping a close watch over you."

"Me?" Hamilton suddenly felt a cloud of dread drift over him. "W—Why?"

"We don't know," Kingston said. "He doesn't talk to us about it anymore. Before our blind training went into effect last year, Julius would sneak into your room while you were away and go through your things. He had no choice but to give up once the blind training began, but I think he's started it again. By the way he's been acting, I think it's safe to say he doesn't much like what he's been finding in your room."

Samuel quickly sat forward, "I told him he shouldn't go through your things, Hamilton, but he doesn't listen to a word I say. Julius doesn't like me very much, and I think it's because I personally like you, but apparently he sees something in you that he doesn't trust."

Hamilton could feel his palms begin to dampen. There was only one thing in his room that would point to the fact that he was in love with a vampire, someone who was supposed to be the mortal enemy of humans all across the world. In a trunk at the bottom of his closet, he'd stored all the letters Demiesius had written to him over the period they'd been together, and a large handful of them clearly point to the sender being an immortal. If Julius had gotten his hands on those, Hamilton knew he should be worried.

"You're not doing anything you'd regret, are you, Hamilton?" Kingston asked. He looked genuinely concerned.

"Not at all," Hamilton said, because of course he didn't see his love for Demiesius as anything other than a healthy relationship that made him happy. What kind of betrayal was there in falling in love with someone? "I think I should have a word with him."

"I don't think that's a good idea," Samuel said.

"Why not?"

Scratching nervously at the back of his neck, the Austrian boy shrugged. "I don't know. Julius in general just gives me a pretty bad feeling right now, so you being alone with him to talk this out doesn't sit well with me. Something in me tells me he'd try to hurt you."

When Hamilton opened his mouth to answer, he stopped when the knob to the door of the room began to jiggle, followed by a hard and demanding knock. "That's him," Samuel lowered his voice. "You should probably go now."

Kingston went ahead and unlocked the room door and in walked Julius. He was dripping wet with sweat, frustration in his eyes, and the instant they landed on his former instructor, he seemed to glare before marching towards the back hall. "I'm going to take a shower," was all he said.

Leaving the room after that, Hamilton concluded that Julius really was upset with him. He hurried to his own flat and un-latched the trunk in his closet. This was where he kept all his personal things such as old photos, his slayer tools, and every letter written to him by Demiesius. It was only now that he realized the letters were mixed up, no longer in order from first to last.

There was no doubt in his mind.

Someone knew he was in love with a vampire, and that person's name was Julius Dalton.

CHAPTER TWENTY-THREE

A Vampire's Sense of Smell Goes a Long Way

Hamilton hadn't been able to get much sleep the night before, and his discomfort about Julius knowing of his relationship with Demiesius was what kept him awake. Sat up in his own bed, he stared towards his closet, the trunk filled with all his private belongings like a mound of evidence on the floor. He couldn't believe after so long he'd been found out, and all because of the suspicions brought to a seventeen-year-old boy.

Had Hamilton really been so naive as to think no one would consider his usual absence to be strange? Was it all downhill from here? He could only hope not. The last thing he wanted was for his life with Demiesius to end...and so suddenly.

Nightfall was finally upon him after a long day of worry. He'd kept to himself most of the day, only coming out of his room for food, and strangely enough he'd had an even bigger appetite than the days before. At first, he'd simply thought it was just because of his need for comfort, and perhaps food was the only thing there for him, but after every rather heavy meal, he still found himself starving. Even now as he stood in his kitchen, he was craving another plate, but he'd managed to clear out his entire fridge.

As his hunger returned, Hamilton touched his lower stomach. When he could feel a mild curve in his figure, he lifted his shirt and looked down at his body. He was confused by the petite bump in his stomach. While he didn't work out as hard as he used to, he still couldn't really see why he'd be gaining weight, even if it was just a little bit. He liked to think he was still in pretty good shape, and whenever he and Demiesius made love, Hamilton never noticed the small change in his body, and since the elder never spoke up about it either, Hamilton just pushed it under the rug.

It was then when Hamilton squeezed his eyes shut, and he felt a bizarre knot form at his lower stomach again. This suddenly worried Hamilton greatly.

Ever since he'd been cured of tuberculosis, he'd taken Dr. Takahashi's word of advice to watch over his own body, making sure that nothing strange or any odd symptoms resurfaced, and although these occurrences didn't match the same ones that'd caused him trouble before, he still wanted to be sure everything was okay.

Having exchanged numbers with the doctor for if he ever needed anything, Hamilton dropped down onto the sofa in his living area. He used his landline to call the doctor, and luckily the man answered on the fourth ring. "Doctor Takahashi speaking, how may I help you?"

"Hello, it's me, Hamilton," the slayer replied. "I wanted to know if I could ask you a few questions if you're not too busy. I'm a little worried."

The doctor had just been in his office for a while reading through some information he'd received, and although he was in the middle of it, he dropped all his priorities to tend to whatever Hamilton needed. "Of course, what is it?"

Sitting back, Hamilton rested a hand at his lower stomach when a minimal pinch started again. "I'm not sure if it is anything at all, but I just wanted to check in with you to be certain I'm not sick in any way. For the past — um — I'm not quite sure how long exactly, but it just came to my attention today. I've been eating a lot more than I usually do and unconsciously gained a bit more weight. I wish I could tell when this started happening, but, like I said, I wasn't paying too much attention to it until now. Oh, and there's this strange pain I get in my lower stomach area. It doesn't hurt, it's just a discomfort that comes and goes."

"Off the bat," Dr. Takahashi chuckled, "Aside from the discomfort, your cravings sound more like a pregnancy, but we both know that sounds utterly ridiculous."

Hamilton laughed along on the other line, "Yeah, would you mind if I came by your clinic for an x-ray just to be extra sure, to see if there might be anything wrong?"

"I don't mind at all," he said, "I'll be here for the remainder of the night, so come by at whatever time is most appropriate for you."

"Thank you, Doctor. I really appreciate it."

After hanging up, Hamilton caught the time and then decided

to head out to see Demiesius. He threw on a pair of jeans that were a little tighter around the waist than normal, and then a black turtleneck with long-sleeves. When he had a trench coat tossed on over himself, he grabbed a small shoulder bag with his personal belongings and keys from the low table in front of his television.

As he left, he stopped there in front of the entry doors when he saw Julius leaving the Administration building. He appeared angrier than ever, and as he stormed away, Hamilton almost couldn't believe he witnessed the boy unstrap his stake holster from around him and throw it to the ground in fury. Julius kicked the weapon across the parking lot, pushing his black hair back as he held in a scream he so desperately wanted to let out.

Hamilton watched silently until Julius disappeared behind the building, headed back to his dorm, and not long after Samuel came out of the Administration building as well. The Austrian boy had his hands on his hips, shaking his head at the ground in what looked like disappointment, and then he picked up the holster from the ground.

Concerned about the situation, Hamilton called out for Samuel's attention, able to snag it before the boy left the scene. When he was standing before the young slayer, he said, "What was that all about?"

Samuel leaned lazily against the brick wall. "Julius is being discharged from the Public until further notice."

"What...?" Hamilton couldn't believe it. "Why on earth would they do that?"

"We were all called into the Gathering earlier in the evening," Samuel informed, "and Julius was being very disrespectful to the Councilors. They didn't want to put up with his attitude, so he's technically being suspended until they think he's ready to come back. For now, he's confined to the House. Even if Kingston and I get handed an assignment, we'll have to handle it without him. To be honest with you, Hamilton, I'm a little relieved."

"I understand why," Hamilton said. "With his anger lately, it's probably a good idea to keep him in a place where he can be watched." The moment another slight discomfort entered him, Hamilton placed a hand on Samuel's shoulder. "I'll get out of your way. I've got a late doctor's appointment to get to."

Samuel nodded. "I hope you're feeling alright."

When Hamilton dropped into his vehicle, he started the engine and let it warm up in the cold weather. As he sat there behind the steering wheel, he thought almost selfishly of Julius. The boy was a mere child in his eyes, seventeen, but Hamilton knew that even someone at that age could be dangerous. Ever since last night, he had grown frightened of being in the same place as Julius for too long. A part of him wondered why the young slayer hadn't spoken a word about his true findings regarding Demiesius, but the other was glad no one else knew. He knew there was nothing in the Public ruling that restricted slayers from entering a relationship with a vampire, but Hamilton also knew that it was more than likely an unspoken rule.

The things that could happen to him if his own Administration found out filled him with constant dread, dread that urged him to get as far from this place as fast as possible before someone else found out.

He'd be killed.

Hamilton knew without a second thought that he would be killed if others in the Public discovered his betrayal. They would call him a traitor, and although he was in love with Demiesius, would never regret falling for him as hard as he had, Hamilton knew that's exactly what he would be considered. A traitor to the Public. A traitor to mankind.

When the car was warmed up, Hamilton started away from Gregor House and towards Demiesius' castle. During the entire drive, he was overcome with anxiousness, but the moment he pulled up to the secluded beauty of a home, his nerves calmed, and he got out of the car.

He was starving when he entered the castle, stomach growling, and the first direction he went was for the kitchen. Surprisingly, Demiesius was already in there making himself something to drink. When the elder laid eyes on Hamilton, a slim smile curved at his lips. He was dressed in black bottoms and a black button down, hair streaming past his shoulders, and he looked just as handsome as always, taking Hamilton's breath away every time he looked over the one he loved. Demiesius was just so pleasing to look at, the slayer thought his overly attractiveness should be a crime.

"Do you mind if I raid your icebox?" Hamilton said with a chime in his voice. "I'm bloody famished."

Demiesius raised his glass of warm blood towards his refrigerator, "You ask as though most of what is inside isn't there for you."

With a joy in his craving, Hamilton pulled out a small tub of strawberries, some leftover stew from the dinner he'd had there the other day, and then after wondering if this would suffice, the slayer grabbed two cups of vanilla pudding from the side door and then closed it. When he turned around, Demiesius raised a curious brow at him.

"Don't say anything," Hamilton shrugged. "I'm hungry, so I'm going to eat however much I want."

Once Hamilton made himself comfortable at the island bar in the center of the kitchen, Demiesius sat down beside him at a vacant stool. "I wasn't going to say anything," he said. "I've only noticed your eating habits lately, but it doesn't bother me at all. It's nice to see this kitchen has become useful to someone after so long."

Jumping up quickly to reheat his stew on the stove top, Hamilton poured the delicious contents into a pot before letting it sit over the fire. He returned to his pudding and strawberries a second later, tossing a tangy fruit into his mouth and savored it. "You mean you wouldn't mind if I ate so much, I gained an impeccable amount of weight?" Hamilton asked after downing the fruit. "Because it's starting, and I'm not sure if I have the willpower to stop. I'm just always so hungry."

Swallowing his warm blood, Demiesius said, "You're still you, my love."

"God," Hamilton shook his head, "You always know how to word yourself." When he scooped a spoonful of vanilla pudding into his mouth, Hamilton looked over the elder's glass of blood when it was set down. The crimson liquid was thick, staining the inside, and when Hamilton sniffed the air, he swore he could smell the beverage, its aroma stronger than he ever remembered it being. Then again, it wasn't always that Demiesius had a drink in front of him.

Hamilton leaned forward a little, hovering his nose above the glass. When he inhaled, he couldn't believe how good it smelled. Quirking his brow up at Demiesius, he said, "Do you put sugar in here or something? It smells so sweet."

The elder thought it odd that Hamilton would be able to

pick up on the true spoor of blood, moreover; pick up on how vampires in general saw blood. To humans the essence of blood was supposed to smell more like iron or rust, nowhere near sugary and sweet. Thinking it odd, Demiesius placed the back of his hand against Hamilton's forehead, feeling for an excess of heat radiating from him, but nothing in the slayer spoke of sickness.

"Don't worry," Hamilton offered. "I'm going to see Dr. Takahashi later tonight. I don't want to think that I'm sick again, but I only wanted to have a little examination with him to be sure."

"Good," Demiesius nodded, glad the slayer was taking it into his own hands to make sure he was alright. "If you'd like, I can go with you. I'm already done with my appointments for the night."

Finishing up his pudding and the entire tub of strawberries, Hamilton smiled, "I would like that very much." He touched unconsciously at his lower stomach again when the discomfort returned for a quick second.

Hamilton watched Demiesius move about the kitchen when his stew was heated, the elder preparing it in a clean glass bowl before setting it in front of him. Thinking it a good a time as any, and since he didn't want to keep secrets, the slayer thought it appropriate to fill the elder in on everything about Julius from the night before.

"Demi," Hamilton said insecurely, "There's something you should know. Something in me wanted to keep him a secret from you, but I love you too much to lie to you about anything."

"What is it?" Demiesius asked, standing on the other side of the marble island. From the uncertainty in the slayer's eyes, he could already tell whatever it was...was something serious. "You know you can tell me anything."

"One of my students," Hamilton started, "Well, I guess he's now one of my former students, but either way...Demi...he knows about us. Not you in general, he doesn't know you're an elder or who you are or how you look, but he knows that I'm in love with a vampire."

Hamilton saw the elder's hands turn into fists atop the counter, clearly not liking the confession at all. "And how does he feel about this information?"

The slayer scooped a spoon of stew into his mouth after it cooled off, chewing it down before giving an answer to Demiesius' question. "He hasn't voiced his opinion to me, but I know for sure he is angry about it. Two of my other students said he just about hates me, and I already know he's gone through my room. He found all of the personal letters we wrote to one another in the beginning."

"He hasn't said anything to you? Done anything to threaten you?"

"No," Hamilton sighed. "But I'm not going to lie, it does make me uncomfortable knowing we're in the same place all the time. Now that he's been confined to the House until the Administration takes him off suspension, I can only imagine it's made him even angrier. If he informs anyone else about this...who knows how the rest of the House will react."

"You're not going back to that place," Demiesius declared. "I will speak with the Councilors to have you essentially transferred to another location, and then you will be able to come live here with me. I won't settle knowing you are in a place alongside an aggravated boy with an apparent temper."

Hamilton simply nodded. Not only did he fully agree with Demiesius, but he was growing more and more uncomfortable with Julius. If Samuel and Kingston couldn't tame the wrathful attitude corrupting their teammate, the slayer thought it safest to put some distance between them.

Through the time he'd remained at their side until the end of their training, tensions hadn't been noticed in the slightest, and Hamilton would have considered everything regarding Julius was fine, but he'd clearly been wrong as the boy had kept his frustrations to himself. Given that, although it might not solve the entire problem, at least he'd be able to sleep easier at night.

Besides, he and Demiesius were supposed to move in with each other sooner or later. Why not now?

When he was finished eating and it seemed like his hunger had been quenched for the time being, Hamilton and the elder prepared themselves for departure into the city. Since Dr. Takahashi's clinic wasn't a distance that would take hours, the two traveled by car, and entered London's city limits by a quarter to midnight. It was a Saturday, so the streets were still rather alive with people, music spewing from different buildings on various blocks with party goers.

They parked in a lot with just a few other cars and got out to enter the respective clinic. There was a front desk area, and as Demiesius stood beside the slayer, Hamilton waited patiently for the woman on the other side of the glass to finish up her call.

After bidding the person on the other line a goodnight, the brunette woman smiled up at the two guests. "How can I help you?" she asked.

"I'm here to see Dr. Takahashi," Hamilton said. "I called him earlier in the evening, and he told me to come by when I was ready."

The slayer furrowed his brow with a frown when he noticed

the woman's attention seemed to stray, instead focusing on Demiesius beside him. "E—Elder Demiesius?" she stuttered.

When he nodded, the woman looked towards Hamilton and then stood hastily, bowing her head in admiration. "Please, follow me," she said, gesturing to the door that led back into the clinic. "I will take you to his office."

Hamilton shrugged and entered the clinic area, the elder still beside him as they were led to the doctor's personal office. The brunette woman opened the door for them, and on the other side was Dr. Takahashi. He was seated at his desk with a mound of research papers and documents in front of him. It seemed he'd been reading up on quite a bit since the slayer's phone call.

"Good evening," the doctor smiled, standing quickly to greet Hamilton and his elder. "I didn't think both of you would come tonight, but the more the merrier. Now, Hamilton, there is absolutely nothing in my centuries of notes that can give me any insight on what may be happening with your body, but that's what x-rays are for, so I would like to get a shot of your entire ventral cavity to see if there is anything to worry about. Regarding your abundant food craving, it isn't hard for one to rule out a possible tapeworm that's found its way into your intestines, but since you've been gaining weight instead of losing it, I would say that is not quite the issue at hand. So, why don't we get a few pictures of you to be sure? Elder Demiesius, you can follow me to oversee the procedure as well."

In no time, Hamilton was in a room all by himself, dressed in nothing but a blue paper gown tied at the back, and a weighted apron draped over his shoulders to cover his thoracic and abdominal cavities. He'd been told to stand before the x-ray machine as a nurse, called upon by the doctor, took care of the quick procedure, telling him to stand completely still as the pictures were taken.

After hearing a few beeps, the nurse handed Hamilton back his clothes so he could get dressed, stepping out a moment later to head to another room where the pictures would be displayed.

Dressed now, the slayer left the room and went down to an examination area. Dr. Takahashi and Demiesius were already inside, two black and white identical images of his internal body held up against a light bolted to the wall. Hamilton hopped up onto the examination table as the doctor studied the pictures.

Dr. Takahashi scanned Hamilton's lungs, not finding any sign whatsoever of illness, and as he moved his eyes further down to the jumble of intestines under the diaphragm, he ruled out the possible tapeworm again when nothing came up strange. There was...something though...nothing that looked threatening in any way, but he noticed that Hamilton's intestines seemed repositioned. When his eyes traveled further down the image, his eyes nearly bugged from their sockets when he finally saw the cause of hunger, discomfort, and the internal shift of his inner organs.

"H—Hamilton," the doctor stuttered, stepping away from the x-rays. "You're...but...that can't be. It's impossible. Aren't you a — aren't you a biological man?"

"Of course," Hamilton said, almost offended, but his nervousness spiked from the doctor's incredulity. "What is it? What did you find? You're scaring me."

Nearing the image of the x-ray again, Dr. Takahashi took it down from the light, amazed by what he was looking at with his own two eyes. "Incredible," he said. "In all my years, I have never seen anything like this before. I've heard stories but—."

"Doctor," Demiesius asserted, "Elaborate at once. What did you find?"

Turning the picture towards the couple when Hamilton stood, Dr. Takahashi pointed to the lower portion of the slayer's stomach region, circling his finger around what looked like a gray oval-like shape. "You're pregnant."

Hamilton froze, his entire body going completely numb when he could perceive the formation of a tiny baby inside himself. Something in his mind wanted to rule the allegation false, but he was no doctor, and the longer he stared at the picture, the more he could see it clear as ever.

He wasn't eating more or feeling an odd sensation in his abdomen due to yet another unfortunate illness...

A dizziness swayed back and forth inside Hamilton's mind, and as Dr. Takahashi continued to speak, no words entered his mind fluently. The moment a weakness overcame his entire body, Hamilton stepped back, knocking up against Demiesius as his mind faded into unconsciousness.

He was pregnant?!

CHAPTER TWENTY-FOUR

To Endanger Another is to Endanger Oneself

12 weeks

That's how far along Hamilton was. It was said he barely showed because of how tight his abs initially were, and although none of this made any sense at all to the slayer, Demiesius was not too shaken to find out Hamilton was carrying his child. These occurrences, male pregnancies, it was anything but an impossible incidence, rather rarer than anything. During his thousands of years on this earth, nothing at all surprised Demiesius anymore, but not just on behalf of his open mind, but there were times during his past when he'd encountered men who had the internal capabilities of becoming pregnant just about the same way a woman could. Genetically speaking, something like this only ever occurred in one out of every one million men, and even still, those men had to of course partake in the necessary intercourse to allow it to happen.

At least now there was an explanation for Hamilton's glowing scent and the irregular heartbeat. As it turned out, the beat wasn't irregular at all. Over these last twelve weeks, Demiesius was just hearing the rhythm of his own child's heart along with the slayer's.

Demiesius and Hamilton had returned to the castle not long ago, the slayer not having spoken a word since he woke up from passing out at the clinic. During the entire ride, he hadn't stopped clutching his stomach. More than anything, he wanted to know what was going to happen now. Even though all of this was complete nonsense to him, after seeing the proper ultrasound of the actual baby growing in his...his womb...there was no doubt in Hamilton's mind that he was keeping it, but how the hell would his life from here on out unfold?

After tonight, he wouldn't be returning to Gregor House, and the decision about that had previously been formed from his fear of Julius, but now he couldn't go back because of this. No other human being would take it lightly to see a man walking around with a pregnant stomach. He couldn't leave this castle. At least not until the baby was out.

Or without Demiesius by his side.

Laying down in the elder's bedroom after being carried up to it, Hamilton couldn't find the willpower to move any more than necessary. Demiesius was seated beside him, brushing his fingers through Hamilton's hair in a manner that would soothe the shakiness inside him.

One thought that worried Demiesius as the silence filled the room, was how Hamilton would properly be able to care for himself while pregnant. Humans who carried the child of an immortal had to follow one specific guideline to ensure they and the baby lived to full term. They needed to consume at least one cup of blood a day to bring the needed nutrition to the baby over the months until birth. If food was scarce within the human, the baby would begin to take what it needed to survive, unconsciously killing the host until every bit of energy was handed over. And the elder didn't want Hamilton to have to resort to drinking from a source that was taboo to him. Besides, he was almost sure that was something his lover wouldn't want to do either.

Demiesius was just glad the slayer was eating more, unknowingly giving the baby a large portion of his intake each time he ate. So long as Hamilton kept these habits up, there would be no need for the baby to draw in further nutrition. From here on, he would make sure nothing went wrong. He'd be there for Hamilton just as he had since he'd first fallen for the slayer. To do anything in his power to guarantee Hamilton and his unborn child's safety, that's what would define him as the true father he needed to be.

"I'm so sorry," Hamilton finally spoke for the first time in nearly two hours. He felt terrible about the condition he was in right now.

Even though he wasn't aware of the fact that he could become pregnant, Hamilton had always insisted they make love without protection. There hadn't been any fears of anything being transmitted between them, or even the current situation they were in, so Hamilton had enjoyed the many intimate nights they'd shared, and the flow of the elder's essence whenever it passed into him on so many occasions. Yet, why had it taken so long for this to happen? Was the timing never right up until twelve weeks ago? Hamilton figured his body hadn't been in the right state until then. That was all he could make sense of about it.

"If I had known my body was like this," the slayer said, "I swear I would have told you the truth. I'm so sorry, Demi."

"Relax, my love," the elder turned a bit more on the side of the bed, cupping Hamilton's face tenderly. "Don't apologize to me for something you couldn't help." His hand moved down towards the slayer's stomach then. As his touch lay still upon Hamilton's bump, he could essentially feel the life of his own flesh and blood alive inside of the one he loved. "How do you feel about this?"

Placing his hands atop Demiesius', Hamilton shook his head, "I'm scared," he said, "but I can't truly explain what it is I'm scared about. There's something in me that, strangely enough, makes me a little excited on the other hand. I mean, I'm a pregnant man, and though that may not be something you're too unfamiliar with, I've spent my entire life thinking I was just like any other biological man in the world, but here I am with a baby inside me. I'm going to be a father, or would it be a mother? Demi, we're going to be parents." A laugh came to him out of nowhere as he brought himself upright, wrapping his arms around the top of the elder's shoulders to hold fast. "We're going to be a family!"

Closing his arms around Hamilton with a delicacy, controlling the strength of his embrace to the best he could, Demiesius breathed in the comforting scent that continued to emit from the slayer's body. It was divine and filled him with an intense boost of security. If he'd already been protective over Hamilton during their previous time together, one could only imagine how he'd be now that there were two lives he had to oversee, and he would certainly do any and every little thing in his power to make sure nothing ever happened to Hamilton and their child.

In Demiesius' human years, he'd been a family man, someone who'd lived to care for those who he loved and had a piece of his blood. His mother and father, siblings from back then, everyone from the young boy he'd taken under his wing, all those caring traits never washed off even after so many years, and they weren't about to go anywhere now. Hamilton, Dominick, and this unborn baby, they were family now, and he'd give anything to keep it that way.

Looking down into the vibrant eyes, Demiesius couldn't help himself when he kissed Hamilton. It was a gesture that the slayer felt like he should have been used to by now, but there was something different about the manner in which Demiesius kissed him this time.

It was softer, more profound than any other kiss he'd ever received from the elder, and it made his heart swell even bigger than before. When irrepressible tears began to tumble down his cheeks, the kiss was broken for a moment as Demiesius looked about the slayer's face. "What is the matter?" he asked, wiping them away with his thumbs.

Another laugh broke from Hamilton, "I'm not crying because I'm sad," he confessed. "I'm crying because I just have so many emotions running through me, I don't know what to do with them all. But I know I'm happy. So...maybe I'm crying tears of joy."

Demiesius smiled mutually, kissing the stream of tears away until he met Hamilton's lips once more. "I will continue to love you through this," he promised. "And I will love our son or daughter from this night on into our future. This family we've made has become my top priority, and it will stay that way forever. I love you, Hamilton. Thank you for giving me the one thing I've always wanted in my hundreds of years on this earth."

"Oh, Demi," Hamilton sighed, cuddling himself into the fold of his lover's arms, "Now you're thanking me for something you shouldn't."

"Why am I not surprised?" Dominick smirked his amusing crooked smile.

He was lounging on a divan in the parlor room of his coven manor, dressed in a dark gray satin shirt with black trousers, his hair tied up into an unkempt bun, strays of his raven hair falling into his forehead. Demiesius and Hamilton were seated beside one another on the Victorian sofa opposite Dominick. They'd come here together after a while to give the coven leader the news, and it was clear by the entertained leer on his face that, evidently, Dominick truly wasn't surprised by it.

"What do you mean by that?" Hamilton asked. He had a small bowl of kiwis and grapes in his hands, having asked for something, anything to eat when his appetite started to pick up again.

Dominick sat forward, looking from his father to Hamilton. "Not to be rude, but look at you. Have you seen yourself in the past thirty-one years? Sport a pair of tits, and you'd be a fit woman."

Hamilton threw a grape across the room, but the blood child dodged it like a bullet. "Just for the way I look, doesn't make it any more plausible for me to be able to carry a baby."

"Yeah, but it helps me make more sense of it. Anyway, you're not the first man I've ever seen with a baby bump. Granted, the last one I'd seen was back in my human days, and the second the mad village people discovered him, he was taken to burn at the stake. This is 1972, and you're going to be more involved with the immortal world than the human, so you don't have anything to worry about."

"Yay, me..." Hamilton joked.

"No, really, this is good for you," Dominick said. "Trust me, if you were out there in the human world, and some guy got you pregnant, you would likely be beaten to death by the time you reached your fourth month, if not by the bloke who stuck it to you in the first place. Everyone knows humans only destroy what they don't understand. You're lucky my father stuck you with his—."

"Dominick," Demiesius interrupted, "I believe that is quite enough."

"Apologies," the blood child snickered, "I got a little carried away. Please, forgive me. I should not say such things in front of the baby. By the way, father, what does this make me to the girl or boy? I am still...I am still your son, aren't I?"

"Of course, you are," the elder assured, picking up on the sudden insecurity inside his blood child. "You will always be my son, Dominick."

"So I'll be an elder brother? Exciting," Dominick stroked his chin, "I'll be able to teach them my ways."

Hamilton shook his head immediately. "If you mean you'll be teaching them manners, then I will gladly agree with you, but I've got an inkling feeling that's not what you mean."

"For the love of Lilith," Dominick scoffed. "Father, I hope you do inform Hamilton on the proper way to raise a human-vampire child, especially once that girl or boy hits puberty. Yes, you can raise them to be a nice, polite little dhampir, but the second those years come around where discipline is needed, you'll have to put on your strict mum jeans and control your child. If not, those Councilors you work for will call someone to put them down."

Hamilton swallowed a nervous lump in his throat. "Dominick, please don't say things like that."

"Well, hold on, you didn't let me finish. My father has some of the most influential blood in the world. His word is law, his blood makes him the one who sets them. I'm sure no slayer Councilor, or even vampire for that matter, would ever be stupid enough to lay a hand on someone who comes from my father's blood. Take me for instance. I am one of the top vampire arseholes in the entire immortal world. I am despised from all over because of the way I speak, but I've brought covens across the globe to their knees under my name. 1) because I have a way with words, 2) I fuck like a gladiator, and 3) my father's blood runs through my veins. Your child is safe from everything."

Hamilton then looked towards Demiesius who was beside him, picturing what it would be like in about four or five more months when all of them were an actual family. "The perks of being in love with an elder, I guess," he said.

When the slayer rose from the sofa to head to the kitchen, Demiesius remained behind with Dominick in the lounge. Ever since the blood child learned of Hamilton's expectancy, Demiesius had been able to feel the change in his son's mood. Though his face and words spoke of the usual arrogance that left his mouth, the elder knew his son all too well not to know he was feeling something totally different.

"What troubles you?" the elder asked.

Dominick looked up at the question, and then shook his head, rubbing at the back of his neck. "It's nothing. I'm just having one of my —."

"Nothing will change," Demiesius said, already knowing what it was his blood child was so reluctant to tell. "You are my son, Dominick. Although you may not be of my flesh, you are my blood, and not a single night will go by where that is not true. I elected you out of a world of millions to accompany me into the years for a reason. The second you opened your eyes to this life as an immortal, you became a part of me, a part of me that I will never see taken away. You are my son, Dominick. Never forget that, for I will never forsake you."

"Ugh," Dominick covered his face when his eyes began to well with sentimental tears of blood. He then stood from the divan and took to his knees before Demiesius. "Father," he said looking up with bloody, tear-filled eyes, "Are you happy? Hamilton makes you happy?"

"Yes, my son. He does."

Dominick rested his head down against his father's knees, allowing the individual streams of crimson to flow down his cheeks, each drop forming a tiny red puddle on the dark wooden floor. "I am glad he does," Dominick said. "It is nice for me to see you this way. I can't promise you I won't be jealous of your new child once they are born, but I will be sure to love them as if we were from the same flesh."

The elder placed a hand atop his son's head, having always known of the possessiveness Dominick carried for him. It was like that for all blood children raised correctly by their creator.

Blood children were probably one of the most dangerous kinds of vampires if their creator was ever threatened. These immortals would put everything they had into annihilating those who stood in their way, and once before, Dominick had lost himself in vengeful mindlessness, all because someone thought it humorous to joke about taking Demiesius' place as an elder. To put it simple, Dominick was as loyal as they came, and Demiesius would never take the esteem his first son held for granted. Besides, if Hamilton hadn't wound up pregnant during their life together, they would still form the same family bonds over time.

"I will always love you, my son."

On his way back from the kitchen with two jelly glazed biscuits, Hamilton stopped in the middle of the dim, antique corridor when he noticed Christoph at the other end. He was heading towards the curved stairwell, but before he could disappear, the slayer called out for him. The vampire gazed down the passageway, offering a nod as Hamilton neared him. "Hello, Chris, how are you?"

"I've been better," Christoph shrugged. "Did you need something?"

"Actually," Hamilton couldn't believe he hadn't thought about this earlier, "Yes, would you mind coming with me to the front room? I think there is something you, myself and Demiesius should talk about since you're my partner in the C.C."

Without question since the elder was here, Christoph followed Hamilton down the corridor. When they were on their way to the parlor, before they rounded into the room, the front double doors of the coven manor flung open, and in shuffled a drunken pack of vampires that'd just finished up an evening of partying in the city. A few were paired with humans, laughing and whispering sweet nothings, while those who hadn't a lover for the night lugged each other in, trying to remain focused during their intoxicated state. Hamilton recognized a couple of them from his previous visits, all but one that was new to the coven, a little wobbly on his feet when he locked eyes with Hamilton.

This vampire reeked of blood and alcohol, had curly dirty blonde hair to the nape of his neck, and he was dressed in black Gothic attire. With features pale as snow, the vampire let go of the friend he'd been supporting himself on, smiling eagerly as he neared the slayer.

"Oh, fuckin' hell, mate," the drunkard said, "You smell like a bloody buffet." He entered the slayer's personal space, causing him to drop his plate of biscuits when his arms were restrained from moving, and when Hamilton squirmed to push him off, he was able to shove the vampire away.

"Don't touch me," Hamilton said, knowing he shouldn't be fighting. "Just leave me alone, please."

The vampire ignored the command and pursued Hamilton further, not hearing the warning given to him by Christoph that this human in particular was one he shouldn't even think *once* about touching. Failing to kick the drunk immortal off him again, Hamilton gasped when a pair of long, dangerous white fangs hissed in his face.

"Demi!" He called out before Christoph could wrench the immortal away, and not a second later, Demiesius was standing in the hall with Dominick by his side.

In the blink of an eye, the drunk vampire was torn away from Hamilton, and slammed up against the opposite wall so hard that the foundation of the entire manor shook like a mild earthquake. Demiesius squeezed his sharp-nailed fist around the immortal's throat so tightly, so fiercely, the color of the blood beneath the other's face began to bring a bright pink hue to his complexion.

The vampire clawed mercilessly as everyone around the elder watched the consequences of touching Hamilton. His eyes bled, a course of crimson draining from his mouth, and then Demiesius' fingers finally dug completely into the vampire's neck with one squeeze, closing around his cervical vertebrae, ultimately snapping and decapitating the problematic immortal.

Blinded by the fury clouding his mind, Demiesius then pulled the remaining length of the vampire's spinal cord out through the blood gushing opening of the broken neck, and then dropped it, allowing the head to tumble to the floor along with the rest of the body.

In a second, the corpse disintegrated into bone and dust.

Hamilton, with his back against the wall, clung defensively around his stomach, trembling from having felt so helpless in those few seconds. When he looked up at Demiesius who was facing him now, he gazed up into pure black eyes, and for the first time in all the while Hamilton had known the elder, Demiesius had never looked more like a vampire than he did right now. His fangs were elongated, eyes like pools of endless black, and his cheekbones were sharper, ears pointed at the tips, and even the shape of his nose was slimmer, his hair like a canvas of the midnight sky passed his shoulders.

"Are you alright?" Demiesius asked, hands finding their way to the slayer's abdomen, able to feel the musical pulse of life growing in his lover.

"Y—Yes," Hamilton nodded, still rather shaken. His eyes drifted to the bloodbath on the floor, not able to feel any form of sympathy for the dead vampire. "I'm sorry I couldn't protect myself. I suddenly didn't know what to do."

Slowly, as if finding himself again, Demiesius' features began to transform back into their human state, his ears rounding off, the whites of his eyes came back, and his nose and fangs all returned to their original appearance. "Do not worry. I will protect you from all that I can. You and our child."

Hamilton nodded, trembling as he pushed himself into Demiesius' arms. "Take me home," he tried to stay calm. Stress wasn't good for his body. "Please, take me home, Demi."

At that, Demiesius guided Hamilton over the dusted corpse and down the corridor towards the front door. Dominick was still standing there at the entryway of the parlor, a little shocked at what he'd witnessed with his own eyes. It'd been a long time since he'd seen his father stain his own hands with blood, the blood of another vampire if anything. "I will discipline them," the blood child assured. "Goodbye, father."

In no time, they were back at the castle, and the longer Hamilton could smell the scent of that vampire's blood on Demiesius' hands, the hungrier and hungrier he got. He'd been told that blood was what the baby wanted, and he wanted to give it to the life in him so badly, but to drink the blood of a fellow human being, it didn't sit well with him.

They went up to the main bedroom together, and Demiesius began to undress from his blood-stained clothes. Hamilton sat up at the foot of the bed as the elder stepped naked into the bathroom for a shower, wanting to wash the night away under the heat of cleansing soap and water.

Hamilton tried his hardest to take his mind off his hunger, but even just the red blemishes on the clothes Demiesius had left on the floor were calling for him.

Not wanting to be tempted anymore, Hamilton slid off the bed and headed into the bathroom. It was humid and the mirrors were foggy, mist rising out of the Sierra glass block shower.

Hamilton could see the blurred silhouette of Demiesius on the other side, and when he was undressed, he entered the shower, hair beginning to frizz until he stepped below the water too. He hugged his arms around Demiesius' body from behind, warmed against his moist skin.

This night truly hadn't been something Hamilton would have ever considered living. For heaven's sake, there was a baby growing inside him, and though he might not understand how it was possible, just knowing he wasn't the only one for this to happen to put his mind at ease. Besides, maybe he could finally have what he wasn't able to have growing up, and now there was this man he loved deeply who would be a part of that.

A part of him.

Together, they would start a family.

CHAPTER TWENTY-FIVE
Talks Amongst the Expecting

16 weeks

Hamilton was standing in front of the full-length mirror inside Demiesius' closet. He wore an oversize lavender jumper he'd bought the day after moving in, and underneath was a pair of small shorts that had an elastic waistband that would hopefully go a long way.

Lifting the hem of the jumper, he eyed the bump in his stomach. It'd gotten bigger in these past four weeks, but there was not much of a significant change in size.

During his days spent alone, since Demiesius was confined away due to the sun during the day, Hamilton filled a large portion of his time reading up on things he should expect in these next months. A part of him wasn't sure if he could trust the guidelines of any human pregnancy book, but he wanted to believe that no matter if the baby inside was part vampire, it would grow just the same as one that wasn't.

According to the book he'd finished in a single day about fetal development, his baby should be about the size of an avocado. Hamilton turned to the side, wondering shortly what his life was going to be like once the baby was born. All his life, he'd kept this solitary mindset that he'd utilize all the time he had on this earth to fight, and now that everything had changed, he was curious to get a glimpse at his life maybe...two years from now.

Would he be here at home in this castle, cooking, cleaning, teaching, reading bedtime stories? Or would he go back to the C.C.? Would he continue his position in the maintenance of the slayer and vampire worlds?

For now, Hamilton wanted to focus on being healthy, and it was time to get something to eat before he collapsed.

Barefoot as he left the closet, Hamilton started out of the bedroom area. At the moment, Demiesius wasn't home, but the elder hadn't wanted to leave Hamilton alone in case anything happened.

As he descended the stairs and crossed the foyer, he poked his head into the library, and there Dominick von Kraige was seated in a large, leather armchair, an ancient book opened in his lap as he read the crinkling pages. He looked up at the slayer and sighed, closing the book, and then set it down on the table beside the chair.

"You must really tell my father to invest in a television or something," he groaned, sinking down into his seat. "I can't see how this place has not driven you mad. Despite what happened the last time you attended my coven, the least my father could allow is for you to stay there during the day, and then you can leave after he is done with his assemblies. All the vampires are asleep during the day, and the humans who stay there could keep you company. Aren't you bored?"

Hamilton entered the archive, taking a seat in an armchair beside Dominick. He lifted his feet up, criss crossing his legs as he folded the long droopy ends of his jumper's sleeves over his hands. "I haven't spent too much time alone these days. Since my stomach has not gotten suspiciously round by this time, I've gone out to the city to buy food and clothing."

"Understandable," Dominick said, "But, pretty soon, you'll require another human to fulfill such tasks for you. Sooner or later, you won't be able to go anywhere."

"Then that is something I will have to deal with," Hamilton shrugged, and then he smiled mischievously. "You'll just have to come over more often to give me company when Demi steps out."

"*Demi...*" Dominick shook his head, amused by the sound of the slayer's chosen moniker for his father. "What would vampire's think if they discovered the silly name you've given the most powerful immortal in the world?"

Hamilton smiled with a light round of laughter. Even though he and Dominick had gotten off to one of the worst starts imaginable, the slayer almost couldn't believe how much this vampire meant to him. Dominick was the blood child of the man he was madly in love with, Demiesius' child under the principles of immortal law, and though they'd nearly been at each other's throats in the past, Hamilton was glad they'd been able to build some sort of mutual understanding. And even with that, Hamilton still didn't know very much about this vampire. He knew Dominick was the leader of a coven, he knew Demiesius trusted him with anything, and he knew of the reason the elder brought him into immortal existence, but...who was Dominick von Kraige?

"I've got an idea," Hamilton said, "Since you're bored, why don't you and I play a game of questions."

Dominick draped an arm over the back of the chair, making himself comfortable, and asked, "What do you mean by questions?"

"If there's anything you want to know about me, you can ask whatever question, and I have to answer it no matter what it is. I get to do the same to you."

Rubbing at his chin as if he were in a large debate with himself, Dominick nodded, "I get to go first."

Excited to learn what he could about Dominick after so long, Hamilton situated himself. "Ask me anything."

The blood child took his time when deciding what to start the "game" off with. There were lots of things he didn't know about the slayer, so finding out where to begin had him in a bind. "Let's see. Where were you born?"

"Where was I born?" Hamilton tucked his hands under the miniature bump of his stomach. "I would like to think I was born here in London, but I honestly am not sure if that is true. You see, Dominick, I was technically an orphan when I was brought into the Public by my instructor. I didn't know who my mother and father were, and don't even know if I've got brothers or sisters out there. Sometimes I used to think that perhaps either my mother or father was involved with the Public, so my instructor, possibly being their friend, went ahead and took me in. But I'll never know if that has any truth behind it. For all I know, my name could have been something other than Hamilton Haven Hamilton before I was taken into the Public."

With a hum of thought, Hamilton asked, "What was your human life like?"

Dominick ran his fingers through his mane of midnight streaks, the waves of black falling gently into place at his shoulders. "My human life, eh? I guess that will always be an appropriate question. I was born in the Tudor period of England, raised until my tenth year; that is when my parents were taken by sickness. By that time, I had to provide for myself, and since I could not afford anything for myself, I began to roam the villages and different regions as a beggar. That was illegal for able-bodied people in my time. I will never forget being tied to that post in the middle of the city, whipped in front of everyone for being a hungry human being who wanted nothing but food and shelter. A job. Not long after, I was taken in by a Gentleman and his family. I worked their land as a laborer for little pay, and there I was taught to read and write. As I spent more and more time around that Gentleman, I learned what made me a peasant and what made them and the nobility rich bastards."

"Demi told me you wrote a speech," Hamilton interjected. "Do you still remember it?"

"No," Dominick shook his head. "When you become a blood child, for some reason, the night before and the night of always become a little hazy. It's a lot like drinking too much. You may recall bits and pieces of the night before, but all in all, it becomes one big blur. How was it being the greatest vampire slayer of all time?"

"What do you mean 'was'?" Hamilton joked. "I'm still the best."

"You know my father won't allow you to do anything after that baby is born, don't you? At least, not for a while. When I was raised, even when I finally got a hold of my hunger, he never let me leave his sight for longer than a couple minutes. This lasted for about five years. He is going to do everything in his power to make sure nothing happens to you two." Dominick huffed a laugh, "That kid is going to be miserable."

Hamilton didn't think Demiesius' protectiveness was a bother. Knowing there was always someone out there that wished the best for him, it was more reassuring than anything. "Did you ever want kids, Dominick?"

"No. Absolutely not. In my time, a child wasn't expected to live past the age of five, and even in that time, you would only be expected to live until about forty-five, but of course the rich were expected to live much longer. I wouldn't have wanted to bring a child into the world, and I didn't have a wife either, so...there's that."

"Dominick?" Hamilton said, his voice sounding more insecure than a second ago, this change in tone catching the blood child's full attention. When he looked up, Hamilton was fumbling with the long sleeves of his lavender jumper, turning them over each other until a loose knot formed at his fists. The neutral mood in the room switched suddenly, and Dominick could feel the atmosphere alter from quaint to tense in a matter of seconds. "Since I've been in this massive castle, spending a good amount of time alone, I've been doing some thinking and—."

"See, it's only been four weeks and you're already overthinking things."

"I have not, I'm just...worried."

"About what?"

It was no surprise that all of Hamilton was still relatively new to everything. Everything from his unbreakable love for Demiesius, to his pregnant condition, and his personal involvement in the immortal world. He knew there was a large chance, or reality more like, that he wasn't the only human being to fall in love with a vampire, to bear the child of a vampire, but all these new experiences were coming along so quickly, and he still didn't quite know how to process the situation he was in.

Carrying the child of a vampire, of an elder of all, was turning his life completely upside down. All he wanted was to do a good job, to be able to situate himself in this life, but he was unaware of just how hard it all might be further down the line when his baby was brought into the world.

"I don't want Demi to know just how frightened I am of our future," he finally said, "He constantly tells me not to worry about anything, but how can I not when just last year I thought of myself to be a fairly normal man? This baby that grows in me, I love them already, I do, but there's something in me that can't help but be afraid of them. How am I supposed to raise a human-vampire hybrid when I virtually know nothing about it?"

Dominick nodded in understanding. It couldn't be easy transitioning from someone who knows nothing, into someone who is now expected to handle said task they know nothing of.

"Hmm," Dominick thought for a moment, hoping to at least be able to calm Hamilton some. Odds are, if the slayer was opening up to him, he truly was desperate for some kind of comfort. "Let's see, you're worried about the child, yeah?"

Hamilton interlocked his fingers under the small bump of his stomach again, "I just don't want to mess up with them. I don't want to accidentally hurt them, or to have someone else hurt them."

"Well, I'm no expert at raising a dhampir, but that also doesn't mean that I'm clueless. I have been around for nearly five-hundred years." Dominick thought back through his long vampire life, recalling any information he'd been able to collect over time. "Alright, let me just give you a little advice for now. One thing that you will always be able to rely on with a dhampir is that there will always be a way to control them no matter how out of control they get. And trust me, Hamilton, they may lose themselves a lot as they grow. Then again, if you and my father ever happen to have a falling out with one another, you alone will not be able to control them if they do slip into hunger and madness somewhere down the line. There was a time, in the late 1620s I believe. It happened in a village in the middle of Romania. After the death of the father of this dhampir child, it pledged revenge against the people who'd done it. Once they'd been able to take that revenge, the boy became addicted to the taste of blood. Without his father to place him back in line, he needed to be put down by the elders."

"They killed him?" Hamilton asked.

"Yes."

Hamilton's heart jumped and he gasped. "Then why are you telling me this? I don't want to ever think about someone having to...kill my baby. Dominick, I'm—."

"Let me finish, Hamilton," the blood child started. "If the father of that dhampir had not been murdered, he would have easily been able to stop the madness of his son with a mere word. Children of their immortal parents cannot resist the command of their father, just as I do all mine tells me, not because I want to, but because it is inherently impossible for me to deny him. My father will keep your child safe from the world and themselves. You don't have anything to worry about." Dominick rose from his seat then, stretching a stiffness from his body before heading for the doorway. "Now, if you will excuse me, I'm starving."

Hamilton trekked to the kitchen with the blood child as well. He watched Dominick groan when taking a cold plastic pack of bagged blood from the icebox. "What's wrong?" Hamilton asked.

Dominick tossed the crimson sack on the kitchen counter, "That *thing* is the problem," he said. "I'm starving my arse off, and my father expects me to feed from that thing? Pardon me, but I like my blood nice and fresh, from a source I can sink my fangs into and feel their life in the palms of my hands." A conniving leer spread across Dominick's lips. The sharp tips of his fangs were visible now. "I love me a nice masochist. You should have seen the boy I had against my lips the other night. I wouldn't mind seeing him again."

Looking towards the bagged blood on the counter before him, Hamilton took it into his hands, the liquid inside moving along a lot like any other. Though the package had yet to be penetrated, the slayer could swear the scent of the contents inside found their way into his nostrils. His mouth began to water, his hearing going hazy as Dominick continued to speak to him. Eyes fixed on the sack in his hands, his own trembled, fingers going for the seal keeping the package closed. Hamilton then tore at the plastic and brought the opening to his mouth. The scent wafting into his sense of smell mixed his thoughts into one realm of focus, and all he could think about was getting this substance inside him.

Without further thought, Hamilton tipped the bag into his

mouth, the strong liquid pouring inside him as he swallowed large gulps of it. His eyes closed in relief as the blood filled his stomach. Savoring the sugary iron concoction, Hamilton's mind went blurry, the whites of his eyes darkening from the black ink-like color that overlapped on top of them, washing out the pure blue of his iris until they were spheres of coal.

Once the sack was emptied into his being, Hamilton dropped it to the tile of the kitchen floor, and his maw was stained with blood. When he opened his eyes, he stared hungrily with a gaze of black, Dominick standing beside Demiesius now, gawking in his direction with looks of disbelief on their faces.

"I was going to drink that, you know," Dominick said. "I just needed a couple seconds to complain about it first."

Losing stability, Hamilton took a step forward, almost collapsing to the hard floor before Demiesius appeared to catch him right away. The slayer could hear his name being called, repeated over and over for any kind of response, but his mind was far too flustered to manage a single word of his own.

A hand tapped lightly at his cheek, Demiesius trying to get his attention, but the only thing that entered Hamilton's mind was what frightened him the most.

The moment his mind settled around what he'd done, Hamilton pushed out of Demiesius' arms, a sharp gasp making his throat cold when recognition hit home.

He touched his mouth, lips and chin soaked in someone else's blood. Still able to taste the sweet flavor of the blood, Hamilton felt his stomach flip internally. His hands began to shake, and his eyes bugged, fear prickling his skin, and he stuttered. "I—I...did I just? Oh, my god. No, no, no!"

"Hamilton," Demiesius tried to settle him, "Calm yourself."

"No, no, no," the slayer panicked. "I just drank someone's —
I didn't mean to — I didn't want to! It was an accident!"

"Hamilton, it's alright."

"No, it's not!" he belted. "I'm a human being! I can't just — I
can't drink someone's blood. I'm not a — that's not for me. I'm
a human!"

"Yes, you are," Demiesius assured, "and what you have done
does not change that. You could have gone without this type of
nutrient, but it is also something your body craves on behalf of
the baby. This blood did not come from a victim of mine, if that
is also something you are worried about. This blood is donated
to me specially from those who are willing to give it. You have
done no harm."

Hamilton could feel his previous hunger go down rapidly, no
longer in the need to fill his stomach with any food he could
get his hands on, but the sweet tang of blood on his breath and
tongue rubbed him the wrong way.

Hugging his arms around himself, Hamilton shook his head,
"I don't want to do it again. Even though what you say is true,
I can't feed on the essence of another person. That is not in
my nature as someone who still lives. Please, don't let me do
something like that ever again."

───※───

Julius was sitting in the center of his bed, Hamilton's old trunk
of belongings opened before him. One by one he took each of the
personally customized pieces of weaponry from inside, placing
all of them on the mattress in front of his crossed legs.

From inside, he pulled out a stake crafted from wood and

silver, his previous instructor's name engraved into the fineness just above the grip. Beside that was a chain and sickle made from pure silver and aligned beside that were numerous daggers that varied in size, some ranging from the length of an index finger to the full-grown length of a forearm. Admiring the craftsmanship of the tools, Julius picked one of the medium daggers into his hand, turning the icy silver over in his grasp.

They all looked worn at the hilt and around the blade but were taken care of to an extent where not one of them was dull along the edge. Running his fingers up the sleek metallic surface, Julius closed his fist around the grip, holding onto it as though he were preparing to drive it into an opponent.

Inside the trunk remained the letters exchanged from Hamilton and Demiesius, the vampire whose name Julius still couldn't identify. Alone, he'd infiltrated the Slayer Public Headquarters, flipping through each immortal file he could get his hands on, but still he came up short as to who this link to corruption was. He wanted to know who Demiesius was, he wanted to know the vampire's face. On one hand, he was curious as to what type of vampire had the ability to lure in someone like Hamilton, but on the other, he wanted to know this Demiesius vampire's face due to Julius' desire to insert him into his...strategy.

Ever since he'd found out Hamilton's secret life outside the Public, Julius wanted to teach his own teacher a lesson he wouldn't soon forget. He believed vampires were not supposed to be treated like human beings. They were supposed to be treated like the nocturnal monsters they were. Vampires needed to be hunted down, expunged from this world in every way, and Hamilton seemed to have forgotten that unspoken rule. Julius wanted to drive it into him if it was the last thing he ever did.

As he sat, confined to Gregor House until told otherwise, Julius plotted, taking into deep consideration how he would make Hamilton pay for the sins he committed against the human race. Right now, it seemed he would have to do it on his own, turn his back on the man who'd inspired him to be the greatest vampire slayer of his generation, and it was beginning to look like this was going to be what tested his determination.

First, he had to get Hamilton alone. Second, he had to let Hamilton know why this lesson was important. Third, Julius needed to make sure Hamilton learned severely from the mistakes he'd made, and once he was sure of that, he wanted to be sure Hamilton never made them again.

Crazed and delusional in this world of his own, Julius Dalton was now the worst possible enemy Hamilton H. Hamilton could have ever made, and it was only a matter of time until he found out why.

CHAPTER TWENTY-SIX

Speak Now or Forever Hold Your Peace

24 weeks

Hamilton officially didn't fit any pairs of his old trousers, but he wasn't really complaining about it. It felt nice being able to walk around in nothing but t-shirts and underwear, especially since he had a valid excuse to. His bump no longer classified as a small, unnoticeable curve in his stomach. It stood out now and anyone in their right mind would be able to tell that he was in fact pregnant.

As the sun began to set below the horizon, he pondered on his busiest days before his life made this complete one-eighty. Back in his regular slayer days, Hamilton was always on his feet, out for hours on late nights, and working his hardest to stay in the fantastically athletic shape he'd previously been in. He remembered training to sleep a minimum of one hour to last several days, conserving his energy for moonlit activities, and spending many of his daylight hours in a gym.

Before Demiesius, before stepping into the immortal world as the human lover he was, Hamilton had barely taken the time to rest, and it was only now that he began to appreciate...being pregnant.

Downstairs with a stereo playing out this year's most popular songs, Hamilton was sitting on the floor before a sofa in the sitting room, and in front of him was a low glass table with a solo game of backgammon set up. He was relaxed and cozy in his briefs and a teal blue shirt that was two sizes too big, a long pair of black socks that cut off above his knees, and his long hair was jumbled up into a ponytail. This was probably the most hassle-free and comfortable he could ever remember being, and for once he appreciated the stillness of his surroundings.

Having grown up to be content in wild environments, Hamilton couldn't be happier as the lazy man he was allowed to be now.

Moving one of the dark brown backgammon chips, Hamilton turned the board around to the light tan pieces. During this game of strategy, the slayer took his time figuring out which chip to move next. With a hand placed underneath his stomach, he chewed his lip thoughtfully, and then gasped sharply when he felt something move inside him.

All thoughts on the solo game before him disappeared and he held his breath, the sound of the music playing out going mute. A couple seconds later, Hamilton gasped again when he felt a soft kick knock within his protruding stomach. He'd read that babies, particularly in women whose first time it was being pregnant, would experience the internal movement of a baby much later on in the months of their perinatal period, so being able to feel even the slightest effort of the baby inside him sent Hamilton into an excited frenzy.

Too eager to hold in his enthusiasm, Hamilton pushed himself up from the floor.

"Demi!" he shouted at the top of his lungs, rushing for the archway of the sitting room. "Demiesius!"

Before he could step foot out in the hallway, Hamilton stopped when he nearly ran into Demiesius' bare chest. The vampire's long black mane was a bit disheveled from his day of sleep, and he was dressed in just night trousers, his strongly built chest shirtless, and the look in his eyes was ready for anything. "Are you hurt?" he asked immediately.

The sun had yet to go down completely and the windows to the sitting room allowed the rays to invade his home, dull streaks of sunlight striking his slightly bronzed skin with its ethereal ability to slowly withdraw the immortal energy from within him.

Suddenly realizing this, Hamilton stepped back in horror, completely shocked to see Demiesius standing here before him with sunlight peeking onto his flesh. Yet, he did not burn.

With trembling hands, Hamilton reached out for Demiesius, mouth sitting open as he placed shaky fingers on the vampire's chest. Their gaze met then, and as if able to read the concern on the slayer's face, Demiesius reassured him by stepping back into the shadows of the hallway. "Don't worry yourself," he said, "Sunlight cannot kill me unless I am reckless. It merely drains my energy before shedding the remaining life from my body. I do not die immediately like ordinary vampires."

Still afraid of the sunlight touching Demiesius in any given manner, Hamilton neared the windows of the sitting room and closed the drapes hung over them. Once darkness returned to this small area of the castle, he breathed a sigh of relief when Demiesius stepped into his line of sight and no sunlight threatened his body. "Don't scare me like that," the slayer said.

"When I heard your scream, I could not stay hidden away. What were you afraid of?"

"I wasn't afraid of anything," Hamilton felt a smile touch his lips again. "I wanted to tell you that I felt the baby move."

"Did you?"

The excitement from before slowly returned and Hamilton neared Demiesius. He took the elder's hand in his own and placed it at the lower curve of his stomach. They waited a couple seconds, but nothing happened. Furrowing his brow in disappointment, the slayer wrinkled his nose, "Maybe he's shy."

"You know it's a boy?"

"Oh, no, I was just saying something. I don't want to call our baby an 'it' until they're born. Then again, I guess I can refer to them as they until we know for sure." Hamilton chuckled to himself, and he took the elder's hand to guide him into the darkened sitting room. "Come be with me," he said, sitting Demiesius down on the sofa and then came down on top of him, straddling his lover as he allowed his fingers to trace shy circles against Demiesius' toned chest. Without warning, he kissed the elder hotly, able to feel the light vibration of a chuckle against his lips when they went for his lover's neck. "Mmm, you smell different. Did you change your body wash?"

Demiesius' hands ventured to Hamilton's hips, caressing them softly as the slayer continued to kiss him. "No, I have not," he said. "Perhaps your sense of smell is being particular tonight."

The kisses pressed to the elder's neck continued, each peck slightly rougher than the one before, and Demiesius let it be. It'd been a while since the last time they were intimate with one another, so he took whatever time he was granted to appreciate the attention the slayer wanted to give him. They hadn't made love since Hamilton's pregnancy began to grant aches about his back two weeks ago, and although Demiesius was doing fine without the craving for sex, he could sense inside every kiss that it was something Hamilton missed.

Hamilton wanted to be touched, needed to be touched in any which way, so these moments where their bodies had even the slightest bit of contact was more of a necessity than anything.

When his kisses began to calm just a little, Hamilton leaned into Demiesius' embrace, keeping his arms around the elder's neck. To think he was carrying the child of one of the most powerful vampires in all of existence, a child that would ultimately be praised and respected by all immortals around the world, was amazingly unreal. He wondered if the vampires of the immortal world would ever truly come to like him. After all, he had once been an active slayer, and though he was a promised lover to their elder, he was certain there would always be those who disagreed with him as a man and as a vampire. Nothing could stop people from having opinions.

"Demi, what's it going to be like?" he said suddenly. "I know we cannot tell the future, but what will it be like to have a child both human and vampire? The way you and Dominick have spoken to me, one could assume that there have previously been hybrids in the world. As parents, is there anything we should expect? What have your past experiences with half-breed children been like?"

Demiesius' chest shook momentarily from a small chuckle, "They've never been too fond of being called 'half-breeds'," he said. "I can give you that much information. They prefer dhampir more than anything and being called hybrids makes them feel like something unnatural, so you might want to refrain from using those terms. But everything will be fine, Hamilton. You needn't worry yourself so much."

"You and Dominick keep saying that, but this is all still like entering a new world for me. I never once imagined getting married and having, well, adopting children. The closest I thought to becoming a parent was when my students were assigned to me two years ago. Dominick tells me always having you near will keep our child under control, tame out in the world, but...where do I fit into the equation?"

Hamilton sat up on Demiesius' lap and the elder met his eyes. "You may not think this now from all you've been told," the elder said, "but you have the most important role in our child's life. Dhampirs bond strongest with their mother, or in our case, the human whose womb they came from. In their first stages of growth, dhampirs are drawn to life, finding comfort near the warmth of a heart that beats. While human children bond with their mother more than their father through contact or breast feeding, dhampir infants would much rather remain close to the person who gave them life to begin with. By the time our son or daughter is one year old, they will associate you as being their everything. Without a human parent to connect with, the bond between myself and the child will never be as strong."

Comforted by the material, Hamilton hugged his bump, "How nice," he said. "The more I am told, the more I can hardly wait to be a dad. When I was growing up, it made no difference for me to have been raised without a mother or father, but I'm glad our baby won't have to live that way. They'll be able to grow up with the love of two parents willing to do anything to keep them safe. Right?"

Demiesius touched fondly down Hamilton's blushing cheek, "Right," he agreed.

Placing a hand on Demiesius' before it could drop from his face, Hamilton held it in his own and brought it to his lips. He caressed the elder's knuckles with a kiss and then pressed one to the back of his hand. "I feel blessed," he said. "To have been given all the things I could have never been able to ask for. Demi...can we...can we get married? But without a ceremony, without a big announcement with a large gathering for others. Can we get married, just you and me, here as we are now? I have been willing to be yours entirely, and to be able to carry your name alongside mine, it would fill me with so much joy. Can we?"

The elder's eyes moved from Hamilton to the necklace resting against the slayer's collar bones, the drop of his own blood still inside from the time he'd handed it over as a token of choice. "Of course, we can," he said. "Before we were expecting, I was going to ask you once you took the steps into becoming an immortal."

"That's in four years!"

"That is quite a bit of time away, isn't it?"

"I don't want to wait four years, Demi."

"Then we'll be married."

Hamilton's face brightened with a smile that resembled what Demiesius could only compare to the sun. "Tonight?" the slayer asked, "Right now?"

"Right now."

With that, Demiesius helped Hamilton from his lap, holding the man's hand in his own as he led the way further into the castle. The sun had finally set a couple minutes ago, leaving the entire interior dark as Hamilton began to turn on light after light. When they made it to the stairwell, the two climbed towards the third floor and into a room Hamilton had become familiar with. It was where Demiesius kept most of the ancient and expensive trinkets he'd come across during his long years as an immortal, presents given to him by historical figures, royals, and those who simply wished to gift him with something from their time.

The room was illuminated by light fixtures bordering the rounded off doorway, dark forest green drapes pulled shut over the windows, and the floor was of polished wood. There were shelves that held cherished books from the past and glass topped compartments housing pieces of jewelry with names and dates underneath each of them.

Demiesius released Hamilton's hand in the center of the room, going for one of the glass compartments and then opened it.

Standing just behind the elder, Hamilton watched as Demiesius chose wisely from his collection of rings, eyes stopping on a gold band with a red garnet ruby at the head, tiny shimmering diamonds encrusted around the wonderful jewel.

"This was personally given to me," Demiesius said, carefully taking the ring from the case, "by the Queen in 1955. She made me promise on that evening, if I were to ever give it to another, I would have to be steady and willing to give up anything and everything in this world for that one person." He then took Hamilton's hand once more, placing it face down in his palm. "I did not know it seventeen years ago, but I promised the

Queen that I would give this ring to you. From this night on," he continued, sliding the fitting gold onto Hamilton's finger, "I am yours in a manner I have never belonged to another. I will love you and protect you from all, return to you always, treasure each moment we have spent and each we will spend together in this long life. Never will I allow a single night to go by where I do not remind you of my feelings. And though I have said such words before, I will say them however many times I must so that it is always known what thrives within me for you. I've discovered that you are truly what I'd been waiting for all this time. I love you, Hamilton. Always and forever, I love you."

Hamilton found his hands trembling as he looked down on them, his left hand was still in Demiesius' tender grasp, and as tears began to blur in his eyes, he couldn't control himself when vibrant laughter shook his lungs.

It was a merriment that confused the elder, but when Hamilton spoke up, he was reassured. " And I—I love you, too. I am so glad my heart was captured by someone like you, Demi. You are everything that is good in the world, my world, and to always be yours, the one you love, I couldn't imagine it any other way."

They kissed then, this one kiss singled out from all the others they'd shared during their time together. Hamilton could feel it in his bones, in his heart that on this night, he and Demiesius' relationship was elevated to another level they could not have imagined ever being able to reach.

This love was founded from the ground up with promises they could virtually only hope to keep, but as hoping remained all they could do, Hamilton would never have to guess that together they would put all they could into this.

Their life as one.

Their eternal love.

⚜

Samuel had been keeping a close watch on Julius all day, and even though the boy was confined to Gregor House, one would think he'd have no place to run off to. He'd been partly right, but Julius Dalton was not the type to be locked away.

As night was headed over the city of London, Julius had closed himself off in his room, one he now shared with no one given his detachment from Samuel and Kingston. He didn't want to be at this House anymore, didn't want to be a part of the Slayer Public anymore, or at least not under the supervision of this Administration. Julius wanted to hunt vampires, wanted to make all immortals pay for being the undead killers they were, but to be given orders from the current Councilmen...

He preferred to work alone under his own authority.

So Julius had managed to sneak out of his flat through the window of his bedroom, leaving behind almost everything, even a note addressed to Kingston, the only person he knew deep down would understand why he was acting as he was now. Before escaping from Gregor, Julius left the note beneath Kingston's pillow, and it was only a matter of time until he would have the answer he was looking for from the other seventeen-year-old.

Having gotten out when he could, Julius was now back at a place he never thought he'd see again. He'd grown up on a patch of rural land about half an hour away from Oxford, and returned to it after stealing a drop-off van from the lot.

The last time he could remember being in this place, in the

home he'd been raised in until he was thirteen, it'd been when the floors and walls were drenched in the blood of his family. He could still hear their screams, the agonized cries that jolted him from sleep.

Julius could recall running into the living room from downstairs, the image of his loved ones bloodied and slaughtered about the room. The face of the vampire who'd committed the crime was at his forefront, forever taunting his nightmares with that sinister leer it'd offered on that night. He couldn't remember ever feeling such anger, soiled with incredible hatred for a monster he'd once thought existed only in myth.

Vampires were the reason he was the way he was now, angry, cold-hearted, desperate for endless rounds of vengeance. It was their fault. All of them.

The secluded house was abandoned now, spotless, as if the events of that time had never occurred within these walls. It was amazing what a copious amount of bleach and cleaner could do to a crime scene. Julius had pulled off all the plastic coverings from the furniture, making himself at home in the place he didn't think he'd ever call home again.

Taking a seat on a sofa in the living room, he waited and waited for his note to be answered, and at just thirty minutes to sundown he was finally greeted.

"Julius!" He heard Kingston call from outside, "Julius, it's me. Are you in there?"

He went for the front door and opened it, faced with Kingston standing at the top of his patio steps. The American boy was dressed in his slayer attire, dark red hair tied in a small ponytail at the nape of his neck, and his face mask was pulled down from his mouth. He appeared tired and afraid, but Julius was sure he knew why.

Coming here for answers would put Kingston's name as a reliable slayer at great risk, but he'd come anyway, and for that, Julius was grateful. "I'm glad you're here," he said.

"I wouldn't be here," Kingston started, pushing by the other boy to get inside, "if I hadn't read and reread your stupid letter a thousand times. Tell me why you're so against Hamilton, Julius. Honestly, what has that man ever done to you? All he's ever done since we were brought in is care for us, and even continued to train us when he was sick and dying of TB. I thought you respected him way more than this."

Shutting the door behind himself, Julius said, "He is not the man you think he is. Hamilton has got you, Samuel, and the entire Public wrapped around his finger, and all because we praise him for supposedly being the best."

Kingston entered the living room area, rounding a low table so as not to trip over it in his heated pace. "What do you mean 'supposedly'? The Public isn't going to crown just anyone as the best. He's rightfully killed more vampires than we can ever dream of all for the good of mankind."

"You sound just like everyone else," Julius sighed, disappointment in his jaded eyes.

Leaving the room for a moment, he returned with something in hand: a loaded backpack filled with papers.

When he unzipped it, he let its contents fall out, collapsing into a pile on a table in the middle of the living room. "I have evidence that Hamilton is nothing but a traitor. All these letters were written to him by a vampire, one Hamilton has been seeing, dating behind the Public's back for almost three years now. Even as we speak, I know damn well he is sleeping with the enemy.

Administration was told by the higher-ups that Hamilton has been transferred? Bollocks! He's fucking a vampire!"

"That — that can't be..."

"Well, it's the bloody truth, Kingston!" Julius shouted, swatting at the pile of papers.

Trying to keep levelheaded, he calmed himself down and neared Kingston. He stood just an inch from the other boy, hands at Kingston's hips as he lowered his voice. "While you and Samuel stayed by his side, I was finding out the liar Hamilton truly is. And I plan to make him pay for the sins he has committed against us, against the Public and mankind. If he thinks he can simply get away with turning his back on everything, he's got a huge fucking wake-up call coming straight from me. It saddens me to see how he's been able to manipulate you into thinking he's innocent." Turning up the boy's chin to meet his own eyes, Julius shook his head, "You're too good to be fooled by someone like him."

Kingston couldn't believe what he was hearing. He didn't want to believe a thing Julius had told him, but even though he and Samuel had previously discredited the English boy as delusional, now that he was faced with evidence of what could only be classified as a crime, Kingston halfheartedly couldn't let go of the idea that Hamilton was involved with a vampire.

Was it willingness that drew Hamilton into the arms of an immortal, or was there a chance he was being manipulated into all this foolishness? It would not be the first time Kingston heard about a vampire using humans for what they wanted by taking over their minds. It was a plausible notion to consider that as an angle, but while Kingston looked down at the letters splayed across the floor, that option jumped out the window.

If Hamilton was being controlled, he wouldn't be writing back and forth to someone he hated.

Rubbing the frustration in his temples away, Kingston couldn't stop himself from feeling a portion of resentment enter him. He thought of Hamilton as a friend, someone he'd been able to learn from, and he'd always appreciated the man for the kind of person he was.

Patient.

Understanding.

So incredibly kindhearted.

"I don't know," Kingston shook his head, reluctantly stepping out of the hands holding him close. "I don't know, Julius."

"You don't know what?" the other boy asked.

"Hamilton is—."

"Scum."

Kingston met the determination in Julius' eyes, staring into the void that was this boy's loathing for someone he'd trusted. Then Kingston turned and started for the door, voice shaky as he repeated, "I don't know, I don't know," until the front door was closed on him again.

CHAPTER TWENTY-SEVEN
The Most Wonderful of Nights

32 weeks

Demiesius had gotten everything in order when it came to him and Hamilton having a life together. Without spilling the details of the slayer's pregnant condition, he'd managed to sort out their personal relationship with the Councilors of the Public.

The three remaining Councilors had been reluctant at first with the idea of simply handing off their greatest vampire slayer to another vampire of all, but they'd eventually come to terms with it given it was Demiesius Titus they were arguing with. They knew this elder in particular had the ability to slaughter more than half the country single handedly if he wanted to, so it was best to abide by the mere request to pull Hamilton from his ranks.

The last thing the United Kingdom needed was a very angry vampire elder on the streets.

Currently, Demiesius was in the middle of a meeting with the other elders, discussing the formation of the first C.C. organization to hit the Americas. There was already one set up in Italy and Japan, but the Americas were unsurprisingly a difficult truce to sort. American vampires and slayers had a hatred for each other that burned far hotter than any other parts of the world, so settling the arguments of the selected C.C. slayers against the chosen immortals was not an easy task. While the vampires Demiesius and the other elders had designated remained quiet and reluctantly consenting towards the order of a C.C. formation, the slayers were not so easy to win over.

The assembly room he was seated in was large, rectangular with a high ceiling, and against each wall was an ascending row of blue velvet seats, like the stands of a jury ready for trial. Two glass chandeliers hung overhead, bathing the entire room with calm light, though the atmosphere inside was well overheated.

At the head of the assembly room was a table where Demiesius was seated with his fellow elders and the additional four American Councilmen. To the left side of the room, the nominated immortals who were to join the C.C. were seated, while the vampire slayers were on the right. There was a back-and-forth dispute going on between the two parties, and while Demiesius merely sat in silence, his mind traveled to another place entirely.

He was about two-hundred and eighty kilometers, give or take, from Hamilton, and all he wanted right now was to be home. This gathering wasn't supposed to take as long as it was, but the longer these American slayers argued about the predicament, the more time would pass where he couldn't be with Hamilton. And he knew his husband was waiting for him. Having left just at sunset, Demiesius had already been gone for more than four and a half hours. He didn't want Hamilton to wait up until he got home, but the slayer was a stubborn one who would do as he pleased.

As the quarreling around him continued, Demiesius' thoughts wandered into a familiar place. For a part of the day, he and Hamilton had sat up in their darkened bedroom, talking for hours about their future together as parents. They spoke of the future their child was in store for, how they would raise the child with love, discipline and understanding.

The more they'd spoken of their baby, the more Hamilton grew excited about his transition from human to vampire. He valued the single drop of blood in the tiny vial around his neck, happy to get the chance to spend years upon years with a family that he would treasure.

Ignorant to the sex of their child, the two expectant parents had spoken of potential names, Hamilton not able to choose between the long list he'd come up with, while Demiesius was fine with anything the slayer had in mind. He just couldn't wait to see them, their baby for the first time and hold them. Because at that moment, all of this would become more real than it was right now.

Right now, he was an immortal, an elder, a husband, the creator of a blood child, but for the first time in all his life, both human and vampire, Demiesius Titus would become a biological father to someone brought into this world by conception.

The closer they got to Hamilton's delivery, the more nervous the elder got. He didn't like to show it, never wanted Hamilton, or anyone for that matter, to see him in a weakened or vulnerable state, but the closer the time got to their baby being delivered into this world, Demiesius couldn't help but stress just a little.

Though he had been on this earth and experienced life through countless generations, this was one of the few things he was inexperienced with.

Raising a dhampir wasn't going to be anything similar to what it was like raising Dominick. Babies weren't his forte, but still he was excited to have someone of his own flesh and blood in the world. This family that was forming slowly over time would become the most important things, something to keep him going even in the darkest of times.

"It is no surprise to me that you all do not wish to cooperate with us," Bethania said. The elder was beside Demiesius in a pantsuit, her mass of curly dark hair tied in a ponytail, and by the mere looks of her she seemed to be in a calm and collected mood, but Demiesius could practically feel the heat radiating from her dark brown skin. She was annoyed that this was taking so long, and he couldn't blame her given these moody humans were starting to get on his nerves as well. "But to be quite frank with you lot, I am a fraction of a second away from losing my patience. We have sat here trying our best to explain just how important this underground alliance is to both our people, but if you all insist on sitting there with your contradictory theories, I think it is about that time we call it a night and part ways. I'm sure we'd all like to be elsewhere."

A man sitting in the slayer section of the assembly room stood as if ready to leave, but he was immediately advised to sit back down by the head of his Public, Councilor Axel.

Councilor Axel was a middle-aged man with jet black, slicked back hair and lightly tanned skin. He was the youngest of the Councilors, having inherited the position from his father who'd once sat in his seat.

Looking more put together and prepared for business, he said, "I, for one, agree entirely that this Coalition is something that needs to happen to minimize the bloodshed between our people. Vampires and slayers have been at each other's throats for many centuries, and a union such as this would cut down on not only death, but grief as well. I know countless slayers whom I once called friends...family...and lost them to the misfortune of death by vampire, and I'm sure you elders can say the same."

Councilor Axel glared at the man who'd been about to walk out on the assembly, "This alliance in the Americas will happen whether you like it or not. If you do not care to join, then I will strip you of your rank and title, and you will be free to leave this place to return to a normal life. Do I have any objections?"

No one moved.

"Good," Axel shared a look with all the other Councilmen, and when they all nodded in understanding, Axel gestured to Bethania for her to continue.

"Then it is settled," she said. "We will set up the main headquarters in New York this coming week. There, those in attendance tonight will be paired accordingly, and then proper orientation will commence. I look forward to..."

Demiesius' attention was captured suddenly when there was a small tingle in the core of his temples. Dominick's voice entered his mind then, his tone not filling the elder with any sort of assurance when he began to speak. *"Um, father, by any chance are you nearly finished with your meeting?"*

"Just about. Why?"

"You should come home. Something is wrong with Hamilton."

Demiesius immediately stood from the head of the room, pushing out of his chair and he stepped around it. Everyone stared his way in confusion, but he did not stop to excuse himself.

"Demiesius, where are you going?" Bethania asked, the rest of his fellow elders raising a brow at him.

"I must go," is all he said, and then he burst through the doors leading out into the hall. *"Dominick, I'm on my way. Contact Dr. Takahashi."*

In a blur of darkness, Demiesius vanished from the building he was in. Though he was several kilometers away from home, it took only a minute to travel through the realms of shadow to get where he needed to be. If his heart could beat, he knew it would be pounding in his chest right now.

Earlier in the night, Hamilton had complained about an insignificant amount of pain in his lower pelvis, but neither he nor the slayer had taken it as seriously as it could have been. Or did this incident have nothing to do with Hamilton's own body, but with the baby growing inside of him? What if something went wrong during this final trimester? Demiesius knew the slayer wouldn't be able to handle the idea of something being wrong with their baby. And neither could he!

Appearing before his castle from the shadowy encasement, Demiesius rushed through the front entryway, bursting open the thick wooden doors so hard that the hinges nearly ripped off.

"Hamilton!" he called out, and he reached into his surroundings with his tracking senses, able to detect where the slayer was in the castle just by feeling for his life force. He could perceive his husband's shakiness was coming from their bedroom, and he shadow mastered to it without further delay.

When he entered the bedroom, he froze in complete worry

at the sight of Hamilton lying down on his side in the bed. Shivering in his pajamas from before, a blanket pulled over Hamilton, and a thin shine of sweat could be seen gleaming on his forehead. Dominick showed up beside him a second later, seeming shaken as well and utterly confused.

Demiesius entered further and neared the side of the bed. He placed a hand on top of Hamilton's head, and immediately the slayer opened his eyes only a small way. He was shivering so much.

Before the elder could ask what was wrong, Dominick spoke from the doorway. "He's in pain. So much that he can't speak. Before he got this silent, he told me it felt like something broke inside of him, but after that he hasn't been able to open his mouth without screaming. He's been holding it in for a couple minutes now."

"Where is Dr. Takahashi?" Demiesius demanded.

"He should be here any second," Dominick promised, "Said he was gathering supplies and an extra pair of hands. Father, he said the baby is ready for delivery."

"Now?"

Dominick shrugged, "He said dhampirs finish development a bit quicker than human babies in the last month, so they don't require the full forty-week due date."

Demiesius ran his touch down Hamilton's cheek and gave a silent nod. "It's alright," he said then, "Everything is going to be fine, my love."

The slayer's half open eyes closed tight, and he reached up slowly from under the covers. Demiesius took his hand and held it gently. A tear shed down Hamilton's face and suddenly his grip on the elder tightened. He gasped sharply and squeezed his eyes shut as his husband took a seat beside him.

"The doctor will be here soon." Even with that said, the elder began to grow frustrated as a couple minutes turned into several, but eventually there was loud knocking that echoed up to the bedroom.

After receiving a nod from his father, Dominick swiftly went downstairs to open the front door. A moment later, he returned with Dr. Takahashi, a nurse and another doctor. Remembering the nurse's face from the medical clinic, Demiesius only grew anxious when he didn't recognize the second doctor and she was a human.

"Don't worry," Dr. Takahashi assured, "She studies vampirism under me and is more well-versed in child delivery than I. Trust me, you want her to orchestrate this procedure far more than you would want me."

Hamilton resisted the urge to writhe about as the pain in his pelvis struck into his abdomen. If he thought a vampire bite was painful, this here was multiplied by a million. Was this really what he was supposed to be feeling? This level of agony? He was aware of the contractions women went through during childbirth, but this was utterly ridiculous.

Through his weeks upon weeks of carrying this baby inside him, he'd grown excited about having a life in his womb. But it appeared all the joys of being pregnant took a quick turn once these internal pains kicked in.

As Demiesius continued to sit beside Hamilton on the bed, the human doctor spoke of all the things she would have to do to get the baby out safely, and that involved something that put Demiesius on edge. The woman would have to cut Hamilton open and perform a cesarean. She explained that the surgery wouldn't have any negative effects on Hamilton or the baby, but, still, Demiesius didn't like the idea of something that involved slicing his husband open.

Cooperating regardless, he stepped aside when the woman, the nurse and Dr. Takahashi got started.

Finding what strength he could to speak, Hamilton asked Demiesius and Dominick to step out of the room. The elder was confused by the request, but also didn't feel like it was his place to argue at a time like this.

"I'll be in the hall," he said before he and the blood child stepped out. He couldn't keep still in the corridor even if he tried, and while Dominick attempted to calm his nerves and tell him everything was going to be fine, and not a thing would go wrong, he couldn't knock the feeling aside.

Pacing back and forth with his hands clasped behind his back, the elder kept his ears open to what was going on inside the room, most in tune with the beat of Hamilton's heart. It was beating at a rhythm quicker than normal, but he was sure that was due to the situation he was in right now. There was something mentioned about spinal and epidural anesthetics, but all in all, the room was rather quiet.

After a couple minutes, Demiesius' senses became very aware of the scent of blood. Hamilton's blood, but given the slayer's heart rate remained the same, he assumed there was still nothing for him to fret over. The aroma became stronger over the span of a couple minutes, and soon there was another loud heartbeat that joined Hamilton's in the room, this one more lively.

Dr. Takahashi and the other doctor both said something at the same time; Demiesius was unable to tell what it was, before he finally heard the nurse inside the room say, "Congratulations, Hamilton, it's a healthy baby boy."

There was no newborn cry that rattled the room, but there was a cry of happiness that emerged. It was Hamilton. "Oh, my god," the slayer seemed to whisper.

Dominick and his father shared a look, and then the blood child patted the elder's shoulder with a large smile.

A few more minutes of mere listening through the door went by before Hamilton called out, "Demi, come inside, come look!"

Surprisingly the elder's hand hesitated to turn the knob, but when he finally did, he almost couldn't believe his eyes. The sheets covering the bed were nearly soaked in blood, but that wasn't what held his attention. Given Dr. Takahashi had healed the slayer's incisions with his blood, Hamilton had been wiped down clean and moved to a black lounge seat nearest to the windows of the bedroom. He was wearing a black shower robe from the closet and looked thankfully calmer than he had earlier. And Demiesius was sure the only thing keeping him so calm was the tiny infant nestled in his arms.

The elder entered the room further, no one saying a word as the father of this dhampir looked upon his child. The baby's skin was fair like the grains of sand on a beach, and the short growth of hair on his head was oddly two-toned. On the left side, his hair was black as night, while on the right it was as blonde as Hamilton's. Everything about him almost frightened Demiesius since he looked incredibly fragile, easily broken, and when Hamilton lifted the baby and said, "Here, Demi, hold your son," he dithered in doing so.

Demiesius put his hands out after gaining the courage, and Hamilton carefully as ever placed the quiet baby in his father's arms.

Remaining in the lounge seat due to his legs still being numb from his anesthetics, Hamilton watched with a smile on his face as Demiesius took a step back, seeming to awe at the mere sight of his child in his arms. He didn't say a word, unable to totally believe what he was holding.

After just one minute, the baby began to stir in his arms and opened his eyes. They were light gray spheres, and when they looked upon the man holding him, the elder could strongly feel the connection he had with the baby. It was far stronger than the simple blood bond he and Dominick had. Suddenly then, the infant's eyes flashed a dark crimson red, and he began to whimper out a small whine before he started to cry.

Unsure, Demiesius handed him back to Hamilton, and surely, he stopped crying almost immediately. "I told you he would want you more than me," the elder said.

Hamilton shook his head and when the nurse came back into the room after having left a second ago, she offered Hamilton a baby bottle filled with warm blood. It bothered him for a second that human blood was going to be the first thing to enter his child's stomach, but he'd been informed already that it was essential to his growth. Dhampirs could be weaned off a purely blood diet a little later, but for now, it was crucial to his early survival.

After about two hours of further coaching from Dr. Takahashi, Demiesius was alone in the castle with his family. While Hamilton was now able to walk about, he was dressed in just a loose fit white shirt and a pair of underwear. He hadn't set the baby in his arms down once, and it seemed that alone was enough to keep him from crying. Walking in circles around the parlor room, he

listened as Demiesius and Dominick talked about the meeting
the elder had attended earlier in the night.

There was a fair amount of disagreement coming from Dominick, speaking of how the elders should just give up on the
American slayers, and leave the tensions right where they were.
Demiesius, on the other hand, was more familiar with how
important immortal and slayer contact was. It was what kept
the bloodshed to a minimum, no matter how much continued
to spill between the two races, and no matter what, he liked to
think his opinion on that would never change.

"Speaking of slayers," Dominick said, folding his arms over
the back of the black sofa, "When do you plan on going back
to the force again, Hamilton, or shall I tell Christoph he'll be
assigned a different partner in crime?"

"I don't know," Hamilton said, not looking up from the baby
cradled in his arms. "For now, I think I just want to focus on
being a parent. I've been away from the C.C. for some time now,
so I'm sure I haven't been missed by anyone. Maybe I'll go back
someday, then again, maybe I won't. I don't know. Aside from
that, I think I finally know what I want to name our baby, Demi."

Demiesius was sitting in an armchair when Hamilton approached him from the side, "What is it?"

"Jeremiah. What about that?"

The elder merely nodded with a delighted smile, "That's a
beautiful name."

"Then that will be his name. Jeremiah." Hamilton pressed his
nose to the baby's forehead; all his maternal instincts ever awake
to the tiny being in his arms. He turned then to walk away,
heading upstairs to his and the elder's bedroom. "I love you,
my sweet boy, my Jeremiah," he spoke softly, climbing the steps

slowly to the second floor. "And I will always love you just as I do now." He smiled down at the watchful eyes gazing curiously up at him, unable to physically feel the connection he and the infant had, but he knew it was there in not only their blood, but in their hearts as well.

This little boy, Jeremiah Titus, was his son and no matter what happened, that was impossible to change.

He entered him and Demiesius' bedroom, humming a pretty lullaby that lulled the boy to sleep. The bed had been made up with everything new given the messy childbirth, but the room was completely back to normal now, except the sheets were now a dark sea green with black pillows and a black skirt.

Beside the bed off Hamilton's side was an oak framed bassinet with comfortable cushioning inside. He set Jeremiah on his back as he slept and sat down at the edge of the bed. He couldn't stop the amazement that had entered him the moment his son was placed in his arms, finally able to hold this baby and look upon a piece of himself.

He desperately wanted to be the kind of father this boy would look up to—be proud of as the man he was. Hamilton couldn't wait to teach his son about the world, watch him grow and thrive in it no matter how difficult raising him could wind up being as he got older. He was going to spend all the time he had making sure nothing happened to his son: love, guide, and shelter him from all who could dare oppose him.

Touching lightly at the boy's two-toned hair, Hamilton looked over his shoulder when a shadow darkened over him and the bassinet.

Demiesius neared him from the doorway. "Dominick has gone back to the coven," he said. "He gives his warmest regards."

When he was beside Hamilton, he placed a hand at the small of the man's back. "It is late. You should find some sleep."

Without answering the elder, Hamilton turned into Demiesius' chest and closed his arms around him. So pent up with eagerness, the slayer couldn't help the tears of happiness from shedding down his cheeks. He pressed his face into the center of his husband's chest and held fast. "I can never express," Hamilton cried softly, keeping his voice down, "just how thankful I am that I met you, Demi. If I hadn't stumbled across you that night, we would have never been gifted such a life." He looked up at Demiesius and the elder wiped away the wet shine of tears on his cheek. "If we hadn't met then, we would not have our baby, our Jeremiah."

"But we did," Demiesius said, "And we do."

Calming down to the best of his abilities, Hamilton quietly readied himself for bed and fell asleep not long after shedding a few more tears of utter happiness. When morning rolled around, Demiesius dressed down and entered the bed after handling some paperwork he'd needed to submit to the American Concord Coalition.

The peaceful heartbeats of both Hamilton and Jeremiah were like synced melodies to his sensitive hearing, songs of life that assured him before closing his eyes and drifting into a most peaceful sleep of his own.

CHAPTER TWENTY-EIGHT

The Price of Living is Paid in Blood

Afraid to take Jeremiah out of the castle on his own, Hamilton had left for the store this afternoon alone, leaving Demiesius with the baby for a couple hours. The elder wasn't sure if leaving him to the duties of a caregiver was smart, but he also didn't quite want his little boy out there either.

It was the middle of the day, and though Jeremiah could withstand sunlight like any ordinary human, to think of Jeremiah being so far from his line of sight itched at the elder's protective reach. Five weeks had passed since the baby boy was brought into the world, and Demiesius' thoughts on the upbringing of his son never left his mind for a second.

Though still an infant that required a watchful eye instead of lessons and schooling, Demiesius already knew what he wanted to teach the boy when he was old enough to understand. He wanted his son to wield as much knowledge as he did: history, languages, personal attributes, what it was to be a dhampir, a man. He wished for Jeremiah to see the world as he did, comprehend the differences of the mixtures in his blood. But there was one single thing Demiesius wanted to make sure his son understood when the time came.

Empathy.

This was something everyone needed. Especially a dhampir.

As he grew older, Demiesius knew Jeremiah would become even stronger than him and all the elders combined. Unimaginable strength was one thing that accompanied a half-human half-vampire child, and since Jeremiah's heritage would be delivered from an elder, the potential of his abilities would be almost tripled. He would be able to withstand anything in his path, take whatever threats came his way, but Demiesius wanted to do whatever he could to stop his son from ever feeling like he had to unlock those dangerous capabilities that lived inside him.

By the time Jeremiah Titus was in his teens, he would have surpassed every other immortal on Earth, so Demiesius knew detaining his emotions was something that needed a lot of focus.

A simple upset could devastate an entire country.

With Jeremiah snuggled in the support of his arm, Demiesius had managed to keep him quiet after a feeding not long ago. While he read over the contracts sent to him the night before, he set the papers down when the telephone at the corner of the desk began to ring. The shrill noise alerted the baby.

Cutting the ring, Demiesius picked up the receiver and

pressed it to his ear. "Who is this?" he demanded. Calls during the day were never something he was used to.

"It is Public Councilor Jamison."

"What do you want at an hour like this? We don't have another meeting until tonight."

"I understand that, but I am calling for Hamilton."

Demiesius glanced down at Jeremiah when the little boy yawned, a tiny sound coming from his mouth, and then he almost appeared to smile at the man holding him. "Hamilton isn't here at the moment," the elder informed. "He's gone into the city for a while."

"When he returns, tell him he must come to the Council Gathering immediately. There may be a dilemma going on and his help has been requested."

Demiesius didn't like the sound of this, "What's going on?"

"I don't mean to sound imprudent, but this is simply a Public matter. I cannot disclose our personal matters to you." By the sound of the man's voice alone, the elder could tell whatever it was that needed to be handled, it was probably something quite serious. It wasn't always that the Councilmen wielded such urgent tones.

"And it seems *you* have forgotten," Demiesius said. "For the time being, Hamilton no longer works under the orders of the Public. Whatever problem it is, I am sure you can find another slayer to do your bidding."

"Elder Demiesius, this is no laughing matter. Hamilton must report to us as soon as he can. This is a command from his headquarters!"

"I think you better realize who it is you are speaking with," Demiesius asserted, and when his voice raised a volume in frustration, Jeremiah fussed against his chest before finding comfort again. Trying to keep his tone leveled so as not to trouble his son, Demiesius settled down, and said, "Either you tell me what it is you so desperately need him for, or he will not be in attendance today."

Given that it was clear Demiesius was adamant, Councilor Jamison gave into the immortal's demand. "There is something going on with his former students, and two of them have sought guidance from him. Samuel Colebrook and Kingston Fisher; they think Hamilton is the only one who can help them."

Reluctant to cooperate with the Councilman on the other line, Demiesius merely agreed with the man before the line was cut. No part of him wanted his husband in a place like the Council, especially since the last thing he wanted was for Hamilton to go back to fighting so soon, but even with his top position in the rule of immortals, he hadn't really any say in what went on with the Public's personal matters. And no matter what, there was no pulling Hamilton out of the Public just for his wanting the man out of it. The only person who could do that was Hamilton himself.

Demiesius sighed and stood from the desk chair, fixing Jeremiah in the crook of his arm. When he stepped out into the corridor with the boy, it was darker than the office since all of the drapes were closed.

His ears became aware of the sound of Hamilton's car pulling up to the castle outside. He waited in the middle of the foyer for the front door to open, and when Hamilton entered with a few shopping bags in his hands, he lit up the very second he laid eyes on his family.

Today he was dressed in tall platforms, bell bottom jeans,

a cream-colored off-the-shoulder top, a burgundy red scarf looped around his neck, and his sunny hair was let down to the middle of his back. "Hello, my beautiful boys!" he exclaimed and then looked around. "Wow, it's so gloomy in here. Why don't you turn on some lights, love?"

Moving along with Hamilton when he went for the grand hall, Demiesius said, "Most light sources during the day, even if it is just artificial, irritates my eyes given I am supposed to be asleep and surrounded by darkness."

Hamilton hummed, "Why are you only telling me this now? And here I've been sticking you in the light since I moved in. I'm sorry."

The elder let it pass and they stepped into the sitting room not far from the entryway. Hamilton set the bags he'd been carrying down on the low center table, and then he turned to the elder and smiled brightly down at the bundle in his husband's arms. "Look at that, still awake, are you? Thought he'd be asleep by the time I got back. Your Papa's been keeping you up, I bet." He laughed and met Demiesius' eyes, "I'm glad he's not asleep at least for right now. I got him this new outfit I've been dying to dress him in since I saw it. He's going to look even cuter than he already is!"

Moving Jeremiah into the slayer's arms, Demiesius watched as Hamilton spoke cheerfully to the alert infant, nothing but the sense of happiness in the vibrant aura he let off. It was something that would never cease to be familiar to him, a unique impression that would always remind him of this pure-hearted man that he loved so dearly.

When the slayer began to hum that same little tune he used when putting the dhampir to sleep at night, he stopped suddenly, and said, "I'm going to miss this when he's older. I know he's only five weeks old now, but time flies and soon he will be a grown man who won't need us to nurture him. He won't need anyone." The look on Hamilton's face softened as he watched his son lying awake in his benevolent hold. "When I become a vampire once I'm thirty-five in a couple years, I'm positive I won't be able to have any more babies even though I still don't fully understand how I had this one in the first place. Knowing that now, I'm going to be a little sad when the time comes."

"You want more children?" Demiesius asked, picking up on the slayer's sorrow.

"Maybe not at this very second, but it would be nice to have one more…or two. What if someday we had a daughter? I'd spoil her senseless just like I have no doubt I'll do with Jeremiah. How would you feel about that? More children?"

"I've always wanted a big family."

The glittering excitement in Hamilton's eyes shone like polished crystals up at Demiesius. "When he's at least a year, let's try for another."

When Hamilton rested Jeremiah down on his back in the middle of a nearby sofa, Demiesius remembered about the phone call he'd received from Councilor Jamison. Everything in him didn't want to tell the slayer of the summoning, but he went ahead with it anyway.

Watching as Hamilton took an infant sized blue and white romper from one of the shopping bags, he clasped his hands behind his back, and said, "The Public called for you this afternoon. In fact, it wasn't too long ago."

Hamilton carefully undressed Jeremiah from the plain black outfit he'd been wearing, being as gentle as he could when putting the baby's arms through the sleeves. "Hmm, wonder what they could want. Did they say?"

"Something about two of your past students Samuel and Kingston. Apparently, they are in need of your assistance with something. Jamison would tell me nothing more than that."

At the sound of the two young slayer's names, Hamilton couldn't help but think of Julius first. Was the boy still angry with him for loving a vampire after all this time? Did he somehow turn his back on his former comrades? But what could they need him for if that was the case?

When he finished buttoning the last of Jeremiah's new outfit, Hamilton looked back at Demiesius with a pout. "Were the words 'immediately' or 'command' used during this conversation you had with Councilor Jamison?"

The elder nodded.

Hamilton released a long breath, "Then I guess I've got no choice. Besides, Samuel and Kingston mean something to me. They became great fighters. I'm sure they'd even make a nice addition to the C.C. one day if they were ever scouted to join." Fixing the small collar of Jeremiah's outfit, Hamilton smirked down at the baby. "He looks just as cute as I predicted. Come on, now. It's time for you to take a nap." When he picked Jeremiah up, he headed for the stairs to their bedroom. "I'll put him to bed for you, Demi, so you can get some sleep. I'm sure you're just hiding how tired you are for the sake of being awake with us. Depending on what the boys want at headquarters, I probably won't be too long."

It thankfully hadn't taken as long as it did to put Jeremiah to sleep. After a bottle, he was out like a light.

Hamilton kept quiet while he undressed from his day clothes.

Since he wasn't too sure what the Public would ask of him once he got there, he thought it wise to travel prepared.

Standing before Demiesius and the large bed, he stripped down until he was in just his underwear, his cheeks warming when he spotted the elder's wandering eyes on his near nude body.

He was so glad for the qualities that came with giving birth under the healing factors of a vampire. With Dr. Takahashi's methods during and after his initial cesarean, his body had bounced back to what it used to be before pregnancy altered him. So it thankfully hadn't taken long for his stomach to go down, his once tight and fit figure returned, and his body was more than presentable. Tucking a strand of hair behind his ear, he grinned cheekily at Demiesius and neared him, a sway in his trim hips with each step he took.

Without a word, his husband reached out and folded him in his arms, but Hamilton let it be as Demiesius clung to him. He softly touched the elder's midnight hair, pushing his fingers through his lover's tresses. When he could feel the light fall of Demiesius' hands glide down his back, Hamilton felt a shiver run through him, and when the sensations working his roused appetite grew deeper, he tipped the elder's chin to look up at him. "It's been a little while since we...maybe I can make them wait just a little longer."

Not wanting to wake the baby, Demiesius picked Hamilton off the floor and took a step back, softly colliding with the medium dresser behind him when he did so. What framed family pictures were on top, as well as the slim vase holding their seemingly everlasting higanbana, shook atop the dresser, but the toppling rattle that sounded in their wake went unnoticed.

The elder guided them into an unused guestroom down the hall, making sure to leave the door open in case Jeremiah began to fuss. When he sat back on the full-sized bed in the vintage style room, Demiesius wrapped his strong arms around his husband in his lap.

Hamilton unbuttoned the row running down his lover's shirt and pulled it off, feeling his hand down the elder's sturdy chest until reaching the clasps of his trousers as they kissed.

Worked out of his underwear next, Hamilton straddled his husband, nothing but his vial and ruby necklaces dangling around his neck. He turned over off to the side, lying down on his back while Demiesius quickly got rid of his clothing. From the small amount of light seeping into the room from the open doorway, the elder's visage fell into shadow when he dipped his head and his hair cascaded down around his face. The only thing Hamilton could perceive for a moment was the blood-like glaze in his husband's eyes when they flashed with lustful hunger.

Their lips met then, and Hamilton moaned lowly when Demiesius' flushed cock stroked against his own. He locked his ankles behind the immortal's back, his entire body seeming to melt just by the sensual manner in which Demiesius handled his tongue. Oh, how he'd missed this kind of attention. The hot, passionate sex, the worlds this man could send him to with one fuck, Hamilton had missed it so much the entire time he'd been pregnant, and this was the first time since giving birth that they had done anything remotely sexual.

Demiesius kissed along the slayer's jaw then, licking keenly down his neck until reaching his collar. Hamilton sprawled his arms above his head, gasping for air when the elder tweaked and sucked at his perked and delicate nipples.

Hamilton curved his back up off the mattress when Demiesius' hands then touched down the underside of his thighs, pushing them up and open as he continued the journey of his kisses. When the tip of his wet tongue touched the head of Hamilton's cock, the slayer's entire body jolted. The elder teased the sensitivity before he closed his lips around the tip, bobbing his head with the dip of Hamilton's groin into the bed beneath him.

Demiesius felt a hand drag through his hair, Hamilton's breath shaking with each pump of his mouth. When the slayer sounded too close to cumming after a minute, Demiesius stole his tongue from the oral pleasure and let a pool of saliva coat his fingers before prepping his husband's entry.

The slayer twitched and moaned with each plunge of Demiesius' fingers into him, unable to control himself as he touched across his own body. His skin felt like it was ice-cold and then a flash of heat would fill him, and the light dots of sweat cooling his entire figure made each transition feel like a shower of affection.

When Demiesius' fingers escaped him, Hamilton turned onto his side, the immortal lifting one of his slender legs up before the hot and glossy tip of the elder's cock pushed into him. Hamilton bit down a rejoicing cry and threw his head back.

The passion in each stroke of Demiesius' hips never failed to send him over the edge, fucking him just right to make him resist all the loud mews he wanted to let out.

On his knees after, Hamilton had his cheek pressed down, clawing at the sheets below as hands gripped into his hips. What words he could speak were either mumbles of moans he couldn't quite get out, or whispers for his husband to keep going until he was a complete mess.

When Hamilton was turned over, his body quivered in need until he was filled again. The elder slowed his passion as if the clock froze the entire world around them, leaning down on one hand as his eyes watched every desperate breath Hamilton took.

"Yes," the slayer exhaled, "Just like that—. Demi—."

Hamilton's mouth fell agape when Demiesius closed his fingers around the slayer's cock, pumping the hard, oozing shaft as he continued to thrust zealously into his husband.

Feeling himself growing nearer to his climax, Hamilton began to squirm beneath the looming immortal, the tightness of his entry constricting more as the need to cum tightened his body. But he couldn't hold it for long and found himself trembling as his load of cum shot from his cock, belting out the tune of his pleasures as his voice rose.

Demiesius released the strain he'd been holding in, clutching his husband's trim hips to hold himself in place, his own course overflowing from within Hamilton.

They didn't move a muscle after the elder collapsed beside Hamilton, resting for a good couple minutes before the slayer finally found the strength to move.

"Come take a quick shower with me before I go. I want to feel your touch one more time."

As they trekked to their bedroom, Hamilton could hardly contain himself from seeking further kisses, walking backwards as he distracted the elder with constant hungry pecks that met his eager lips. He chuckled lightly at the manner in which Demiesius never missed a kiss that happily reached up for him, but their attention was snagged when they each felt a crumble of something under their feet.

Looking down, the slayer and elder looked to the floor to find they'd stepped on the fallen arrangement, Hamilton's barefoot crushing the red higanbana as Demiesius' accidentally smashed the white spider lily beneath his own foot.

When they stepped off from them, Hamilton placed the toppled vase back atop the dresser and frowned at the flattened and destroyed flowers. He'd loved their unique and stunning splendor, but there was no repairing what couldn't be fixed, especially with how the petals of each were half strewn about the floor now.

"What a shame..." Hamilton uttered, mostly to himself. "I guess they lasted as long as they were meant to, huh?"

Demiesius received the two wilting stems and placed them on the dresser, a bizarre flow traveling through his chest when his fingers grazed what petals remained of the red flower. Before he could dwell on it too long, Hamilton pulled him into the bathroom with a smile, and they entered the shower together.

Hamilton stepped into the disguised library of the Gathering of Councilors, traveling down into the headquarters far into the bowels of the building. He was dressed in his black slayer attire, a coat over him to hide the utility belt of stakes and other weapons he used whenever in combat.

It'd been a while since the last time he was dressed this way, so Hamilton felt odd, almost out of place when he'd strapped on his last boot. There was just something inside of him that didn't feel like a slayer anymore, and while he was still confident enough in his skills as a fighter, this felt like something he wasn't cut out for.

Perhaps after tonight, he could make it clear with the Councilors that he no longer wanted to be part of their Public community.

He headed down the winding corridors until reaching the Gathering room and entered. There were no Councilmen sitting in their posts at the head of the circular room, but Hamilton was not alone when the heavy door closed behind him. Samuel and Kingston were in the center of the gathering area. Both boys were dressed in their combat attire, Samuel's blonde hair parted to the side with a genuine scared look on his face. Kingston looked like he was having an easier time keeping a hold of himself, red hair tied into a ponytail to keep it out of his face.

"Hey, lads," Hamilton greeted. "I feel like it's been so long since we've seen each other. You both look fantastic."

Samuel hurried for his former instructor, not wasting any time in getting his worry out. "You have to help us stop Julius. He's gone completely off the deep end."

Just the mentioning of Julius churned Hamilton's stomach, knowing without the need of a reminder that that boy was one person who hated him more than anything. "What's going on? Where are the Councilors?"

Kingston stepped up beside Samuel, "They're all getting ready for some kind of meeting being hosted tonight, so Mister Jamison told us you would be able to help us on your own. Samuel and I are afraid Julius has lost it. He's planning to stalk the streets of London all night to kill as many vampires as he can."

Hamilton was having trouble following the problem at hand. "Why can't the Administrators at Gregor restrain him? It's their job to keep all slayers in the House in line. Why do you need me?"

"Julius ran away months ago," Samuel said.

"And, honestly," Kingston started next, "I've known where he's been for a while, but I was too scared to tell the Administration in fear they would hurt him. Julius is my friend, Hamilton. He's been so close to me since before we even started this whole thing. It's just...it's all gotten to his head, and I'm afraid my best friend is going to get himself killed. Even with you being transferred and him growing distant afterwards, I know Julius still respects you more than anyone. He looks up to you."

Hamilton felt terrible for leading these kids on. He was almost sure they didn't know the full extent of Julius' hatred for him, but to think about the lost teenager preparing to face droves of vampires on his own was a scary thought. Samuel and Kingston had shown themselves to be the two more proficient fighters of the bunch, and even if Julius had been honing his skills for the past almost two years since the last time they'd seen each other, he was confident in saying the young slayer wouldn't be able to take down more than a handful of vampires at once.

"I feel like I'm the last person he'd ever want to see," Hamilton admitted, voice insecure. "I feel like I'm just another person who abandoned him."

"Help me show him you haven't," Kingston begged. "My best friend, your former student, is out there getting ready to throw his life away with the confidence that he'll actually make it out of this night alive."

"He's going to get himself slaughtered," Samuel said. "I'm sure he just needs a good talking to."

Hamilton wondered if his love for Demiesius had aided in giving Julius such an insane idea. The boy held a hatred for vampires that burned hotter than anyone else in the world, and to find out one of the people he'd trusted in so much was virtually in league with them; it must be something that could shred the heart. If he could stop this flame from spreading any further, he at least wanted to give it a shot.

"Are we the only ones going?" Hamilton asked.

"Yeah," Kingston sighed, "Mister Jamison said that was alright."

With that in mind, Hamilton turned and headed for the doors of the Gathering room. "Let's go."

The three got into Hamilton's car, Samuel in the back seat while Kingston directed him to where Julius had been hiding out all this time. He was surprised at the amount of distance they had to travel, entering Oxford after forty-five minutes of driving.

While the majority of the ride had been quiet, he wondered to himself how Demiesius and Jeremiah were doing, hoping that his son wasn't giving his husband such a hard time so the elder could sleep after spending most of the day awake. Even with the worry of one of his previous students on his mind, Hamilton wanted to be with his family, to make sure Jeremiah was taken care of while his husband was.

There was a brand-new nurturing instinct inside of him that hatched the second Jeremiah was born, and that was the fierce desire to be with him at all times. Hamilton wanted to feed his baby, care for him the way a parent felt the need to after their baby was born, and even with Hamilton being a biological male, this was an internal makeup he couldn't ignore. Right now, he just wanted to get Julius stable enough to get back to his family.

The sun was on its way down by the time Hamilton reached a

country road that led to a secluded house. "Is this his childhood home?" he asked.

"Yeah," Kingston said from the back seat. "He's been living here since he ran away from Gregor."

The closer they got to the house, Hamilton could see someone sitting out on the porch. It was Julius, and when he parked his car behind a stolen drop-off van that belonged to Gregor, he could see Julius was dressed in his slayer attire, equipped with all of his weapons, and the chain of the sickle in his hands rattled as he twirled it in a small circle close to the floor.

The black-haired boy stood when Hamilton cut the engine and got out after taking off his coat, Samuel and Kingston following suit.

"Listen, Julius," Samuel called out, moving past Hamilton to the porch. "Please, just hear us out for a second."

Hamilton looked up at the sky when an uneasiness came down over him. He couldn't explain what it was, maybe just a change in the wind, but when he looked towards Julius and the boy gave him a sly grin, he couldn't say the joking expression gave him any relief.

"Julius," he said, "I just want to talk with you. Samuel and Kingston, they're worried about you, and so am I after what they've had to tell me."

Julius stopped twirling the chain and lifted the silver handle of the sickle instead. Pointing the curved blade in Hamilton's direction, he said, "I'm afraid there's nothing we have to talk about tonight. In fact, this will be the last night you ever speak again." Taking a confident stand at the top of the porch steps, Julius glared sinisterly at his former instructor. "I'd just like to thank my best mate for bringing you to me."

Samuel rutted his brow and looked towards the two standing behind him.

When Julius' words quickly registered in his mind, before Hamilton could go to look over his shoulder to Kingston, he felt a harsh, piercing sensation burrow into his lower back. He gasped sharply as a numbing pain entered his body. When he looked down, his hands touched at the bloody tip of a blade that'd been stabbed through his lower right abdomen.

A scream echoed around Hamilton, and even with how shrill the holler had been, it was like he could hardly hear it. He watched, frozen, as the blade was pulled from his body, and the second it was out, it was like everything around him hit play.

Blood poured from the open wound.

Agony rippled through him suddenly as Samuel's horrified scream entered his ears. "What the hell did you do!?" the boy yelled out in anger and confusion.

Hamilton dropped to a knee, shaken by the blood on his hands as he gripped his stomach. When he looked up to the boy who'd stepped around him, Kingston showed no remorse for the act of betrayal he'd blindly committed. There was a bloodied dagger in his hand and a cold look in his eyes as he joined Julius on the steps.

Please, no...

Hamilton's thoughts cried the words he could not speak.

Please, don't let this be my end.

CHAPTER TWENTY-NINE

Vengeance is a Flame that Burns the Brightest

"Do you have any idea what you've just done?!" Samuel bellowed, his resentment for the two equally young slayers seeping out of each of his pores. He dropped to Hamilton's side, kneeling beside the bleeding man as he cupped the lesion punctured through his abdomen. "I'm so sorry," he apologized fearfully. "I swear, I didn't know these two lunatics were planning this. I'm so sorry!"

Hamilton met the Austrian boy's eyes, surprised he hadn't passed out from the blood loss. There were scared and livid tears blurring his vision, and before he could think to say something in return, Julius began to approach him from the porch steps of the house.

"Move aside, Samuel," he ordered as if he had all the power in the world. "I didn't want to have to kill you, too, but seeing your clingy sentiment to our wonderful instructor, allowing you to leave this property after this evening probably isn't such a good idea."

Samuel glared up at the dark-haired boy and rose to his feet. From his utility belt, he withdrew two sharpened blades and fisted their leather grips. He held them in front of his face in a semi-crouched stance, heart pounding in his chest at the thought of what he had to do. "If you think I'm just going to stand back and watch you kill him, you're sadly mistaken. If you want to get your hands on him, you'll have to face me first!"

Looking down at the chain and sickle in his hands, Julius slid the rattling silver against his palm. "Funny how you think it will be that easy to defeat Kingston and I. If you haven't noticed, it's clearly two against one, and if you're thinking I'm still a little rusty when it comes to fighting, you're the one who's sadly mistaken. I've perfected this weapon and your little daggers will do you no good. Not that I wanted to fight you anyhow. My enemy here is Hamilton and Hamilton alone, and it's time I taught him a lesson he clearly needs to learn."

When Julius took a step off the porch, Samuel dug his feet into the dirt, "Stay back!"

Aggravated by the Austrian boy's interference, Julius met Kingston's eyes and nodded towards their partner. "Take care of him, please."

The way Kingston moved without delay reminded Samuel of someone who was possessed, somehow manipulated by the words of the dark-haired boy, and he wanted to understand why. How could these two turn on the man who'd worked so hard in the beginning to teach them what they knew now?

"Kingston," Samuel said almost woefully, "Please, stop and think about what you're doing. I don't want to have to fight you. I thought — I thought we were friends."

Getting closer and closer to Samuel, Kingston shook his head, and said, "We can still be friends after tonight, Samuel. Trust me, that is something I want, too, but if you're going to protect this vampire fucker, then I have no choice but to strike you down here. Move aside and I'll reconsider."

Even after hearing the allegation of Hamilton having an intimate relationship with an immortal, Samuel continued to stand protectively in front of his former instructor. "I don't care what you have to say about Hamilton, true or not, we are vampire slayers. Killing one of our kind is worthy of a death sentence."

Julius knitted his brow, "I'm sick of hearing him bicker, Kingston. Kill him!"

At the drop of a hat, Kingston sprinted towards Samuel, the same effective dagger in his fist that he'd used to stab Hamilton in the back. With the sun going down, the land before the isolated house in Oxford began to darken as well, the dancing shadows of the two quarreling slayers stretching across the grass. They were similarly matched, knowing what move was coming next no matter how fast.

Taking his eyes off the combative slayers, Julius laid his gaze on Hamilton. The man was still knelt there on the ground, holding onto the strength leaving his body with each pump of blood that gushed from his open wound. It was like he was a kid on a holiday morning, ready to open a present gifted to him, except it was not a holiday, and his present was a human being he aspired to carve open with the deadly blade of his sickle.

When he neared Hamilton, he knelt in front of him. He smiled at the scent of iron blood filling the air, and said, "It is probably sick of me to say I'm going to enjoy this, but I am really going to enjoy killing you tonight. Ever since I found out you've been fucking a vampire, I've wanted to get my hands on you so badly. I just — I want you to know what you're doing is wrong."

Julius furrowed his brow when Hamilton merely trembled before him, having wanted to hear what the man could use to back up his actions.

The second he opened his mouth to speak again, Julius didn't have time to get a word out when the butt of a spear point knife knocked him across his face.

Hamilton rose to his feet quickly and stumbled. Weakened from the amount of blood he'd lost, he pressed a hand to the open abrasion while wielding his weapon in the other. He wasn't about to die on his knees. If this was going to be his last night on earth, he was going to go out fighting for his life.

The faces of Demiesius and Jeremiah in his mind kept Hamilton strong. "You hate me so much," he spat. "Then come at me!"

Spitting a wad of blood from his mouth, Julius ran the back of his hand across his lips. Kingston and Samuel had stopped their brawl to watch the two, Hamilton standing in a prepared and defensive position as Julius began to circle him like he was prey. This reminded him of almost every situation he'd ever been in with a vampire, being stalked like a wounded animal under the spotlight of the moon, except...this was the first time he would be fighting as weak as he was.

Hamilton was ready when Julius attacked from behind, the boy yelling out when he swung the heavy weighted knot at the end of the chain.

Turning quickly on his heels, Hamilton ducked before the

weight could knock against his temple. Before the moment Julius could pull back the chain, Hamilton then grabbed at it, entangling his pointed blade into the loops and tugged with all the force he could muster. The handle of the sickle was pulled from the young slayer's hands so fast that the sharp crescent point nearly sliced into his chest as it was seized from his possession.

"Maybe you should have chosen something else to fight me with," Hamilton's voice was shaky even with his confidence. "This is my specialty."

"No matter," Julius leered. "Face it, you're still dying!"

The young slayer quickly pulled two tiny throwing knives from his belt and twirled them around his fingers. He flung them in Hamilton's direction a second later and darted for the man.

Though he was a little slower than he was used to being, Hamilton dodged the small daggers and used the chain and sickle to the best of his abilities. This weapon had been what his own instructor had drilled him to perfect, but even with that in mind, he couldn't set aside the fact that with every move he made, he was losing more and more blood.

Putting as much effort into each of his attacks, Hamilton held his own against Julius for as long as he could, getting a couple hits that managed to knock the boy away long enough to catch his breath for a few seconds.

Wrapping the chain around Julius' ankle, Hamilton dragged the boy off his feet, a heat in his eyes that wanted nothing more than to live, to survive this fight and go back to his family. He dragged Julius to the dirt and came down over him.

"You think I'm a traitor?" he snarled, raising the blade over his head, "Fine, I'll be the traitor!"

Hamilton brought the deadly point down, but when it was on the verge of piercing Julius' left eye and expunging him from this world, Hamilton was tackled by Kingston who'd run for him.

Groaning out from the wave of pain that swelled through him, Hamilton tried to lash out as Kingston rolled him over. When he succeeded in pinning the boy to the ground, he winced when a fistful of his long hair was grabbed and yanked.

Like a bolt of lightning struck him, Hamilton's blue eyes shot wide open when Julius plunged a knife into his chest, not once, not twice, but three devastating times. Each assault punctured his lungs, grazing arteries when the razored edge was ruthlessly withdrawn, and caused the truest amount of damage that could reach his mortal body.

"Oh, my god..." Samuel couldn't believe his eyes as his former instructor collapsed like a limp corpse to the earth. He would have put forth more effort to protect Hamilton, but Kingston had stabbed him in his thigh before going to Julius' aid.

Kingston was helped to his feet then, and they looked down on the blood-soaked man lying on the cold ground. The two boys looked towards Samuel, unknowing that Hamilton wasn't totally dead yet.

 The agonized man's trembling hands reached for the thin chained necklaces gifted to him by Demiesius, tears blurring his eyes when his fingers finally found the vial looped around his neck. He unscrewed it from the chain, hoping for what would become of him the second this single drop of elder blood found its way into his system. Would it be enough? Would it work? Just when death gripped Hamilton, the shaky crimson drop fell against his tongue, and his entire body went completely still.

His once vibrant and worldly ocean eyes glazed over with an emptiness only seen in those who knew what the end looked like, and as a long, final breath escaped his still lungs, his heart shuttered its last withering beat.

The man once known as Hamilton H. Hamilton was dead.

It was nightfall when Demiesius awoke from his seemingly short slumber, but it was not his nocturnal instincts that roused him on this night. He looked towards the bassinet Jeremiah still slept in that was beside the bed, almost startled by the fierce cry escaping the tiny boy's mouth. It was like he was screaming bloody murder.

Afraid something was wrong with his son, Demiesius quickly got up from the bed and peered at the baby lying on his back. Jeremiah's face was a bright red and streams of tears trickled down his puffy cheeks.

Demiesius raised the writhing boy out of the bassinet, figuring maybe he just wanted to be held, but even that wasn't enough to calm him down. He carried the boy downstairs after getting dressed, not fully buttoning his white dress shirt when he entered the kitchen area. Usually when Jeremiah cried, it was either because he wanted to be fed, needed to be changed, or wanted Hamilton to hold him, but since his diaper was clean and Hamilton still wasn't back yet, the elder tried to see if a feeding was what his son wanted.

The entire time he prepared the blood bottle for Jeremiah, the baby kept crying, and even without being an expert when it came to figuring out what exactly each cry meant, Demiesius couldn't help but think this one was different from all the others. With the tears shedding down his son's face, this cry began to sound more agonized than anything, as if he were letting out an internal sorrow only he could feel.

When the bottle was ready, Demiesius tried to feed him, but Jeremiah turned from the nutrition and continued his lament.

"What is it?" the elder asked, knowing he wouldn't get a proper response. There had to be some way for him to stop crying, but with being unable to find this source, Demiesius felt utterly powerless.

He caught the time on the grandfather clock in the entrance way of the foyer, wondering when Hamilton would be done with his duties so he could come home. Demiesius had a meeting with the Councilors scheduled for tonight, and he couldn't afford to miss it. This was the night Hamilton's C.C. replacement would be chosen to partner with Christoph, so he needed to be there to oversee the induction.

Calling upon Dominick through their telepathic connection, Demiesius ordered the blood child to his home as fast as he could make it. A minute later, Dominick showed up on his doorstep in black trousers and a violet wine shirt. His long mane of black hair was still a little muddled, and by the look in his dark colored eyes, the elder could see he was quite tired still.

Dominick winced when he entered the front area of the castle, covering his ears as the strident ring of Jeremiah's distress vibrated the air around him. "What the hell is wrong with that kid?" he protested. "Please, make him stop!"

Demiesius looked down at the hollering baby in his arms, touching a hand to the top of Jeremiah's blonde and black hair. Curious if it would work, he reached into the baby's mind with his thoughts, twisting a sense of assurance into the small boy in hopes it would be enough to settle him down. He forged a wall of serenity inside Jeremiah, and when the tiny boy finally stopped crying, Demiesius wiped away the tears on his reddened cheeks. "I need you to watch him for me," he said to Dominick. "Just for an hour or so, or until Hamilton makes it home before me."

"You're kidding, right?" Dominick laughed. "Father, I am not fit to be a nanny."

"Dominick," Demiesius asserted, "You're the closest person I would trust with him right now. It won't be for long."

Dominick grumbled under his breath as Demiesius handed him the baby, Jeremiah's newly calmed gray eyes looking at him. He held the boy out in front of him, weirded out by the cloudy look in the baby's eyes. "What would my coven think of me babysitting? This is ridiculous, father."

"Stop complaining," Demiesius said, buttoning the remainder of his shirt. "And don't hold him like that."

"Can he walk yet?"

Almost reconsidering leaving his blood child with Jeremiah for even a minute, the elder wished Hamilton would hurry with the duty he was handling for the Public and come home. He wondered if his husband would have a heart attack knowing Dominick was alone with their child. But desperate times called for desperate measures, and apparently that measure was going to be Dominick von Kraige.

"If he's not in one piece by the time I get back," Demiesius warned, "you will be in pieces. Do I make myself clear?"

Dominick rolled his eyes, "Yes, father..."

When Demiesius then disappeared into a formation of shadows that closed around him, Dominick looked down at the baby in his arms. Jeremiah smiled happily up at him with a toothless smile, letting out a giggle when the blood child raised a brow at him. "Can you try to grow up a little faster?" Dominick said. "We'd have a lot more fun if you were at least...five or something."

***

Demiesius reached the European Public Council Gathering and stepped out of his encasement of shadow. He'd materialized in the center point of the room, the other four elders already in their seats at the front, and the C.C. vampires were standing against the semicircular wall off to the side.

The Public Councilors, Homer, Jamison and Richard were seated atop their podiums as well, and while the slayers who'd been previously partnered with vampires early on stood off to the side, there was one who hadn't joined the gathering yet.

"Good evening, Elder Demiesius," the Councilors greeted. "We are glad you could make it tonight. Please, have a seat."

The immortal neared his placement at the elder's table, receiving nods from each of the vampires in the C.C. before taking his seat between Bethania and Minerva.

For about two hours, everyone discussed the topic of a man named Luis Dalca. He was a thirty-year-old man who was born and raised in Romania, introduced to the Slayer Public at the age of ten since his father had been in it before him. He was being chosen as Hamilton's replacement, and if everyone in the gathering approved of his background, Christoph would have another person to call his partner.

While they were in the middle of deliberating Luis Dalca's

experience, everyone in the room became quiet when the tall double doors to the room opened. A blonde-haired boy who looked no older than seventeen or eighteen walked in, his legs seeming to drag behind him as he lugged himself further.

Samuel Colebrook.

His movements were lagging, cuts and bruises littering his arms, the stench of blood hanging in the air. His slayer attire was torn all over, and the weaponry lined along his belt was still touched with blood.

The C.C. vampires in the room tensed up at the sight of a foreign slayer, worrying suddenly if he'd entered here to make any moves. No one who didn't know about the underground relationship between vampires and slayers was allowed inside.

As he severely limped to the middle of the gathering, all eyes were on Samuel. He looked worn, beaten, as if he'd just finished brawling a pack of skilled fighters only minutes ago. He looked half dead already.

"Mister Colebrook," Councilor Richard narrowed his curious eyes, "What is the meaning of this?"

Demiesius remembered the surname and wondered if this was the same Colebrook that his husband had come to see some hours ago. He could acutely hear the boy speaking softly under his breath, and when the elder listened closer, his throat tightened when he heard the boy say, "They killed him. There was so much — so much blood."

"Samuel, speak up," Councilor Jamison commanded. "You are intruding on a private meeting. What has happened?"

"How could they...?" Samuel said.

Demiesius rutted his dark brow at the quiet mutters coming from the boy, nervousness coming over him like a quick storm arriving over an unsuspecting city.

"Hamilton," he finally spoke so the entire room could hear. "He is dead."

Each elder at the table looked towards Demiesius in that second, fearful of what their brother would do when those words left that boy's mouth.

"So much blood. There was so much."

Demiesius stood from his seat, stepping in front of Samuel faster than the human eye could follow. "What did you just say?" he demanded. "Repeat yourself, boy."

The young slayer didn't flinch for a second, clearly far too traumatized that he began to separate from his slayer dispositions. "Hamilton is dead," he said shakily once more. "I — I tried, but they were..." Samuel stepped forward, losing consciousness against the elder's chest before the strength in his knees gave out.

Not about to lose the only source of information he had, Demiesius grabbed the boy by his wrist and broke the bones inside. Samuel shot back into consciousness, screaming in agony as he clutched his now stinging wrist to his chest.

"Demiesius, calm yourself this second!"

The elder looked back at the podiums in which the Councilors were seated, his intense gaze striking uneasiness into the three old men. "You so much as think a command against me," Demiesius threatened, "And I will tear this boy apart before your very eyes."

At the warning, all of the C.C. slayers on the opposite side of the room stepped forward, each of them looking ready to police any actions taken against their leaders. And just when the slayers stepped forward, so did the vampires, fangs and claws ready for the attack. Even though each of them had been partners bound by the Coalition only seconds ago, they were all ready to stand up for their kind.

Demiesius tossed Samuel to the hard stone ground, "What happened to Hamilton?!"

"He's dead!" Samuel screamed out, hugging his wrist as he curled up on his side. "Kingston and Julius, they tricked him into thinking Julius was about to kill as many London vampires as he could." He was sobbing uncontrollably, drowning in his own tears as the remembrance left his mouth. "When we got there, Kingston stabbed him to weaken him. Julius — he fought Hamilton to the death and then they tried to kill me."

Could all of this be true? Demiesius took a step away from the crying teenager. Could mere boys have taken the love of his life from him? No, Hamilton...he was too strong for something like that to happen.

"Where is he?" the elder growled.

"I don't remember..." Samuel sniveled.

"WHERE?!"

"I don't know!" The boy trembled with horrid memories of the night. "It was too far. I can't remember the exact location!"

Demiesius turned from Samuel and switched his crimson glassed eyes to the Councilors, his rage directed at Jamison more than the other two. "You sent him to those bastards. Hamilton should not have been the one to deal with your problems. He was out of commission!" Shaking inside in uncertainty and aggravation, Demiesius almost couldn't control himself from letting go of all the words and rage he'd put aside to retain the peace between his people and humans. How could he, if humans couldn't even level with their own kind?

He didn't want to believe that his husband was dead, killed by the traitorous motives of his former students, but by listening to the grief in Samuel and seeing the boy so battered, the truth was lying directly at his feet.

"I won't be a part of this any longer," Demiesius asserted. "As of this night I will not associate with the Public in any manner. Anyone who stands in my way from here on will die at my hands. I do not care how many slayers, how many humans stand before me, if you interfere with my search for Hamilton, for these murderers, I will tear each and every one of you bloody mortals from this fucking world!"

Two Coalition slayers withdrew stakes from holsters on their boots, "Not if you die tonight, vermin!" one of them shouted and they darted for the elder.

Everything in the gathering suddenly turned upside down, the once aligned immortals and slayers now fighting against each other. As the mutual hatred filled the atmosphere, blood spilling across the floor in thick red puddles, Demiesius grabbed Samuel by the back of his shirt and dragged him out of the room. As he descended the narrow walkway, the other elders joined him, Bethania in shock after what she'd witnessed; centuries of underground cooperation between life and death thrown away for a mere broken heart.

"I hope you know there is no turning back from this," she said, the skirt of her black gown flowing as she walked to keep up with her brother's pace. "We won't be able to mend an alliance after the bloodbath taking place tonight."

Minerva, the sixteen-year-old-looking girl shrugged, "I'm actually glad we're finally out of that alliance. It was such a waste of time."

Eros and Nabadias strode behind them all, not caring for the detachment either. Given Demiesius had thought this whole alliance up in the first place, and he was the one tossing it aside after all this time, the other elders weren't too affected by it. Bethania even shrugged it off when it seemed this was how things were going to go now.

Drenched in shadow, they all disappeared into shrouds of darkness, Demiesius bringing Samuel along with him when they reappeared inside the property of Dominick's coven.

Entering the manor, Demiesius tossed Samuel to a female vampire dressed in nothing but a white bra and a pair of underwear that'd been coming out of a nearby room. She was stunned to find all the elders here without a word of notice, and when she caught the suffering boy against her, she looked down at him in pure confusion.

"Heal that boy," Demiesius ordered. "I'll need him for later."

One by one, every immortal resident of the von Kraige coven emerged from what they were doing, everyone coming together on the first floor for an announcement they anticipated.

When Demiesius was sure every vampire was standing before him, he said, "To those who were unaware, I forged an alliance with leaders of the Slayer Public long before all of you were ever raised. I did so thinking it would decrease the amount of blood spilled by our kind, but as of now, I no longer care for the union I once made, for tonight I was informed that Hamilton was murdered by his own students for a reason I'm sure had to do with his relationship with me. I want to find those boys who took him from me, and I want them to suffer for what they have done. My question is, who here wishes to assist me in that quest?"

After only a few seconds, the entire household took to a knee, lowering their heads in respect for their elder. If Demiesius didn't find any sign of Hamilton or the boys who'd killed him, the immortal knew he would never be able to feel peace within his heart ever again.

CHAPTER THIRTY

The Unfortunate Events of 1973

Samuel couldn't keep himself from thinking the worst as he sat still. He was a slayer surrounded by vampires, and while not one of them had made a move to harm him, he thought it impossible to imagine himself walking out of this place alive. The near nude woman who he'd been thrown to upon arrival was beside him on a black and ivory Victorian sofa. She'd ordered him to take off his shirt, and while he'd been reluctant to do so, she'd promised that no harm would come to him so long as he didn't do anything "funny". So here he was, shirtless beside a half-naked vampire.

After piercing her index finger with the point of her elongated fangs, she'd run streaks of her own blood against each of his wounds. In amazement, Samuel watched as she healed him of the scars Julius and Kingston had given him earlier in the night, almost thankful his wounds would no longer be the death of him. Even still, he couldn't escape the idea that these vampires would likely kill him the second they found his presence useless.

He could still envision almost everything that'd happened tonight, and his heart was bruised after the sight of such a brutal event that'd taken place against someone he'd respected so much. He didn't care if Julius was right about Hamilton falling in love with a vampire. It wasn't like their former instructor was out there killing his own kind. That was where Samuel would have drawn the line, but Hamilton was a gentle man. Even with his previous reign of being the strongest, deadliest, and most skilled vampire slayer on the face of the earth, he was still someone who had enough heart to care. Samuel might not have known everything about his teacher, but if there was one thing he did know, it was that Hamilton hadn't deserved to meet such an end.

When the woman at his side healed the final scar on the side of his rib cage, she smiled kindly at him with her fangs still protruding from her gums. "There, all better. You're as good as new."

Samuel rolled his wrist, feeling his bones rotate without any stings from when Demiesius had broken it. Swallowing anxiously, the boy tugged on the long sleeved, black leather breasted shirt he'd been wearing, the piece of clothing still torn here and there and carrying the scent of his blood.

"Am I free to go?" he asked.

Before the woman could answer him, Demiesius stepped through the threshold of the room.

Samuel felt his entire body tense up at the sight of the glaring vampire. He couldn't explain why, but this one...he was different from the others he'd come across in his few years as a member of the Public. This man gave off a profuse aura that recited just how strong he was, and Samuel wanted nothing to do with him. Just the solid black scowl in his eyes caused the boy to clench up inside to make sure he didn't piss his pants.

"You're sadly mistaken," Demiesius said, his voice noting every bit of unadulterated anger in his being, "if you think I'm going to let you walk out that door without the answers I'm in search of." He then switched his gaze to the vampire woman sitting beside the boy, "Leave us."

With a bow of her head after standing, the woman was gone, and Samuel was alone.

Demiesius stalked into the sitting area, his coal-colored eyes never leaving the shivering slayer sitting down across the room. Nothing but fear radiated from Samuel, and when the elder slipped into the boy's thoughts, they were occupied with quiet pleas to be with his mother.

"Tell me what I want to know," Demiesius said, "and I will make certain no harm comes to you. Refuse to give me what I want, and every vampire inside this manor will find pleasure in sucking the life from your veins."

Samuel was quiet and when his scared eyes looked towards the doorway, he spotted a handful of protective vampires blocking the entrance. Even if he could provide Demiesius with what he wanted, the boy was almost sure he wouldn't make it out of this house alive.

"Hamilton," Demiesius started, "Where is he?"

Is this him? Samuel wondered.

This had to be the vampire Hamilton had fallen in love with. "I really can't remember," he answered, "I wasn't paying too much attention to where we were going, and when I was coming back, I could hardly focus when I was driving. Honest. I almost got into three wrecks on my way to the Councilors."

"Don't make me carve into your mind to find what I'm looking for," Demiesius warned. "It is very unpleasant for humans to have a vampire burrowing into their memories."

"You don't want to do that," Samuel shook his head frantically. "You don't want to see what I witnessed out there. It'll drive you mad."

Demiesius scorched from within, "What's going to drive me mad is not finding Hamilton!"

He couldn't go on not knowing where his husband was even if he truly was dead. This man whom he loved so much was what kept him going. They'd become pieces of each other, and now that they had Jeremiah in their lives, he refused to accept a life...especially an immortal life without his true love. He needed his family! What he had with Hamilton was nothing like the two preceding relationships he'd had in the past. His present lover hadn't made Demiesius feel like he was just a vampire walking through each century. Hamilton made him feel what it was like for time to pass at standard speed.

Hamilton made him feel...alive.

Though he was unprepared for the torment that would follow his actions, Demiesius grabbed at Samuel, his entire hand covering the boy's eyes and his extended nails closely squeezed into the boy's temple bone.

Samuel gasped and grabbed at the elder's forearm, but his attempts proved impractical when he was driven back until his shoulder blades hit a wall, causing the painted pictures hung on the walls to tremble from the impact. Demiesius dragged the boy off the floor, legs kicking out hopelessly. "No, please!" Samuel tried to reason. "You don't understand!"

Ignoring him, Demiesius closed his eyes, searching through the dark for the opening of the cerebral portal that led into the boy's memories. This invasive procedure caused a prickling sensation to occur inside the area of Samuel's brain which clung to his memories. The aggressive disruption sent the boy into spasms in the elder's grasp, and as Demiesius' mind traveled into the realm of Samuel's, he was able to witness what had been seen during the last few hours. It was more like the flickering of past events, quick sparking images that all appeared from Samuel's point of view.

Demiesius saw a boy with dark red hair, Kingston, pacing back and forth inside the empty Council room. A second later, the image flushed away and revealed Hamilton entering. They spoke of a boy named Julius, and when that moment in time passed, the elder watched as the three entered Hamilton's vehicle. They drove for a while, Demiesius trying to pick up on any of the surroundings that would provide him with any hint as to where they were headed. Unable to determine anything other than they'd entered Oxford, the memories focused again on a dark-haired boy, Julius, standing on a porch with a chain and sickle in his possession.

The elder's blood grew hot as he listened to Julius' cocky speech, burning the face of this human boy into his own mind so as to never forget it. Quickly after, Demiesius heard the voice of his husband trying to talk Julius down from what he was doing, failing to do so when suddenly Kingston drove a blade into Hamilton's backside. He heard Samuel scream after beholding the treachery, but the wounded slayer hadn't given up so abruptly.

While a piece of the memories flowing into Demiesius' mind dove into a flash of combat between Samuel and Kingston, the elder felt every nerve in his body catch fire when Samuel's sights turned onto the image of Julius assaulting Hamilton with a dagger before his husband keeled over.

Demiesius pulled out of Samuel's mind after seeing the vicious stabbing. He then released the boy in his grasp, sending Samuel to his knees, minor streaks of blood running down his cheeks and his eyes burnt horrendously.

The elder backed away from the young, tormented slayer. Blood was running down his cheeks as well, but unlike Samuel, it was not caused by the mental incursion.

These streams of blood that ran down Demiesius' face were brought on by the horrid reality that his husband was in fact...gone. There was no doubt about it.

What was he going to do now?

He couldn't possibly make it without Hamilton by his side, he didn't want to think about having no choice in that. This point in time was supposed to be the beginning of their settlement together. And what the hell was he supposed to tell Jeremiah when the boy was old enough to wonder who he'd come from, and why they were no longer with them? Demiesius didn't want that for his son; to grow up without the key element that would have assisted in sculpting his character. How does one tell their child that their birth parent had been murdered in cold blood?

Demiesius feared such news would fuel an indescribable anger inside his son.

Jeremiah needed Hamilton!

Not ready to give up hope, Demiesius cleared his face of the bloody tears and turned to the coven standing guard outside the room. "Julius and Kingston, these are the names of the two slayers who took Hamilton from me. They were students at the Gregor House training facility. There I am sure lies information about what they look like, and I want each and every one of you to know their faces."

"We're going on the hunt, Lord Titus?" one of the vampire residents asked with an eager pitch.

Providing a nod, Demiesius added: "Those who do not wish to follow my vengeful path, I will hold no ill will if this is something you wish to stay out of. I cannot guarantee you all will make it back." When everyone remained ready to follow their elder to the ends of the earth, Demiesius continued. "Once the faces of Julius and Kingston are known to us, we will head up to Oxford to search. I don't care if you have to break into every household in that city to find them, I don't want a single stone left unturned, and I will not rest until Hamilton's murderers are found."

West of London and hidden within an enclosed forest of elm trees, the von Kraige coven stood outside of Gregor. Blocked in by a blessed silver fencing all around, the immortals thought it comical that these humans would believe in such superstitions that vampires were afraid of "holy powers".

Demiesius was at the head of the pack of immortals with Samuel by his side, the only elder in attendance now given he'd advised the others to head back to their homes. This was a personal matter that didn't involve them, so letting them get back to their own lives seemed like the right thing to do.

Concealed under the darkness of the surrounding forest, the vampires went unnoticed by the two guards standing watch in two towers that boarded the entrance gate. The elder turned to a woman standing behind him. She had shortcut blonde hair and hazel eyes, dressed in tight fit black bottoms and a dark gray crop top. Her name was Sara.

Demiesius gestured for the towers, and she went for them right away.

They all watched as Sara climbed the right tower like a silent feline stalking up towards her kill, and when she reached the top, she quickly snapped the neck of the guard inside. When the body dropped, the man in the second tower called out into the darkness for his partner, worried about the loud thud that followed the strange crackling sound.

When he received no response, the guard picked up a pair of night vision goggles that dangled around his neck. The moment he looked through them, the man jumped back when Sara smiled directly in his face, her fangs like long, glinting barbs.

"I think I'll eat you instead," she giggled.

The guard was too late to call out when Sara jumped him, covering his mouth as she dug her fangs into the side of his neck and took him down.

"What else is there that may cause a problem?" Demiesius questioned Samuel.

Samuel was clearly tired, but the elder wasn't done with him yet. He sniffled as his eyes still stung and pointed to three tall darkened light fixtures inside the gated facility. They had large bulbs, one just inside the gate, while the other two were inside on opposite sides of the parking lot. "They're motion detector

UV lights," Samuel said. "So powerful that they'll kill all of you if they're triggered."

"How far do they shine?"

"Just the lot and the sides of the buildings. Some are located on the training field as well, but the Administration has been meaning to get them fixed. They're currently broken. You don't have to worry about those."

Demiesius looked down at the utility belt buckled around Samuel's waist. There were three silver stakes tucked in their straps, and he took them out. Almost immediately he could feel the lethal weapons burn into the flesh of his palms, but he could hardly feel the pain of it.

"Once everything goes dark," he told the pack of vampires behind him, "Get to work."

Evaporating into his veil of shadows, Demiesius rematerialized inside the gates of Gregor House. The UV lights on the property instantly illuminated, but just as the sun was not so lethal of an opponent, it did nothing but slowly try to drain the energy out of the elder's body.

Before that could be done, Demiesius' eyes locked onto the elevated light posts, and he chucked the silver stakes accurately in their direction. One by one, each bulb shattered, blanketing the entire House in darkness once more. With that done, the gate closing off Gregor was torn from its joints and all the blood-sporting vampires rushed inside.

From here, they didn't need a command to be given, because they knew what was to be done. No one inside this slayer training ground was to be left alive on this night.

Screams could be heard from every which way, slayers in each building of the House caught off guard when hungry, excited vampires infiltrated their nightly lives.

This would be the first time in history that a House was target-ed like this, and Demiesius knew for sure this would also be the first time in a long time, where vampires killed so many humans in one sitting, but he didn't give a shit about that anymore and didn't think he would ever again.

Searching for Samuel after he was brought inside, Demiesius closed a hand behind the trembling boy's neck. "Take me to the Administration building."

Like a well-trained dog, Samuel did as he was told. He could hear the massacre taking place all around him, knowing each of the people he'd lived with here at Gregor were being killed one at a time, but he was far too haunted to show how he felt about it all. A part of him couldn't help but think the rest of these slayers would have been just like Julius and Kingston, deceiving, unfaithful liars who'd have been quick to fall in league with Julius if they'd discovered the truth about Hamilton as well.

After all, each one of them had joined this organization due to their own vengeful desires. Maybe...just maybe...they all de-served this.

He led Demiesius into the Administration building. There was a clash between an immortal and slayer taking place in the middle of the walkway, but when the vampire gained the upper hand and tore the slayer's throat open with a clawed hand, the elder and Samuel were let by. When they entered a lobby area, the scene looked like a storm had gone through it. Armchairs were knocked over on their side, small tables tipped with broken legs, and blood was smeared across the once clean, dark blue painted walls.

A man in his early forties was sitting up against the wall below a counter that'd once been guarded by glass, but now that glass barrier was sprinkled on the floor. The man was still clinging to life, wounded by jagged claw marks on his chest, and it wasn't until Demiesius and Samuel drew nearer, that they were able to see a pile of bones and ash nearby.

"You?" The man looked up at Samuel, recognizing him as a fellow Gregor occupant. "You brought these monsters here? F—Fucking traitor!"

When the man rose to his feet as if ready to take on both Samuel and the vampire at his side, Demiesius seized the man before he could make a move and crushed the man's throat before throwing his limp body across the lobby.

"All files on the slayers who live here," Samuel said, seemingly unfazed by the brutal act, "are back in the office."

Demiesius pushed the boy along, "Go get the ones on Julius and Kingston."

When Samuel entered the doorway into the office, Demiesius waited for him to return with the information he was looking for. While he was alone, his thoughts went back and forth from Hamilton and Jeremiah.

Though he was familiar with the feeling of loss when it came to the people he'd loved, Demiesius had high hopes that, with Hamilton by his side, he would not have to feel such dreadful things again.

Regret entered him when he remembered the very first time he'd laid eyes on the beautiful slayer. He'd cared dearly for the man back then, even when Hamilton hadn't known who he was, secretly working through the Public and immortal alliance to make sure he was always safe enough to do his job. Demiesius had admired Hamilton's courage, his strength and his beauty,

everything that made the wonderful man who he was. To think
about losing all of that in just one night, it crushed the faith the
elder had once held on to.

This is my fault, he believed, *if I hadn't allowed him to pursue
me...if I hadn't fallen so carelessly...he'd still be here.*

He wanted to apologize to both his husband and his son;
to Hamilton for his inability to have seen this coming, and to
Jeremiah for losing the baby's birth father before he could know
who Hamilton H. Hamilton truly was as a man.

"*Father?*" Dominick's telepathic voice entered the elder's
mind, "*Are you almost finished for the night? Or can Hamilton come
relieve me of my babysitting duties? I had a rendezvous with the coven
leader of Japan scheduled at midnight and it's fifteen till.*"

The burning inside Demiesius was so massive he could virtually feel it in every part of his body. He wondered how Dominick
would take the news after he told him Hamilton was never
coming back. Would he care? "*I'll be right there, son. I apologize
for handing you my responsibilities.*"

"*Father, are you alright?*"

"*I will tell you once I return.*"

Samuel came out of the back office with two manila files in his
hand. He moved much like a zombie, slowly as if he weren't in a
hurry, and when he reached where Demiesius stood, he handed
him the files holding all of Julius' and Kingston's material. The
elder looked through the entire file provided about Julius in
particular, discovering everything from Julius' blood type to
where he was born and raised. When he saw that the location
was in Oxford, Demiesius had no doubt that was where the boys
had lured Hamilton to his death.

"Mister...?" Samuel spoke up from beside Demiesius, "Are you going to kill me?"

The elder looked down on the young slayer at his side. Just by looking at him, Samuel was visibly torn on the inside. Although he was no longer in pain from the extreme beating he'd taken from Julius and Kingston, he truthfully couldn't get over all the things that had happened to him tonight. First, he'd accidentally brought his former instructor to death's door, was almost killed as well by his own partners, and now he was being ordered around by resentful vampires who cared little for his life. He could only see this going in one direction, and that was down a path that led to a dead end. If he was going to die tonight, he at least wanted to see it coming.

"I did not plan to kill you," Demiesius made clear. "Given that you tried to save my husband from such a fate, I haven't a reason to hold any ill-will towards you."

"Hamilton was your husband?" Samuel asked.

The elder started out of the lobby and stepped into the corridor leading from the Administration building. The moment he was outside, Demiesius glanced up to the window on the third floor when two bodies crashed through it. An immortal had tackled a slayer through the glass, and while their bodies fell, the vampire rotated on top and slammed the man into the concrete before getting to his feet. When the animated vampire made to dart away for another kill, Demiesius stopped him with a single command.

Handing the vampire the manila folder, he said, "When all is done here, take a faction of you to this location. Report back to me with your findings."

"Yes, Lord Titus," the vampire smiled.

"Wait!" Samuel called after Demiesius, rushing after him.

"What am I supposed to do now? I don't have anywhere else to go. I've got no family, and I don't want to...I don't want to be a slayer anymore, so I can't just go to another House. Please, help me?"

Majority of Demiesius' sentiments were already occupied, so not a very large part of him felt too bad about what this young slayer was feeling, but when he reflected on Hamilton's previous connection with Samuel, he figured opening whatever regard he could offer the boy wouldn't hurt.

As the carnage of Gregor's annihilation continued around them, the elder said, "Are you willing to make peace with immortals?"

Despite the wreckage taking place all over, Samuel nodded.

Demiesius took hold of the boy's forearm then, and soon they were both sheltered by the shield of darkness in which the elder traveled. The strange occurrence was still such a bizarre ability to the young boy. It made him feel like he was losing all the pieces of his body, only to be put back together once his feet touched solid ground, and when that happened after a short minute, Samuel found they were both standing before a royal-looking castle. The first place his mind had gone to upon seeing it, was if this place was a real living quarters, and not just some tourist destination out here in the obscurity of the countryside. But, no, this was the home of a vampire.

When they were inside the entrance hall, Samuel was taken aback by the grandness of the interior, made speechless as his eyes wandered the regal white and gold space. As they moved down an extensive walkway that led to a twin staircase, before they could ascend the steps, Dominick came out from a hall on the second-floor balcony. The blood child wasn't holding Jeremiah, but he did have a curious look on his face when spotting the unfamiliar boy beside his father. "Who's the lad?"

Demiesius climbed the stairs while Samuel stayed at the bottom, "Someone who will be calling your coven home for the time being."

"First question, why?" Dominick said, "Second question, who the hell is he? No, as a matter of fact, where's Hamilton? That guy hasn't spent more than two hours away from that baby, and now all of a sudden he wants to take his sweet time out there? When is he coming back?"

The elder went ahead and took his son aside and filled him in on everything that happened tonight. He hadn't expected a colossal reaction from Dominick in the least given his past issue with Hamilton, but when the blood child showed immense signs of upset, the elder felt every sense of sorrow melt back into him.

Dominick quickly embraced his father with a tight hold, telling him over and over again that he was sorry for the loss of his lover, and how he would do his best to see that Julius and Kingston got what they deserved once they were located. The blood child took a step from Demiesius, his own eyes threatening to shed crimson tears for the grief he knew his father was feeling and would feel for years to come.

After giving his honest condolences, Dominick took Samuel with him back to his coven, leaving Demiesius in the castle. The elder stood there at the top of the balcony for a few seconds, despising the piercing silence that filled each room. When he then heard the soft complaints of Jeremiah coming from down the hall, he went into the baby's nursery to find him lying in the crib Dominick had placed him in.

Jeremiah's eyes flashed a shade of red when he looked up at

his father, tiny arms reaching up towards him as if asking to be held. Demiesius' chest felt hollow suddenly when he touched the blonde half of Jeremiah's hair, and it was only when he spotted a drop of blood on the boy's olive-green pajamas that he noticed he was crying.

Demiesius raised his son from the crib and held him close, squeezing his eyes tight to force back the tears. "I will never allow anything to harm our child," he said. "This I promise you."

CHAPTER THIRTY-ONE

The Curse that Closely Follows

"What the hell are we going to do with the body?" Kingston asked. He was sitting on the guard rail of the front porch, watching as his partner stood at the bottom of the steps. "You got a couple shovels somewhere, so we can bury him?"

Julius had his back turned to Kingston, and what the other young slayer couldn't see was that Julius was having a hard time stopping himself from laughing and smiling so much. He'd done it! He killed the greatest fighter to ever grace the Public with his bare hands, and he couldn't feel prouder of himself. Sure, he'd had a little help from the American boy, but it was him who'd delivered the fatal blows.

Killing another human felt a lot different from killing a vampire. There was a life in his hands, a life that could be felt leaving while vampires were only hollow creations of their former selves.

The body of Hamilton was still laid out in the yard, curled up in the position he'd fallen in. When Julius was finally able to compose himself, he started towards the still corpse and stood over it. "I think I want to send a further message," he said. "I know the Public knows about his disgusting involvement with a vampire, and I want them to see what happens when such behavior is allowed."

"You want to take his body to the Gathering?" Kingston raised a brow at the idea. "Don't you think that's a little on the dangerous side? I mean, we already let Samuel get away after not being able to kill him, so don't you think that would be one of the first places he'd go? Sorry, Julius, but I have to be honest...that's a stupid idea."

The dark-haired boy glared at Kingston from over his shoulder, meeting him at the bottom of the porch steps when the other boy hopped down from his seat on the rail. Just as he'd been able to before, he twisted Kingston in his direction with one easy influence.

For as long as he and Kingston have known each other, Julius had been aware of the affections this red-haired American had for him. And with that small piece of leverage in his pocket to do with as he pleased, it wasn't as difficult as one would think it'd be to convince Kingston to follow his path of destruction.

Softening the look in his eyes, Julius brought his hands to the other boy's face, touching Kingston's cheeks fondly. He leaned in close, brushing their noses together, and said, "If you're scared of what the Public might do, then I guess I can go by myself, even though I want you by my side."

Kingston felt his body warm despite the surrounding cold,

and when the dark-haired boy kissed lightly against his lips, he nodded. "I'll go with you," he said. "After all, you'll need someone to watch your back."

"Thank you," Julius smiled as their lips hovered together. "I need you, Kingston. You're all I have left."

When he stepped away from the love-blind slayer, Julius and Kingston looked out to the body of Hamilton...and gasped in disbelief. The man was sitting up, supporting himself on his hands and knees as his blonde river of hair curtained down to hide his face.

"What the fuck?" Kingston retreated intuitively, truly afraid after seeing that his former instructor was still alive after all this time, after enduring the assault he'd completely bled out from.

Julius swallowed a nervous stone in his throat, keeping his eyes on the man he was positive had been dead only seconds ago. The two watched on as Hamilton looked down at his trembling hands now, and then, as if merely hearing the rapid beats of their hearts, the blonde man moved his gaze in their direction.

"Impossible," Julius whispered, "He'd have to be a—."

Hamilton rose to his feet, sluggish at first as he seemed to take in the realization that he was somewhere he didn't belong. Hamilton seemed to search his body for something, feeling the wounds all about his body close before he could see them do so.

Julius couldn't believe what he was witnessing with his very eyes. There were no longer any stab wounds riddling his chest, not even a single scar was left behind to show remnants of an attack or his past rising as a slayer.

Suddenly irritated by a strange stinging around his neck, Hamilton grabbed at the silver jewelry and pulled at the latch. When it broke from the force, he threw the thin chain that the blood vial had been attached to. As he stood there in the darkness of this unfamiliar place, he couldn't remember getting there, couldn't remember what he'd been doing.

What's going on?

He looked up when he heard a soft whisper, confused by the presence of Julius and Kingston. "What am I doing here?" he asked, covering his ears when everything unexpectedly became louder.

He could hear the nature around him taking place, everything no one would notice, from the distant flaps of a bird's wings, to the trampling of dirt beneath a buck's hooves, even crickets chirping, frogs croaking, and the bothersome pulse of Julius' and Kingston's hearts within their chests.

Covering his ears, he wanted it all to stop, but he didn't know how to silence it.

Looking down at the oddly bright silver necklace he'd thrown, Hamilton noticed the vial was missing but the cap was still intact. That could only mean...

Hamilton brought a hand to his mouth, shocked to feel the sharp points of fangs elongated from where his canines would have been. He gasped and covered his mouth, stumbling onto his bottom in fear. What had he...why...when had he become a vampire?!

"Oh, god," Hamilton shivered all over, but not from the natural coldness of his body temperature. He was terrified. Not only was he unable to remember a thing that happened in the last several hours, but he was also a newly turned vampire all alone with no clue as to what was going on.

"Julius," he took a step towards the two boys, "Kingston, I don't know what's...I don't know what's going on."

Julius looked down at his utility belt and in a second, the silver chain and sickle were in his grasp. Without putting a thought into his actions, he ran for Hamilton and whipped the chain out at the vampire standing before his childhood home. Before Hamilton could think of how to react, he was taken to the ground, the burning chain causing him to scream in unimaginable pain as it wrapped around his neck. He clawed at the chain to no avail, feeling like his flesh was being singed off by hot flames.

"How did this bloody happen?!" Julius yelled out, his right foot unknowingly driving the silver necklace Hamilton once wore deeper into the ground.

"What are we going to do now?" Kingston asked, "You still want to take him to the Gathering?"

Not hearing Kingston's worry, Julius tightened his hold on the chain in his hand, pinning Hamilton to the ground as he cried out in agony. "You were dead! How is this possible? Who turned you? Who turned you, you vampire fucker?"

"Loosen up just a little if you want him to speak," Kingston said. "I doubt he can talk while you're choking the shit out of him."

Julius stood, dragging Hamilton's thrashing body to the drop-off van he'd stolen from Gregor House. "Go get a blanket from inside," he told Kingston, "We're still taking him."

The pain Hamilton was in when the two boys tied him up in silver chains was indescribable. He couldn't move an inch or else the discomfort would worsen. They'd stabbed stakes through the palms of his hands to make sure he couldn't break free, and then finally covered him with a blanket to hide him on the floor of the van.

Hamilton tried to remember whatever he could about what had gone on before finding himself in the middle of nowhere. If anything, the only thing he was sure of was that he'd drank the drop of blood Demiesius provided for later use, which meant...he'd died. No, he was still dead. With a body chilled by death's grip, and a frozen heart in his chest, Hamilton the vampire slayer was now the very creature he used to hunt.

While he laid there in the moving drop-off van, unable to budge from the agony keeping him still, Hamilton wanted to cry out in despair. He and Demiesius had talked about him becoming a vampire someday, and he thought he'd be ready for when that time came, but with it having been planned for a few years down the road, he was unprepared for this new existence to take over. He still wanted to walk under the sun, he still wanted to have babies, he still wanted the chance to say goodbye to his prior self. To open his eyes to a totally new world...it frightened him.

He didn't know how to be a vampire.

Jeremiah.

Hamilton felt his eyes tear up at the mere thought of his son. Would he ever see him again, hold him close? With the predicament he was stuck in right now, Hamilton saw doubt dancing before him. No, he wouldn't be able to watch his beautiful son grow into a man. He wouldn't be there to help Jeremiah when he needed a loving shoulder. Just that thought alone hurt far more than the silver charring his pale skin beneath this covering.

"Demi," he cried softly, desperately wanting his husband to save him.

"Shut it back there," Julius ordered, looking onto the floor of the back seats, and then he sat forward again. "I've got a plan to make sure we're out of this clear," he told Kingston as the other boy drove. "When we get to the Councilors, I'll threaten to tell all the other Houses about their allowance of human and vampire relations. Imagine how pissed off a lot of people would get about that, everyone threatening to disobey the Council all at once. I would imagine that's something they'd want to avoid at all costs."

Kingston glanced toward Julius before putting his eyes back on the road. "What are your plans for Hamilton now that he's a vampire?"

Julius huffed a confident laugh, "The only way I'll make a deal to keep my mouth shut about this whole thing, is if the Councilors will give us a new designated position in the Public, and they have to keep the *great* Hamilton locked away in the prison ward. I think I'd like to oversee our dear teacher's punishment for turning his back on the human race."

Kingston nervously gripped the steering wheel, "I thought — I thought you said we could be together when we made it out of this. No more Public orders, no more vampires, just us. That's the whole reason why I agreed to do all of this...so we'd be together."

Holding back his annoyance, Julius placed a hand on Kingston's leg, giving the other boy's thigh a light massage that aroused him at the same time. "If you promise to stay by my side, I swear we'll never be apart as we see where this new path takes us. I need you with me, Kingston. We'll see where all of this goes together. Alright?"

The American boy's breath released with a slight smile, "Yeah," he nodded, "I understand."

After a while of driving, the agony all over Hamilton's body hadn't stopped for a mere second. He thought he'd go numb once his nerves leveled with the intensity of the burning, but he was wrong as time went on, and he still hurt just as much.

When the van came to a stop, Julius kept a lookout on the streets before getting out. It was well past one o'clock in the morning, and given this block already received little traffic even during the day, the two slayers opened the rear door of the vehicle and hauled Hamilton's bundled body inside the sizable medieval structured library.

They were puzzled to find the building on the main floor was completely trashed, bookcases shoved over, furniture broken everywhere, and books were soaked in blood, study desks and chairs appearing to have been torn apart by bare hands. When the doors slammed shut behind them, the loud echo clapped through the large concrete space.

"What the hell happened here?" Julius pondered. The hair on the back of his neck stood on end as he looked around, expecting to find dead bodies laying all over, but blood was all they saw.

Walking over broken bookcases and around destroyed furniture, the boys heaved Hamilton along until they reached the entrance to the underground. It was behind a set of doors that was usually always guarded by someone, but given no one was here to question them, Julius shoved open the doors when they wouldn't move the first time. There'd been a comatose body positioned up against them on the other side, a woman the boy's recognized as someone who worked in the weapons crafting wing of the underground. Her head was twisted in a disturbing angle, and it looked like her neck had a chunk bitten from it.

They headed into the cellar of networking tunnels, all the while spotting dead body after dead body, each of which looked like they'd been attacked by a wild horde of ravenous animals.

"Hey," Kingston kept his voice down, "Do you think all of this is our fault? We don't even know who Hamilton was dating. What if he was some kind of big shot that could command something like this?"

"Then we'll kill him if he's still here," Julius assured.

Inspecting each chamber of the underground, the two boys finally reached the Gathering and entered. Inside were several shredded bodies of grown men and women, all of which had been dressed in their combative slayer attire, weapons were here and there, and there did seem to be a couple piles of bone and ash on the floor as well, meaning these fighters had managed to take out a few vampires before being killed themselves.

Julius laid eyes on Councilors Homer and Richard lying dead beside the base of their podiums, but when he saw signs of life in old man Councilor Jamison, he set down Hamilton's body and gestured for Kingston to follow him. They knelt beside the old man who was having trouble breathing. He had a trail of serrated scars on his face, and when the boys helped him sit up all the way, he appeared relieved that they were human.

"Julius, Kingston, oh, thank the heavens it's you. I don't suppose you ran into any others out there?"

Kingston shook his head, "No, the place seems clear now."

"Who did this?" Julius asked, his question sounding more like a demand.

"Demiesius Titus," the old man said without bother. "He virtually commands the entire vampire population. Since *you* had Hamilton killed, he commanded his followers to destroy this headquarters out of revenge. Why, Julius? How could you do something like that?"

"How did you know that?" Julius said in an upset. "If I'd known this had happened—."

"Shut your mouth, boy." Councilor Jamison sat up further on his own. "Samuel showed us some courtesy to speak of your betrayal. You dare kill one of your own kind and then speak of remorse? I will have you thrown in prison for all the damage you have caused this Public faction."

Angered by the threatening words spoken to him by one of his higher-ups, Julius narrowed his eyes, fingers inching closer to the grip of a blade tucked at the back of his belt. "You would have me rot in a cell for years to come? Maybe you should reconsider doing so, or I'll walk out that door right now. I'll go to every House under this Public's command and tell them of the things you all let happen between vampire and slayer. I have no doubt in my mind people would find you traitorous if they knew you allowed vampires a right to their people."

Councilor Jamison glared warningly at the young dark-haired boy, "You wouldn't..."

Julius laughed heartily and neared the wrapped body of Hamilton, pulling the covers off to reveal the suffering of the newly turned slayer. Jamison gasped upon seeing the blonde man, perplexed as to why his skin burned against the silver chains binding him, but all he needed to see were the fangs in Hamilton's mouth to realize he was in fact an immortal.

Instead of spending hours wondering how something like this could have happened, he met Julius' eyes again with a dark look when the boy said, "He's all the proof I need to get everyone to believe me."

"What do you want?"

"Protection," the boy said. "For Kingston and I. I wouldn't

be surprised if Hamilton's vampire boyfriend already knows my name by now and everything about me since Samuel doesn't know how to keep his mouth shut. I want you to give us new identities and document us as leeway slayers so we can move freely."

Jamison agreed, not wanting to risk losing control of the Public due to more hateful slayers. "What becomes of Hamilton?" the older man asked then.

Julius looked down at the man he once wished to be like more than anything. "We'll build another headquarters and keep him in the dungeons so he may rot with time. That's all I want. It's what he deserves."

Jamison gave in to anything this young slayer wanted, all for the sake of keeping the past relationship of vampires and slayers under wraps. No one could know, lest more slayers threaten to follow in Julius' vengeful path.

After helping Councilor Jamison to his feet, Kingston and Julius dragged Hamilton further into the underground, down narrow stone passageways, and into a cell block that smelled of stale water and generations of age. They opened the heavy steel door to the last cell and lugged their former instructor's body inside. Julius then unwrapped the scorching chain and sickle from around the blonde man and pulled the stakes from the vampire's palms, but before Hamilton's body could heal, and he could think to find his way out of here, the chain was replaced with a restraint bolted to the south wall of the cell. It was a silver-necked collar with leather around the inside of the clasp so his skin wouldn't burn anymore, but if he tried to tear it open, his hands were in for a painful sting.

The moment it was locked around his neck, Hamilton tried

to grab Julius, but the young slayer moved just fast enough to avoid being caught. The dark-haired boy and Kingston stood outside the opening of the cell, "Don't worry so much," Julius said, his voice oddly assuring, "I'll only keep you in here until you've learned your lesson. Hopefully when that time comes, you'll have seen the wrong in your actions. But...until then...try to have a nice immortal life. It might not be a very pleasant one."

Julius slammed the loud squealing door and the second it shut; Hamilton dashed for it only to be choked back by the chain around his neck. He couldn't be kept in here forever, he had to get home, and he had to get back to his family.

"No!" he screamed, "Let me out of here! Julius, Kingston, please, you don't understand!"

When no one answered him, and he could hear the footsteps disappearing, Hamilton closed his hands around the silver chain and pulled. The harmful element worked against his attempts to free himself, quickly searing and draining the energy from his body as he continued to struggle. How was he supposed to get out of here? He hadn't anyone to rely on anymore, no one knew where he was, no one knew what he'd become. This was a disaster.

Looking down at his hands after letting go of the chain, Hamilton watched the pale skin heal on its own, thankful at least to not feel the pain any longer. As he stared at his quivering hands, the man's blue eyes stopped on the golden band on his left ring finger. It was the marriage ring Demiesius had given to him before becoming pregnant with Jeremiah. He touched the piece of jewelry, glad it hadn't the capabilities of hurting him.

Hamilton sank to his knees then, clutching over his still heart as an overpowering cry escaped his chest. He couldn't ever remember crying so hard. The grief built up inside of him was so strong he figured he might drown in the bloody tears falling down his face.

Hamilton then slammed his fists into the cobblestone under him, the rock cracking from the force. "Demi," he cried, sinking further into a sorrow he would feel for years to come. "Jeremiah, I'm so sorry."

Sorry he didn't have the strength to get out of this mess alone.

The last thing Demiesius wanted was to come to terms with the fact that his husband wasn't coming home, but as the night went on and Hamilton was not beside him, there wasn't much else he could do to change that. For now, all he had the power to do was hope the von Kraige coven would discover something at the location in Oxford. Even if it was just Hamilton's lifeless body that they found, he would be content with at least having something to bury, the ability to show his husband what respect he hadn't been given in his final moments.

As he stood outside in the gardens of his castle's courtyard, Demiesius held Jeremiah tenderly against him, the small boy having found sleep in his arms not long ago. He remembered sitting out here with Hamilton a couple months when the man still carried their son. It'd been a night where Demiesius was free of any duties as an elder, unrestricted and welcomed to do as he'd pleased, and on that night, Hamilton had wanted to sit here beneath the stars. They'd spoken for hours then, and the immortal would never forget the words that'd been said to him.

"You are the first person I have ever loved," Hamilton had

said. "For so long, I was alone, bound by my blind loyalty to the Public. At the time, I think I was alright with that...being alone, feeling like I had a purpose in this mad world. But now that I know what it's like to experience what true love is, not one piece of me wants to go back to such an isolated life. You are the first person I have ever loved, Demi, and I just know you will be the last. You are my one and only and I'm quite proud of that."

Recalling it now, the elder wished he could go back to the moment they'd shared, go back to say a little more. Ever since the night he'd become the vampire he was, Demiesius had never been much of a talker, had never been one to say everything that was on his mind, but he hoped all the words he'd spoken during he and Hamilton's time together had been enough, enough for the beautiful man to know that he felt the exact same way.

They'd been so lost in their deep and unrelenting pool of honest love and commitment, that now it was impossible for him to visualize what an existence without the other man could be like. The memories they'd made over the few years that'd bonded so earnestly were now seared into the elder's aching chest, would never fade, would remain ever-present in his mind and body.

Not that he would ever want such a memory to fade.

To forget, to remember, they were curses in their own right, but he would welcome them to his side wholeheartedly for as long as he continued this journey through time.

When he turned from the garden to head inside, wanting to get Jeremiah out of the cold, Demiesius stopped in the open doorway of the atrium. An almost familiar feeling caused a sort of pulsation within the core of his frontal lobe. It was so insignificant that it would have gone unnoticed if he hadn't felt it just once before, but he couldn't quite mark the point in time where this sensation came from. The tingling stopped after one second, vanishing as quickly as it'd come.

With the vanishing of the occurrence, he glanced down at the baby in his arms and the curious, treasured gaze of his small son stared up at him now. This was...it was so terribly difficult to look upon him, even more so when a coo left Jeremiah's mouth and his tiny hands reached up toward his father.

A babble of laughter left the five-week-old, causing the tear dragging down the center of Demiesius' chest to worsen, just about shredding what was left of the elder's heart into fragments of nothing. He couldn't fathom this world without the one person who'd brought this boy into the world in the first place, so much so that faith in his ability to raise Jeremiah without Hamilton at his side seemed an unattainable feat. Things weren't supposed to be this way...

Why did it always have to be this way?

His heart was no stranger to what it was to mourn, and yet—this hurt was unbearable. This pondering of a future absent the face of the man who'd only laid beside him, stood beside him what felt like a moment ago was far worse than any hurt that'd once gripped him in the past. Together, he and Hamilton had created so much more than aspirations of a future as one, and now that future would be missing a crucial piece of his past. As much as it grieved Demiesius to be without the man he'd come to admire and see so much in, an ache also settled in his chest for their son.

While Demiesius would continuously mourn the loss of a soul once linked so perfectly with his own, he could bear the pressure of such a crushing weight. But Jeremiah didn't deserve this;

their son didn't deserve to experience what it would be like to come to terms and deal with what sorrows would follow him the moment he understood what death truly was.

True death—it was permanent.

Once the cold wind began to pick up around him, the elder's priorities lay with taking his son inside and putting him to bed. The doors to the atrium shut behind him, and he made his way up to the boy's nursery. When he laid Jeremiah down, he turned on a music box that filled the silence with a soft tune, strumming a melody similar to the one Hamilton often hummed to the infant as he cradled the boy to sleep. Demiesius pursed his lips, able to imagine the very picture of his husband beside him, and as if the tune itself was enough, Jeremiah shifted where he lay before finding comfort in his warmth.

Demiesius heard footsteps coming towards the nursery then but given he could already feel who it was approaching, he remained where he was and waited to be joined. The elder looked to the archway of Jeremiah's bedroom to find Dominick standing there, watching him worriedly given the gloom clouded around the entire castle.

"Father," the blood child said, his tone woeful. Regretful. "I thought I should be the one to tell you the location where Hamilton was taken...no one was there anymore by the time of arrival. I'm so sorry."

Not speaking a word, Demiesius took a step forward and into a rising cloud of black mist, his Mastering carrying him out to the courtyard once again where he could be alone. It was the only place he could think to go.

To escape.

The night whispered its nocturnal tunes from all around once more, and he closed his dark colored eyes, as if simply shielding his vision would be effective enough to hide him away from the world and its truth. Even still, the shut of his eyes only brought about the haunting vision he'd witnessed upon discovering the cruel fate of his lover. He flinched internally, able to see as that boy drove such determined and vicious killing blows into Hamilton's chest, and then the final collapse as the love of his eternal life slumped over and hit the ground. Demiesius wished he could forget it, wished now he hadn't sought such answers if that was the outcome. For as long as he continued to walk the earth, he would never forget it.

Such a plague, it was.

Gritting his teeth as he opened his eyes now, Demiesius' stare reached the stars and the moon overhead. His gaze burned hot, and his vision blurred from the rise of crimson tears taking over. They washed down his once unblemished cheeks, each drop hanging onto the end of his chin before falling to the ground.

It couldn't possibly end this way, he swore on the inside, tired of this curse that seemed to follow him no matter where his heart resided.

Was this his punishment, he wondered, to never be granted peace with someone to call his own? Having now bore witness to the death of each of his fallen lovers, Demiesius could only believe such a thing to be true.

This hurt, this agony, he didn't want to go on with it, he couldn't possibly. Yet, Jeremiah crossed his mind, and he saw Hamilton's face as well, saw the utter happiness and glow that reached his lover upon first holding their infant son. With Hamilton now gone, his son would need his father's focus, need his father's strength, and Demiesius promised Hamilton then and there to make certain he would do at least that.

Always, Demiesius would protect their son from all he could, raise him to know every piece of good that had been the man who birthed him. From here on, that was the least he could do to lift and nurture his husband's shining legacy, for it now lived within their son.

He will be alright, my love, Demiesius promised. *I will shelter him as you would have wanted. From now and into forever.*

For you, Hamilton.

Read ahead for a sneak peek of the contents of book two! Titled: *'The Tale of Two Killers: To Kiss a Killer'*, the continued journey through time will follow Dominick von Kraige as his rule over the London area is seemingly challenged. On a quest to understand the love filtering itself into his heart, he'll also be faced with the trials brought on by tensions from a past and present whose paths have finally merged.

CHAPTER THIRTY-TWO

Book Two: Chapter One

DARKNESS

Year — 2007

The two boys were petrified as they were dragged down the long, lonesome corridor, each of them held harshly by two individuals on either side of them. Their own towering grandfather walked with a bold stride as they were led to what was promised to be their end, a boundless cold in the older man's eye that never spoke of affection — seemingly not even for his own family and loved ones. The youngest boy sobbed relentlessly, trying as he might to push with his feet to free himself. Just sixteen, he'd never been so terrified in his life, so hopeless as he only wished to take his twin brother's hand and run — run to the ends of the Earth where this heartless man could never find them.

"I warned you," their grandfather spoke, his English accent gruff over the sound of footsteps echoing all around. "This is what happens to traitors, this is what happens to those who disobey and turn their backs on the Public."

As the youngest continued to struggle, blinded by his own tears, his brother attempted to wrench himself free as well, the effort proving useless no matter if he did manage to slip from the man's hands holding strongly onto him. Even if he freed himself, he wouldn't leave without his brother, wouldn't leave his brother to suffer the fate of what came to all who disobeyed down in this dark, dank hidden part of the underground world.

"Grandfather, please," the oldest begged, most of his fears meant solely for his brother. "Please, stop this. I beg you, please!"

A light chuckle was heard. "You beg now that your fears are coming true, yet you refused to listen to my demands in the beginning."

"We're sorry," the oldest besought, "We'll do anything, I swear!"

The older man stopped, causing his followers to halt as well, and their grip on his grandchildren didn't lighten up for a second. With an ever-present arrogance that'd clung to his heart for decades, the man glared down at the two sixteen-year-olds. They shared little to no likeness to him whatsoever, yet they were still his grandchildren. The connection he had with them was almost non-existent, save for the request he'd thought to make of them when they were older, but after overhearing, witnessing their disloyalty to the Slayer Public, he thought to teach them a much-needed lesson. If they died in the process — so be it — if they lived, perhaps their loyalty would be restored. Either way, these boys were going to learn something; whether that be what the touch of death felt like, or the importance of obedience. It didn't matter anymore.

Glaring down at the two boys, the older man smirked cruelly and balled his fist. As his brother looked on in terror, he slammed his powerful fist across the younger boy's face.

"Stop!" his brother screamed, witnessing the sharp line of blood burst from a gash that tore just below the other boy's eye.

The older man then grabbed at the oldest brother's neck; his hand fixed firmly to nearly stop his air passage. "You'll do anything, yeah? Then impress me, grandson. Impress me and I'll give you and your pathetic excuse of a brother a ticket out of here. Can you do that for your beloved grandfather?"

The smirk upon his face vanished the moment a blotch of spit landed on his cheek. He shoved the boy back then, wiping the sleeve of his shirt down his face to get rid of the saliva. Nodding further down the hall then, the two boys were dragged a bit further toward the heavy metal door at the end of the corridor.

Continuing to sob as he tried to control his breathing, the youngest looked to his brother when the door was opened. There was nothing but a wall of darkness looking back at them, a pitch blackness that looked like it would swallow their very existence whole.

Shoved then, the two boys fell to the hard stone floor, and the door was slammed behind them. Unable to see given the wash of darkness surrounding them, the frightened boys felt around until their hands came together. "It's alright," the oldest wanted to promise, to calm his trembling brother. He didn't believe his own words, but it was all he could say to calm himself as well. "He'll come back for us. He can't leave us here forever."

"I'm scared," the youngest sniveled, every breath he took struggling to fill his lungs.

Before the oldest could think to speak of any more comfort,

he and his brother's hearts skipped a beat upon hearing a terrifying sound. It was a guttural rumble, an animalistic snarl that sounded like they were locked in the same room as a hungry tiger. There was an eerie atmosphere that surrounded them then, sending an iciness down their spines. With the room as trapped in darkness as it was, they couldn't see, could only hear as the sound of a chain rattled against the stone floor.

"Brother," the youngest felt his tears sting his vision once again.

A dangerous hiss was heard, the sound of a footstep that approached from what could have only been a meter away. The oldest shoved his brother away from where these footsteps originated from, causing the boy's back to strike the door that'd been closed on them. Cowering at the fierce sound of combat, the youngest covered his ears, so filled with fear until the familiar embrace of his brother wrapped his arms around him. "It's alright," the oldest said, "It can't reach us from here."

If they could see in this shroud of obscurity, the two boys would have met the ravenous, piercing eyes of a being ready to rip them to shreds, not only for the hunger eating it alive, but the abhorred familiar scent that traveled through their veins. They were lucky to not know what such malice resembled. Such a glare resembled an alienated man bathed in decades of blood, untapped bitterness, and a passionate need for reprisal.

The door came open then and the two boys tumbled out, scurrying back to the only safety and guardian they knew. They wrapped themselves around their grandfather, shaking as if they'd never let go, and never think twice about questioning him again.

The older man looked down on the boys, noting the blood

trickling from the elder brother's forehead. "Impressive," he said smugly. "Now what will you do, boys?"

Together, they said, "Whatever you wish, grandfather."

Made in the USA
Las Vegas, NV
25 September 2024

95777444R00249